P9-DGL-066

Praise for *New York Times* bestselling author

SAMANTHA YOUNG

"This is a really sexy book and I loved the heroine's journey to find herself and grow strong. Highly recommend this one."
—*USA Today*

"Will knock your socks off . . . [an] unforgettable love story."
—RT Book Reviews

"Humor, heartbreak, drama, and passion."
—The Reading Cafe

"Truly enjoyable . . . a really satisfying love story."
—Dear Author

"[Samantha Young's] enchanting couples and delicious romances make her books an autobuy."   —Smexy Books

"Hot, bittersweet, intense . . . sensual, with witty banter, angst, heartbreaking moments, and a love story you cannot help but embrace."   —Caffeinated Book Reviewer

"Filled with heart, passion, intensity, conflict, and emotion."
—Literary Cravings

"[Young] is a goddess when it comes to writing hot scenes."
—Once Upon a Twilight

continued . . .

"Ms. Young dives deep into the psyche of what makes a person tick emotionally . . . [The] one thing you can count on from Ms. Young is some of the best steamy sexual chemistry."

—Fiction Vixen

"Smart and sexy, Young writes stories that stay with you long after you flip that last page."   —Under the Covers Book Blog

"Charismatic characters, witty dialogue, blazing-hot sex scenes, and real-life issues make this book an easy one to devour. Samantha Young is not an author you should miss out on!"

—Fresh Fiction

ALSO BY SAMANTHA YOUNG

THE HART'S BOARDWALK SERIES

Every Little Thing
The One Real Thing

THE ON DUBLIN STREET SERIES

Moonlight on Nightingale Way
Echoes of Scotland Street
Fall from India Place
Before Jamaica Lane
Down London Road
On Dublin Street
One King's Way (novella)
Until Fountain Bridge (novella)
Castle Hill (novella)

Hero

Fight or Flight

SAMANTHA YOUNG

JOVE
New York

A JOVE BOOK
Published by Berkley
An imprint of Penguin Random House LLC
375 Hudson Street, New York, New York 10014

Copyright © 2018 by Samantha Young
Excerpt from *The One Real Thing* copyright © 2016 by Samantha Young
Penguin Random House supports copyright. Copyright fuels creativity, encourages diverse
voices, promotes free speech, and creates a vibrant culture. Thank you for buying an authorized
edition of this book and for complying with copyright laws by not reproducing, scanning, or
distributing any part of it in any form without permission. You are supporting writers and
allowing Penguin Random House to continue to publish books for every reader.

A JOVE BOOK and BERKLEY are registered trademarks and the B colophon is a trademark of
Penguin Random House LLC.

Library of Congress Cataloging-in-Publication Data

Names: Young, Samantha, author.
Title: Fight or flight/Samantha Young.
Description: First edition. | New York : Berkley, 2018.
Identifiers: LCCN 2018015165| ISBN 9780451490193 (paperback) |
ISBN 9780451490209 (ebook)
Subjects: | BISAC: FICTION/Romance / Contemporary. | FICTION/Contemporary
Women. | FICTION/Romance/General. | GSAFD: Love stories.
Classification: LCC PR6125.O943 F54 2018 | DDC 823/.92—dc23
LC record available at https://lccn.loc.gov/2018015165

First Edition: October 2018

Printed in the United States of America
3 5 7 9 10 8 6 4 2

Cover design and illustration by Colleen Reinhart
Back cover image of airplane by Best Vector Images
Book design by Laura K. Corless

This is a work of fiction. Names, characters, places, and incidents either are the product of the
author's imagination or are used fictitiously, and any resemblance to actual persons, living or
dead, business establishments, events, or locales is entirely coincidental.

Fight or Flight

One

SKY HARBOR AIRPORT, ARIZONA
MARCH 2018

Food. Food and coffee. I knew those should be my priority. The grumbles in my belly were making that perfectly clear. And considering the purpose for my visit to Phoenix, it was no wonder I was marching through the terminal after having my bag searched in security, feeling like I might claw someone's face off if I didn't get a shot of caffeine in my system.

Even though I was hangry, my priority was to get upgraded to first class on my flight home to Boston. I could be hangry all I wanted in an airport. But as I was someone who suffered from mild claustrophobia, sitting in coach—with my luck stuck beside someone who would take their shoes *and* socks off during the flight—would be a million times worse than being hangry. I couldn't chance it. A pair of strange, hot, sweaty, smelly bare feet next to me for four and a half hours? No, that was a hell my current state of mind couldn't deal with. I shuddered as I marched toward the desk at my gate.

Seeing a small group of people crowded under a television screen,

I faltered, wondering what had drawn them to the news. I slowed at the images of huge plumes of smoke billowing out of a tremendously large mountain, my curiosity drawing me to a halt.

Within a few seconds the news told me that an unpronounceable volcano in Iceland had erupted, creating this humungous ash cloud that was causing disruption in Europe. Flights there had been grounded and consequently travel chaos ensued.

The thought of being stuck in an airport for an indeterminate number of hours—days even—made me shudder in sympathy for my poor fellow human beings.

I couldn't imagine dealing with that on top of the week I'd just had. I liked to think I was someone who was usually cool and collected, but lately my emotions were so close to the surface I was almost afraid of them. I asked the universe to forgive me my self-absorption, thankful that I was not someone who wasn't going to make it home today, and continued on my path to the gate desk. There was no one in line, and the man behind it began to smile in welcome as I approached.

"Hi, I was wondering—*Oof!*" I winced as a laptop bag attached to a big guy whacked against my right shoulder, knocking me back on my heels. The big guy didn't even realize he'd hit me as he strode right past and cut in ahead of me.

Rude!

"I'd like tae upgrade tae first class, please," he said in a deep, loud, rumbling, very attractive accent that did nothing to soothe my annoyance with him for cutting in front of me.

"Of course, sir," the gate agent answered, in such a flirtatious tone I was sure that if I'd been tall enough to see over the big guy's shoulder I would see the agent batting his lashes at him. "Okay, flight DL180 to Boston. You're in luck, Mr. Scott. We have one seat left in first class."

Oh, hell no!

"What?" I shoved my way up next to Rude Guy, not even looking at him.

The gate agent, sensing my tone, immediately narrowed his eyes at me and thinned his lips.

"I was coming here to ask for an upgrade on this flight and he"—I gestured to my right—"cut in front of me. You saw him do it."

"Miss, I'm going to ask you to calm down and wait your turn. Although we have a very full flight today, I can put you on our list and if a first-class seat opens up, we will let you know."

Yeah, because the way my week was going, *that* was likely.

"I was first," I insisted, my skin flushing as my blood had turned so hot with anger at the unfairness. "He whacked me with his laptop bag pushing past me to cut in line."

"Can we just ignore this tiny, angry person and upgrade me now?" the deep, accented voice said somewhere above my head to my right.

His condescension finally drew my gaze to him.

And everything suddenly made sense.

A modern-day Viking towered over me, my attention drawing his from the gate agent. His eyes were the most beautiful I'd ever seen. A piercing ice blue against the rugged tan of his skin, the irises like pale blue glass bright against the sun streaming in through the airport windows. His hair was dark blond, short at the sides and longer on top. And even though he was not my type, I could admit his features were entirely masculine and attractive with his short, dark blond beard. It wasn't so much a beard as a thick growth of stubble. He had a beautiful mouth, a thinner top lip but a full, sensual lower lip that gave him a broody, boyish pout at odds with his ruggedness. Gorgeous as his mouth may be, it was currently curled upward at one corner in displeasure.

And did I mention he was built?

The offensive laptop bag was slung over a set of shoulders so broad they would have made a football coach weep with joy. I was guessing he was just a little over six feet, but his build made him look taller. I was only five foot three but I was wearing four-inch stilettos, and yet I felt like Tinkerbell next to this guy.

Tattoos I didn't take the time to study peeked out from under the rolled-up sleeve of his henley shirt. A shirt that showed off the kind of muscle a guy didn't achieve without copious visits to the gym.

A fine male specimen, indeed.

I rolled my eyes and shot the agent a knowing, annoyed look. "Really?" It was clear to me motorcycle-gang-member-Viking-dude was getting preferential treatment here.

"Miss, please don't make me call security."

My lips parted in shock. "Melodramatic much?"

"You." The belligerent rumble in the Viking's voice made me bristle.

I looked up at him.

He sneered. "Take a walk, wee yin."

Being deliberately obtuse, I retorted, "I don't understand Scandinavian."

"I'm Scottish."

"Do I care?"

He muttered something unintelligible and turned to the agent. "We done?"

The guy gave him a flirty smile and handed him his ticket and passport. "You're upgraded, Mr. Scott."

"Wait, what—?" But the Viking had already taken back his passport and ticket and was striding away.

His long legs covered more ground than mine, but I was motivated and I could run in my stilettos. So I did. With my carry-on bumping along on its wheels behind me.

"Wait a second!" I grabbed the man's arm and he swung around so fast I tottered.

Quickly, I regained balance and shrugged my suit jacket back into place as I grimaced. "You should do the right thing here and give me that seat." I didn't know why I was being so persistent. Maybe because I'd always been frustrated when I saw someone else endure an injustice. Or maybe I was just sick of being pushed around this week.

His expression was incredulous. "Are you kidding me with this?" I didn't even try not to take offense. Everything about this guy offended me.

"You"—I gestured to him, saying the word slowly so his tiny brain could compute—*"Stole. My. Seat."*

"You"—he pointed down at me—*"Are. A. Nutjob."*

Appalled, I gasped. "One, that is not true. I am *hangry*. There is a difference. And two, that word is completely politically incorrect."

He stared off into the distance above my head for a moment, seeming to gather himself. Or maybe just his patience. I think it was the latter because when he finally looked down at me with those startling eyes, he sighed. "Look, you would be almost funny if it weren't for the fact that you're completely unbalanced. And I'm not in the mood after having tae fly from Glasgow tae London and London tae Phoenix and Phoenix tae Boston instead of London tae Boston because my PA is a useless prat who clearly hasn't heard of international direct flights. So do us both a favor before I say or do something I'll regret . . . and walk. Away."

"You *don't* regret calling me a nutjob?"

His answer was to walk away.

I slumped in defeat, watching him stride off with the first-class ticket that should have been mine.

Deciding food and coffee could wait until I'd freshened up in the restroom—and by freshen up I meant pull myself together—I wandered off to find the closest one. Staring out of the airport window at Camelback Mountain, I wished to be as far from Phoenix as possible as quickly as possible. That was really the root of my frustration, and a little mortification began to set in as I made my way into the ladies' restroom. I'd just taken my emotional turmoil out on a Scottish stranger. Sure, the guy was terminally rude, but I'd turned it into a "situation." Normally I would have responded by calmly asking the agent when the next flight to Boston was and if there was a first-class seat available on that flight.

But I was just so desperate to go home.

After using the facilities, I washed up and stared long and hard into the mirror. I longed to splash cold water on my face, but that would mean ruining the makeup I'd painstakingly applied that morning.

Checking myself over, I teased my fingers through the waves I'd put in my long blond hair with my straightening iron. Once I was happy with it, I turned my perusal on my outfit. The red suit was one of the nicest I owned. A double-breasted peplum jacket and a matching knee-length pencil skirt. Since the jacket looked best closed, I was only wearing a light, silk ivory camisole underneath it. I didn't even know why I'd packed the suit, but I'd been wearing black for the last few days and the red felt like an act of defiance. Or a cry for help. Or maybe more likely an act of denial.

Although I had a well-paid job within an exclusive interior design company as one of their designers, it was expensive to live in Boston. The diamond tennis bracelet on my wrist was a gift on my eighteenth birthday from an ex-boyfriend. For a while I'd stopped wearing it, but exuding an image of success to my absurdly wealthy and successful clients was important, so when I started my job I'd dug the bracelet out of storage, had it cleaned up, and it had sat on my wrist ever since.

Lately, just looking at it cut me to the quick.

Flinching, I tore my gaze from where it winked in the light on my arm, to my right wrist, where my Gucci watch sat. It was a bonus from my boss, Stella, after my first year on the job.

As for the black suede Jimmy Choos on my feet, with their sexy stiletto and cute ankle strap, they were one of many I was in credit card debt over. If I lived anywhere but Boston, I would have been able to afford as many Choos as I wanted on my six-figure salary. But my salary went into my hefty monthly rent bill.

It was a cute, six-hundred-square-foot apartment, but it was in Beacon Hill. Mount Vernon Street to be exact, a mere few minutes' walk from Boston Common. It also cost me just over four thousand dollars a month in rent. That didn't include the rest of my bills. I had enough to put some savings away after the tax man took his cut too, but I couldn't afford to indulge in the Choos I wanted.

So, yes, I'd reached the age of thirty with some credit card debt to my name.

But I guessed that made me like most of my fellow countrymen and -women, right? I stared at my immaculate reflection, ignoring the voice in my head that said some of those folks had credit card debt because of medical bills, or because they needed to feed their kids that week.

Not so they could live in a ridiculously overpriced area of Boston (no matter how much I loved it there) or wear designer shoes so their clients felt like they were dealing with someone who understood their wants better.

I bypassed the thought, not needing to mentally berate myself any more than I had since arriving back in Phoenix. I was perfectly happy with my life before I came home.

Perfectly happy with my perfect apartment, and my perfect hair, and my perfect shoes!

Perfect was good.

I straightened my jacket and grabbed hold of the handle of my carry-on.

Perfect was control.

Staring at the pretty picture I made in the mirror, I felt myself relax. If that gate agent had been into women, I *so* would have gotten that first-class seat.

"But forget it," I whispered. It was done.

I was going to go back out there and get a much-needed delicious Mediterranean-style salad and sandwich from one of my favorite food stops in Phoenix, Olive & Ivy. Feeling better at the thought, I relaxed.

Once I stopped being hangry, it would all be fine.

Two

Apparently, the universe *didn't* hate me, because there was a seat free at Olive & Ivy. It was popular, so it didn't surprise me that there was only one stool left at one of the counters around the small restaurant. The young twentysomething woman sitting next to the open chair looked up as I approached, her dark gaze skimming down my body and back up again. A flirtatious welcome smile lit up her face. Huh. I had hoped her obvious interest meant she would hold the seat for me while I ordered food. I rounded her, feeling her follow the movement. I was just about to ask her to keep the seat for me when the thump of a laptop bag on top of the counter at the open seat caused me to flinch.

"This seat is taken."

I squeezed my eyes closed at the familiar voice.

No way.

Nuh-uh!

No!

I whirled around and stared up at the source of irritation that had recently entered my life. "Yes, it is. By me!"

The Scot's stare was calm, stolidly so, annoyingly so. "Have you bought food yet? Because I have. As a paying customer, I think I take precedence over a tiny, entitled fruitcake with a stick up her arse."

I glowered up at the ceiling aka The Universe. "This is not happening."

"Aye, 'cause you're not a fruitcake, talking tae yourself."

My glare transferred to him. "Again with the totally un-PC language."

"Babe, look at me." He curled his lip. "I *am* un-PC."

"Don't 'babe' me. That is incredibly overfamiliar of you."

He bent his head toward me, those icy blue eyes momentarily freezing me to the spot. "And I am not having another altercation with you in public. Now bloody shoo."

He just shooed me?

Shooed me!

The Scot pulled the stool out forcefully, so I had to move back or be clobbered by it. He assessed my surprised expression and his countenance, to my confusion, transformed from merely irritated to total disdain. "I realize you're probably used tae men falling at your feet, so I'll let you have your two seconds of shocked horror. But if you're not gone in five seconds, I'm going tae embarrass the shit out of you."

"You curse a lot," was the only thing I could think to say under the onslaught of such distaste for me.

His face clouded over. "Five. Four. Three—"

I made a sound of disgust, cutting him off, and was about to walk away when the twentysomething woman next to us placed a hand on my arm to stop me. "I'm just finishing up, if you'd like my seat."

I gave her a sweet smile. "You're so kind, but"—my voice grew louder—"I'd rather sew my eyes shut with cocktail sticks than sit next to an ill-educated *dickhole* who defies the rumor that Scottish people are the nicest people in the world." I finished it with a triumphant spin that made my hair flip dramatically, and I would have continued to feel like the last-epic-word victor if I hadn't heard a ragged, too-attractive chuckle, which I knew had originated from the Scotsman.

That chuckle made me falter visibly.

He couldn't even let me storm off in style.

grabbed a sandwich from a refrigerator instead and ate it even though it tasted of nothing, while sitting at a gate that wasn't mine and staring out at the mountains. Using the time to cool down, as memories of the week pricked me and helped to put everything in perspective, I grew calm enough that I felt confident in striding back out there to grab a coffee from one of the barista carts. There was a line already forming at the closest one and I hurried a little to make it before it got too long.

At the sight of the imposing figure of the Bastard Scot marching toward the cart from the other side, I picked up my feet and almost ran toward the spot. I skittered into place behind a man in a suit, accidentally hitting his carry-on with mine. He threw me an annoyed look over his shoulder and I gave him a quick smile of apology before bestowing a *you can suck it* grin on the Scot as he pulled up to the line after me.

"You snooze, you lose," I said over my shoulder, not caring how infantile I sounded.

"You're four years old, you know that?"

"I finally beat you in line—that's what I know."

"Fruitcake."

"Ignoramus."

"Shrew."

I scowled at the insult, which was even worse than "fruitcake." *"Dickwad."*

"You seem tae be obsessed with my dick."

I spun around. "Excuse me?"

"Dickwad. Dickhole."

"Those are insults."

"With a very specific focus."

To my horror, my eyes flew to his crotch with a mind of their own. Oh dear God! My face blazed with color and I quickly lowered my gaze down the length of his dark blue jeans to the loosely laced black leather biker boots on his feet.

Big feet.

You know what they say—Shut up! Who cares what they say?

"It's really hurtful tae be objectified in this way."

Sure that my cheeks were tomato red, my eyes shot to his smug face.

"Look, as fun as it is wiping the floor with you in these verbal battles, I really need a coffee." And without further ado the Bastard Scot got out of line and walked to the front of it.

Uh, hell no!

I followed, my carry-on bumping on its wheels with my fury.

"My flight is about tae board," I heard him say to the woman who was next in line to be served. "Would you mind if I cut in front?" He was almost charming to her.

And *she* definitely thought so. "Of course." She practically swooned. "Where are you from? I love your accent."

"Scotland," he answered curtly, and stepped in front of her without saying thank you. This guy had no manners. But I did.

"Hey." I smiled at her. "I'm on the same flight as him. Would you mind?"

The Scot turned slightly at the sound of my voice.

She eyed him in disappointment. "Are you two together?"

He appeared nauseated by the thought. "I've never seen her before in my life."

The woman raised one very unimpressed eyebrow at me. "Nice try. Back of the line."

I'd never *actually* wanted to claw someone's face before, but I would definitely make an exception for the Bastard Scot.

"Your people would be ashamed," I said to his back.

To my disbelief, his shoulders started to shake. Was he laughing? I looked at the metal espresso machine and saw in its shiny reflection a distorted image of him grinning, teeth and all.

Ugh, he was so abrasive!

Spinning around, feeling sweaty, flustered, and so far from perfect it wasn't funny, I ignored the glares from the people in line and made my way back to the very end, which was now five people longer than it had been.

Two minutes later the Bastard Scot sauntered by me, shot me a wicked self-satisfied smile, and saluted me with his cup of coffee.

"Go to hell!" I shouted after him.

The guy in front of me gave me a wary look and stepped so close to the woman in front of him they were practically touching.

"He's an asshole," I tried to explain.

But the stranger's look told me he thought *I* was the asshole. And the truth was, the Scot was making me into an asshole. Or my bad mood was. I didn't know. Christ, I needed to get home, and as unfair as it was to blame an entire country for one man, I never wanted to speak to another Scottish person ever again.

Visiting Scotland was *so* off my bucket list.

Suddenly something in the loudspeaker announcement caught my attention. "Wait, what?" I stilled, listening.

". . . Flight DL180 to Boston has been canceled. Please see the gate for alternative flight arrangements."

Abandoning my quest for coffee (again!), I hurried down the terminal toward my gate in time to hear the gate agent from earlier explaining to the small crowd that had already gathered the reason why our flight had been canceled. Apparently, the volcano eruption and consequent ash cloud that had grounded flights in Europe had had a domino effect on domestic flights in the U.S. "The crew for this flight has been delayed because of the canceled flights in Europe. We're currently understaffed because so many of our crew members have been grounded in Europe on international flights. This means we unfortunately do not have a crew or a plane available for the scheduled flight to Boston. Please form an orderly line so we can make other arrangements for you."

I heard a few people complain about the late notice because "surely they knew there was no crew or plane before this." I also heard a lot of people make arrangements to stay at the airport hotel and get the next flight out to Boston whenever it became available. As more and more decided to do that, the antsier I became.

There was no way I could stay in Phoenix another night.

Two days had been long enough.

I needed to get home. ASAP. Or I was going to lose myself in gigantic, uncontrollable sobs.

My fingers were shaking by the time I handed my ID and ticket over to the gate agent. He recognized me from earlier because his lips pinched together.

"Is there an alternative route to Boston? A flight to another airport that has a flight to Boston?"

He relaxed at my tone and offered me a sympathetic smile, seeming to hear the tremble in my voice. "There is a flight out of Chicago tomorrow morning that will get you to Boston before noon. And a flight to Chicago is leaving from here in an hour." He checked his computer and threw me a wry smile. "There are first-class seats available on both flights."

Relief made me slump against the counter. I didn't even care how much it was going to cost. I just handed over my credit card. "Thank you."

Then I stared up at the ceiling again. *Thank you, Universe.*

Three

stared at my ticket, at my seat number. And then I stared at my seat.

And proceeded to glare at the person sitting in the seat next to mine in first class.

"You have got to be kidding me." *Screw you, Universe. You and I are done.*

The Bastard Scot looked up from his newspaper and gave a slight shake of his head. "Please tell me you are *not* sitting next tae me on a three-and-a-half-hour flight?"

"I'm just as unhappy about it," I said, opening the overhead bin. Lifting the carry-on that weighed a ton (seriously, it was a miracle I got it shut), I stumbled a little, losing my grip, and it whacked the Scot on the head. At the sound of his grunt, I smiled. "Sorry! That was a happy accident."

"Here, let me help you." A guy around my age in a tailored business suit stepped forward to assist but was brusquely brushed aside by the Scot as he stood up, dwarfing us both.

"I've got it." He grabbed the carry-on out of my hand. "Safer I do it or I'll land in Chicago with a concussion."

"Well, that would be a shame." I skirted past him so I could slide into my seat while he dealt with my luggage.

I'd already removed my e-reader from my carry-on for the plane ride and had it booting up before the Bastard Scot got back in the seat beside me. And even though there was a double arm divider between us with little cup holders in them, he still managed to make me feel overwhelmed by his size.

My plan had been to sink right into a good book and get on with my life like I wasn't sitting next to an uncivilized, too-attractive-for-his-own-good guy who definitely had to have some Viking blood in his genetic history. I was going to ignore him because I was certain he'd say something rude about the weight of my luggage. However, I didn't get the chance to slight him because he did it to me first. He pulled out the table from the side of his seat and propped a laptop open on it. And he acted like I didn't even exist.

"Mr. Scott." The flight attendant who had greeted me when I entered the plane appeared above us with a tray of drinks in his hand. "Can I offer you a preflight drink? Champagne?"

"Water." *Mr. Scott*—the Bastard Scot—responded in what seemed to be his typical abrupt fashion.

The flight attendant handed him a glass of water and then smiled at me. "Miss Breevort?"

"Champagne, *please*," I responded instantly, throwing my neighbor a filthy look for being discourteous. "*Thank you.*" Again, I don't know why, but I'd expected commentary from the Bastard Scot as I reached in front of his face for the glass of bubbly. But there was nothing.

My toes twitched with irritation, and my fingers gripped tight to the glass with annoyance as I sipped the champagne. I side-eyed Mr. Scott as he sipped his water with one hand and tapped the mouse pad on his laptop with the other.

I should have been glad he was ignoring me, but for some reason that felt as insulting as his behavior in the airport.

I didn't want to admit it, but his indifference bothered me. I'd spent the last few days being ignored by people in my hometown of Arcadia. And I mean treated as if I was invisible.

As much as I told myself I didn't care, it stung.

And now here I was being treated to the same by a complete stranger who had obviously made a snap judgment about me. That shouldn't have irritated me, but I was tired, I'd had a tough week, and it did royally annoy the crap out of me.

I glared out of the corner of my eye at him, my gaze drifting to the laptop screen his eyes were glued to. A wave of surprise moved through me. He clicked between tabs—spreadsheets with figures, complicated drawings that looked like technical specs, dense documents, e-mails. All of which suggested the Bastard Scot was more business guy than motorcycle gang member.

"Planning a big bank heist?" I said before I could caution myself against engaging in another verbal battle with him.

His stunning gaze turned my way. Confusion mingled with aggravation radiated from those unusual eyes.

I pointed to his laptop in answer to his silent question.

He looked back at it and then at me. The confusion left his expression, abandoning the aggravation that seemed to grow into full-blown vexation. "Do you always put your nose where it doesn't belong?"

"Well, if you don't want anyone realizing you're planning to rob a bank, you should probably hide the plans."

"It's my work," he bit out.

"You're a businessman?"

Somehow his reply was sarcastic without even saying a word. I took his silent retort for a yes.

"You don't look it."

"Aye, well, it doesn't surprise me someone like you would judge people based on what they look like." He sneered. "He's covered in tattoos, doesn't wear a suit, so of course he's a criminal rather than a businessman, right?"

"You do realize you're doing what you accused me of doing? You're judging me based on what I look like. Come to think of it, you have been doing that since the first time we ran into each other at the airport. Also . . . if you can afford to fly first class, you can afford to buy a sense of humor. And I would get on that because you're in serious need of one."

"How am I judging you based on what you look like?"

"'Someone like you,' you said, right?" I cocked my head to the side as I studied his rugged—and right now harsh—countenance.

He gave me a taut nod.

"You don't know me. You met me a few hours ago in an airport, where admittedly people don't always act like their normal selves because of high levels of stress, fatigue, and often fear of flying. So if you don't know who I am as a person, the only logical conclusion I can draw is that you're judging me based on what I look like and not on who I am."

The Bastard Scot contemplated me a moment. "True," he finally said. "To a certain extent. But you can often tell a lot about a person from the way he or she looks. It's just whether or not you're intuitive enough tae get it right. You saw tattoos and thought—what . . . motorcycle club?"

I tried not to blush, squirming uncomfortably that he'd guessed correctly.

"And you were wrong about me. But you are right, I dinnae know you, but I can tell by the time you spent on your hair and makeup, on the money you spent on your suit, on those designer shoes, the diamonds in your ears and around your wrist, that for whatever reason—and I dinnae know what those reasons are—you care what people think about your appearance. By the weight of the carry-on I just stuffed in the overheard bin I'd also say you overpack, which along with how you look, suggests you're high maintenance. And I would be very, very surprised if I'd gotten that wrong about you."

His tone more than the words caused a heat in my cheeks brought on by hurt feelings. "So you think you're better than me because you don't care about your appearance?"

"I didn't say I dinnae care about my appearance. I care. I'm covered in tattoos that say I care. I just dinnae care what *anyone else* thinks about my appearance."

"Well, maybe that's how I feel. *I* like to look well presented. It's got nothing to do with anyone else."

His answering expression suggested he didn't believe me and it bothered me that I cared. So I scoffed, "I don't care what you think of me."

"Of course you do. I'm probably the first straight man you've ever met who hasn't fallen at your feet." His eyes scanned my face first before moving down the length of my body in a way that made me involuntarily shiver.

That only made his words more provoking. They prodded an old hurt that had already been reawakened this week. I was determined to bury it where it belonged and did not need this stranger messing with my efforts. "You accuse me of being judgmental, but you are way more judgmental than me."

He shrugged. "Didn't say I wasn't. I'm just usually right. And I'm right about you."

The urge to prove him wrong was so strong and yet all that proved was that he was right. I cared too much what people thought. Despite his dismissal of me, of how much it opened old wounds, I decided the best thing I could do was just ignore him as previously planned.

I drank the rest of the champagne and put the empty glass in the cup holder beside me. The Bastard Scot turned back to his laptop like he hadn't just insulted me. *Again.*

Truthfully, I'd never met a more impolite, ill-mannered, impertinent man in my life.

Trying to ignore his existence, I opened up my current book on my e-reader, my body humming with awareness of the large guy beside me and growing steadily more pissed off about it. I hated that I kept getting faint whiffs of cologne—a decidedly delicious musky, woodsy, spicy scent that suited the bastard way too much. After I'd read the same paragraph for the fifth time, relief flooded me when my phone started to buzz in my suit pocket.

"That's supposed tae be switched off," he grumbled beside me.

I sniffed in derision as I pulled the cell out of my pocket. "The man who is trying so hard to prove he doesn't care what other people think of him is a stickler for the rules? Shocking."

Watching his lips pinch in annoyance gave me more pleasure than it should. Pleasure that transformed from smug to tender at the sight of the name on my phone screen. "Hey, sweetie," I answered.

"I'm sorry I missed your call. Lunch hour, you know." Harper's voice made me instantly relax. My best friend's voice on the other end of the line had kept me sane these past few days.

"I just called to tell you my flight got canceled. I'm on a flight to Chicago, but I'll have to stay overnight at O'Hare. My flight home isn't until tomorrow morning."

"What happened?"

"Some volcano in Iceland."

"I thought that was just affecting European flights?"

"Apparently not."

"Huh. That sucks. You okay?"

Aware of the man sitting next to me, I turned slightly toward the window and lowered my voice. "I just want to get home."

"I should have come with you." Harper's voice was filled with regret.

"No, sweetie. I had to do this alone. We both know that."

"We both don't know that. You are always there for me. You should have let me be there for you with this."

Maybe I should have. But the truth was, I didn't want the way I was treated back in Phoenix to affect Harper's perception of me. She knew my side of the story, of course, but I was afraid that all those people would somehow convince her everything was my fault. And it wasn't my fault. It was a ridiculous fear, because Harper loved me, but still it had snuck under my skin. "You didn't have to be there for me to *be there* for me."

Harper sighed. "Okay, babe. Just call or text me when you land in Chicago and let me know when your flight gets in at Logan tomorrow. I'll see if I can cut out of work to come get you."

"You don't need to do that."

"Well, I want to, so shut it."

I laughed softly. "Okay. I'll call you. Bye, sweetie."

"Bye, babe."

When I hung up, switching my phone off, I could have sworn I felt the Bastard Scot's eyes on me. When I glanced over at him, however, he was frowning at his computer screen.

The announcement that we were getting ready for takeoff came over the PA and we were asked to stow away larger devices like laptops. I surreptitiously watched my obnoxious neighbor as he put away his laptop and settled back in his seat.

He closed his eyes, and I used the moment to study him. The sleeves of his henley were still rolled up, so I could see up close some of the tattoos on his left arm. In among smoke, dust, and what looked like debris from buildings was a modern-day soldier running with his rifle. Above him there was what looked like the foot of another figure, but the rest of it was hidden by his shirt. My wayward gaze moved upward to his interesting face. His lashes were a fair golden brown color, so I hadn't realized how long they were until now. His full, pouty lower lip surrounded by that short beard drew my attention. Stubble was usually a turnoff for me, but I had to admit the pain in the ass suited his.

I wondered if it scratched or tickled when he kissed a woman.

The mere thought caused a tingle between my legs that shocked me.

Flushing at the thought, I wrenched my gaze off his face, intending to return to ignoring him and the physical response he'd elicited in me, when my eyes caught on his big hand curled around the arm divider.

Not curled.

Gripped.

Tight.

White-knuckled.

Looking back at his face, I saw the wrinkle between his brow and the slight flare of his nostrils.

Was the badass Scotsman afraid of flying?

I was instantly reminded of Harper. She was terrified of flying. We'd gone on vacation with each other a few times to Europe, and every time I'd felt powerless to help her. She was a ball of nervous energy as soon as we boarded an airplane, pale and trembling until we were up in the air. Even then she'd stay tense in her seat, her whole body clenched with fear. On long flights, I'd walk her to the bathroom and stand outside the door for her, a constant reassurance. Still, I hated how scared she was. I'd even tried to convince her to vacation in the States in places we could drive to. But Harper never let fear control her. That was one of the things I admired most about her.

Reminded of my friend, I felt an unwanted and unwarranted sympathy flood me.

"Excuse me," I called to the flight attendant as he was passing. I saw the Scot's eyes fly open out of the corner of my own. "May I have another glass of champagne?"

"We're getting ready to take off, Miss Breevort."

"I'll be super quick. Promise."

He didn't look happy about it, but returned quickly with a glass for me. I smiled my thanks and then turned to the Scot, whose eyes were closed again. "Drink up." I held the glass out to him.

Those icy blues flew open. "What?"

I shoved the glass toward him. "It'll help."

He lifted his head, grimacing. "What are you talking about?"

"Is it a fear of flying or just of taking off?"

Instead of answering, he shot me another baleful look. "I don't drink champagne."

"You'll drink this. It isn't whiskey, but it might take the edge off."

When he ignored me, I sighed. "Jesus, I don't think you're any less of an alpha pain in the ass because you're afraid of flying."

At that he snatched the glass out of my hand and threw back the entire lot. Wiping droplets off his lips, he glowered at me. "It's just the takeoff and landing."

The words were bitten out, and I had to quell a smile. "I'm not surprised. A plane isn't exactly a longboat."

His lips twitched. "Scot. Not Scandinavian."

"If you're telling me you don't have an ounce of Scandinavian blood, I don't believe you."

The flight attendant appeared to take the empty glass, but my seatmate didn't even seem to notice as he was too busy staring at me like I was suddenly a puzzle. "Swedish."

"What?"

"My great-great-grandfather was Swedish."

"I knew it. And here you were getting prickly because I called you Scandinavian. Technically I was kind of right."

"You're also more than kind of annoying."

"Well, you should be comfortable around annoying. You're the king of it. Although I'm beginning to wonder if this 'mean guy' thing you've got going on has more to do with you being afraid of flying than you actually being a mean guy."

He narrowed his eyes. "Mean guy?"

"Uh, yeah. You've been mean to me from the moment we met."

"I beg tae differ. You got in my face the moment we met. How else was I supposed tae respond?"

"You practically knocked me off my feet barging past me to get to the gate check-in desk."

"I didn't see ye."

"Seriously?"

"You're five foot nothing. Seriously."

"I'm five foot three. Five foot seven in my heels."

His gaze drifted down my body again, lingering on my legs. "You dinnae look it."

I frowned. "Are you suggesting I have short legs?"

"No, your height suggests that."

"I have surprisingly long legs for a short person."

"You can turn anything into an argument. That's quite a talent."

"You are distracting me from my point. Which is that you were clearly acting out because of your fear of flying, the same way I perhaps have not been myself due to exhaustion."

If I wasn't mistaken, I thought I saw a hint of curiosity in his expression. "Exhaustion?"

I shrugged. "It's been a trying week."

"Separated from your boyfriend?"

Huh? "What boyfriend?"

"The 'sweetie' on the other end of the phone."

I smiled. "That was Harper. She's my best friend."

"I'm surprised someone as annoying as you has a best friend."

"Everyone else loves me. If you weren't currently acting out, you might like me too."

"Look, I'm not acting out because I'm afraid. I didn't see you earlier in the airport, didn't know I'd clipped you with my laptop bag, but maybe if you hadn't come at me like a wee harpy, I might have apologized."

"I doubt it. You have no manners. I mean, what was your excuse for embarrassing me at Olive & Ivy? For being rude at the barista cart? Huh?"

He grinned suddenly, a sexy flash of his teeth that sent a fizz of pleasure shooting low across my belly. My physical response to his smile stunned me. "I did that because it was fun. You make it too easy tae wind you up."

I sniffed in an attempt to squash my absurd physical attraction to him, but even to me it came off sounding haughtier than I'd intended. "You are a very twisted, belligerent individual."

"And *you* might want tae consider having that huge stick rammed up your tight wee arse surgically removed."

"I'm sorry, I think you've mistaken me for someone who actually gives a damn what you think."

He scoffed. "Babe, like I said, I dinnae even know you and I know you care too much what other people think."

Infuriated that he kept pushing that particular button but refusing to let him see how much he was getting to me, I started calmly patting at my jacket pockets and then riffled through the magazines in the seat pocket in front of me.

"What are you doing?"

I turned to find him scowling at me. "Looking for some paper and a pen."

He raised an eyebrow in question.

"I thought I'd take some notes on your sage advice . . . and then you should take the paper and shove it up your ass."

"Do you want tae shut up and let me get through this?"

My smile was admittedly supercilious. "You almost are."

He frowned and then glanced around, only then realizing that we were in the air. We hadn't leveled out yet, but the plane had juddered up into takeoff minutes ago. The Viking/Scot had risen his voice to be heard over the engines, but he'd been so focused on me, he hadn't been paying attention.

He turned back to me, seeming uncharacteristically taken aback. "You're welcome."

Four

aybe I really was exhausted beyond rational thinking, because for a second I almost thought the Scot would thank me for distracting him during takeoff.

The surprise in his expression abruptly transformed into surly with a curl of his upper lip. "I hope you dinnae expect a thank you."

His tone was so cold I almost shivered. I realized at some point in our conversation I'd started leaning toward him. Pressing back against my seat away from him, I mirrored his expression. "Silly me to even expect it."

"Aye, well, annoying me tae distraction doesn't count as being helpful."

I returned my attention to my e-reader, readying myself to ignore his existence. "You are a miserable bastard, do you know that?"

"Babe, when I start caring what pampered princesses think about me, I'll know my life is no longer worth living."

Hurt flashed through me hot and unwanted, making my cheeks prickle. This guy was horrible. Just horrible! My fault for feeling sorry for him and mistakenly thinking his behavior could be excused due to his fear. I wouldn't make that mistake again. "Stop calling me 'babe.' My name is Ava."

He didn't respond and I wished I'd just ignored him entirely.

When they announced that we could start using larger devices, my loathsome neighbor pulled his laptop back out and returned to disregarding my presence—something I decided was a blessing. I was no longer insulted by his pretending I didn't exist. Clearly, it was better for my self-esteem that he did.

However, either it was the book I was reading or he was affecting me more than I'd have liked, because I could not get into the story. I would have turned to sketching, whether it was designs for work or just random sketches for my own pleasure. But Stella had told me not to pack my laptop and to set an out-of-office notice on my e-mails so I wasn't distracted by work, and I'd decided not to bring my sketchpad either. My boss was covering for me for the next few days, because she wasn't just my boss; she was my friend. There were only four of us at Stella Larson Designs. Stella, myself, Paul, and our junior designer, Gabe. We handled projects all over the world, not just in the U.S. I was used to flying out to a project, taking specs, measurements, an abundance of photographs, so I could design the space from our office in Boston. Depending on the size of the project, I'd maybe have to fly back to the site a number of times.

The budgets we worked with ranged from the mid six figures to well into millions of dollars. And we were dedicated to Stella's company. She made it easy, demanding excellence with a no-nonsense attitude, but treating us as more than employees: as friends who could talk to her when we had a problem. There were not a lot of employers like Stella, and she'd won our loyalty with her own. The day she approached me after seeing the results of my first big solo project out of college (I'd convinced my uncle to let me overhaul his office, and he just happened to be Stella's accountant), was one of the luckiest days of my life.

But right now, I was cursing Stella for being a good boss. I wish she'd demanded I stay on top of my work because right then I could have been answering a bunch of e-mails—e-mails I was sure were piling up between the two projects I was currently working on. Sometimes I had clients who turned the reins fully over to me; most times my clients just wanted to have the overall aesthetic (maybe even fabrics and palettes) run by them. And then there were the few who wanted to be involved in every choice I made. They were the exhausting clients and right now I had one of them.

I could only imagine she was going nuts waiting on me to get back to work.

Well, I knew the feeling.

I enviously watched my seatmate work away on his laptop.

The only bright spot was when the flight attendants offered us a light lunch and I got that cup of coffee I'd been longing for. It was instant, so it wasn't great, but it was caffeine and I could not help the little sigh of pleasure that escaped my lips after the first sip.

I thought I felt the Scot tense at the noise, but when I side-eyed him, he was digging into his lunch, ignoring me.

My lunch could wait. First I savored my coffee.

"If you're not going tae eat that, I will," he said, sounding annoyed.

How I managed to rankle him just sitting there I did not know.

"I *am* going to eat it. I'm enjoying my coffee first."

"I thought maybe you were one of those women that doesn't eat." He shrugged, throwing back the rest of his coffee.

"I think we've established you're a judgmental pain in the ass." I smiled sweetly before turning to my lunch. Feeling his eyes on me, I ate it slowly and deliberately, knowing intuitively that it would bother him. And it was not my imagination that the tension between us thickened as I brought bite after bite of the ham salad to my mouth at a snail's pace.

"Take that," he grunted out, and I turned my head to see he was holding his empty tray out to the flight attendant. The flight attendant stared at it, momentarily stunned.

"Of course, sir," he said calmly, practiced, before taking it and walking away.

Irate at his behavior, I couldn't help myself. "Do you ever say please or thank you?"

He cut me a dark look. "What?"

I gestured with my plastic fork to where the flight attendant had been standing. "People aren't your servants. The flight attendants are not your servants. They're doing a job and trying to make this flight easier on you. You can be forgiven for being abrupt and standoffish and maybe unintentionally insulting because you're anxious about flying. I was trying to tell myself that, anyway. But the way you speak to people in customer service makes you an arrogant, entitled prick."

"If I were you, I'd shut up and mind my own business."

"Yeah, well, if I were you, I'd reach into that goddamn dark soul of mine and pull a thank you out of there every now and then."

I didn't know if it was the honest pique trembling in my words, but the Scot's eyes widened marginally before he glowered and pulled his laptop back out with a clatter on top of his table.

Hateful, hateful man.

Ignoring him now came much, much easier. In fact, after lunch (and another coffee) I actually got into my book. The urge to use the bathroom about fifty minutes from our estimated arrival, however, made continuing to ignore my neighbor impossible. I was going to have to ask him to move. Plus, I was too warm and was dying to take off my jacket.

"Could you please let me out?" I asked in a carefully neutral tone.

Equally lacking in expression, he grabbed up his laptop, pushed his table back in, and gestured for me to get out.

I stared at the barely-there gap between his knees and the seat in front of him. Was he kidding? He wasn't going to get out of his seat? My gaze flew to his face, but he was staring determinedly ahead.

Fine!

If I happened to step on his feet and then grind my stiletto into his toes, that was his fault. Huffing, I got up, grabbed hold of the top of the seat in front of him, trying not to touch the head of the woman sitting in it, and I shoved my right leg into the teeny gap he'd left. If he'd been an average-sized man, I probably would have squeezed past no problem in the spacious first-class seats.

But he wasn't an average-sized man.

My leg touched his and my fingernails dug into the headrest in front of me. I shimmied into his space, bringing my left leg into the mix, and I heard him curse when my heel came down on his left foot. A fizzle of satisfaction moved through me and I pushed farther into his space. I felt his legs tense and I was suddenly very aware that my ass was in his face. Thankfully, it was mostly hidden by the peplum of my jacket.

With one last shimmy I stumbled out into the aisle and looked back at him, hoping he was seared and scorched by the heat of my glower.

The bastard already had his laptop back out.

Wondering how it was possible a person as ill-mannered as he hadn't been caught by karma by now, I marched down the short aisle and into the bathroom at the entrance of the galley.

Inside, I did my business, washed up, and yanked out of my jacket, feeling unbearably hot. Thankfully, the silk camisole I wore was cut low enough under my arms that there were no damp patches on the material. I patted under my arms and sniffed to make sure I didn't smell. Though I didn't, I'd need to freshen up soon in order to avoid it. Not that I cared if I smelled while sitting next to that asshole. I'd do anything to make the rest of his flight uncomfortable.

Knowing I couldn't stay in the restroom any longer, I slipped out, nearly bumping into the woman who had been sitting in the seat in front of the Scot.

"Sorry." I smiled apologetically. "Have you been waiting long?"

She shook her head, her expression filled with a sympathy that didn't make sense until she said, "It's okay. If I were sitting next to that jerk-off, I'd want to stay in there forever too."

Of course the people around us had heard our conversation. Weirdly, when I was talking to the miserable bully, I forgot everything else around me but him. That knowledge was not welcome. "Yeah," I managed feebly.

"Good for you, though. You know how to handle him. I think I'd probably have been thrown off the plane before we even took off. You know, for swinging a punch at him."

I laughed and thanked her, walking back to my seat feeling relief move through me that our flight was nearly over. As I approached, the Scot looked up at me. His gaze dropped to his computer but only for a millisecond before it flew back up. That arctic stare of his moved over my cleavage, now visible in the cami that was tucked into my high-waist pencil skirt.

A shiver I detested for betraying me skated down my neck.

His eyes flew back up to my face and he no longer looked right through me.

He appeared displeased.

Narrowing my eyes, wondering what the hell I'd done now, I gestured to my seat. "Can you let me back in?"

He snapped his laptop shut, dropping his table again. "High maintenance," he murmured quietly.

I gripped the now empty seat in front of him and turned my back to him as I shimmied in. "Yeah, needing to pee is so high maintenance."

My left foot hit his left foot and he pressed his knees in closer to the back of my thighs, trapping me.

I glanced over my shoulder, about to snap at him, only to catch him glaring at my ass. There was an angry heat in that stare, heat he hadn't looked at me with before. The kind of heat a guy usually had in his eyes when he wanted to find the nearest bed and throw me on it.

Suddenly, the image of him looming over me, his body pressed between my legs, flashed through me in a surge of fire that shocked and pissed me off in equal measure.

Huh.

I snapped my head back around, not going there. "Would you move?" I bit out.

His knees suddenly pulled back and I stumbled out of his space and tumbled into my seat with less grace than I'd have liked.

Feeling his gaze on me, I shot him what had to be the hundredth filthy look of the day. "What?"

Instead of answering, he turned, bent down toward the aisle, and came back up with my jacket in his hand. I hadn't even realized I'd dropped it. He shoved it at me and I snatched it out of his hold.

"What? No *thank you*?" he mocked.

"I'm not going to thank you for not getting out of your seat to let me into mine like someone with good manners would have done."

He grunted and turned back to his laptop.

"Ladies and gentlemen, we're now approaching Chicago O'Hare," the head flight attendant announced over the cabin PA. "Please put any larger devices like laptops safely in the overhead bins, stow tray tables, and return your seats to their upright positions for landing . . ." Her words faded out for me as my gaze unwittingly moved to watch the Scot put away his laptop. He stowed his table and got up out of his seat, stretching to his full height. He easily reached the overhead bins, putting his laptop away in its bag. I let my eyes wander down his long body, wishing that people with ugly insides could have some kind of monstrous appearance on the outside. In fact, if I was wishing for things I'd wish that my body wasn't as fickle as it was, that it had somehow evolved past cavewoman mentality, that it didn't lust for this kind of masculine virility I didn't even know still existed.

Need gripped my lower body, a clench of desire followed by a tingling I couldn't deny. Flushing, I wrenched my gaze away from him and began to shrug back into my jacket.

God, I hated him.

Our seats jolted a little when he threw himself back into his. He immediately clipped his seat belt on and I side-eyed him. His fingers were curled tight again over the ends of the arms of the divider between us.

Okay, if I was really wishing for things, I would wish I wasn't so softhearted, because I still felt a little sorry for him. Although I truly did not like this man, I also disliked the idea of someone who could clearly take care of himself being held captive by fear. I had a feeling that would bother this guy more than it would most people.

We sat in tense silence as the plane gradually descended, closing in on landing.

"I can feel you stewing over there."

I shouldn't have engaged with him, but I, unlike him, did not lack a heart and I knew that the only reason he was talking right now was because he needed the distraction. He was just too much of a baby to admit he needed me to distract him. So I answered, infusing the annoyance he wanted from me in my answer. "I'm not stewing."

"You're stewing."

"You don't know me well enough to know if I'm stewing."

He sighed. "Babe, no one would need tae know you tae know you're stewing. Everything you're feeling you wear on your face."

"Not true. I bet you don't know what I'm feeling right now."

"You're feeling murderous with a hint of sympathy."

My lips parted in amazement at his intuitiveness.

He rolled his eyes. "Murderous, fine. But to hell with your sympathy."

"You're awful. You know that, right? Like, truly awful. Is there anyone in this world who doesn't think that?"

"My entire family. Colleagues. Friends. The women I've had sex with."

Heat bloomed in my cheeks at his bluntness and the imagery it brought to mind. "I think you're probably delusional about the last one."

"I dinnae think so." His cold gaze drifted over me again, and then he abruptly looked away. "Uptight princesses just dinnae understand. They choose the wrong men who dinnae know how tae pleasure them and write sex off, thinking women who enjoy it are lying."

That's what *he* thought. "I've had good sex. Great sex." It had been years ago and it was followed by heart-wrenching betrayal, but it had been great sex.

He stared at me, I think trying to discern if I was being sincere. "That's surprising."

Uncomfortable with the way his eyes bore through me, I decided it was definitely time for a subject change. "So this family of yours . . . do they know you're obnoxiously rude?"

"Why would they? I'm nice tae *them*."

"Oh, so you admit that you're mean to me?"

"Maybe I am. Maybe I need tae be."

That enigmatic answer infuriated me almost more than anything else he'd said. "What does that mean?"

The freeze in his eyes suddenly warmed. "It means"—his deep voice juddered a little as the plane bounced onto the runway—"I need you tae hate me."

I screwed up my face. "What kind of bullcrap is that?"

His lips twitched as he studied me. "The kind that means you won't be amenable tae sleeping with me."

Genuine surprise locked me in place. "Excuse me?"

"You don't want tae sleep with me, do you?"

"No," I answered emphatically, because as much as I was unwillingly attracted to him, I *really* didn't like him. More than that, I didn't respect him.

I thought I saw a flicker of displeasure in his expression at my sincere reply. "Good," he bit out, and looked away. I knew the moment he realized we'd landed because he turned back to me. His countenance softened just a little. It was a look that said the words he was apparently incapable of saying out loud.

I thought I might have imagined the silent thank you until he gave me a curt nod.

I nodded back.

Quite abruptly he snapped off his seat belt and got up as everyone else did. Maybe it was his appearance, but the other passengers seemed to move out of his way after he grabbed his laptop bag out of the overhead. He strode past them down the aisle to wait in the galley to be let off the plane first.

Without another word.

Without even looking back at me.

"So rude."

Five

For the life of me, I couldn't remember the last time a shower had felt so good. The water pounded down on my shoulders, easing the tension, and they automatically dropped from where they'd been hunched up around my neck. As much as I wanted to be back in Boston, I was happy to be out of Arizona. I usually found O'Hare intimidating because of its size and how busy it was, but right then I didn't care. All I cared about was that I had made it to a hotel room, that the concierge had arranged to dry-clean a few of my outfits so I'd have something to wear down to dinner that evening, and that I'd finally sleep well miles away from my hometown.

Rather than get on a shuttle to some other hotel farther from the airport, I decided to stay at the hotel with an indoor walkway between it and the domestic terminals. The rooms boasted sound-resistant windows, I had a great view of the runway from the floor-to-ceiling window in the separate living room, and it meant I could sleep in a little longer before my flight in the morning.

As soon as I'd arrived at the hotel, I'd called Harper to let her know I'd landed and confessed to her how much my whole body had seemed to relax as soon as I'd stepped off that airplane. Just knowing I was out of Phoenix had a massive effect on my body. It was like

King Kong had snatched me up, squeezing me tight in his whole fist from the moment I'd landed in Arizona, kept hold of me during my stay in Arcadia, and finally as soon as I knew for certain I was in Illinois, the big ape let me go to return from whence he came.

Nick's face flashed across my mind. Grief-stricken. Confused. Angry.

It was followed by the accusatory expressions of all the people who used to be my friends.

"She died still thinking this was all her fault. It wasn't all her fault. We were to blame too. But you couldn't let it go, Ava. You couldn't forgive her. Now you can live the rest of your life knowing I'll *never forgive you."*

I didn't care if Nick would never forgive me. But I cared that I had never forgiven Gemma.

Once upon a time Gem had been the closest thing I had to a real family.

And just like that, memories I'd been trying to hold at bay flooded in . . .

T   *his is going to be the greatest three days of our lives!" Gemma whooped, throwing her hands in the air as the wind whipped her shoulder-length dark hair behind her.*

I threw my best friend a wide grin before turning my attention back to the road. Excitement filled me as I drove my blue convertible west down the I-10. It was the end of April, we had all but graduated from high school since the ceremony was just a few weeks away, and we were about to have our first real taste of freedom.

"Coachella 2006, baby!" Gem yelled again.

"Could you be any more excited?" I shouted over the sound of the car radio.

I felt her warm hazel eyes on my face. "Bree-Bree"—she called me by her childhood nickname for me—"this is the first day of our lives. For the last three years we've had to suffer under the authority of my parents at Coachella. Finally, we are eighteen, fully grown adults who can set up camp without my father complaining that the music is too loud while my mother whines about sleeping in a tent. Now, I love that they love me so much they would put up with going to a music festival for me every year. But I can't say I'm not freaking excited that me and my best girl get to do Coachella on our own together."

"I can't believe your parents agreed to it." And I couldn't. My parents didn't even flinch when I told them Gem and I had bought a parking spot at Coachella and were cutting school for two days to drive to California. We'd arrive that night, stay at a hotel, and then park up the next day, a Friday, in the spot we'd paid for. All by ourselves.

"They trust me."

I snorted, thinking of all the crazy stuff Gem got up to behind her parents' backs. The only reason they thought she was trustworthy was because I was there to make sure she was always okay. That was me. Miss Responsible.

"What?" She chuckled. "I'm trustworthy."

"Well, of course your parents think that. They don't know about Kade Moreno and his pickup truck three years ago."

"Well, yeah. No parent should ever know how their kid lost her virginity."

"Or that they lost it to the biggest manwhore in the entire state."

"He was experienced."

"Yeah, because he's a manwhore."

She rolled her eyes. "Whatever. Just because I have crappy taste in boys does not mean I'm not trustworthy."

"You took their Range Rover on a joyride to impress Styler James and let your mom take the blame for the dent you put in it."

"Yeah, but I felt bad about that. Styler so wasn't worth it."

"And what about the time you challenged Pete Manning to a beer-

chugging competition and Nick had to carry you out of there? We kept you hidden until you were sober and well enough to go home."

"Are you, like, keeping a journal of all my misdemeanors?" Gem laughed. "You make me sound way more wild than I am."

"You are wild."

"Luckily I have you to always make sure I don't go too far over the line." She threw her arm around my shoulders and gave me an affectionate squeeze before releasing me.

The familiar citrusy smell of her shampoo tickled my nose and with it I was suddenly flooded by love and concern for my best friend. My whole life my best friends Gem and Nick had been more like family to me than my own. Especially Gem. She was the sister I never had. The one person I could turn to for everything. I could turn to Nick for a lot of things too, but he was my boyfriend. It was different.

I could tell Gem absolutely anything and she would never judge me. I had her love and her loyalty and she had mine in return, plus my overprotectiveness toward her. In a few short months we would be at college and it would be the first time since we were four years old that we'd be apart.

"I'll be three hours away when we go to college," I said. "I won't be there for you then."

Gem reached over to turn down the volume on the radio. "No. No worries, no melancholy. Not this weekend." I saw her shake her head out of the corner of my eye. "And if it makes you feel any better, I'll have Nick."

It did make me feel slightly better knowing Nick would watch out for Gem. He was in his freshman year at Georgia State studying computer science. He played football and he was smart. Totally the whole package. Gem would be following him there to study law, which Nick and I both thought was hilarious because Gem was the biggest rule breaker we knew.

"I just can't believe after this summer we won't be together." Tears clogged my throat anytime I thought about it too hard. "I should have chosen to do interior design at Georgia."

"Okay, first off, we've already had that argument. And I won! Savannah is the better school for you. End of story. Two, let me repeat that there will be no sadness this weekend. This is Gem and Bree-Bree do Coachella! We have a tent, a case of beer you're adorably nervous about having hidden in the trunk, and a weekend of Daft Punk, Metric, Massive Attack, and more to look forward to. And you know what makes it even more awesome? The fact that Coachella isn't really your thing. It's my thing. But you came so I can share something I love with you. So it makes it our thing. And we are not going to be sad at our thing."

I knew she was right. I smiled at her before returning my attention to the road. "Coachella, here we come." It was true that a music festival wasn't really my thing, but I'd started going with Gem every year, not only because she wanted me there so we could escape into the festival away from her parents, but because I loved getting away from my house and my parents for an entire weekend. When I was with Gem and her mom and dad, I felt like I was part of their family.

Perhaps it sounded pathetic, but I was afraid of losing the family I'd made with her.

As she had an uncanny ability to do, Gem sensed my thoughts. "A three-hour drive isn't going to change us, Bree-Bree. Best friends forever."

My hands tightened on the wheel. "Promise?"

I glanced at her and saw her draw a cross in the air above her chest. "Cross my heart."

Determined not to be a wet blanket, I exhaled shakily and then shimmied my shoulders as if I was shuffling a melancholy grip off of me. "Coachella, here we come!" I repeated more forcefully.

Gem whooped beside me. "Hey!" She fidgeted excitedly in her seat. "I have an idea. Let's do Coachella every year. I mean, we've already started it as a tradition, but it's different now that it's just you and me. Let's make it always just you and me. No matter the new friends that enter our lives or how serious you and Nick get. You. Me. Coachella. Every damn year."

Warmth suffused me. "Definitely."

Gem turned the volume back up on the radio. We drove for another few minutes when she suddenly reached across to turn the volume back down. Feeling her gaze, I looked at her. Her expression was serious, sincere. "I love you, Bree-Bree. You're my family. Family is forever. I'm yours and you're mine and nothing will ever change that."

We kept our promise, and no matter what was going on in our lives, we got in a damn car and drove to Coachella, just the two of us, until the year after I graduated.

I'd never been to the festival since, and anytime I heard mention of it on the radio or television, I felt a sharp pain in my chest. Harper had brought up the idea of going once. After my grim reaction, she never mentioned it again.

I tried never to think back to my times with Gem there, because I was afraid of what I'd remember. Afraid to remember that once upon a time we were two young women who loved each other as deeply as sisters.

My knees buckled, a sob bursting out of me before I could stop it, and I slid down the wet tiles of the shower, pulling my knees into my chest. For the first time since my mom had called to tell me Gem had died, I cried.

I cried as pressurized water bounced and rolled off my skin, disguising my tears in the shower, unable, even when in private, to admit, even to myself, that I was crying. Admitting that was like admitting my guilt, and right then I couldn't bring that guilt to the surface. I was afraid if I did I'd never get to my feet again.

Perhaps I chose this particular dress to be dry-cleaned in defiance. It was the dress Nick's mother—who once upon a time had loved me like a daughter—had told me was inappropriate for the occasion. I'd worn it to the dinner my parents had insisted we attend the night before Gem's funeral.

It was black, figure-hugging, with a conservative hemline tight around my knees. There was a small split at the back of the knees, but nothing risqué. I think what Mrs. Kane had found inappropriate about the dress was the neckline. It was sweetheart-shaped and showed cleavage. Problem was, I had boobs and plenty of them and I gave good cleavage no matter how high or low a dress was cut. This dress was supposed to be conservative.

My boobs didn't know what the hell conservative meant.

Mrs. Kane had even side-eyed me at the funeral when I was wearing a black dress with a Peter Pan collar. If she wanted to blame anyone for my abundance of cleavage, she could blame my mom, who could have been Dolly Parton's long lost hippy daughter.

I noticed Mom didn't get the side-eye at the funeral in her long, floating bohemian dress with its revealing neckline. Not that Mom owned any article of clothing that didn't have a low-cut neckline.

The memory of Mrs. Kane's distaste for me and this dress somehow bolstered me. It tore through my grief and fired my anger. And I needed my anger more than I needed any of the rest of it.

"You're beautiful, Ava, but it's not enough. You feel empty."

Those words Nick had spoken to me so long ago still haunted me. Still knifed through my gut. Then: because they hurt so much. Now: because I'd never defended myself. Back then there had been a part of me that believed the words were true.

Suddenly I remembered the Scot's disdain for me all day. The way he'd judged me because of how I looked. That defiance in me grew, and as I readied myself to eat dinner alone, I rebelled by taking time with my appearance. Yes, maybe a long time ago I'd relied on my looks too heavily. But I was older and wiser now, and looking good wasn't about anyone else. Doing my makeup, slicking red matte lipstick across my full lips, putting on three coats of mascara that made my big jade green eyes pop, using my curling iron to create loose waves in my long blond hair, pairing my black dress with black stilettos and their signature red soles—all of it was for me. It was me saying, *Screw all of you.* My physical appearance was just a small fraction of who I was. I was more than a pretty bauble to hang on the tree of a man's world.

Tears burned in the back of my eyes and I blinked them away as I stared in the mirror. Years of moving on was not going to be obliterated by a few days in Arcadia.

When I was feeling stressed or distressed, I would run. Run for miles. Sweat it out. Let it all go. Running was my self-medication. But I didn't have my running gear with me and I was in an airport hotel. Without my usual avenue of relief open to me, I decided getting out of the hotel room would just have to do.

Armor on, I swiftly turned away from the mirror, grabbed up my purse and key card, and left the room.

I made my way down to the hotel restaurant, giving the hostess a blinding smile when she asked me if it was a table for one. "Yes, please."

The restaurant had a traditional look about it—dark wood furniture, dark wood floors, and intimate low lighting. I stared straight ahead, following the hostess to a small booth at the back of the restaurant. Suddenly feeling as though I was being watched, the skin on my neck prickled. Out of my peripheral vision I caught sight of a table of businessmen staring in my direction and put the feeling down to that.

"Is this okay? Or would you prefer a small table?" She gestured to one in the middle of the room.

But I preferred the privacy of the small booth. I slid into it. "This is great, thank you."

She handed me a menu. "Your waitress, Emily, will be with you shortly."

I thanked her again and dropped my gaze to the menu. My stomach grumbled loudly as soon as I saw filet mignon.

My waitress, a tall, willowy young woman with an English accent appeared to take my drink order. I asked for champagne, because screw it. After the week I'd had, I was treating myself to a goddamn filet mignon and a glass of champagne. Or two.

As I sipped at my glass of bubbly, I pulled my phone out of my purse and trolled through the work e-mails I wasn't supposed to be looking at until my return.

However, the skin on my neck continued to prickle, distracting me. It wasn't a wonder, then, when I felt someone approach my booth and stand over me. Slowly I lifted my gaze, annoyance already heating my skin when I found a tall, rangy guy in a business suit grinning down at me.

"Dining alone?"

I didn't reply and let my deadpan expression do the talking.

It didn't deter him. "That is a diabolical sin." His dark gaze drifted down to my cleavage, which he blatantly ogled. My skin crawled. "I'm Matt. Let me join you."

In hell, maybe. "Matt, I appreciate the offer. But I just want to have a quiet dinner alone. Thank you." I dropped my gaze, returning my attention to my phone.

It took him a second or two—I could almost feel his confusion—but he eventually walked away and I breathed a sigh of relief. Dear old Matt was likely thinking to himself, *Why would a woman dress that way if she wasn't looking to grab a man's attention?* And that there was one of the things still wrong with our society. There was this obnoxious misconception that women only dressed well to attract a mate. Hello! Some of us were just obsessed with clothes, shoes, and makeup and liked to look good, you know, for *ourselves*. Shocker.

So I wasn't at all taken aback when the feeling of being watched didn't dissipate with Matt's retreat.

My toes curled inside my shoes with agitation as I felt another person approach. This time he slid into the bench across from me in my small booth. I lifted my gaze to the stocky blond guy who bore a faint resemblance to a handsome Australian actor. Clearly, he thought this made him irresistible, if the cocky, assured smile he shot me was anything to go by. "Sorry about my friend Matt. I tried to tell him a beautiful woman like you wouldn't be interested in sharing a meal with a guy like him. I came to rescue you instead. I'm Chuck."

Of course he was. I stared through him stonily. "Well, Chunk—"

"It's Chuck."

"I don't mean to be rude, but I couldn't care less if your name was Tallulah. Like I told your friend, I just want to eat alone. If you wouldn't mind . . ." I gestured for him to get out of the booth.

He leaned over the table, his blue eyes moving over me in a way that made Matt's staring feel benign. "I get it. You're alone. You feel vulnerable, a little defensive, but you don't have to. I promise you I'm a nice guy who just wants to share a meal with a pretty woman instead of the assholes I'm on a business trip with." He smiled.

I guessed I was supposed to melt now.

"Chuck." I smiled sweetly and his eyes lit with triumph. "If you don't get your ass out of my booth, I'm going to scream bloody murder."

The grin promptly fled, replaced with astonishment. "There's no need to be rude."

"I'm not the one who sat down at a table I wasn't invited to sit down at."

"I think we've gotten off to—"

"Chuck. Get the hell out of my booth."

Chuck flushed angrily and shuffled out of the booth, shooting me one last glare before he marched back to his table.

My heart pounded in my chest, my fingers trembling slightly as

I reached for my glass. Confrontation was never fun. Some people might think I was the one who had turned it into a confrontation by being defensive—a bitch even—but I was watching these men from under my lashes. They were laughing as another one of them stood up, grinning my way, shrugging his suit jacket down as if readying for battle. So was I a bitch? Or was I fully in my rights to feel defensive and wronged when men treated me like prey?

Yes, I was *absolutely* within my rights.

I felt my stomach plummet as the next one began to walk toward me. This was a game to them. To see which one of them broke me.

Deciding I'd rather eat in my room alone than endure their assholery, I reached for my purse and began to shimmy out.

"Stay."

My eyes flew upward at the familiar voice and a flip low in my belly betrayed me.

The Bastard Scot towered over me for a second before he slid into the bench opposite me. I could only stare at him, stunned. Somehow, I still wasn't used to how striking and pale those blue eyes of his were. They held me fixed in their snare, and the hair on the back of my neck stood up. Was *he* the one who had been staring at me? Was it his eyes that made my skin prickle? Finally, able to relinquish my eyes from his, my gaze drifted over him. He was wearing a white shirt open at the collar, the sleeves rolled up to the elbow so his right sleeve of tattoos was visible again. His blond hair looked a little darker and I realized it was still wet from the shower he'd obviously taken.

The thought of him naked with water rolling down that fine body made me flush hot, and I was more discomforted than ever that I could be attracted to someone I did not like.

"Better this than me layin' one of those assholes out, no?" he suddenly said from his place opposite me.

My eyes flew over to the table of businessmen. The one who was standing threw us a disgruntled look before slumping back into his seat. His buddies shot my new companion displeased frowns.

I turned back to the Scot, utterly confused.

His expression was sour, and I realized why when he spoke. "My presence will deter them. We'll just pretend we're at different tables. But this way we can both eat in peace."

Clearly I was putting him out so . . . "Why help me?"

"You might be a pain in the arse, but I wouldn't let any woman be harassed. And I owe you. I don't like owing anyone. This way we're even."

His words from earlier came back to me. "I hope you don't expect a thank you."

The Scot's lips twitched, as if desperate to smile at my teasing. He got hold of that impulse, however, and didn't reply. Instead, he sipped the whiskey he'd brought over to the table with him.

Tension immediately sprung up between us as we sat looking anywhere but at each other.

Really? We were supposed to sit there and ignore each other?

I rolled my eyes. "They're not exactly going to be deterred if we look like two strangers sharing a table."

His gaze returned from its perusal of the room to meet mine. "Believe me, they will."

Considering how he dwarfed the booth, he was probably not wrong. But . . . well . . . the thing of it was that he was doing a surprisingly nice thing for me. I was weirdly not uncomfortable around him even though he was obnoxious and rude, and I think—maybe because of my physical attraction to him more than anything else— I wanted the chance to discover that he did in fact have a redeeming quality.

"I'm Ava Breevort."

"No one said anything about exchanging names."

I sighed. "Okay. I could continue to think of you as the Bastard Scot in my head, if you'd like."

The look he gave me said he found me more than a little insufferable. Well, hey, the feeling was mutual. Still, he answered, "Caleb. Caleb Scott."

"Why do men do that?"

"Do what?"

"Say their name followed by their name *and* surname. Is it just an unconscious desire to be James Bond?"

"I'm already regretting this favor."

Redeeming quality? Really, Ava? "Well, Caleb, I didn't ask for the favor and I didn't need it. I don't need some man to save me. I was taking care of it myself."

"You were leaving, you mean."

The businessmen had returned their attention to their dinner and one another. I shrugged. "If it had just been the one guy, I would have stuck it out. But they were obviously gearing up to make this a game, and I just wanted to eat in peace."

"Why accept my help, then? Why not just get up and leave?" He seemed genuinely curious about the answer.

"Not all men are assholes. I know that. But those that are fall into different categories. You are an asshole but you're not *that* kind of asshole—" I gestured to the men who had bothered me. "That makes you less of an asshole than they are and one I'm willing to put up with so I can eat my medium-rare steak and not whatever dry lump of meat resembling filet mignon they send up as room service."

"Fair enough." He took another sip of whiskey.

"So, what is it you do, Caleb?"

He raised an eyebrow. "Small talk?"

"I could keep insulting you instead, if you like?"

I thought I saw his lips begin to smile, but, again, he fought the reaction. *Hmm.* "I'm the CFO of the UK division of Koto."

Shocked by this information, I sought to clarify. "The tech company?"

"The very one." He gave me an arrogant, knowing smirk. "Didn't expect that, did you?"

"Honestly, no. That's a pretty big job title you've got there. I heard Koto is becoming a real competitor for some of the bigger tech giants."

Caleb's eyes glittered suddenly with a fierceness I'd understand when he said, "We're almost there. And we plan tae surpass them."

"So you must enjoy numbers?"

"I'm *good* with numbers."

I frowned. That wasn't really an answer, but before I could re-mark upon it he spoke. "What do you do for a living? Personal shopper?"

"Close." I shrugged, not letting his snide tone get to me. "I'm an interior designer."

"Well, either you do very well or you're a kept woman."

My plans to not let him get to me flew out the window pretty quickly. Why was the latter even a choice? Did I really say he was any different from those other assholes in the restaurant? My mis-take. "Because I flew first class?"

He didn't even flinch at my snarky tone. "Aye. That, the designer shoes, and the diamonds in your ears and on your wrist."

"Well, of course I'm a kept woman. And it's not just one guy I spread for cash. I've got three sugardaddies. Lucky girl, huh?"

Caleb rolled his eyes. "You take offense tae everything."

"*Everything* you say is offensive."

"Ah, there you are." Emily suddenly appeared at the booth, look-ing a little flustered as she eyed Caleb. "You switched tables."

"Aye." He held out his hand for his plate of food, which I noticed was also the filet mignon.

"There you go. Can I get you anything else, sir?"

"No." He immediately started to dig in without a thank you.

I looked up at Emily and she gave me a pained smile. "I'll be right back with your order."

"Thank you so much."

As she walked away, I eyed Caleb with a mixture of distaste and longing. Distaste for him, longing for his steak.

My belly grumbled loudly and I quickly drank the rest of my champagne. Caleb looked up from his plate, amusement in his eyes. Amusement that made him five million times more attractive than the haughty chill did. "Hungry?"

"Starving. Is it good?"

"Aye." He grinned, one of wicked taunting, and took a huge bite.

Thankfully, Emily returned with my dinner before I could consider stealing Caleb's plate out from under him.

"Oh my God. Thank you," I said, practically ripping it out of her hands.

She laughed. "You're welcome. Can I get you anything else?"

"Champagne, please." I tapped my glass with my fork.

"Would you like a bottle instead?"

If I was going to get through dinner with an arrogant Scot, I was thinking yeah. "Oh, yes, please." I threw her a quick smile before I started cutting through my filet. I squished pomme purée onto the fork with the steak and rubbed it in the sauce before shoving a huge mouthful through my parted lips.

I closed my eyes and groaned around the tasty beef. When I swallowed, my eyes popped open in preparation for the next bite, but instead of going directly to my plate they got stuck on Caleb's.

He was staring at me with a forkful of food halfway to his mouth, frozen, his features taut with tension while those ice eyes had melted into blue pools of heat. My breath caught in my throat. "What?" I whispered.

His eyes narrowed. "Do you always eat like you're having an orgasm, or is the show just for me?"

Blush blazed across my cheeks. "Excuse me?"

"On the plane with your coffee. Now here with the steak?"

My cheeks felt hot enough to cook on. Did I really do that? "I . . . I just like coffee. And steak."

What happened floored me more than his insinuation that I got the same kind of pleasure out of food and coffee as I did from sex.

Caleb Scott grinned.

And it was not a wicked smile or an arrogant smirk. Just a wide, amused grin that caused a strange flutter in my chest. "You really are something else, babe."

I had wanted to find something likable about him to feel better about my physical attraction, but the sudden compression on my chest, the feeling of breathlessness that I remembered from when I first realized I had a crush on Nick, stunned me for a moment.

It scared me.

One moment of normality didn't eradicate the last day of him being a total prick to me. I frowned, busying myself with my food. "Don't call me 'babe.'"

There was no response and we continued to eat in silence. When we finished up, Emily returned to take our plates and offer us the dessert menu.

"Thank you," I said as she gathered the plates in her hands.

I waited for Caleb to follow suit and was not surprised when Emily walked away without receiving a thank you from him.

"Why?" I took a huge gulp of champagne.

His eyebrows drew together. "Why what?"

"Why do you never say please or thank you?"

"I noticed years ago at work that my staff responded better tae me when I stopped saying please and thank you and just started expecting them to do a good job. It's psychological."

"One, that's still shitty. But two, okay, that's your staff and maybe that really does work for you in the office. But you're not in the office. People are doing you a kindness and you don't thank them."

"They're not doing me a kindness. They're doing their bloody job."

"True. So say you got a shitty waitress or crappy flight attendant . . . you're right. You shouldn't thank someone when they're doing a shitty job. But none of these people today have been doing a shitty job. It's just good manners to thank them."

"Why does it bug you so much?"

"It's common courtesy. I know when I spend weeks, sometimes months designing a space or a house, that it feels amazing when the client thanks me. And it feels horrible when they don't say anything. You know they like it because they've called a national magazine to have them photograph it or you see them plastering it all over their social media showing it off. But they never said thank you or good job.

"Being underappreciated is like being a ghost. They know once upon a time you were there, that you made a mark, but they already stopped caring before you even said good-bye. That's shitty. And maybe being a flight attendant isn't making someone's home or office a place they love to spend time in, and it's not making sure a tech company stays on the right path upward financially . . . but it's making sure someone who is afraid of flying, or is tired and grieving, has a good flight at least. That they didn't have to put up with obnoxious service. The same with Emily tonight. She got our food out to us and she did it with a smile. And we don't know what kind of day Emily is having. If those assholes over there have been giving her a hard time.

"So maybe a please or a thank you doesn't seem much to you. But I'm pretty sure that every time I say thank you to Emily—including the thank you I'll leave in my twenty percent tip—it helps her deal better with the assholes who were rude to her while she stands on her feet for a twelve-hour shift in the four-inch heels her boss insists she wear."

I drew in a breath after my rant and sat back in my chair, waiting for his sarcastic reply. It didn't come. Instead, he just stared at me, his expression inscrutable.

"What?"

His answer was to look at the menu. "Are you getting dessert?"

Would it have been wrong of me to pour my champagne over him?

Yes, yes, it would have. That didn't mean I didn't feel the urge. I sighed and looked over the menu. "I am."

We didn't speak as we waited for Emily to return. "Dessert?"

"I'll have the chocolate fudge cake."

"Whipped cream or ice cream?"

"Ice cream, please."

"Great." She turned to Caleb.

He shook his head and handed her the menu. "Nothing for me."

As Emily walked away, I frowned at my companion. There was a possibility if I stuck around him any longer I was going to form permanent wrinkles between my brows. "I thought you were eating dessert. I wouldn't have ordered if you weren't."

"Why not? Frankly, it's refreshing that you eat steak and choco-late cake."

"I don't normally. It's a treat."

"Because you're grieving and tired?"

Stunned that he'd picked up on that and that he was curious enough to ask, I attempted to shrug it off. "I'm not drunk enough to talk about that."

"Fair enough. But I'll still wait with you while you have your dessert."

"Well, as begrudgingly as it is given, I'm grateful." I snorted. "I'm looking forward to that damn cake."

This time there was no mistaking the male appreciation in those spectacular eyes. "Aye. Me too."

He was obviously referring to my reaction to eating good food. I flushed and hoped he attributed it to a champagne blush. But if that cocky smirk of his was anything to go by, he didn't.

Oh boy.

Six

S omehow after cake we still hadn't left the table. After we'd
paid for dinner (separately!), Caleb said he needed another
drink. When I stood up from the booth to leave, he'd put a
hand on my lower back and led me to the bar.

I was so hopped up on sugar and bubbles that I followed, completely bemused.

An hour later I was still sitting at the bar with this obnoxious
Scotsman I didn't like very much, sharing my wisdom about life in
general and teetering over the edge into drunk. I was perfectly aware
of my surroundings, but all the snark and defensiveness had leaked
out of me as my alcohol consumption increased. Suddenly, I didn't
hate Caleb. We were just different people, and just because you didn't
agree with someone on everything didn't mean he was a bad person.
Caleb had sat with me during dinner to stop other men from harassing me, which was very thoughtful, I thought.

"It was thoughtful, Caleb," I found myself saying.

He smiled at me over the rim of his third glass of whiskey, and I
felt that now familiar flutter in my stomach. God, he was handsome!
"What was, babe?"

And being called "babe" by him wasn't so bad. When Harper

called me "babe," I found it cute. I felt something a little different when Caleb called me "babe." "Sitting with me. Acting as a barrier between me and those awful men. That was thoughtful. You can say it was you owing me, but it was still thoughtful."

"I thought you didn't need me tae rescue you?"

"I didn't. I don't. That doesn't mean I don't appreciate the effort."

His lips did that twitchy thing again. "Noted."

"I mean, it has been such a shitty week. I just . . . I didn't need guys acting like their usual asshole selves and bugging me. Just because a woman dresses nice"—I gestured to myself—"doesn't mean she's advertising that she's looking for a guy to take notice."

"No, you're right. It doesn't. But it would be naive tae think that some men dinnae still think that it does."

"Oh, I know that. But I refuse to let misogyny and sexism and sexually aggressive a-holes dictate what I put on my body and how I do my makeup or my hair."

"So this is all just for *you*?" Caleb waved a finger over the air in front of me.

I scowled at him, momentarily forgetting I didn't hate him anymore. "Yeah, it is! This is my 'Screw you, Nick!' 'Screw you, everyone!' Being pretty doesn't mean being empty."

Caleb lifted an eyebrow. "Who is Nick?"

I laughed bitterly. "Ah, the million-dollar question. Nick, Nick, Nick. Nick Kane. He doesn't like me very much. He used to. But he stopped. He . . . he was married to my best friend, Gemma." Tears glittered in my eyes before I could stop them. "She died. Childbirth. They struggled to get pregnant and then . . . God . . . she needed a C-section and there were complications. She and the baby died." I brushed a tear away, sucking them back. "I went back to Arizona for the funeral this week and, uh . . . I wasn't welcome. It was a crappy experience and, you know, burying my ex–best friend and all, my expectations were already kind of low. But, shoot . . . those people managed to take that experience and make it shittier than fleas on shit. That, my friend"—I leaned toward him—"is a gift."

Either I was getting really drunk or Caleb's expression softened. "I'm sorry tae hear that, Ava."

"That's the first time you've called me Ava instead of 'babe.' You're nicer than you let on."

He scowled instantly. "I'm not nice."

"Okay." I leaned away from him and drank the rest of my champagne. "You may not be nice, but I am grateful to you tonight. This is the first time I've relaxed all week. It feels good."

"Ava."

"Mmm."

"Ava, look at me."

I looked at him.

Oh boy, he was so attractive. I wondered what those unshaven cheeks would feel like between my thighs. "Hmm?"

And as if he read my thoughts, he leaned into me. The scent of his sexy cologne made my senses prickle and tingle. "How drunk are you?"

"How drunk are you?"

"I'm not drunk but I'm not sober."

I nodded. "I'm that too."

"So if I ask you tae come up tae my room, I wouldn't be taking advantage?"

My breath faltered as I stared into those beautiful eyes of his. I tried to remember how only a few hours ago I didn't even like this guy. But that was hard to remember when he was so yummy and Scottish and talking to me in that accent. The only conclusion I could come to was that I'd been feeling uptight and defensive earlier. Now . . . not so much.

And I hadn't had sex in a really long time.

Like a really, really, *really* long time.

Suddenly there was a tall Viking with a hot accent asking me up to his room and I was not really sure I wanted to say no to that.

The tingle that was growing in intensity between my legs and the tightness in my breasts also seemed kind of unsure that they wanted to say no.

"You don't even like me. You said you wanted me to hate you so I wouldn't want to sleep with you."

His lips curled up at the corners. "I dinnae need tae like you tae want tae have sex with you." He leaned in, making my breath falter. "And aye, I was going tae ignore the urge but it seems you keep getting thrown in my way. And just because you dinnae like me either, babe, doesn't mean you dinnae want tae have sex with me tae."

In that moment, I thought he was wrong. Not about the wanting to sleep with him part, but the liking him part. He didn't seem so bad. And I wanted him. That in itself was unusual enough to make up my mind. "I could come up to your room."

"Just sex, Ava."

"Oh, I don't do relationships," I assured him honestly, staring at his beautiful mouth. "They just rip you open and eat your carcass and then leave it there for some other animal to finish you off. If you're smart, you heal and you get your ass up out of those woods and make sure no animal gets the chance to rip you back open. But I'm amenable to having wild animal sex with you." I reached up and ran my fingers over the prickle of thick stubble on his face and whispered, "Will it tickle my thighs?"

Caleb's eyes flashed and I swear I heard him growl, before he slapped a lot of cash down on the bar and got up off the stool. Then my hand was in his, helping me off the stool, his fingers tightening around mine as he marched us through the bar and down the lobby toward the elevator.

Oh my God. I was really doing this. I couldn't blame the alcohol, because the world wasn't spinning or anything and I felt totally aware of what I was doing.

And very turned on.

My gaze drifted upward from Caleb's black boots, to his black jeans, to the white shirt that attempted and failed to make him look civilized. Finally I settled on his strong profile. The proud, straight nose. The bristles of his blond stubble that did nothing to hide the sharp angles of his cut jawline. His full lower lip was so sensual it made me want to nibble on it.

Feeling my intense gaze, he looked at me and I found myself falling into those eyes. I'd never seen eyes like them. They were like wolf eyes. He looked like he was going to eat me up, and I sucked in a breath.

I couldn't remember the last time a guy had looked at me with such sexual voraciousness that I welcomed. More than welcomed. I wanted him to wreck me in the bedroom—give me so many orgasms that it made up for the years of abstinence.

"You're going to be as good at this as you look, aren't you?"

His answer was a devastatingly arrogant grin as he pulled me none too gently into the elevator and pushed me up against the wall as the doors closed. He pressed his long, hard body against mine. "Never fear, babe. I'm about tae ruin you."

The elevator dinged and quite abruptly he hauled me out and down the hall. I vaguely noted we were staying on the same floor, but Caleb marched me in the opposite direction from my room.

He let go of my hand to let us into his room and I found myself standing in the middle of a suite identical to mine.

The first thing he did was grab a remote control to lower the blinds over the window facing the runway. Then Caleb turned to me and studied me carefully for a moment. "Still sober?"

I swallowed hard, feeling more sober than I had downstairs. "Yup."

"Still want this?"

There was a doubtful voice in the back of my head, the one that was quickly sobering up, telling me to stop this nonsense. But my blood was too hot and my inhibitions were down. I wanted sex. End of story. I nodded. "Do you still want this?"

Caleb's response was as straightforward as ever. He crossed the distance between us, slipped his hands into my hair, and tugged me toward him. His mouth slammed down on mine, his kiss hard, hungry, needy—everything I couldn't remember ever having.

I wrapped my arms around his waist, my fingers curling into his shirt as I tried to match his ferocious kiss. His tongue swept against mine and I groaned as lust shot through me, making my breasts tingle and my belly tighten. I found myself being pushed toward the bed as his large hands gently extricated themselves from my hair, slid down over my breasts, the pads of his fingers just tickling the swell of my cleavage. My nipples peaked against my bra as his fingers trailed down my stomach and his hands gripped my waist. All the time he kept kissing me.

I was jolted out of the kiss when he abruptly spun me around and moved my hair out of the way of my zipper. "You have gorgeous hair."

"Thanks," I whispered, shivering as he tugged the zipper down on the dress. He brushed the fabric away from my shoulders and I took over, releasing my arms from the short sleeves and pushing it down from my waist until it dropped to the floor. I stepped out of the fabric, wobbling a little in my heels as I undressed.

I felt his breath on my neck as he dragged the back of his knuckles down my spine. "Perfect," he murmured.

Feeling hot—way too hot—I spun back around, reaching for him, but suddenly he gripped my waist again. He lifted me up like I weighed nothing and dropped me on the bed with a bounce. I made a little squeak of surprise.

Caleb towered over me, his body tense, his features taut, his eyes hot as they dragged over my body. I wore a matching black lacy bra and underwear. Something flickered in his expression—something I didn't like—and he took a step back from the bed.

Confusion made me tilt my head. "Where are you going?"

He didn't answer but a muscle ticked in his jaw.

Feeling vulnerable, I felt the snarkiness that had left me down in the bar return. "I'm sitting on your bed in my bra and underwear. Don't be an asshole. Are we doing this or am I putting my dress back on?"

And just like that, he grinned at me. God, the man gave mood swings a new meaning! "Underwear off, babe."

"*Please.*"

He shook his head. "Not even for sex."

I rolled my eyes but reached for the clasp on my bra. I shimmied it off and dropped it at his feet. I knew I had great boobs. Right now they were swollen and my nipples were tight. I sat back on my hands, the natural arch of my back thrusting my favorite assets out.

The Scot's gaze devoured me. "Jesus," he muttered.

The tingling between my legs worsened. "I'm going to assume that means you like what you see."

"Was it the hard-on that gave it away?"

My eyes lowered to where a bulge was straining the crotch of his jeans. A fizzle of deep, gnawing need hit me in the gut. God, I hoped he knew what he was doing because if so this was going to be delicious.

Caleb began unbuttoning his shirt with quick fingers, and my mouth really did go dry as I watched him rip the damn thing off. Only his left arm was covered in a full sleeve of tattoos, and the design continued onto the muscular left pec. There was a solo tattoo at the top of his right arm. Now I could see that above the modern soldier on his left arm, there was a kilted soldier like the ones I'd seen depicted in *Outlander*. The smoke above him gave way to a Spartan in among the ruins of an ancient building with broken columns. The clouds of smoke, debris, and ribbons of tattered material were drawn downward from his shoulder and collarbone to his pec, where words on two ribbons, one above the other, were tattooed. They read: "I don't know how I'm going to win. I just know I'm not going to lose."

My eyes wandered over the muscles of his six-pack and those broad, delicious shoulders to the other tattoo. It was of a skull sitting on a huge black rose.

His large bicep flexed as he began to unbutton the top button of his jeans. I licked my lips as I dragged my eyes back over to his muscled stomach. Lust flooded me. "Oh dear God."

Caleb's smile was full of ego. "Did he finally answer your prayers, babe?"

"Depends on what you've got in the pants."

It was unclear who was more surprised by his sudden bark of laughter, me or him. It made me smile, though. Laughter suited him. *He should laugh more.* I grew steadily more turned on as I took in the sight of him and thought of all that masculine beauty becoming mine. Not that I dated, but when I did find myself attracted to a guy, he usually had lean muscle rather than brawn.

But I wasn't complaining about Caleb's physique in the least.

My eyes dropped to where the Scot's jeans, now open at the top, hung low on his narrow hips, the hard-cut V of his obliques so goddamn sexy I was about to self-combust.

"Please take those off now."

"Always so well mannered."

"Just take them off."

His answer was to kneel down and quickly unlace his boots. Staring at me, that arrogant heat in his eyes really far too attractive to be fair, he kicked them off.

I physically shivered, shuddered even, at the sound of his zipper cutting through the tense silence of the room. Caleb curled his thumbs into the waist of his jeans and his boxer briefs (black, of course) and shoved them down. He kicked them off too.

"Oh my." I practically wheezed at the sight of his straining erection. "That . . . well . . . that's . . ."

"I think the word you're looking for is 'impressive.'"

"It seems a little unfair actually to all the other penises."

Caleb's grin this time was just all pure boyish amusement, and I decided it was my favorite of his smiles so far. He reached toward me and grabbed the heels of both of my shoes and slipped them off.

Every inch of me was a live wire, restless, too hot, sensitive. I never knew it was possible to be so sexually hungry. I'd had great sex in the past but I'd never felt like I might just explode at his first touch.

"We need to have sex. Now."

Caleb placed his hands on my knees, his thumbs on the inside of my legs, and he slowly coasted them upward.

"Oh boy."

His lips twitched but he was too focused on his destination to really smile. He reached the apex of my thighs but he kept going, his thumbs meeting in the middle over the lace of my underwear. I gasped as he pressed his thumbs down.

I immediately flopped back on the bed and let my legs fall open. "Oh God, yes."

"You keep calling me God, lass, and my ego might get out of control," he murmured.

"Your ego is already the size of Mars—nothing I say can make it any worse." My hips arched off the bed into his touch, but he only rubbed his thumbs over me once more before he stopped. I lifted my head to glare at him. "Why did you just stop?"

Caleb didn't reply. He didn't need to. I could see all patience had fled his expression. Suddenly his fingers were brushing my lower belly, curling into my underwear. He wrenched them down my legs. A little huff of excitement escaped me.

Caleb's eyes darkened. He moved over me, straddling me, his hands braced at either side of my head. The heat of him engulfed me as he stared into my eyes and smoothed his hand up my naked thigh.

"Caleb." I breathed, any vulnerability I should have felt at lying so small beneath this big stranger obliterated by the voracious need I felt for him.

He reached between my legs, watching me with an intensity that caused my breath to catch as I lifted my hips into his touch.

"You're so beautiful." He stopped teasing my clit and slid three thick fingers into me. My inner muscles clamped around him in desperate need. "You feel beautiful too."

Something about the words didn't sound like a compliment. "Your tone suggests that's a bad thing," I gasped out.

"It is." His gaze was suddenly calculated. "You think your beauty gives you power over me. It doesn't." He thrust his fingers in and out of me and my toes curled into the bedding.

"You are such an ass—*Oh!*" He caught my clit with his thumb again, sending sparks of pleasure shooting through me.

"You were saying?"

I reached for him, laying my small hands flat against his hard chest, and I stared him straight in the eye, attempting to push through the fog of lust. "We don't like each other. For a second I might have thought otherwise in the glow of champagne. But we don't. So let's not pretend that physical attraction isn't the only reason I'm letting you touch me right now. You think I'm beautiful and I think you're hot and that has power over both of us even though we'd rather it didn't. So stop being an imperious prick."

For a moment he appeared pissed off. Then the anger melted. "True enough." He removed his hand and then gently took each of my wrists in his hands and pinned them to the mattress at either side of my head. I felt overwhelmed by the size of him. We were two people giving in to the power of physical attraction, and in that we were even.

He wanted me just as much as I wanted him.

That I could deal with.

Caleb bent his head to mine, and that masculine, earthy scent rushed over me, sending a new jolt of desire.

"I promised I'd ruin you, lass," he murmured, and then kissed me. His tongue pushed between my lips and slid over mine, dancing with it in a dirty, deep, wet kiss. My hips pulsed toward him at the feel of his hardness rubbing against my belly.

And then he was gone, taking his mouth from mine as his grip on my wrists loosened. His fingers trailed teasingly down the soft skin of my inner arm and down the sides of my breasts as he stopped to pay attention to them.

His stubble scratched against my skin in the most delicious way as my body writhed, bucking off the bed. I wrapped my arms around his shoulders, stroking his hot, smooth skin. My fingers curled tightly into the longer section of his hair as he paid lavish attention to my breasts. He brought me to the edge of orgasm and then stopped, kissing them sweetly.

"Caleb." I groaned, tugging on his hair.

He reached for my hands, gripped my wrists, and slammed them back above my head. Then his lips were moving down my stomach, his tongue licking my belly button, before moving south. My lower belly rippled as his mouth neared closer to where I wanted it the most.

My legs fell open, inviting him in. I heard his grunt of satisfaction seconds before his tongue touched me.

Need slammed through me and my hips pushed into his mouth. He gripped them, pressing them back to the mattress, and then he truly began his torture.

As his thick stubble scratched and tickled my thighs, he suckled. He studied my body, my reactions, and just when I was about to reach blinding satisfaction he'd lift his head and press a sweet kiss to my inner thigh.

I cried out in frustration. "You *are* a bastard."

Caleb's grip on my hips became almost bruising.

And then his tongue was back. I shuddered, but it still wasn't enough. Hearing my whimpers, the Scot introduced his fingers into the equation.

"Caleb!" I jerked against him. "Yes, yes! Don't stop!"

Cool air blew over me suddenly as he got up off the bed. I glanced up in confusion, wondering what the hell he was trying to do to me! My body relaxed when I saw he was pulling a condom out of the wallet in his jeans. His eyes ate up the sight of me sprawled naked on his bed as he readied himself.

"Are you done?"

"So impatient." Laughter trembled in his voice as he moved back up onto the bed, moving over me with intent. His lips brushed mine, softly, sweetly, surprising me, and then he pushed up onto one hand and curled his other around my thigh, opening me . . . and he thrust inside me.

Hard.

I gasped his name in pleasured pain. Our eyes held as my breath scattered as he moved inside me, the feel of him so perfect it electrified my lower spine. I whimpered and he let go of my thigh only to lift my legs so my hips and ass came up off the bed. His large hands held the back of my thighs, holding me at this angle as he got up on his knees. And then he powered hard into me.

And something happened.

He seemed to hit this sensitive part inside of me I'd never felt before and my whole body was seized with this incredible pleasure.

I wasn't aware of anything but the heat flushing through me, of the feel of Caleb's hot skin and hard muscle beneath my hands.

He kept hitting that spot until I wasn't cognizant of anything. I knew I was saying words but they were incoherent even to me. I heard his grunts, I heard my whimpers, I smelled his cologne and his sweat mingling with mine and my perfume.

But it was all a blur against the coiling bliss building inside of me.

And then I splintered, shattered apart, exquisite pleasure undulating through me. "Caleb!" I cried, my eyes fluttering closed as it rushed through my entire body, its focus in my center. The sensation was so sexy, so raw, I never wanted it to end. It felt like it *was* never going to end. Caleb's hips stilled. And then his lower body seemed to shudder long and hard against me.

I lay stunned, limp, as Caleb grunted and buried his face in my neck. Our chests rose and fell against each other as we tried to catch our breath. I remembered the look on his face as he came. His gritted teeth, his flushed skin, the dazed lust in his wolf eyes.

God, that was hot. It made me curl my fingers in his hair to tug his head up. I kissed him, sweet, deep, wet, loving the scratch of his short beard. He kissed me back, and I rolled until I was on top of him. His hands caressed my back, my hair, my ass as we kissed, and I pressed against him, needing more, wanting him ready again.

Not too long later he was, and I explored him and the raw masculinity that fascinated me despite myself.

The desperation of our need eased by our first time, I dragged my nails down his hard stomach as I rose up and down on him and felt my power over him. The power he hated that I had over him.

It felt good.

Whatever satisfaction he saw in my face made Caleb climax first, and as his hips bucked beneath mine he tipped me over the edge, and we came together.

We stared at each other for a moment, two strangers who had just shared something extraordinary, and I felt the moment reality returned.

I'd just had sex with a man I didn't even like.

And he'd had sex with a woman he didn't even like.

Somehow I didn't think that was such a big deal to him, but it was to me.

Even more so that it had been so physically epic.

With the ache in my body now satisfied, the heat of pleasure dissipated and I felt cold. I eased off him and he let go of my hips so I could slip off the bed. I grabbed my clothes from the floor around the bed and disappeared into the bathroom.

Misery overwhelmed me, and I wondered how I could go from enjoying the most pleasure I was sure any woman had ever felt to feeling wretched with myself. Disappointed in myself.

And wondering how the hell I could get out of there without losing face.

I took my time until I panicked that maybe he thought I was trying to stick around.

However, when I stepped out of the bathroom, Caleb was lying sprawled with the sheets over him, his arms above his head, his lips parted slightly, and his eyes closed.

The asshole had fallen asleep.

"Caleb?"

He didn't even twitch.

I stepped closer to the bed. "Caleb?" I shook the mattress a little.

Still nothing.

Wondering if he was pretending to sleep as an immature way to get rid of me, I held my finger under his nose. The lack of movement from him and the steady, even breaths he took convinced me he was asleep. Relief moved through me. I slipped on my shoes, studying the potently beautiful and masculine man lying in bed.

It was the kind of sex I would never forget, even if I had been getting sex regularly.

And I decided right there and then to get over myself. So what if I didn't like Caleb? Being attracted to someone I didn't like didn't make me a bad person. It made me human. And you know what? For a couple of hours everything had been simple and good.

Knowing he was asleep, I approached him quietly and acknowledged that if he was clean shaven he'd look almost boyish in his sleep. I wanted to kiss that pouty mouth one last time, but I was afraid it would wake him.

"Thank you," I whispered. "I'd never say this if you were awake because . . . well, we both know you're an asshole . . . but I needed this. It's . . . it's been a shitty week. And this was nice. Uncomplicated. Thanks for being just the guy I could have sex with." I smiled. "And thanks for living up to my grand expectations. Not that you need your ego stroked."

I turned and moved across the room, grabbing my purse off the floor. Then I stopped and looked back at him, sleeping peacefully. "And P.S. You win when you realize that anyone can hurt you, even those you never expect it from. Once you know that . . . you'll never be knocked off your feet long enough to lose."

As I slipped out of the hotel room, I knew deep down I hadn't said those words to a sleeping man who couldn't hear them. I'd said them to myself. Because as much as I didn't like the bastard . . . he'd somehow still taken something from me in there, and I couldn't have that.

Even though he had slipped past my defenses, I needed the reminder that it didn't mean I could trust him.

Seven

Although I had to get up early to catch my flight, I woke up feeling refreshed, realizing I'd slept better than I had in ages. I didn't walk away from Caleb filled with regrets and I didn't overanalyze. I truly appreciated our one-night stand for what it was: a major stress reliever. As soon as I'd gotten back to the room, I'd passed out on my bed, out like a light.

The overthinking came the next morning while I was in the shower. It wasn't so much overthinking or regret as really the wish that I hadn't said as much as I had about Nick and Gem. I wasn't so drunk the night before that I couldn't remember every second of it. I didn't mind my inhibitions being lowered enough for me to have sex with Caleb, but I did mind that they'd been lowered enough for me to talk about Gem's death. Reassuring myself that it wasn't a huge deal because I'd never see Caleb again, I was suddenly hit with harsh reality. I *would* see Caleb again. He was on my freaking flight to Boston.

I really, really hoped we would not be sitting next to each other. "Awkward" didn't even cover it.

Still, it wasn't worth getting worked up about, so I attempted to shrug that niggle off my shoulders and sweep away the nervousness in the pit of my stomach. To my relief, I didn't see Caleb in the hotel as I checked out and headed along the walkway to the airport.

The more I thought about my epic sexcapades with the Norse God (in my head I allowed myself to call him that because, seriously, the man had found my *G-spot*), the chirpier I became despite my anxiety over seeing him again. I had not once in my life engaged in a one-night stand, but it would seem that I did it perfectly. I chose a seriously sexy (if unlikable) man to sleep with, he gave me the best sex of my life, and the cherry on top of the icing on that cake? He was from an entirely different continent, and after this flight I would never see him again in my life.

"What you grinning about, girl?" the cheery security personnel said, smiling at me as I handed her my passport and ticket.

I hadn't even realized I was smiling. I lied, "I'm happy to be going home."

"Well, you have a nice flight," she said, handing my documents back to me.

"Thank you," I returned sincerely. Seriously . . . good manners *did* matter.

And positivity really did attract positivity.

After I got through security, which was heaving with people— even the fast-track line for first and business class—I strolled into the busy terminal, heading for the nearest coffee cart. Miracle of miracles, there was only one guy in front of me, and soon I was holding a grande macchiato in my hand, relieved to be going home, and feeling so sexually satisfied that I thought maybe the universe was looking out for me after all. Last night with Caleb had been a much-needed diversion. *Thanks, Universe. I owe you one.*

Only a short time later, reality intruded far too quickly and I wondered if the universe and I really were on such good terms after all. It *was* awkward seeing Caleb again.

I looked down at him, sitting in the aisle seat adjacent to my aisle seat in the first-class cabin. His eyes pierced me as he sat there with his food tray out and his laptop open at the ready. Today he wore a black henley, sleeves rolled down, with dark blue jeans and biker boots.

"Excuse me," an annoyed voice said behind me. I turned to see that while I was staring at my one-night stand, there was a line building up behind me.

"Sorry." I moved to the overhead bin above my seat and had just bent down to pick up the carry-on when it was out of my hands and up into the bin. I blinked in confusion at finding Caleb standing so close beside me that our bodies brushed.

He looked displeased that we had to share another couple of hours together.

Well, why help me with my carry-on, then? I dropped down into my seat. As soon as he was seated, I said through the line of moving people, "You knew we'd be on this flight together, so I don't know what the dirty look is for. Why are you going to Boston anyway?"

"Why are *you*?"

"*I* live in Boston."

"Koto's North American division is based out of Boston. I have a meeting there."

"If your meeting is in Boston, what the hell were you doing in Phoenix?"

"It's called a *layover*." He smirked and turned back to his laptop.

"Ha ha ha." I glared at him. "Your wit is unparalleled."

Caleb shot me an assessing look. "You seem awfully upset I'm on this flight, considering you were fully aware I would be."

"You have to admit, it is a little awkward."

"Facing your sins, you mean?"

"Actually, yes." I lifted my chin haughtily, my voice lowering as I lied, "I can be forgiven, however, because I was drunk."

Indignation claimed his features. "You were as sober as I was. You regret it, fine. But own your actions."

I stiffened at the derision in his voice and realized he was right. The truth was, I didn't want to feel vulnerable around him, and that was pretty much how I was starting to feel. The lie had slipped out as a defense. "Fine, I wasn't drunk."

When no response was forthcoming, I side-eyed him and saw he was working on his laptop, ignoring me once again.

Sighing to myself, I pressed the power button on my e-reader, determined to ignore him for the duration of the flight. At least it was a short flight.

"Excuse me."

I glanced up at the smooth voice to find a guy around my age looking down at me.

"I'm in the window seat."

"Oh, of course." Unlike Caleb yesterday, I got up out of my seat to let the guy in.

"Thank you." He flashed me a flirtatious, charming smile. "Must be my lucky day."

Normally I'd just wave a comment like that off, but I was too aware of the Scottish bastard, and I wanted him to know I was just as unaffected by our one-night stand as he was. "Some guys have all the luck," I joked affably, hoping it came off as charming versus conceited.

The guy chuckled, moving past my seat and into his. He wore a suit that fit him so perfectly it had to be tailored. He hunched over a little in the space to shrug out of the suit jacket.

"Would you like me to take that, sir?" A flight attendant appeared at my side.

"Yes, please." He handed the jacket to her. Handsome. Check. Well mannered. Check.

Not that I was interested, but it was safe to say today's seatmate was a step up from yesterday's already.

"Could you take mine?" I began unbuttoning the red peplum jacket of my suit. I'd had the hotel dry clean it too.

"Of course, madam."

Ugh. *Madam.* I missed the days of being a "Miss." Still, I smiled gratefully as I handed it to her with a thank you.

I slid back into my seat well aware of my new companion's eyes on the black silk cami I wore tucked into my skirt. Turning to him, I gave him a small smile, which he returned. The guy had dark chocolate brown eyes, long sooty lashes any woman would have killed for, and a smooth Rob Lowe circa *St. Elmo's Fire* look about him, minus the hair. This guy's hair was thick, dark, and waved so perfectly back from his forehead he had to be using product. And a very expensive barber.

I took in the crisp white shirt he wore along with the dark blue silk tie he was currently loosening. He had a slim, athletic build, more to my usual appeal than the man across the aisle from me. Yet he was doing nothing to my hormones. Which, as it turned out, was a good thing. My gaze snagged on his left hand as he tugged on the knot of his tie.

There was a white band around his ring finger.

The jerk had removed his wedding ring.

Between the one-night stand on my right side and this ass on my left, I was beyond exasperated.

"I'm Hugh." He held out his hand to me.

I shook hands, even though I was quietly cursing him in my mind. I didn't understand guys who got married if they had no intention of staying faithful. "Ava."

"A beautiful name for a beautiful woman."

Ugh, he wasn't even original. "Thank you."

I thought I heard a grunt across the aisle, but I ignored it.

"You live in Boston?" Hugh asked.

He was giving me good eye contact, so much so it was like he was deliberately trying not to look anywhere else.

"I do. You?"

"Yes. Arlington Street." He said it pointedly, with more than a hint of pomposity.

God, the guy lived across the Common from me. And he was basically telling me he had lots of money.

I don't need your money, pal. There was no way I was telling him he could find my place just a ten-minute walk from his. "Nice."

"We like it."

Bingo. "We?"

"Uh . . ." He gave me another charming smile. "I have a dog."

Did he just refer to his wife as a dog? "Oh, breed?"

"French poodle."

I raised an eyebrow and Hugh gave a little self-deprecating laugh. "She was actually my ex-wife's, but when she left me she also left La Roux."

A laugh bubbled up out of me before I could stop it. "She named the dog La Roux? And your name is Hugh."

He chuckled. "She had quite the sense of humor."

Past tense. Really?

Okay, so there was the small possibility that this guy was recently separated . . . but my gut told me otherwise. Or maybe that was just my cynicism.

Thankfully, before my distaste started to show, the flight attendant arrived to offer us something to drink. I almost flinched at the sight of the champagne and opted for a water. Out of the corner of my eye I saw Caleb working away on his laptop.

The jerk didn't even care some other guy might be flirting with me, and honestly . . . I didn't want to flirt with this leech just to make a point to Caleb when I'd never see him again after this flight.

"You know, I think I'm going to use the restroom before we take off," Hugh said.

"Sure." I got up out of my seat to let him out, and this time he did let his eyes drag down my body.

Not so well mannered after all.

"Excuse me."

I turned to see the flight attendant behind me and stepped back to let her past, only for my ass to bump into the guy behind me. I spun around, my cheeks flushed as I met Caleb's gaze. "Sorry."

He stared back, deadpan. "I'm familiar with having your arse in my face, babe. It's not a problem."

Thankfully, he had no one beside him to overhear. Still, I leaned down so none of the other passengers could hear me, and a pleasurable but traitorous tingle of awareness shot through me as our noses almost touched. "Well, treasure the *memory*, Scotty Boy."

He gestured to the restroom beyond us, his expression neutral. "Planning on giving Vanilla there a look at it tae?"

"It's a nice ass—it would be a shame to keep it to myself," I taunted, and the dark look he cut me made my breath catch.

"A pain in the arse, aye. But I didn't take you for being manipulative or a game player. But I guess what you said last night was right. Nobody really knows anybody else enough tae really trust them."

My breath caught and I straightened, needing distance from him. "You were awake."

"Aye, I was awake."

I decided to ignore the fact that he'd heard me say something so personal and so revealing and went with being pissed that he'd deliberately pretended to be asleep. "You didn't need to pretend to be asleep to get rid of me. I was leaving anyway."

He shrugged. "It made it easier, though, right? No awkwardness."

I moved back to my seat. I'd been planning on standing until Hugh returned from the restroom, but I didn't want to be near Caleb. As soon as I sat down, Caleb shut his laptop and swung the table out of his way to stand up. I tensed, wondering what he was planning on doing, but he ignored me and stood in the aisle.

Despite myself, my eyes drifted to his ass, and I remembered rolling around in bed with him last night and feeling every finely crafted detail of his body. I was shocked by the bolt of longing and mourning that hit me in the chest as I realized I was disappointed I'd never get the chance to feel his lips on mine again.

The man could kiss.

And I didn't mind the scratch of his short beard. There was something so erotically masculine about it.

The sound of the restroom door opening brought my gaze up and I watched as Caleb strode toward Hugh as he came out of it. Instead of giving him space to pass, Caleb knocked his big shoulder into him, making him stumble.

"Sorry," Hugh mumbled, looking up.

Why was he apologizing?

Caleb didn't apologize. No, Caleb cut him a look so chilling, I shivered. Then he disappeared into the restroom, having to duck and maneuver his large body in there.

"Whoa." Hugh was suddenly at my side, wearing a wide-eyed look. "Big guy. Scary guy."

I nodded and got out of my seat.

"Wouldn't want to get on the wrong side of him." He laughed as he slid by me.

Apparently, you already did, I thought, disoriented by the idea.

Did it bother Caleb that I couldn't care less about our one-night stand? Why would it? He was the one who'd pretended to be asleep so I could sneak out and avoid any awkwardness.

Hugh talked about his work as a lawyer in Boston, but I was only half listening. I was too aware of the guy in the restroom. I looked out for him in my peripheral vision as he stepped out of the bathroom, and suddenly I remembered that Caleb was afraid of takeoff and landing.

I shouldn't care.

I really, really shouldn't care.

Dammit.

"So, maybe when we get back in Boston, Ava, you and I could meet for drinks or dinner?" Hugh asked as Caleb returned to his seat. I shot Caleb a look and found him staring back at me in derision.

I gave him a dismissive look and turned to Hugh. And in a not so quiet voice I responded, "I don't date married men."

He looked stunned. "Married? I'm not—Why would you—?"

"You slipped your ring off while you were taking your jacket off, right?" I guessed.

He flushed guiltily, giving himself away.

"Yeah. There's a white ring of skin where your band usually sits. Oh, and your pickup lines are awful." I gave him a wide, carefree smile and slipped out of my seat.

Crossing the aisle, my e-reader in hand, I began easing my way past Caleb's legs.

"What the hell?" He pulled his laptop toward him as I clambered by his knees and fell into the seat beside him.

"Don't say a word." I glared into his scowling face. "This doesn't mean anything. You are just currently the lesser of two evils, and do not tell me you wouldn't rather have me beside you to annoy you and distract you during takeoff."

Caleb glared at me. "I dinnae need you."

Inwardly I flinched. Outwardly, I smirked. "Yeah, you do."

He sighed and glanced over at Hugh, who was staring at us in confusion. Caleb turned to me, his upper lip curled in a sneer. "Realized he was married, did you?"

"I saw the white band on his finger the moment he sat down."

"I saw him slip it off as soon as he saw you."

"And if I hadn't noticed it, were you planning on sharing that information?"

Ducking his head toward mine, Caleb put on a patronizing expression. "I'm not your rescuer, babe. You want tae screw a slimeball, that's your business."

"Oh, don't worry. Last night I made my quota on slimeballs."

He shrugged and sighed. "Guess I walked intae that one."

One of the flight attendants interrupted us to announce that we were readying for takeoff. Caleb put away his laptop and stowed his tray table.

"So . . ." I shifted uncomfortably. "You heard everything I said last night?"

"You mean the part about me living up tae your grand expectations?"

I covered my eyes with my hand. "I blame it on being under the influence of endorphins. Postorgasmic chitchat." I removed my hand and frowned. "That means it doesn't count."

"Oh, it counts." He bent his head toward mine, eyes drifting over my face, to land on my mouth. "And I'm thinking you sitting here means you're after more of the same when we get tae Boston."

I jerked back from him in denial. "Uh, no. When we land in Boston, it is the last time we ever see each other. I'm not going to sit here and lie that last night wasn't great sex—"

"Fantastic sex."

I flushed, pleased that he thought so. "Okay, fantastic sex. But I still don't like you."

His expression chilled. "So? I still don't like you either. Doesn't mean I dinnae want tae sleep with ye again."

"You weren't of that opinion when you pretended to be asleep."

Caleb grinned, and I hated how that flash of smile sent a ripple through my belly. "That really bugged you, eh? And that was last night. I'd just had you and didn't expect tae want you again. Now that you're here, though . . ." His eyes trailed down to my breasts and on down to my crossed legs. "Aye, I wouldn't mind another go."

Incredulity and fury raged through me. "Another go? Another go?"

His lips trembled with laughter. "Poor word choice?"

"You're a pig. Last night I got what I needed and I don't want to go there again."

In answer, Caleb bent his head until his lips gently brushed my ear and he whispered, "Liar."

I shivered, my breasts tightening at the mere caress of that mouth near my skin. His laughter warmed the skin at my neck and I whipped my head around until our lips were inches apart. "You are a cocky son of a bitch."

"Aye."

"Boston is filled with beautiful women. They'll be happy to see to you. I'm sure that accent gets you pretty far here."

"It usually does. It's not my first trip tae Boston."

Of course, I was just one in a long line of American women. My jaw locked with annoyance and I couldn't help glaring at him.

Something flickered in his gaze, and I really hoped it wasn't triumph, because I would swing for him if it was. And then his lips were back at my ear. "I can't remember the last time any of them felt as good as you did, though, Ava."

Heat flushed through me as I remembered just how good *he* felt. I licked my suddenly dry lips and somehow managed to turn to look him in the eyes. Leaning in, I brushed my lips over his, a barely-there kiss that made them tingle deliciously. "Like I said, Caleb . . . treasure that memory." I sat back in my seat, staring defiantly at him.

Instead of blasting me with a dirty look like I'd half expected, he gazed at me with something new in his eyes. Something almost like respect. Then he seemed to remember where we were and he looked around, realizing we were already in the air.

His beautiful gaze bored into me with a thoroughness that made me tense. "Looks like I owe you again."

I shook my head. "We're not going to be around each other long enough for you to pay up."

Hearing the sincerity in my words, Caleb finally nodded. "Your loss."

Despite the niggling voice in my head that told me I was an idiot for not taking him up on his offer for another go-around of guilt-free best-sex-ever, I stared determinedly at my e-reader.

Minutes of silence stretched between us as Caleb got his laptop back out and started to work. I couldn't concentrate on my book. I started to stew over the fact that I couldn't deny I did feel a sense of longing for this guy. Did I really need to like him to have sex with him? Really? Wasn't sex just sex?

I glanced at his hands typing away on his laptop and flushed, remembering how skillful those fingers were. I could feel myself giving in.

Just as I opened my mouth to tell him so, he spoke first. "Stop worrying yourself over there. Like you said, there's plenty of beautiful women in Boston. I won't go lonely."

Arghh!

My fingers bit around my e-reader to the point I was afraid I might crack the screen. He was horrible.

Just horrible!

And I had had sex with him.

"I hope it falls off," I muttered.

"What?"

I gave him a blinding smile. "I hope they fall all over you."

"You said, 'I hope it falls off.'"

"Did I?" I shrugged innocently. "Slip of the tongue."

"Aye, if I remember correctly you're good at that too."

I glowered at him, scowling harder as I felt the seat shake with his laughter.

Bastard. Scot.

Eight

"S o . . . what you're telling me is that you had sex for the first time in seven years with a hot stranger who talks like a guy out of *Outlander*?" Harper asked.

Hiding a smile at the shock on her face, I nodded casually.

She leaned forward from her curled-up position on my couch to say, "Are you kidding around or not? Because I'm starting to think not."

"I'm not kidding around."

"You slept with a hot Scottish stranger at O'Hare?"

"Yup."

Harper broke out into a massive grin. "You know you were pretty much my hero before this, but you just upped the hero worship by a hundred and ten percent."

"Because I slept with a stranger?"

"Uh, correction—you had sex with a kilted Highlander."

I burst into laughter. "They don't all go around wearing kilts and swords, you know. I'm guessing most of them stopped doing that about a few hundred years ago."

"You know what I mean!" she cried, bouncing up off the couch and making my heart leap into my throat at the way her wine sloshed around in her glass. "Just when people think they have you figured out . . . *boom!* You do something completely out of character." She raised her glass precariously again and rolled her eyes at me when she noticed my wince. "Which is a nice vacation from coaster girl." She placed the wineglass down on a coaster and took her seat again.

I sighed. "What is so wrong about not wanting to leave ring marks on my furniture?"

"I could say something dirty to that but I'm going to refrain."

"Talk about shocking," I teased.

Harper rolled her light gray-blue eyes again and shook her head. "I can't believe you had a one-night stand."

"Not just any one-night stand. An epic one-night stand." I could admit that to my best friend. We told each other everything. People were often surprised by my friendship with Harper. I was thirty years old, slightly conservative, reserved with most people, well educated and, yes, I could admit it, a bit overly organized. Nothing in my apartment was out of place . . . or on me either. Even lounging at home with Harper, I wore yoga pants and an off-the-shoulder blouse. Makeup on and hair done. I didn't own a pair of jeans.

Harper, on the other hand, was twenty-six years old, and had very short platinum blond hair that was cut close at the sides and left long on top so she could style it. Some days she styled it into a sharp, messy quiff, other days in a softer one with a retro vibe. The cut did not at all detract from my friend's femininity—it just gave her an edge. She had soft features—pert nose, full lips, wide eyes, and long lashes. Then there were her dimples. Every time she laughed or smiled, these adorable dimples flashed in her cheeks. Harper was multifaceted in many ways. Looks-wise, when she was straight-faced and staring at you with those soulful big eyes, she was downright beautiful and striking with her daring haircut. But when she smiled, she was absolutely cute as a button.

In her right ear were multiple piercings. As a pastry chef in one of Boston's best restaurants, she wore only studs and tiny hoops. Three close-to-the-skin hoops on the bottom and then five studs up along the cuff of her ear, each a different-colored stone that winked and sparkled when the light caught it. In her left ear was only a hoop and a stud.

Right now, on her day off, she wore gold rings on nearly all her fingers, some that sat below the knuckle and others above.

I thought of Harper as a glamorous punk. She liked edgy, but she liked her edginess to glitter and sparkle. Today she wore skinny jeans that were ripped at the knees, biker boots, and a cropped T-shirt covered in rose gold sequins that reflected light everywhere she turned.

She was the most beautiful person I'd ever met—on the inside as well as the outside—but because of her past she had a hard time believing it. Yet it was exactly because of her past that I admired her so much. Harper had been through the unimaginable and yet she didn't let it affect who she was. Someone outspoken, opinionated, open-minded, brave, loyal, and determined. She'd left home at eighteen with very little money, had been just a step up from homeless when I met her . . . and now she was the pastry chef in the only Michelin-star restaurant in Boston.

"Ava? An epic one-night stand?"

"Huh?" The sound of her voice pulled me out of my musings.

"Why are you looking at me like that?"

I shrugged. "I just missed you."

She gave me a sad smile, her dimples appearing and disappearing so quickly it was almost like I'd imagined them. "I wish I'd gone with you."

Thinking about my trip back to Arizona made me want to curl up in a dark room and not leave for a good long while. Instead, I shrugged it off with a joke. "And have you cockblock me? No, thanks."

Harper chuckled. "I wouldn't have."

"He would have taken one look at you and forgotten me entirely."

She snorted. "Okay. Yeah. Sure."

"No, really." I studied her, thinking I wasn't wrong. "You are probably more this guy's type."

"How so?"

"Uh . . . he looked like something off that show . . . *Vikings*. He was covered in tattoos. And his hair was a guy version of yours."

Her lips parted in shock. Again. "No. Way."

"Yes way."

"Not exactly *your* type."

"Nope. And I wasn't his. We didn't even like each other," I admitted. "He was so rude and obnoxious, had no manners . . ."

"But . . . ?"

I huffed in exasperation. "My body disagreed with me. I can't explain it . . . the attraction was inexplicable but explosive and . . . he found my G-spot."

Amazement brightened Harper's eyes. "He sounds like a god."

"A Norse god. A bastard. An asshole. But the man sure knows what he's doing in the bedroom."

"Do you think we could find him and have him teach Vince about the G-spot thing?"

I raised an eyebrow. "I thought you and Vince were good?"

Vince was the guy Harper had been dating for the last two months, which was a long time for her. Like me, she didn't trust people easily. Plus, her job might sound fancy, but it entailed a lot of long hours and none of the men she'd met so far had been able to deal with the fact that Harper's job came first. Vince was different. He was a drummer in a local band that had found some success playing bars and clubs all over Massachusetts. He seemed to understand her dedication and admire it. I liked him.

"We are and the sex is good . . . but G-spot? I've only met one guy who found that." She wiggled her fingers suggestively.

I laughed and blushed a little. "He didn't find it with those."

She gasped. "Oh my God . . . how . . . what?"

I buried my face in my hands, embarrassed but amused. "I'm not giving you details."

She understood the muffled words and cried, "I need details!"

"Oh Lord." I dropped my hands and looked up at the ceiling, unable to meet her gaze. "He—he—"

"Stop stuttering. He what?"

"He just . . . he positioned me . . . you know, at an angle, and, well . . . he knew what he was doing, okay," I rushed out, my cheeks burning with mortification. I told Harper pretty much everything, but an explanatory description of how I reached orgasm was crossing a line I didn't want to cross.

She eyed me in awe. "I have to meet this man."

"No, you don't." I stood up with my empty wineglass and strolled over to my kitchen to put it in the sink.

"You're telling me that you met a guy who was that great in bed and you don't want to see him again?"

The truth was that part of me did, but his words from the plane came back to me and I hated that they had the power to hurt me even a little. I glanced over at her. "He wanted to, you know. See me again while he was here. I said no because I didn't think it was smart. And you know what he said? He told me not to worry about it, that there were plenty of beautiful women in Boston and he wouldn't be lonely."

Anger suffused Harper's pretty features. "That asshole!" She stood up, her hands going to her hips. "Who the hell does he think he is? Does he not know that he was lucky he even got near you? You're Ava Breevort. There is no one better than you."

Warmth and gratitude flooded my chest. "Except Harper Lee Smith."

The left side of her mouth pulled up into a rueful grin. "What have I told you about full-naming me."

"Oh, I thought that was only in public." She thought her mother naming her after the author of *To Kill a Mockingbird* was too cutesy and did not at all reflect her personality.

I loved her name. I thought it suited her.

"Whatever. Back to the Scottish guy. You're right . . . he sounds completely unworthy."

"It's almost a sin, you know, that someone that gorgeous and sexually gifted is so unlikable."

"You really didn't like him?"

"I mean . . . he was smart. CFO of Koto. And witty. Plus, like I told you, he stopped those annoying guys in the restaurant from harassing me. I guess he wasn't all bad . . . but he was fundamentally rude to almost everyone he came in contact with, and he was mean to me. I was mean to him too but . . . I thought we maybe just had this insulting banter thing going on. But I was wrong. There's a coldness about him. High spiked barriers on that one."

"Well, you know something about barriers."

"Yes, but I'm generally not mean or ill-mannered to people because of them. Unless provoked."

"True." She rounded my coffee table and came to stand by the kitchen counter. "At least it distracted you from Gemma, though, right?"

I winced, reminded of my time in Arcadia.

"Nick had no right to say those things to you—you know that, don't you?"

I looked away, staring at the large bay window in my living room that looked down onto tree-lined Mount Vernon Street. "I know. I *do* know that. But I still feel guilty. I can't help it."

Suddenly I was pulled into a deep hug. Harper was a couple of inches taller than me, so I could rest my head on her small shoulder and hold on tight. We were from two entirely different worlds, two entirely different people, but years ago she'd stepped in to protect me when I was a stranger, and from that moment on I'd vowed to protect her back.

But these days it felt like *she* was saving *me*.

I hugged her tight before stepping out of her arms. "I'm okay," I assured her.

"Promise?"

I nodded. "I just need to get back to work and back to my life."

"Hmm." She eyed me carefully. "Have your parents called to check that you got home safe?"

I made a face and shook my head. At Harper's answering expression of contempt, I sought to remind her, "Harper, don't worry. I'm used to it."

"Doesn't make it right."

My parents liked to think of themselves as free spirits, but they liked their money a lot. I grew up in a nice house with nice cars and clothes. They didn't believe in parenting me at all, so if I'd wanted to, I could have gotten away with murder. They gave me and Nick and Gem weed when we were sixteen, but I refused to smoke it—though Gem and Nick did. I didn't like the idea of being out of control.

There were no rules in my house growing up. No boundaries. No checking in to see where I was or if I was okay.

And I guess that made me go the opposite way. I was responsible and conservative. It didn't take a therapist to tell me that I liked being in control since everything had been so out of control with my parents.

"Honestly, I was just surprised my mom made me go to the dinner the night before Gem's funeral. Very un-Mom-like to care about what people think." I shrugged. "But she loved Gem, I guess."

"Yeah." Harper scowled. "Even when she screwed you over."

"Let's not go there." I shook my head and squeezed her shoulder. "I've been going there for the past ten days and . . . I want to leave *there* behind and move on."

My friend sighed heavily. "Okay. But I'm here if you need me."

"I know." I reached over and kissed her cheek. "Now you need to get home and get some sleep before work tomorrow."

She nodded and walked over to the couch to grab her leather jacket and purse. "Back to work tomorrow?"

"Yes." I grinned. "I can't wait."

"Even with the Shrew breathing down your neck every fifty seconds?"

Harper was referring to one of my current clients. I was redesigning her summer home in Nantucket and the woman drove me crazy with constant phone calls and demands for me to send her hourly updates. "Even then. I have a bajillion voice mails from her. Apparently, my attending a childhood friend's funeral has seriously messed up her schedule."

"Ugh, what a cow," Harper said as I led her to the door. "Seriously, how do you work with these people?"

"Says she who works with Jason Luton, the most intimidating and scary man I ever met until I got to know him." Jason was the English head chef of Canterbury, the restaurant Harper worked at. He opened it six months before Harper started working there as an apprentice chef. Two years after that he was awarded a Michelin star and had held on to it ever since. The man was exacting and ambitious.

"Yeah, but he's not that scary now, right?"

"Not to me. But I've heard him yelling in the kitchen."

Harper grinned, not at all intimidated by Jason's yelling. She respected him, but she didn't fear him, and I suspected that was why Jason liked her so much. He had invested his time in her and helped her become one of the finest pastry chefs in the state. Speaking of . . . "When you put those little chocolate tart things back on the menu, remember to sneak me one."

"They're seasonal," she replied. "Winter only. But . . . if you play your cards right, I might make one especially for you."

"Oh, like the Kylie and Jason song?"

"Huh?"

I winced. "Sometimes the four-year age gap between us feels like thirty."

Harper laughed as I opened the apartment door. "That's because you're older than your years. Or, well . . . you were before you reverted to your early twenties and had a one-night stand with a hot Scottish guy."

A throat cleared and we both jerked our heads around to see my neighbor Brent, from the apartment above me, hiding a smirk as he climbed the stairs with his King Charles spaniel. "Ladies."

I blushed and gave him a wave.

As soon as he disappeared out of sight, Harper burst into laughter and I cut her a filthy look. "Thank you for that. You do know it's the first thing he'll tell his husband, and once Ian knows, everyone in the building will know."

"So what?" Harper shrugged. "You don't think anyone else in this building has ever had a one-night stand? Own it. You finally did something for yourself and there's no reason to feel ashamed."

"Even if he's an asshole."

"An asshole who found your G-spot."

I chuckled. "Okay, then."

She smiled, giving me those dimples. "I'll call you, babe. Be good to yourself."

"You too." I watched her leave, not closing the door until she was out of sight. Then I turned and leaned against the door, staring around at my apartment.

A fireplace in the center of the wall. A coffee table set in front of it and between two chesterfield sofas in ivory velvet. Soft cream deep-pile carpet Harper told me I was crazy to put down. Crisp, Hessian-colored walls, lush oyster silk curtains that draped the bay window and pooled on the floor. A small country-modern kitchen of cream-colored cabinets with a Belfast sink and thick oak counter-tops. I had a few paintings on the wall, and the odd ornament. Scatter cushions on the sofas.

Everything precise, perfect, and in its place.

And for some inexplicable reason I wanted to take the half-opened bottle of wine on my kitchen counter and dump its contents all over the room.

Nerves shaken, feeling lonely when I never felt lonely, I decided it was jetlag. It was the only explanation, so I got ready for bed, despite the early hour, and willed sleep to come and take me away from thoughts of Arcadia and the intrusive stranger I'd met in an airport.

Nine

Curled up on a small armchair beside the patio doors in my bedroom, I stared out at the pool lit up by the lights my dad had installed in fake rocks around it. Mom had told me our house was built back in the sixties. It was all on one level with lots of glass and gray brick curving around a huge backyard and ridiculous outdoor pool. And by ridiculous, I mean it had a mini waterfall rock feature.

Sounds of my parents' party filtered down the hall to my bedroom and I squeezed my knees closer to my chest. My parents were social. To the point that they'd started throwing parties for their friends at our house nearly every month. Parties that went on into the early hours of the morning. Parties I was not invited to because that would mean my parents would actually have to spend time with me.

Nope. I was ushered into my bedroom and told to stay there.

The music and laughter made me feel resentful and I glared at my bedroom door.

My parents were not like other people's parents.

The thing that really made them stand apart from my friends' parents was the fact that they never bothered to hide the act of sex from me. Sure, they'd never openly started going at it in front of me, because that would have been traumatizing, but they also didn't do sex quietly like my best friend Gemma's parents. At least, Gem and I assumed they were doing it quietly. Either that or they never had sex. But Gem thought they got along too well for that to be the case.

And then she asked me to stop talking about it. Which was, like, totally fair enough.

My mom and dad lacked consideration for me, and these loud parties were just another way in which they didn't seem to care how I felt. When I told Gem about the parties my parents were throwing, she felt bad for me. That didn't bother me. What bothered me was Nick's reaction.

He was worried about me, and Nick never worried about anything. However, at fifteen he was a year older than us, so maybe he knew something we didn't. Whatever he knew, his unease made me anxious, creating horrible butterflies in my stomach as I listened to the party beyond my door.

"I want you to come to me if you ever feel scared," Nick had said.

I'd nodded but wondered what I had to feel scared about. It was just a loud, annoying party.

Still, something made me get up out of bed that night. It made me stare at the door. And it wasn't the dry, heady heat of a July in Arizona, because I had a separate air-conditioning system in my bedroom suite, and while my parents liked it tepid in the rest of the house, I liked it cold. Gem said she didn't believe for a second I was born in Arizona. Surely, I should have acclimated years ago. I hadn't. And when I was older and I didn't have to live with my irresponsible parents, I was moving to a state that had all four seasons.

No more Christmas in the sun.

I wanted snow.

I even used to ask Santa for it when I wrote him letters back when I believed in him. It sucks that he isn't real, I moped. If he was real, and

I was wishing for things, I'd ask him to abduct my parents and replace them with the kind that remembered parent evenings and taking me to dental appointments and, you know, feeding me and stuff. I started cooking my own meals at the age of seven.

A creak of the floorboards outside my room made me tense.

My pulse started racing so hard I struggled to hear anything over the whooshing in my ears. I saw my door handle turn. I saw the door open and the crack of light that spilled into my dark room.

Goose bumps erupted all down my arms and spine as a tall masculine figure stepped into the room, his head turned toward my bed. I couldn't make him out in the dark, but I knew it wasn't my dad. He was too tall.

Seeing I wasn't in my bed, the man turned his head toward me and he grew still at the sight of me on the chair. After a moment's hesitation, he closed my bedroom door behind him and then began unbuckling his belt.

Instinct made me jump up and lunge for the patio door. I was running barefoot across the backyard and climbing the stone wall into our neighbor Mrs. Munro's backyard before I could even think about what was happening.

Tears burned in my eyes as I ran in my pajama shorts and tank, heading toward Nick's house three blocks away. The streets were quiet, empty, as I ran faster than I did in my tryout for the cross-country team.

By the time I climbed the fence into Nick's backyard, my tank was damp with sweat, my feet stung, and I was shaking so hard my teeth chittered together. I grabbed a pebble from the multitude of pebbles that made up Nick's mom's patterned landscaping, and I threw it gently up at Nick's bedroom window. He didn't hear it, so I threw another.

I saw his light come on and then his head appeared at the window.

Nick pushed it open. He wasn't wearing a shirt. Lately, ever since joining JV football, Nick had taken to half-nakedness. I was used to nakedness à la my moronic parents. But not Nick's nakedness. And even though he was only a year older than me, he looked older than that. He had just sprouted this last year and filled out too. When he first moved on

to high school without me and Gem, I thought he'd forget us, think of us
as babies.

But he didn't.

I put it down to history.

It had been the three of us since preschool. Even though he had guy
friends, including his best friend, Judd, he still hung out with me and Gem.

"Ava?" he whisper-shouted, squinting at me under the moonlight.

"It's me," I acknowledged, my voice trembling.

He must have heard it, because he instantly disappeared and a few
minutes later the French doors in the kitchen opened. Nick rushed out to
me in a T-shirt and long shorts, as tall as my dad at five foot eleven already and still growing.

"What happened?" He took hold of my arms, concern in his soulful
dark eyes.

And without meaning to and completely mortified, I burst into tears.

Nick enfolded me in his arms, his voice shaking as he said, "Now I'm
really worried. Talk to me."

I managed to calm, scared I'd wake his parents and have to explain
why I was there in the middle of the night crying my eyes out. And then I
whispered what happened. Nick's hold on me tightened.

"He didn't touch you, though?" He bit out.

I shook my head. "I got out of there."

Gently prying me from his chest, Nick gave me a severe look, seeming
so much more like a man than a boy in that moment. "We have to tell my
parents."

"No," I whisper-shouted. "Nick, no, please. I don't . . . I don't want to
make a big deal out of this, okay? My parents won't care anyway."

"If they won't care about that, then they won't care if you live here
instead."

"Your parents will never go for that and . . . look . . . I don't want
anyone knowing, okay? I don't want to be the girl whose parents let a
pervert into the house."

We had a staring match. Something he and I had gotten good at from the age of four.

I always won.

With a heavy sigh, Nick kept a strong arm around me and led me toward the house. "Fine. But I'm putting a lock on your bedroom door. And anytime your parents say they're having a party, you either stay here with me or stay with Gem, okay?"

I nodded in agreement, relief flooding me that I didn't have to go home.

"You can sleep in the guest room."

I grabbed his hand, not wanting to be alone. "Can't I stay with you?"

He paused at the French doors, seeming to ponder it. Then he nodded. "But we have to be quiet."

We tiptoed upstairs and down the creaky hall toward his bedroom, the smell of boy hitting me as soon as I walked in. It was a little musty and sweaty, but I didn't care. I felt safe here with him.

"I'll sleep on the floor," Nick whispered.

I eyed his bed, which was definitely big enough for us both. We'd shared a bed before—not in a while, but still. "We can share." More than comfortable around him and his stuff, I hopped up onto the bed and relaxed back against his pillows. I was so happy to be away from home and with someone I could trust. Still, my insides felt shaky and I couldn't stop shivering. I wanted Nick near me to help abate the feeling.

My best friend, however, stood across the room and stared at me.

He seemed . . . uncertain.

"What's going on?" I whispered, leaning forward. Uneasiness crept over me and I wondered if Nick was secretly sick of having me and Gem around. Was having me infiltrate his space, like, the last straw or something? "Nick?"

"You're in my bed," he whispered.

"Technically, I'm on it," I joked stupidly, wanting to defuse the sudden tension between us.

Finally, he took a few steps toward me, and the chill the strange man had put in my blood suddenly dissipated under a wave of warmth. My cheeks grew flushed and my palms sweaty and I didn't know why. Except . . . except Nick was looking at me . . . differently.

Like a boy looks at a girl.

"Oh." I tensed in realization.

Nick threw me a lazy, almost shy, self-deprecating smile. "Yeah. Oh. I, um . . . I shouldn't get on the bed with you."

"Since when?" My breathing sounded a little funny. It felt funny too. Like I couldn't quite catch a complete breath.

His eyes pinned me to the spot and he seemed so nervous I wanted to hug him. He swallowed hard. "Since a while." He exhaled. Shakily, making the butterflies in my stomach spread their wings and come to life again. "I . . . I love you, Ava. And not like how I love Gem. I don't want to kiss Gem."

Wow.

Oh my God.

How did this night turn from the worst night ever to . . . well, kind of freaking epic?

I stared at him in total shock.

Nick was always the "boy next door," but lately I knew my feelings toward him had been changing. I just wasn't brave enough to admit it like he was. And I never, ever thought he would feel the same way back.

It wasn't like I didn't get asked out, and I'd been on a few dates. I'd even dated Michael Crawley in the seventh grade for eight months. But this was Nick. I never imagined Nick could love me romantically.

"What if I'm glad?" I whispered, my heart racing. "What if I love you too?" And I did. He was Nick. My protector and my best friend.

His eyes widened ever so slightly and then he rounded the bed, getting onto it beside me. I turned into him and he reached out to tentatively cup my cheek in his hand.

"It's okay." I sighed, nuzzling into his touch, amazed how the ugly

shivers from a mere few minutes ago had transformed into excited trembling. "You can kiss me."

When he did, it was the sweetest, softest kiss I'd ever been given. Boys usually just stuck their tongue in my mouth, wiggled it around a bit, and then grinned smugly like they'd accomplished something great instead of something yuck.

Not Nick.

My best friend could kiss.

I laughed softly at the thought, amazed that this was happening.

Nick smiled, caressing my cheek with his thumb. "What?"

"Only you could turn the worst night ever into the best."

He grinned and wrapped his arm around me, pulling my head down onto his shoulder. "I can't believe you like me back."

"You thought I wouldn't?" I asked in disbelief.

"You're the most beautiful girl in school. Even the guys on the varsity team talk about you."

"They talk about a freshman? Perverts," I joked.

He chuckled. "My point is, you could have anyone."

I frowned. "But I don't want just anyone."

"Not even Styler James?" he teased.

I rolled my eyes. Styler was Gem's big crush, and I indulged her by oohing and aahing over him sometimes. He was a junior and admittedly extremely cute. "His name is Styler, Nick."

My head rose with his shoulders as he laughed quietly. "Doesn't seem to bother every other girl, including Gem."

"Gem can have him. I want you."

I felt his lips on my forehead. "You have me," he whispered. "I'll always protect you, Ava."

Snuggling deeper into him, I believed it. I believed it with every bone in my body. He had all my faith.

"So you're my girl?" he asked. "I get to tell everyone to back off now, 'cause you're my girl?"

"Yes." I reached for his hand. "I'm yours. And you're mine."
"Always."

woke up in a jolt from the dream. The memory. Sweat soaked the hair at the back of my neck and my skin felt flushed.

So much for sleep taking me away from the ghosts my time back home had stirred up. If sleep wasn't going to do it, then I hoped running would. I got up just as the dawn was breaking, changed into running clothes, and took off.

A few miles later I felt marginally better, but I knew keeping busy would be the only way to distract myself from the shaky hangover dreaming of my past had left me with. Which was why I was so happy to return to work that morning.

Stella Larson Designs was located on Beacon Street, just a few doors down from XV Beacon Hotel but on the opposite side of the street. It hadn't always been in such a prime location, but as Stella's company took off, she relocated, taking the risk on an expensive office location in the hopes that it would appeal to wealthy clients. And it seemed to work. We had an airy reception room with muted gray tile flooring, a white leather corner sofa scattered with a few different-sized pillows in a gray palette, and a gray throw. At the back of the room was a sideboard in a gray-painted finish that held our public portfolios. Hung on the wall above it were photographs from some of our favorite designs framed in thin lemon-colored frames. That tiny burst of color continued in the vase on the sideboard, the handblown glass bowl on the coffee table, and the miniature button-back armchair in the corner of the room.

We had a glass reception desk, chosen so that it would seem to almost disappear into the room, but it was only for show. There was a bell that sounded in each of our offices when someone entered our reception area, and one of us would go out and greet the client. Stella didn't see any point in wasting money on a full-time receptionist when most of our clients came in by appointment.

The great thing about our location on Beacon Street was that I could walk there from my apartment in less than ten minutes.

As I strolled into the office, relief flooding me at being home, my cell rang. Of course it did. I sighed, digging through my purse to locate it. Not even two seconds into the place and my clients needed my attention already.

However, caller ID told me it was my uncle David, not a client. "Good morning," I said as a greeting, always happy to hear from him.

"Good morning, sweetheart. Just checking in to make sure you got home okay."

It must have been the stress of the last few days, but his words caused a burn of tears in the back of my eyes. Grateful for his concern, I smiled. "I'm home, safe and sound. Just walked into the office, in fact."

"And you're okay?"

Here was the thing that you needed to know about my family. My childhood had been tumultuous since my parents didn't really know what to do with a kid. They'd wanted one, but when they got me, they seemed to flounder. They were never outright unkind to me; they also never provided me with any real affection, beyond whatever they gave to anyone else. Their philosophy was to let me find my way, believing it would make me a freer, more independent person. They also didn't believe in grudges or arguments. So when I was bullied in the seventh grade, they told me to just forgive Amanda Pointer for pushing me facedown in the dirt until I almost passed out, and get over it.

I could have been out smoking dope and stealing cars, and they would have shrugged it off as me "trying to find myself." They knew very little about my personality, never taking the time to get to know me, and the only compliments they ever gave me were on my physical appearance.

One bright light in my upbringing was my uncle David, my mom's big brother. He was totally different from my mom, and he disapproved of the way they brought me up. I'd heard him attempting to say so to my mom when he visited, and my mom would tell him they didn't invite negativity into the house. I knew she and my dad frustrated my uncle to the point of real anger, but he still visited whenever he could to check up on me.

He even sent me money when I attended Savannah College of Art and Design. With his support, and with Nick and Gem only a few hours away studying at Georgia State, college had been the happiest time in my life. A year after graduation, however, after I'd been convinced to move back to Phoenix, the two people I trusted the most destroyed my faith and broke my heart. It was my uncle who stepped in to help me pick up the pieces. He insisted I move out to Boston to stay with him and his wife while I got on my feet. I'd been working as an intern with an interior design company, so my hope was to find a new position with another company. My uncle was a successful accountant and I convinced him to let me redo his office so I could add it to my small portfolio. Instead, Stella Larson noted the changes on her next visit to my uncle's office and inquired about it. Being the super supportive guy he was, my uncle waxed poetic about me to her and got me an interview. Seven years later the rest was history.

It wasn't the only time my uncle David had come through for me. He was also the reason Harper got a chance at Canterbury. Jason Luton was not only his client, but they'd become friends, and I asked him to ask Jason to give Harper a shot as an apprentice chef when she was nineteen.

My uncle was semiretired and lived in a beautiful house in Hyde

Park. One they didn't stay in that often because his wife liked to travel. Still, Uncle David stayed in touch as much as possible. And I knew he'd been worried about me after the news broke of Gem's passing.

"I'm fine," I replied, strolling past Stella's office and waving to her as she looked up from her computer. My office was just as I'd left it—spic and span. All my work put away and organized. It didn't look like that normally. It was the one personal space of mine that was usually covered in drawings, fabrics, photographs, and papers. "I'm just glad to be home."

"I would have dropped by, but we're in New York. When we get back, let's have dinner."

"I'd like that."

"And how is my sister?" he asked, almost reluctantly.

"The same."

He grunted. "Okay. Well, I'll let you get back to work. Call me if you need anything."

"I will. Love you."

"Love you too, sweetheart."

We hung up and I slumped into my chair, looking around my office, preparing myself. First coffee. Leaving my bag and phone at my desk, I headed back toward reception and to the fancy coffee machine that had taken me months to figure out how to use correctly.

"Welcome back."

I glanced over my shoulder and spotted Stella leaning against the doorway to reception with her arms crossed over her chest. She wore a white blouse with balloon sleeves tucked into an oyster pink pencil skirt. On her feet, nude patent Louboutins. I could admit I may have modeled my own style on hers, because I thought she was pure class.

Her dark brown hair was cut short and blunt so that the shiny ends touched her chin. She had it tucked behind her right ear, revealing a large diamond stud. Her dark eyes were filled with concern.

"I'm fine," I said, without her having to ask.

"You should have taken today off."

"And what would have been the point?" I approached her with my coffee. "What I need is to get back to normal. I have a ton of work to catch up on. You know, as my boss you should actually be pressuring me to do that."

Stella snorted. "I like to think I'm a human being as well as a boss."

I laughed as she walked back to my office with me. "You're an anomaly among your kind."

"Since you aren't taking me up on my offer for time off . . . is there anything I can do to help?" She gestured to my office, thus indicating my work. "And by help, I mean off-load some of your work to Gabe."

As our newest and youngest employee, Gabe worked with only one client at a time, so he technically had more availability than me, Stella, or Paul, the other senior designer.

"I'm really okay. And you know I would never off-load work to someone else. The thought makes my chest hurt," I joked. But it was true. I was maybe too much of a control freak sometimes, but that was just who I was.

"Fine." Stella regarded me seriously. "I want to know, however, if you can't handle things. Not just out of the kindness of my heart either. We can't afford for any screwups on your current projects. Both are longtime clients."

"I know that. I'm good," I promised her.

My boss left me to it and I booted up my computer to start working my way through e-mails. Patrice Danby, the forty-eight-year-old daughter of an oil baron and wife to a high-powered attorney, had been using Stella Larson Designs for the past six years. It seemed she had a new project for us to do every six months, whether it was personal or part of her philanthropic work. We found ourselves designing space for hospital common rooms, retirement homes, free clinics, and once even a charity-run veterinary hospital. I liked Patrice. She didn't seem like some bored housewife who needed something to do and so turned to charity work. She genuinely appeared to care about her philanthropic projects, and while some people might be of the opinion that it was silly to put so much work into making a space look pretty, Patrice believed in the power of beautiful things. She believed the perfect space could help healing or provide comfort to people and animals. And Stella was more than happy to work with her on that.

For the past three years Patrice had worked exclusively with me after enjoying my collaboration on a retirement home.

I was also working with Roxanne Sutton aka the Shrew. This was my first time working on a project with Roxanne, because her usual designer had said he was too busy to work on her latest project. It became clear to me quite quickly that that was an excuse, and Paul had landed me with Roxanne for a reason. She was rude, demanding, and interfering. However, she had been a client for ten years, and as the young wife of Marcus Sutton, of the New England Suttons, she had more money than God. That family had their fingers in all kinds of different pies, and their wealth had accumulated for generations. They were the kind of wealthy that was difficult to wrap your head around.

My latest project with Roxanne was redecorating not one room, but the entirety of their summer home in Nantucket.

After making a few calls to the tradesman I was collaborating with on the project to see where things stood, I called Roxanne. She lambasted me for a while about being unavailable for the last few days, and although I tried to explain the situation once again, she pretended like she couldn't hear me. Once I'd promised to send over the latest photos I'd received from the work on the house, and resend samples and drawings I'd already sent her, I managed to get off the phone.

Then I called Patrice. I was redesigning the guesthouse at the back of their property in Wellesley Farms. They had family from Europe coming to stay with them over the summer, and Patrice wanted them to feel like they had privacy, but the guesthouse hadn't been redecorated in ten years.

"Darling, it's so good to hear from you," Patrice said. "I've been worried. I was so sorry to hear about your old friend. It's such a tragedy."

Did I mention I really liked Patrice? "Thank you. I'm okay. Honestly, I'm happy to be home and getting back to work. Which is why I'm calling. The seven-seater corner sofa we ordered for the main family room is no longer available in that specific dark blue velvet. Why they couldn't tell us this sooner, I don't know, but they have provided me with alternative fabric samples. They express-mailed them, so I can send those to you ASAP and you can decide whether you like any of the options. Depending on the change of fabric, we may have to tweak the rest of the design in that room." We'd based a lot of it around that piece of furniture.

"Well, I'll have a look at the samples and we can discuss. Preferably in person, darling, because I have a bit of a favor to ask of you."

"Oh?"

"Did you hear on the news about that volcano in Iceland erupting?"

That was random. "Yes, I did, actually."

"It's causing quite a lot of air travel disruption in Europe, and a guest of ours is a little bit stranded. Now, normally that wouldn't be a problem, but Danby is working on a huge case and is too busy for any kind of entertaining." She referred to her husband by his surname instead of his given name, Michael, because they had a twenty-six-year-old son who shared the same name. "As for Michael, he's stranded in London on a business trip so he isn't here to help keep our guest entertained either, and I'm organizing the annual Sophia Claymore Benefit for Breast Cancer next week. I am snowed under. We have no idea how long our guest will be stranded in Boston. He was only supposed to be here for four nights, but right now they're estimating a week or two for the ash cloud to clear. I know you are so very busy, but our guest is around your age and I was hoping you might be able to see him. I want him to have a good impression of Boston, darling, and I couldn't think of anyone better than you for him to get to know. Also, I know you're single . . ."

Stunned, and cornered, and wondering how I could get out of this without upsetting a longtime client I admired, I stuttered for words. "Well . . . um . . . Are you . . . Is this an attempt at matchmaking, Patrice? I'm flattered, but I actually am very busy with work right now."

"It's not an attempt at matchmaking, I swear. I just thought it might be nice for you to have something other than work as a distraction during such a trying time. Plus, to be blunt, my other friends are either boring fusspots, functioning alcoholics, or middle-aged housewives who would hit on him. It's only for a week, maybe two. It wouldn't take up too much of your time. I just . . . thought perhaps you could show him around town, take him to dinner a couple times."

I could practically hear Stella shouting in my head to say yes. We couldn't afford to hurt Patrice Danby's feelings or piss her off. And it was only for a week or two. I just had to hope that she was kind enough not to land me with an obnoxious sleaze. "Well, I'd be happy to if it would help you out."

"Oh, you are a sweetheart!" she exclaimed happily. "Let's meet for lunch with those samples so I can introduce you two. He's here on business so he's occupied during the day but did promise he could meet us for lunch if you said yes."

"So you've told him about me?"

"Well, yes, your name came up. I must have been going on about how wonderful you were because he seemed intrigued."

Great. Now he had expectations.

"That's nice." I winced.

She laughed. "Don't worry, darling. He's perfectly charming. We'll meet at Deuxave, yes. One o'clock."

"I'll see you both there."

Not five minutes later, Stella poked her head around the door. "How's it going?"

"Patrice Danby is trying to set me up with a guest of hers who's stranded here because of that damn volcano eruption."

She grinned. "And you said yes, of course."

"You owe me."

"Ava, it's Patrice. She would never try to set you up with a cretin."

Ten

Yet, apparently, Patrice *would* try to set me up with a cretin.

My heart was thudding hard in my chest as the hostess led me to Patrice's table at Deuxave, a French restaurant in Back Bay. Confusion and anger were my foremost feelings.

Because the man rising to stand from Patrice's table at my approach was none other than Caleb Scott.

The Bastard Scot.

"Darling, don't you look beautiful as always?" Patrice moved toward me before I'd reached the table and gently took me by the shoulders to kiss my cheeks, one after the other.

I smiled at the attractive older woman, hoping it didn't come across as brittle as it felt. Patrice Danby wasn't what anyone would call a typical beauty, but there was something striking and charismatic about her that made her lovelier than mere ordinary beauty. Tall, extremely slender, she had, according to photographs, always had the kind of figure expected of a model. Clothes hung beautifully on her, like works of art, and the designer houndstooth shirtdress she wore with black leather heels was no exception. Her dark blond hair was cut stylish and short, much like Stella's.

"As do you," I responded, my eyes involuntarily glued to Caleb Scott as he stared impassively at me.

"Let me introduce you to our guest, Ava." She guided me over to him and I was sure my expression was screaming at him, *What the hell is going on?*

He looked different. Although he was still unshaven and his hair was the same, he was wearing a beautifully cut tailored suit. No tattoos in sight. He could have passed for a civilized gentleman, and this look on him was almost as hot as the henley and biker boots.

To my shock, he held out his big hand to me and politely said, "Miss Breevort."

"Oh, call her Ava, Caleb. Ava, this is Caleb Scott."

Gingerly, I reached out and took his hand, staring into those amusement-filled ice blue eyes, trying to find the explanation for my current predicament.

"Ava." His voice rumbled over my name as he gently squeezed my hand. I felt a sparkle of lust fizz in my belly.

Damn him.

"Caleb," I said softly, all the while feeling extremely confused. About a lot of things.

For some reason my saying his name made his hand tighten around mine, but then it was almost like I'd imagined it, because suddenly we were no longer touching. He took his seat quite abruptly in that well-renowned ill-mannered way of his.

A gentleman always waits for a lady to be seated first.

Oh, who cared? I wanted to know what the hell he was doing here. I took my seat across from him, ignoring the way Patrice was glancing back and forth between us as I studied his face. He just stared dispassionately at me. Had he orchestrated this? How did he manage it?

"Well." Patrice's voice drew my gaze back to her. Her eyes were bright, her lips tugging into a delighted smile like she knew a secret we didn't. "Isn't this lovely?"

"Lovely," I murmured, taking a sip from the water glass at the table. "So, Patrice, how do you and Mr. Scott know each other?"

"You must call him Caleb." She smiled fondly at him, a smile he returned, dumbfounding me even further. "Caleb is good friends with my nephew, Duncan. My nephew and his family are the ones we're decorating the guesthouse for."

Understanding dawned. "Your family from Scotland."

"Exactly. And I was telling Caleb why we couldn't give him the privacy of the guesthouse during his stay, and got a little carried away on the topic of the redesign. But he was so impressed by your work, Ava, I thought I should introduce you. Caleb is the CFO of Koto's UK division. Isn't that impressive?"

I managed only to stare at him as my brain whirred with a million questions. Had Caleb really arranged this somehow? "Very impressive."

There was a lull of silence that caused a crease between Patrice's brows. She opened her mouth to speak but was stalled by the appearance of the waiter. Once he'd taken our orders, Patrice continued, "Caleb was staying at the Four Seasons and we were having dinner when he told us of this whole volcano fiasco disrupting his travel plans. Well, of course we couldn't see him stuck at some hotel for a possible two weeks. The expense is ridiculous when you have friends nearby. Even though our house is outside the city, it's not far—just a short drive to the Koto offices."

I looked at Caleb and found him studying his water glass. Why did I get the impression he would have preferred to stay at his hotel? And if that was true, why was he humoring Patrice? That was something someone who cared about other people's feelings would do. Hmm.

Silence fell over the table again and I saw Patrice frown in concern. Not wanting to upset her by being rude to her guest, I offered, "Do you have a rental car to get back and forth from Wellesley Farms? I can recommend somewhere."

He gave me a slight shake of his head. "Danby kindly offered me the use of his Maserati while I'm here."

I almost laughed. That sounded like Danby. He and Patrice were two of the most generous people I'd ever met. "He must really trust you to remember to drive on the right side of the road."

Patrice chuckled while Caleb smirked at me. "I suppose he must."

My eyes narrowed at his restrained answer. Where was the cutting, biting kind of insults from the man I'd slept with?

As the seconds ticked by, we got locked in a staring contest, his expression challenging, mine likely suspicious. It was only when Patrice cleared her throat that we broke eye contact. My client's gaze moved from me to Caleb, that frown deepening between her brows. "Perhaps it's just my imagination, but I've had the feeling from the moment Ava walked in here that you two already know each other."

Did I also mention that Patrice wasn't stupid? I flushed, hating to be caught in any sort of pretense, and worrying over whether I should continue to bury us in more lies, which I hated to do. But I didn't know what would be worse—

"You're not wrong, Patrice. Apologies." Caleb threw me a taunting smile. "I met Miss Breevort in Phoenix. We were on the same flights tae Chicago and Boston. When you said her name, I couldn't help but want tae surprise her. Sorry for the mischief."

"Ahh." Patrice's whole face lit up. "How wonderful. And what a coincidence. I bet you thought you'd never see each other again."

"You're not wrong." I laughed a little hysterically and saw Caleb's grin widen. Alarm pierced me. "I didn't mean to pretend otherwise, Patrice, but I was caught off guard and not really sure what Mr.

Scott was up to over there. He's full of *mischief* all right." I said it cheerily but my teeth were gritted.

The bastard let out a huff of laughter.

"I think it's fabulous. In fact, I really feel like I shouldn't even be here." Patrice reached for her purse, giving me a knowing smile. "You two should spend lunch together alone, get better acquainted. I have so much to do, I should really run."

Panic flooded me. "But, Patrice, you've already ordered."

"Oh, I can cancel that." She placed a hand on Caleb's shoulder. "I'll see you back at the house when I see you. But please don't feel like you have to put in too much of an appearance. I know you're busy with work and"—she glanced at me—"you'll have Ava to keep you company."

"Thank you again, Patrice. Your hospitality is appreciated."

My jaw dropped.

Did he just say thank you?

"Oh, no no. No thank yous. We like having company in that big house." She rounded the table to me and bent down to kiss my cheek. "We'll talk soon, darling. Have fun."

"But Patr—"

She was already strutting away over to the hostess to cancel her order.

And then she was gone. Without her fabric samples, I might add.

Reluctantly, I turned back around in my seat and stared across the small table at Caleb. "What the hell?"

He cocked his head slightly, frowning. "Patrice was so sure you'd be accommodating. I dinnae think she knows her interior designer very well."

"Stop messing around. Last time we spoke I got the sincere impression it would be the *last time*. What with all those other beautiful women in Boston just waiting for the chance to jump on board Caleb Scott."

His lips twitched, drawing my attention to the thick stubble he was sporting, which immediately sparked the memory of it tickling and scratching my skin. Damn. My legs automatically squeezed together, trying to quell the insistent tingling sensation between them.

"There are plenty of beautiful women in Boston, I'm sure many of whom are good in bed . . . Very few are fantastic in bed, however." His now heated eyes blazed at me meaningfully, making my clothes feel too tight, too hot.

I scoffed, trying to dampen the arousal he awakened in me. "I'm sure there was a compliment in there, but I'm not interested."

Caleb calmly reached for his water glass and took a sip. When he was finished, I found myself recaptured in his gaze. "One thing you should know about me, Ava, is that I'm a very determined man. When I want something, I usually get it."

My heart stuttered in my chest. What exactly did that mean? "And you want . . . ?"

Quite abruptly he scowled. "I'm stuck here, which frankly pisses me off. Now I can spend my free time in the evenings being pissed off or I can spend them in bed with you. I know which one I'd prefer. And if you'd stop lying tae yourself, you'd admit that you want another go-around with me."

Was there ever a more obnoxious man alive? My blood was hot with anger. "Do you ever think about what you're going to say before you say it?"

"You're offended?" He raised an eyebrow.

I leaned across the table, lowering my voice to his. "You just told me that you want me to be your entertainment while you're stranded in Boston." I sat back in my seat, my pulse racing even harder because the truth was, despite my aversion to him, I was still stupidly attracted to him. As in seriously wanted to launch myself across the table at him and rip off his clothes right then and there. What was wrong with me?

"No. I suggested we screw this attraction out of our systems."

"We are in a nice restaurant," I said between gritted teeth.

"Then let's take this conversation elsewhere."

"I'm hungry." But I wasn't sure I really was. I was just stalling.

Caleb glanced impatiently at his watch. "I have tae get back tae the office in forty-five minutes."

Understanding what he meant, I decided I didn't care where we were and threw my napkin across the table at him. "We are not having sex on our lunch break."

He didn't even look at the napkin. "But we are having sex?"

I shook my head at his single-mindedness. "I suppose I should feel flattered that you went to so much trouble for a booty call."

Caleb didn't even flinch at my sarcasm. "It didn't sit right leaving things the way we did. I only walk away when I'm bored, Ava. I'm not bored yet. Are you?"

"When you say you only walk away when you're bored . . . what about the women? Do you care if you break their hearts?"

He gave me a condescending smile. "It's only ever about attraction. No one gets attached long enough for feelings tae be involved."

"So you think."

"Are you telling me that you dinnae want tae sleep with me because you're afraid you might develop feelings for me?"

"You know I don't even like you."

"Exactly. So what's the harm in it? Live a little, Ava."

His comment made me think back to the other night in his hotel bed and how everything else had disappeared for those few hours we were together. It was just him and me and the pleasure we could bring to each other. There was something compelling about how lovely it was to disappear into something new. Especially now.

Our food arrived before I could answer, and Caleb unexpectedly stayed patiently quiet as we ate and I mulled over the pros and cons of sleeping with him again.

The pros were obvious. Unbelievable satisfaction with no strings attached. And Caleb would be gone again in a week or two, so I wouldn't have to face him once we'd gotten each other out of our systems.

On the other hand, I'd once again be sleeping with a man I didn't even like. How would I feel about my integrity when it was over? Or was I making too big a deal out of it?

"You think too much," Caleb said, pushing his empty plate away from him.

I finished up too. "Just sex?"

His expression sobered and he nodded.

I lowered my voice. "I know I should have asked this in Chicago, but . . . are you clean?"

"I get a regular health check. You're the first I've been with since my last. I can e-mail you the results if you want."

"I want." Maybe it would sound crazy to him, but I needed to be careful. I wasn't the reckless type.

Caleb didn't seem perturbed by my response. "And you?"

"You don't have to worry about me. I had a health check after my last relationship. I'm clean. I can try to get those results if you want."

"I want." His eyes darkened to a sliver. "So does that mean you're up for this?"

I felt like my heart was in my throat, my pulse was beating so hard. "Yes."

Thankfully, he didn't respond with a smug smile. "Your place or mine?"

The idea of carrying on with him under the Danby roof made me shudder. It was so horrifically unprofessional. Yet I wasn't sure I wanted him inside my apartment, my private space. "I'd prefer neither, to be honest."

"I still have my room at the Four Seasons." He stood up abruptly and pulled out his wallet. "Patrice is very kind, but I like my privacy. For now I need tae get back tae work. Do you have a card so I can contact you?"

Betraying my desire to be cool, my fingers trembled a little as I opened my purse to find a business card. I held it out to him as he dropped a pile of bills on the table to cover lunch. "Thanks for lunch."

Caleb took my card with a carefully neutral expression. "I'll call you when I'm free."

Suddenly I felt a flush of annoyance that he thought we could do this on his time. "And I'll let you know if *I'm* free when you do."

Rounding the table, he bent down to brace one hand on my chair and the other on the table, trapping me. My heart took off at his nearness. His face was so close I almost felt the bristle of his short beard on my skin. Mirth danced in his eyes. He brushed his lips over mine and straightened, towering over me like a well-dressed conquering Viking. "See you soon."

I watched him walk away, my whole body electrified with anticipation. In that moment I realized I was sorry to see him go. I was sorry that I had to get back to work and wait for his phone call. Part of me regretted not ditching lunch, but I reminded myself I wasn't an animal, controlled by my base desires.

Once I left the restaurant, I jumped into a cab to take me back to the office.

All afternoon I cursed Caleb Scott for the distraction he presented. It took me a good hour to really sink into my work and let his proposal drift off into the background. And just when I had put him to the back of my mind, my cell binged.

Unknown number: Room 201. 9 p.m. You'll need a key card to access the floor. I'll leave it at reception for you. Caleb.

The Four Seasons was just a walk across the Common from here. Desire rolled through my belly at the thought of meeting him there later that night. I squeezed my eyes closed, overwhelmed by my physical response to him.

Thank goodness I didn't even like the guy. I could only imagine what danger I'd be in if my emotions were involved on top of such intense physical feelings.

I opened my eyes and looked down at my cell. First I saved his number and then I replied:

Fine.

Happy with my short response, I sat back at my desk and tried to remember what I'd been doing. My cell chimed again before I could.

Caleb: You'll be more than fine when I'm done with you.

I glowered at my phone, warring between irritation and desire. I'd never met a man so unromantic and blunt, and would never have imagined being turned on by that bluntness. Pretending, however, to be anything else was beneath me and childish. I'd agreed to have this affair with him. That meant he knew I wanted him. Playing the prude to save my pride just made me a different kind of obnoxious.

I should hope so. There are expectations to be met.

His response was almost immediate.

Caleb: Surpassed. There are expectations to be surpassed.

I smiled and felt myself start to really relax for the first moment since our lunch. This interlude with Caleb for a week, perhaps two, depending on how long he was stranded here, would be something to remember on those nights I was alone. I'd remember this as the time I let go of my responsibilities and did something just because I wanted to.

Eleven

There was this light, fresh, floral scent in the air at the Four Seasons. I didn't know if it was something they spritzed out through an air-filtering system or if it was whatever they polished the marble floors with, but it was so pleasant and calming every time I visited I was often tempted to find one of their beautifully placed pieces of furniture and sit there for hours. Especially at that moment as I strutted through the main entrance door held open for me by a tall, traditionally outfitted doorman. I nodded my thanks, hoping I looked calm, collected, and aloof enough that no one here would suspect the reason that had drawn me to this hotel.

My heels clacked against the black, gold, and white diamond-patterned floor as I strode straight ahead to the reception desk.

A young blonde smiled at me from behind it. "Good evening. Welcome to the Four Seasons."

"Good evening." I hoped my smile wasn't strained or nervous-looking. "My partner left a room key for me. Room 201 for Ava Breevort." I didn't care if calling him my partner pissed off Caleb. It could be construed as professional partner or otherwise. I just didn't want anyone to think badly of me, especially not at the Four Seasons, where I often dined with clients.

"Ah, yes." The young woman's eyes lit up. "Mr. Scott did leave a key for you." She reached under the desk and pulled out a Four Seasons card and card holder. "There you are, Miss Breevort. Is there anything else I can do for you?"

"No, that's great," I said, taking the key card and feeling my cheeks start to heat as the reality of what I was about to do sunk in.

"Have a wonderful evening."

"Thank you. You too."

I headed toward the elevators, feeling like my heart might explode. My stomach was filled with flutters so wild they seemed to be diving up into my chest and panicking my heart into acceleration. I let out a shaky breath as I got into the elevator, thankfully alone.

If I was feeling so anxious about this, why was I doing it? I stared at the bank of buttons and saw Caleb was right. There was a small panel I needed to flash my room card over to get onto Caleb's floor. Which meant he was more than likely staying in a suite.

"Maybe I should just go home," I whispered to myself.

But almost immediately on the back of the thought came the image of Caleb leaning down over me at lunch, his lips whispering near mine, and the sensual promise in his enigmatic eyes.

No, I didn't like the man.

However, I really, really liked how he made me feel.

Shake it off, Ava, I hissed at myself. *You made the decision to have fun for once so don't back out now.*

I swiped the card over the panel and pressed the button for Caleb's floor.

Once I got off the elevator, the click of my heels now dulled against the thick carpeted floor, I followed the signs for room 201 and sucked in a huge breath when I stood outside it, the flutters from my belly rising right up into my throat.

What was I so nervous about? It wasn't like I hadn't done this with him before. Although my inhibitions were slightly lowered by alcohol last time. Dammit, I should have had more than one glass of wine with my dinner to relax me. Instead, I'd gotten home around six thirty, barely able to concentrate on cooking or eating. I'd rushed through it so I could shower, shave, and primp. What I should wear had posed a dilemma, but I went for a simple black shift dress with simple black stilettos, silk hold-ups with a lace band around the thigh, and black lace underwear. Understated sexy.

Ava, you put on sexy lingerie for a man you don't even like, I chastised myself as I raised my finger to the doorbell of the suite. *You're sure you want to do this? Last chance to turn back.*

I wavered.

Then I pressed the doorbell.

Not a second later I heard movement from behind the door and a few seconds after that the door opened. My breath caught at the sight of Caleb Scott standing tall and imposing before me. He stared at me, his expression almost neutral, if it weren't for those paradoxical eyes of fire and ice blazing at me.

This big, physically and verbally intimidating man, who I imagined never let anyone have a piece of him. What he didn't realize was that his desire was a big part of him, and he was handing it over to me. He wore a white T-shirt that delineated his amazing physique and a pair of jeans that hung well on his narrow hips. Who knew a simple pair of jeans and a T-shirt could be that goddamn sexy?

"Are you going to invite me in or just stare at me?" I arched an eyebrow.

"Both." He stepped aside and I hesitated for a moment, which of course he picked up on. "Are you going tae come in or live the rest of your life regretting that you didn't have one more night with the Bastard Scot?"

I tried to quell my smile but my lips turned up at the corners despite my best efforts. "You remembered my endearment. How sweet." And with that I lifted one foot in front of the other and walked by him, my elbow brushing his stomach, his delicious scent causing a shiver to ripple down my spine.

I doubted very much the hotel suite was decorated to Caleb Scott's taste. He struck me as a black and chrome kind of guy. Not the kind of guy to dig striped pale jade wallpaper, pale gold carpet, dark mahogany furniture, traditional New England essence. We stood in a living room that had a pale gold velvet sofa opposite a mahogany sideboard with a television. There was a matching coffee table between them. At the end of the room was a bay window I knew overlooked the Public Garden, but I couldn't see the view because Caleb had drawn the curtains. Beside the window was a chair and a desk where he'd put his laptop and papers. To my left were glazed double doors, open to the separate bedroom, where I could see the king-sized bed.

I decided to peer inside the bedroom area out of curiosity, since I'd never been inside a suite here before (not to mention a need for distraction from the Scottish Viking behind me). On the left side of the room was an open doorway leading to the bathroom. From there I could see a long marble sink.

"Nice room," I said quietly as I felt him step up behind me.

Caleb didn't reply. Instead I felt his hands slide down over my shoulders to grip the lapels of my light coat. He tugged and I let my shoulders relax and drop so he could remove it.

I turned my head slightly to see him put the coat on the sofa.

And then goose bumps flared and sprinkled along my neck and back as his knuckles brushed my nape while he gathered my hair in his hand and moved all of it over one shoulder.

"I guess the talking part of this is over," I whispered, trying to sound amused instead of breathless and aroused. I failed.

At finding no zipper on the dress, his hands caressed their way down my sides until he found the hem. "You can still talk, Ava." His voice rumbled behind me as he lifted the dress slowly. "Tell me how slow, fast, hard you want it."

I shivered, raising my arms above my head as he pulled the dress up and over. There was silence behind me as I lowered my arms, so much so I felt a burst of nerves that caused my knees to shake a little. "I don't do this," I whispered, the words out before I could stop them.

"Do what?"

"Casual sex with men I don't like." Or casual sex at all.

He grunted. "You've already done it. Turn around."

I did so slowly, hating that I was trembling. Hoping he couldn't see it. Not wanting to be vulnerable to him in any way. Reluctantly, I raised my eyes to his face and felt that hard tug of need at the way his voracious gaze roamed over me.

"The Scot likes black underwear and hold-ups," I teased, attempting to relax into this, to bring back our banter and ease instead of this volcanic sexual tension that was much too intense. I slipped off my heels.

Suddenly he took hold of the hem of his T-shirt and pulled it up over his head and off, throwing it to the couch with my dress. God, I didn't even know men like him existed outside of movies and myths. I couldn't wait to explore his body again, remembering how much fun I'd had last time doing it.

"Babe, you could walk in here wearing a plastic garbage bag and

I'd still want you. Now get on the bed," he demanded as he unbuttoned the top of his jeans.

"*You* get on the bed."

Caleb shook his head as he divested himself of his jeans and underwear. "Why is everything a bloody battle with you?" He looked up from staring at me to glare hungrily into my eyes. "You're not my type. Your hair, your makeup, your clothes, your attitude. You're too beautiful and you know it. And yet I'm desperate to have you again."

I glowered, hating him and hating that my body was still hot and flushed and needy for him even after he'd said that to me. "I *hate* you."

His jaw clenched, fire flashed in his eyes, and he growled, "Good." His mouth crashed down on mine, sweeping me up into a hungry, punishing kiss that I instantly responded to. His strong arms bound around me, crushing my breasts against his naked chest, and I felt the shivery thrill of being pressed against the strength of him.

His hold was almost too tight, but there was something desperate about it that ignited the fire in me, and I slid my arms around his back, my fingers digging into his muscle as the kiss turned almost savage. Our tongues mated, mimicking what our bodies wanted to do, our teeth scraped against lips, biting, possessive, our breaths hot, pants and growls and gasps filling each other's mouths.

No one kissed me like he did.

No one.

It obliterated the insecurity he'd caused only moments before.

It obliterated everything.

Suddenly he was helping me out of my underwear and then I was on my back, his kisses still deep, still ravaging, as I felt his hard length caress my belly and move down to nudge between my legs. I felt him push inside me and I whimpered against his kiss, my fingernails biting into his skin with need. Caleb groaned into my mouth. "You feel amazing."

Through the fog of desire, realization of why this felt so incredibly good hit me. "Condom." I stilled against his movements.

His eyes flew to mine and I saw the astonishment he couldn't mask. Apparently protection wasn't something he forgot about that often. He gritted his teeth as he began to withdraw.

"Dinnae move an inch." He growled, disappearing into the living room.

Seconds later he was over me again, laughter bubbling on my lips at how frustrated and harassed he looked. The laughter instantly died as he gripped my right thigh against his outer hip and thrust back inside of me.

It wasn't the same, but it was still excellent.

Afterward, when both of us were breathless and satisfied, he loosened his hold on me. He dropped to his elbows, his slick, warm forehead resting between my breasts, his hot breath puffing against my stomach. He kissed my belly, softly, almost reverently.

It was sweet and not at all what I expected of him.

It felt nice. Too nice.

So I immediately sought to spoil it. "I guess I should go."

Caleb tensed. After a few seconds of silence, he lifted his head, but only far enough to bring his mouth to my breasts. He covered them in kisses and swiped teasing licks against my nipples until I felt desire building inside me again. Without thought I lifted my hands to grasp his shoulders and my touch brought his eyes up. They were hard with determination. "I'm not done with you yet."

And just with those simple words I was back under his sensual spell. "What do you want to do to me?" I whispered.

"What will you let me do tae you?"

My heart skittered because somehow I knew we wouldn't be done after just one more night. The thought of returning here tomorrow and possibly the day after filled me with a weird mixture of anticipation and trepidation. But the trepidation wasn't going to stop me.

I was addicted to the pleasure he gave me. "Well . . . why don't you try and see?"

Twelve

T ry as I might, it was difficult not to daydream at work the next day. My mind kept drifting back to the events of the night before, and it was unlike me not to approach my work with single-minded focus.

Thankfully, I had an appointment with Fred Russo, the talented man who brought to life the designs for my soft furnishings and window dressings. He had a small, talented team that consisted of curtain makers and upholsterers. They did everything from cushion making to curtain making to creating one-of-a-kind duvet covers. There had also been more than one occasion where I'd been unable to find a sofa or chair I had in mind, so I'd designed it, had one of my master carpenters make it, and Fred upholstered it.

I was there to check up on their work for Patrice's guesthouse and make some final decisions on the fabric choices for each room in Roxanne's summer home.

Fred's shop was fabric heaven, bolts and bolts of expensive, luxurious fabric that often made it difficult for my more involved clients to come to a decision. *I* was decisive. While designing a room, I knew exactly what kind of fabrics and palettes I wanted to use. Clients like Roxanne, however, who didn't trust you (and made you wonder why she hired you in the first place), played lovely games of back-and-forth that slowed the project down. And then they complained about how much time it was taking.

I was done waiting. Roxanne's last okay to fabric choice was now the final decision.

Working with Fred was a wonderful distraction that morning. The entire time I barely thought about the night before, but as soon as I left his shop my mind automatically went *there* again. After our quick, desperate, but extremely satisfying first round, Caleb and I had taken our time exploring each other. I could still feel his beard scratching and tickling my skin as he discovered every inch of it with his mouth. There were little patches of red skin this morning on the places he'd lingered the longest. But I didn't mind. I flushed remembering his attentiveness. And he'd let me touch and kiss every inch of him too.

I hadn't left the hotel room until almost one in the morning, and Caleb had insisted on calling me a cab even though my apartment was walking distance from the hotel.

Despite the chaos of my thoughts, I was so wrung out that I'd fallen asleep as soon as I'd gotten into bed. And this morning when my alarm went off I'd felt surprisingly fresh and awake despite having slept for only four and a half hours. I'd even managed to fit in a run.

But there was something that niggled at me and had been niggling me all morning.

Because last night didn't feel like a quick, satisfying, casual affair. Come to think of it, our first time together in the hotel at O'Hare hadn't exactly felt like that either.

The way Caleb overwhelmed me in bed, the way he completely owned me until there was nothing else in the world but him and me, made me feel uneasy. It wouldn't be difficult to begin to *like* the man he was when we were together like that. He was an amazing partner. Simultaneously wild and rough and savage, yet sweet, reverent, and generous.

No man should be that good. The truth was, however, that he made me a different kind of lover. Sex with Nick had been great, but we'd always just been satisfied with a bit of foreplay followed by the main event. Once that was done, we were finished for the night. I couldn't remember rolling around in bed with him for hours or striving to make him groan with pleasure the way I had with Caleb.

So I had to wonder if Caleb had ever been like this with a woman before, or if our sheer need to pleasure each other just made us more exceptional than ever.

The reality was that our physical appetite for each other felt dangerous to me.

I didn't want to admit out loud that sex with Caleb had confused me, considering the sensible part of my brain knew he was still rude and unappreciative to people. A huge personality no-no for me.

But still, I needed to talk to my best friend before my brain exploded with overthinking. Harper was contracted to work five days a week at Canterbury, but sometimes she worked extra days when she was helping train new apprentices. She worked twelve-hour shifts in the kitchen doing everything from devising dessert menus to developing and testing new pastries and desserts, from overseeing the pastry department budget to procuring ingredients and maintaining the inventory of supplies, as well as overseeing the training of new staff members. I knew all this because I wanted to learn what I could about her job, why she was there for twelve-hour days, and what it was about it that made it worth it to her.

She had a passion for it, but I worried that the sixty- to seventy-two-hour weeks were going to cause her to burn out quickly.

Having such a demanding job meant she and I had to fit in our time together whenever we could. I called her as I was leaving Fred's and asked if she had a moment to spare.

"I'll make time," she said, sounding concerned. "I'll take a quick lunch break early. You okay to meet me at the restaurant or do you need more privacy?"

"Grab one of the booths in the back and we'll be good."

"Okay, babe. See you soon."

Canterbury was on Pearl Street in the Financial District, and Russo's was on the corner of Washington and Waltham, so I decided to jump in a cab. Kelly, the daytime hostess at Canterbury, recognized me and led me to Harper.

My friend was dressed in her chef whites and ripped black jeggings with a pair of black and silver sneakers. She loved her biker boots, but running around a kitchen for twelve hours required comfortable footwear. Harper got out of the booth to hug me in greeting and then we settled down.

She gestured to the small samples of the lunch menu sitting on plates that covered our table in the back of the restaurant. Canterbury had a modern rustic design; it was all glass, heavy dark woods, Spanish brick tiling, and copper, wire, and naked lightbulbs. Jason was from Canterbury in England and the style of the food was British gastropub. "Eat," she said. "And talk."

So I did, cutting into a miniature gourmet burger. I told her everything that had happened with Caleb yesterday, wondering how only a day had passed from the moment Patrice had "introduced" us to now.

"Holy shit. I want to meet him."

"No," I said adamantly. "He's only here for a week or two and this is nothing serious. Meeting my family does not scream 'casual.'"

She squeezed my arm at being referred to as family. "Okay. Whatever you want. But can I ask something?"

"Shoot."

"You wanted to talk to me about this because you needed to tell someone, or you wanted to talk to me about this because something about it is bothering you?"

My smile was reluctant. "You know me so well."

"So what do *you* think is bothering you?"

"Why? Are you going to tell me what *you* think is bothering me?"

"You know me so well." She grinned cheekily.

"Okay, you first."

Harper sighed. "I think that you try to control everything in your life because your parents were flakes when you were a kid and because you couldn't control your life falling apart after college. Controlling everything now makes you feel safe. But you can't control this guy. And you can't control how he makes you feel. And that freaks you out."

My heart thumped hard at her words and I felt an uneasy roiling in my stomach. "You should have been a psychologist, Harper."

She glared at the bite in my tone. "You asked what I thought."

I studied my glass of water, unable to meet her eyes, because for some inexplicable reason I wanted to burst into tears. Why couldn't I just enjoy being with this guy without overanalyzing everything! I wiped at a nonexistent smudge on my glass and said softly, "I don't even like him, Harp. How can I possibly want him this much and not even like him? What does that say about me?"

"What don't you like about him?"

I looked at her, recognizing the curiosity and concern in her gray-blue eyes. "He's arrogant. He's rude to people in service—never says please or thank you. Just treats them like servants. There's a coldness to him. Not in bed. Not at all. But outside of it, yes. And sometimes . . . he looks at me like he can't stand me and hates himself for wanting me."

She was quiet a moment, her brows drawing together at my last sentence. "Maybe you're right to be uneasy about this, then. Casual sex is supposed to be uncomplicated. He sounds way complicated."

"You say that . . . and it makes total sense." I nodded. "That's what I think too . . . and then I'll think about not seeing him again and I feel . . ."

"Yeah?"

"Agitated." I smirked as I encountered the right word. "Like an addict would."

Harper—adventurous, grab-life-by-the-balls Harper—didn't tell me to just ignore my concerns and go for it. Instead, she touched my arm and said, "I thought sex with this guy would be a nice distraction. That it would maybe shake off the shadows in your eyes. The ones Gem's death put there. But they're not gone, Ava. Maybe you should quit it with this guy and find someone else to do the casual thing with."

Her concern made me pause.

If Harper was telling me that, then I should listen. I nodded and looked away, my gaze skimming distractedly across the restaurant.

Wait. What?

My eyes swung back toward the hostess podium, where none other than my Bastard Scot was standing with a group of three other men. He was wearing a different suit but wearing that same brooding, intimidating expression.

"How is this happening?" I groaned.

"What? What is it?" Harper's eyes followed mine.

"He's here."

"Who's here?"

"Caleb," I snapped, turning to her with what I was sure was a look of horror. "Seriously. Some omnipresent being is playing with us. No two people can keep bumping into each other like this without the help of some twisted Fate."

"Oh my God." Harper's lips parted in awe. "Is he the tall blond who hasn't shaved in a few weeks?"

"Yup."

"I thought you said he was a biker Viking dude?"

"He wears suits for work. He's the CFO for Koto, remember. But yes, biker boots, jeans, and tattoos are his usual deal. None of which matters because they're on the move. Oh God, please don't see us."

However, my pleas went unheard as Caleb's eyes came up from the man he was walking beside as they were shown to their table. He scanned the restaurant and his gaze promptly snagged on the sight of me.

I saw them widen a little as I schooled my expression to neutral.

I gave him a nod, not wanting to be rude, but hoping he would just nod back and otherwise ignore me.

Apparently, Caleb didn't feel like being his usual rude self. He excused himself from his group and began making his way over to us.

"Oh my God, he's gorgeous," Harper said under her breath.

"Shut up."

A smile played around his beautiful mouth as he slowed to a halt in front of our booth. "I'm really beginning tae think you're stalking me, Ava Breevort."

I rolled my eyes. "I was here first, Mr. Scott." I gestured to Harper. "My best friend is the pastry chef. Harper, this is Caleb Scott. Caleb, meet Harper."

Harper reached out her hand and he shook it. "Pleasure."

She grinned. "You too."

Her grin gave away too much about her knowledge of him and he shot me an entertained, knowing smile. "Lunch break?"

I nodded. "We both work long hours. We grab time together when we can."

"I look forward tae trying your food, Harper."

Who was this charming guy?

"I can promise you'll like it," she said confidently, making him grin at her in a way he never smiled at me. "Where in Scotland are you from?"

I hadn't asked him that. I was too afraid to ask him anything because we weren't about that.

Caleb was unruffled. "I live in Glasgow, but I grew up in a wee place in central Scotland. Linlithgow. It's not far from Edinburgh."

"I've always wanted to visit. Ava and I try to travel somewhere once a year, and Scotland's on our bucket list."

Stop telling him things about me. I threw her a tight smile, which she ignored.

"Well, call me biased, but I'd recommend visiting it over any other country."

"Straight to the top of the list, then. So you here with your work people?" She gestured behind him.

"Lunch meeting, aye." He frowned distractedly.

It was on the tip of my tongue to ask him what was wrong, but I stopped myself.

That wasn't what we were.

His gaze moved to me, the frown only deepening. "I'd best get back."

"Sure," I said casually, as if I didn't care one way or the other.

Caleb's frown turned to a full-on scowl. "See you later, then. Harper, it was nice tae meet you."

"You too. We should all have drinks together while you're in Boston."

He nodded but didn't give her a definite answer (thank God) before he shot me one last enigmatic look and turned around.

As he was walking away, Harper huffed. "Rude? Really? Because I found him perfectly charming."

I cut her a look. "He's not normally like that. Although . . . he *was* like that with Patrice." A bitter chuckle of realization escaped me. "He's only a shit to me."

"You're right about the way he looks at you," she mused. "When he first came over he looked almost happy to see you . . . and then . . ."

"And then?"

"Pissed off at you." She rested her fist on her chin. "But it could have been because you were as warm as a frozen waffle to him."

"I wasn't that bad."

"You were cooler toward him than I've ever seen you toward anyone. Even to the many men you've shot down in the past."

"I'm protecting myself," I admitted. "I don't see what is so wrong about that."

"Well, have you thought that maybe he's reacting to your coldness by being cold in return?"

I thought of last night, lying vulnerable beside him on the hotel bed. There was nothing cold about me then. I was feeling playful even. And then he'd told me in that sharp, resentful tone that I wasn't his type, that everything about me was the opposite of what he really wanted.

"No. His defenses were up before mine ever were." I smiled sadly at her. "He said something to me last night that hurt. I told him I hated him. Do you know what his reply was?"

My friend's concern was back. "What?"

"He said, 'Good.'"

"Okay." Harper shook her head. "I was momentarily charmed by the whole sexy accent and that body, but if I was telling the same story to you, you would tell me that it sounded super unhealthy, right?"

I heaved a sigh. "Right."

"Babe, I have to get back to work. Lunch is on me." She leaned over and kissed me on the cheek. "But I expect that the next time we talk you'll have called this"—she gestured over to him—"off."

She was right.

She was totally, totally right. I just had to ignore the way my body clenched in agitation at the thought. "Right."

"Okay, good. We'll talk." She threw me a loving smile and got out of the booth, heading toward the back of the restaurant.

Feeling a little shaky and not really knowing why, I grabbed my purse, left a tip on the table for the server, and got out of the booth without looking at Caleb. I would have to pass him, but I decided to delay it by visiting the ladies' restroom first. It was down a low-lit, brick-walled passage at the back of the restaurant.

Inside, I stared at my reflection as I was washing my hands. I looked a little pale. Dark circles were beginning to bruise under my eyes from my lack of eight hours' sleep the night before. But more than that, I looked melancholy. Harper was right. The shadows were still there.

My gaze lowered, unable to bear the fact that I couldn't hide it. How could Caleb not see that when he was with me? Or did he just not care? And why would I want him to consider my feelings? That was never what we were supposed to be about.

A shuddering sigh escaped me as my decision formed into resolve. This was really why I wanted to talk to Harper: because I knew she'd be honest with me. And she'd tell me to do what was best for me, even if it went against her adventurous nature and personal philosophy.

I would call Caleb later to tell him our interludes were officially over.

Patrice would just have to understand that I was too busy with work to "entertain" her guest.

My heels clacked on the tiled floor as I crossed the empty bathroom and hauled the heavy door open, but the sound stuttered as I stumbled at the sight of Caleb leaning against the opposite wall out in the corridor.

I stepped out of the restroom, letting the door swing shut behind me. Glancing left and right, I found we were alone. Slowly I returned my attention to him and felt unwanted desire thrill through me at his hungry gaze. "Hi."

He pushed off the wall and was suddenly pressing into me, his hands braced above my head on the frame of the door behind me. His hot eyes searched my face. "Problem, Ava?"

Bewildered, I shook my head. "What?"

"Don't lie." His breath whispered across my lips.

Annoyance rippled through me. "Why do you care?"

"You're overanalyzing last night. Letting it mess with your head." He gently tapped my temple.

I smacked his hand away. "I'm not." Liar.

He heaved a sigh in obvious frustration and dropped his arms but didn't move back. Instead he studied me, almost curiously. "Harper. She doesn't seem like the type of lass you'd be friends with."

Anger flushed through me, my protectiveness toward her flaring. "What does that mean?"

He shrugged. "She's pierced, punk, not reserved. You're conservative—" His eyes dragged down my body. "Haughty and reserved."

I decided there was no point in waiting to text him. I could tell him my decision now. But first . . . "Harper is smart, ambitious, loyal, protective, and kind. As for me, I have many flaws that I am well aware of, but I like to think that it's exactly those good qualities we share that make us best friends. No, actually, we're family. Not that I owe you any explanation of who I am or who she is." When I glared up at him, I finally allowed him to see the hurt and anger his judgments were causing me. "I don't owe you anything—and I am done."

Caleb's expression blanked. "With me?"

"Yeah, with you."

"It's just sex, babe. I keep telling you that."

"No." I shook my head. "It's sex with a guy who somehow manages to make me feel this small"—I gestured with my forefinger and thumb—"every time he opens his mouth. I don't know what it is about me that you despise so much, but it's kind of killing my lust." I tried to shove by him, but he wouldn't let me, his strong hand circling my bicep tightly. "Let go."

"And what about *you*?" He scowled. "How many times have you told me you dinnae even like me, that you hate me even? What do you really know about me that you can draw any real conclusion about who I am and whether I'm worthy of your like or dislike?"

I tensed. And then my shoulders slumped.

He was absolutely right.

His grip on my bicep loosened.

"You're right," I whispered, staring at his chest as I tried to gather the courage to meet his gaze.

"Ava."

His tone drew my eyes to his face, where his expression had softened, a weary amusement filling his gaze. "This was supposed tae be fun."

I let out a huff of laughter. "Sometimes it has been."

"Well"—he gave me that arrogant smirk of his—"why don't we agree tae agree that we dinnae know each other enough tae judge each other? I'll quit making assumptions about you if *you* admit you dinnae really know me well enough tae hate me."

I raised an eyebrow. "You still want to see me while you're in Boston? Surely it would just be easier to pick up a random woman in a bar?"

His eyes grew smoky. "Do you really think it would be the same?"

My breath caught.

He heard it and gave a small huff of self-deprecating laughter. "Hard for two people like us tae admit it, but no one else quite does it for us the way we do it for each other, right? I'm here for a few more days, then I'm back tae Scotland. So why don't we just take advantage of this opportunity while we can. It's all right tae be that tae each other, Ava. Tae look back and remember that Bastard Scot that gave you bloody brilliant orgasms and for me tae look back and remember the American beauty who was the best sex I ever had."

Surprise and pleasure filled me that he would admit that, and he shook his head at my expression. "Are you gonna lie and say I'm not the best you've ever had?"

Usually, I would take his words for annoying overconfidence, but I knew that wasn't how he meant them. He just knew, as I did, that sex between us was on a whole other level of epicness. Still, it discomfited me. "Well, I don't have a lot to compare it to."

Irritation flickered across his expression and he took a step back.

"I'm not lying," I hurried to assure him. "I—I've only ever been with one other man before you."

His eyebrows shot up. "No way."

I blushed, feeling vulnerable and suddenly wishing I hadn't been so honest. "Uh, yes way."

"You told me you'd had great sex before."

"It was great sex."

"But ours is better." It wasn't a question.

"With you it's . . ." I flushed harder and didn't enjoy being so honest with him. "Yes, sex with you is off the charts. Happy?"

Caleb grinned and I rolled my eyes at his arrogance. "That wasn't so hard tae admit, was it?"

"Shut up."

He chuckled and stepped back into my space, so I had to tilt my head back to meet his eyes. "No more judgments. No more over-analyzing it. Let's just enjoy what we have while it lasts."

My body was already inching toward him, craving his touch, so there was really no other answer to give. "Okay. But no more telling me I'm not your type."

To my astonishment, he looked chagrined. "I won't do that again. It was an arsehole move and I regretted it as soon as I said it."

My lips parted in shock. The man could admit when he was wrong. Wow.

He suddenly gripped my chin gently and brought my lips to his, where he brushed the sweetest kiss across them. He pulled back but didn't release me, and he said softly, "I know you're sad, Ava, about your friend. It's not up tae me tae take that away, tae make you happy. But I can distract you, babe. I can give you somewhere tae disappear."

Tears burned in the back of my eyes before I could stop them at his sweet words. This was a side to Caleb Scott I was afraid to admit might exist. This was a man who could be dangerous to me. But I was going to choose to ignore the danger in favor of the rush and escape he was offering. I blinked back the tears and nodded. "To-night?"

"Same time. You've still got the key card?"

"Yes."

He kissed me again, longer, deeper, his tongue dancing with mine until I was clinging to the heat of him, overwhelmed. I felt his hand slide down over my ass, pulling me tight against him, and I felt the thickening of his arousal against my belly. Just like that he jerked away, like he had to force himself to let go of me. "You best go." His voice was hoarse with need. "I'll need a minute before I go back tae my table."

That feeling of power returned and I gave him an arrogant smile that made him chuckle. With one last wave of my fingers, I walked away, feeling his gaze burn into my back. As I left the restaurant, I couldn't shake off a residual feeling of uncertainty. It had changed from what I was feeling when I first walked into the restaurant. It was no longer worry that I could have such strong desire for a man I disliked. No, now I began to wonder if I'd been lying to myself all along. That maybe I'd been able to see past Caleb's brusque rudeness, and that maybe I could like him.

And liking him was concerning to me.

But not being able to kiss and touch him again was even more of a concern. Dominating my uncertainty was my relief that it wasn't over. I'd explain the conversation Caleb and I had to Harper so she wouldn't worry about me. He and I had reached a new understanding.

As I walked back to my office, I began to wish away the rest of the day, desperate to get my next fix now that we'd cleared the air between us.

Thirteen

A s soon as I strolled into the Marquess, one of the most exclusive restaurant-clubs in the city, I couldn't help but feel like I didn't belong there. However, I suspected if the people who frequented the club caught even a hint of insecurity, they'd be on me like a shark scenting blood in the water. In an effort to seem confident, I wore a careful expression that said, *I belong here, but don't talk to me.* I, of course, *didn't* belong there. Patrice and Danby had invited me to dine with them along with Caleb that evening.

Two more days had passed since he and I had had our little tête-à-tête at Canterbury. And two more nights of passion in his hotel room. Last night he'd been so desperate to have me, he pounced on me as I let myself into his room.

My eyes locked with Caleb's as the host of the club led me across the elegant library room toward him. Apparently, Patrice and Danby hadn't arrived yet, so Caleb and I were to wait for them before being led into the dining room.

There were only a few other people in the room sitting near the open fireplace, but Caleb was sitting in the back. He'd been frowning at his phone, yet had looked up from it almost as soon as I entered the room. As if he'd felt my presence.

I couldn't help but shiver at the way those wolf eyes of his dipped down my body as I approached. The heat in his gaze made me glad I'd worn this dress. It was one of my favorites—a modern twist on a flapper dress. I felt like a 1920s movie star whenever I wore it. Champagne colored with silver detailing, it sparkled subtly as I moved, hugging my body but not too tightly. The kind of dress that made me feel playful but classy at the same time. I'd matched it with a pair of strappy silver stilettos and I'd swept all my hair to one side in a loose, elegant braid.

Caleb stood up as I approached.

"As soon as Mr. and Mrs. Danby arrive, I will inform them that their guests are here," the host said.

"Thank you," I replied, watching him walk away, feeling Caleb's focus on me. Finally I turned to meet his eyes. "Hello."

He pulled a seat out for me at the coffee table. I thanked him as I sat down, trying to ignore the way his eyes lingered over my legs as I crossed them. The truth was, I was nervous to be in a normal situation with him. For the last three nights, we'd been lost in a sex bubble together, and because of that it felt like we'd been sleeping together for longer than we had. I knew intimate details about this man, as he did about me.

We had, however, planned to keep our interludes restricted to the physical desire we shared. When we talked in the hotel room, it was about what we wanted to do to each other. Yet, despite our best-laid plans, Patrice had turned the tables on us. She'd called me to tell me she felt terrible for neglecting Caleb, certain that he wasn't staying in one of their guest rooms at all, but still at the hotel. Upset at failing in her hostess duties, she had insisted she and Danby make time to have dinner with him, and had also insisted that I join them.

And at their private club no less.

Floor-to-ceiling bookshelves surrounded us, with leather-bound books filling every inch of them. Coffee tables and elegant armchairs were strategically placed throughout the room, and there was a small free bar near the entrance.

"Oh, how the other half live," I muttered.

"You look beautiful."

Caleb's compliment brought my gaze swinging back to his rugged face. He wore a small smile, as if entertained by my startled expression. "I've called you beautiful before. Why so surprised now?"

"Because you said it without sounding pissed off about it."

He flashed me a grin. "Is that so?"

"It is." I gave him a quizzical smile. "And thank you. You look very handsome."

He leaned an elbow on the armchair and braced his fist against his mouth. Though the movement shielded his lips from me, I saw the thoughtful amusement in his gaze. I didn't know what was so funny about my compliment, but I shrugged it off since he *did* look handsome in his dinner suit and black tie.

There was something kind of erotic about the fact that he dressed like such a gentleman here and hid the wild, tattooed guy that only I got to see when we were together. I'd traced every inch of his tattoos with my tongue, so curious about them I'd almost asked him about the significance of the warriors and the phrase he'd decided to have permanently inked on his skin.

Thankfully, I'd stopped myself before I could cross that line.

Caleb continued to study me, his eyes taking in every detail of my face until I shifted uncomfortably. "Why are you staring at me like that?"

Lifting his head away from his hand, he shrugged. "Nothing else is worth looking at when you're in the room."

Stunned, I felt my breath catch in my throat. It was quite possibly one of the most romantic things anyone had ever said to me, and it came from the most unexpected source. It took a few attempts to compose myself and ignore the way my heart turned over in my chest; I struggled for once for a retort. Instead, I decided on a subject change, breaking my rule about not asking him personal questions. "Why were you frowning at your phone when I walked in?"

If Caleb was perplexed by the probing question, he didn't show it. Instead he glanced at his phone where it sat on the coffee table. "They think flights tae Europe will be available again by the end of the week, but it looks like I'll be here for at least a week beyond that." He stared at me as I felt a warmth in my chest that couldn't possibly be happiness. "The men I was at lunch with the other day . . ."

"Yeah?"

"One of them is the CFO of the North American division. And he's a complete and utter nightmare. He does nothing. Delegates everything—and I mean everything—tae staff members who are struggling under the weight of their own duties and now his. Staff members who aren't qualified and aren't paid the six figures he's being paid. He deflects my questions because he can't answer them. He's lazy, arrogant, and clueless and—" He cut off as his voice began to rise in anger.

Sympathy moved through me. He sounded so stressed. "What are you going to do about it?"

"I'm not his boss. In fact, the little shit thinks he's my superior because the North American division brings more money in than the UK."

"Well, I'm sure that's true for most companies—we're a bigger country."

"Aye, but the figures aren't adding up. The company should be doing better here than it is. I suspect he's mismanaging the financial risks the division is taking, but I can't know for certain without getting a look at his files. And he won't let me look at his files."

"So how do you alert the head honchos without pissing everybody off, right?"

"Right." He sighed. "And is it my place tae alert them?"

"Yes," I answered immediately. "It's obvious you care about your work and this company. You don't cross me as the type of man who would let an injustice go on without doing something about it." And weirdly, despite my misgivings about him in the past, he really didn't. I suppose I'd started to realize that when he sought to protect me from the assholes at the restaurant in O'Hare.

Caleb studied me with an intensity that made my skin flush hot. "Ten days isn't much time tae do it."

I smirked. "But you're going to do it anyway."

He let out a low laugh but didn't answer either way. Still, I knew deep down he was going to do something about it.

We shared a look of mutual appreciation, and I felt emotion begin to well up inside of me. Emotion I had not expected to feel toward him. It was exactly as I had feared. Was I beginning to like my Bastard Scot?

"There you are, darlings!" Patrice's voice carried across the room and we both turned to watch her and Danby walking toward us. She wore a long, figure-hugging, black-beaded dress. Her arm was looped through Danby's. Michael Danby Senior was the same height as his wife, with a trim, athletic build and a handsome boyish face that never seemed to change as the years passed. His dark eyes were always lit with good humor and kindness.

Caleb and I stood at their approach and were immediately engulfed in Patrice's expensive perfume as she kissed our cheeks in turn. When his wife released me, Danby stepped forward to kiss my right cheek.

"You look beautiful as always, Ava," he murmured.

"And you handsome as always."

He smiled at my compliment and then offered his hand to Caleb. "Nice to see you again. We keep missing each other at the house."

Caleb shook his hand. "Tae be honest, I've been working so late at the office, I've been crashing at the hotel instead. I hope you din-nae mind."

"Of course not," Danby said. "But the room is there if you need it."

"Thank you. I appreciate it."

Did he just say thank you?

"You really should use it, though, darling," Patrice admonished gently. "Our cook, Andrea, makes the most wonderful breakfast. I'm quite sure the Four Seasons's doesn't compare."

Caleb gave her a placating nod. "I'll keep that in mind."

"Well." Patrice stepped back to look at us standing together. "Don't you two look absolutely ravishing together. Danby, don't they look ravishing?" But before he could agree, she frowned at Caleb. "Although, darling, I would really like to see that handsome face of yours. Danby, make an appointment for Caleb at your Ray's Barbers."

"No," I blurted out without thinking about it.

Patrice seemed bewildered by my outburst while mirth danced in Danby's eyes. Caleb looked at me with knowing laughter twitch-ing his lips. I flushed, giving him a side-eyed glare before I smiled somewhat sheepishly at Patrice. "I just mean . . . that . . . I, uh . . . well, I think Caleb should make that decision. Maybe he likes all that stubble."

She eyed us in suspicion and growing understanding. Something like delight crept across her features. "It's no longer stubble, Ava. It's a beard."

I wasn't sure I agreed. You could still see the shape of his jawline. Surely that didn't count as a beard? And quite suddenly I realized I was studying him while he stared back at me, apparently still trying not to laugh.

"You seem awfully invested in the subject, darling?" she teased.

I frowned and looked away. "I'm . . . I'm not."

"Ava's right." Caleb came to my rescue. "I told her myself I'm not really the clean-shaven type. That's why she spoke up for me."

"Oh." Patrice nodded, eyeballing us dubiously. *"I see."*

Oh God.

"Time for dinner, I think." Danby slid his arm along his wife's waist to turn her back the way they'd come. "I'm starved."

"Yes, dinner, all right." Patrice looked over her shoulder at us, but we waited a moment or two for them to get ahead of us.

I felt Caleb's hand on my lower back, gently nudging me forward, and I tried to shrug off my embarrassment. Apparently, he had no intention of letting me. "So what is it you like about the facial hair the most?"

Hearing the repressed chuckle in his voice, I tensed. I felt vulnerable all of a sudden. Like I'd revealed to him something I hadn't meant to. Perhaps I was discombobulated by the rush of affection I'd felt toward him earlier. I scolded myself for making more out of it than there was, realizing he basically already knew all there was to know about how I felt about him physically.

I lowered my voice and glanced up to meet his gaze. "I like how it feels between my thighs. I'd prefer you keep it during your stay in Boston."

He inhaled sharply at my response. I felt Caleb's hand fall away from my back and watched as he clenched his jaw. Finally, as we wove our way through the elegant, busy dining room with its domed ceiling lit by a magnificent crystal chandelier, he seemed to have gotten control of himself again.

"Dinnae worry." He bent his head to whisper. "I have no intention of shaving. Especially not now."

I grinned, a womanly grin of victory, which made his expression darken with want. He wrenched his gaze away and held out my seat for me at the table, just as Danby did for Patrice. I marveled at Caleb's manners, wondering where they'd come from. First a thank you, now seating me at a table.

My wonder was promptly halted when the waiter took our drink order and Caleb didn't thank him. He proceeded to forget the words "please" and "thank you" throughout the meal, as always. However, it was less obvious because Patrice and Danby weren't effusive with the words either, although they thanked the waitress as she cleared away our dessert plates.

Still, preoccupied, I stared at Caleb, trying to figure him out. He could be so abrupt with people in a service position, and brusque in general, but he'd shown good manners to his hosts. Even toward me lately. Not that his manners bothered me so much anymore, I realized, a little shocked. It was just . . . Caleb. I was beginning to think he didn't mean anything by it. He wasn't the type of guy who was demonstrative in general, about anything, until we were in bed. In many ways, he was more reserved socially than even I was. "Taciturn" was probably a better word for it.

His apparent lack of manners wasn't an issue now because I felt I understood him better than I had before.

Danby and Patrice were playfully arguing over who remembered the correct details of a story she'd been telling us about a vacation they'd taken in Aspen. Caleb took the opportunity to lean toward me. "You're staring at me."

I answered honestly. "Your lack of please and thank yous don't bother me anymore."

Caleb rolled his eyes and sat back in his chair. "You and your manners. You're as bad as my sisters."

Sisters?

Plural?

"You have sisters?"

Caleb nodded. "Two sisters."

"Really?" Patrice suddenly cut into our conversation. "I didn't know that. Duncan never mentioned it. And where do you sit? Youngest, oldest, in the middle?"

"I'm the oldest."

Which raised the question: what age was he? As if he read the question in my eyes, he offered, "I'm thirty-five."

Five years older than me. I'd suspected he was around that age. It made me wonder why some sexy Scottish woman hadn't snapped him up already. Or was Caleb Scott the permanent-bachelor type?

"Thirty-five. Then it's definitely time for settling down." Patrice's gaze flew to me. "So have you two been spending much time together?"

Caleb smirked. "Ava has been very accommodating with her time."

Do not blush, do not blush. I tried for a serene smile.

"Oh? Have you been showing our guest around Boston? Where have you taken him?"

For a moment, my brain went blank as I tried to think of a reply. I didn't want to lie to Patrice. Thankfully, Caleb extricated me from the decision. "Neither of us have really had time for sightseeing. But Ava's kept me company in the evening. For dinner."

"Oh, well, I'd thank you, darling, for the sacrifice"—she grinned at me—"but having dinner with a handsome Scotsman can hardly be called one."

I could practically feel Caleb's smug smile on my skin. "Well, you'd be surprised, Patrice. Mr. Scott is a challenging individual sometimes. For example, he often forgets his manners," I teased.

Danby laughed outright, but Patrice's eyes grew round with apprehension—I assumed because she considered my comment rude.

"It's true," Caleb told Patrice as he locked gazes with me. "But Miss Breevort here has such fine manners. I've heard so many pleas from her lips they've got stuck in my head."

I was going to kill him. "Please and thank yous," I said. "You mean please and thank yous."

Laughter twinkled attractively in his eyes, but he didn't agree.

Thankfully, Patrice either didn't pick up on his innuendo or was choosing to be polite and ignore it. Not so thankfully, she began to wax poetical about me. "Yes, Ava is very refined. I said that to Danby after the first time I met her, didn't I, Danby?"

I blushed, uncomfortable with the sudden focused attention.

Her husband gave me a kind smile as if sensing my discomfort. "She did."

Instantly engaged in her subject, Patrice leaned across the table to Caleb. "I said to Danby, that girl is a breath of fresh air. All the refinement of a society girl and none of the haughty, catty, spoiled brattishness. Not that all ladies of society are that way—" She gestured to herself. "I have some lovely friends, very generous, kind friends. But on a whole one must agree that being born into privilege can have its negative effects on a person's perspective."

"True enough," Caleb agreed.

"And Ava was born into money, weren't you, darling. Not society kind of money," she continued before I could reply or, you know, slide off my chair and hide under the table in mortification. "But a very comfortable upbringing as far as material wealth goes. As far as parental guidance goes, that is an entirely different topic, and knowing what I know of Ava's questionable emotional upbringing it is even more of a credit to her how spectacularly she turned out."

Dear God, I was regretting that one afternoon Patrice and I had shared too much champagne over a lunch meeting and she'd probed about my life until I'd spilled like a split bag of M&M's.

Aware of Caleb's gaze on me, I opened my mouth to stop Patrice, but she forged on. "And let's not get started on those so-called best friends of hers. It amazes me that she has faith in anyone after what she's been through. But she is the kindest—"

"Patrice," I exclaimed, attempting to draw her to a halt.

She blinked like an owl at me and I fumbled for a way to make her stop without upsetting her. I knew she meant no harm, but frankly this was the one time I couldn't accept her lack of boundaries. However, I also couldn't be impertinent to her. I scrambled for an excuse. "I forgot to mention that Harper has created a new dessert for Canterbury. You told me to tell you when she updates her menu and I thought I better mention it before I forget again."

"Oh. Well, fabulous." She turned to Danby, who shot me a sympathetic smile. "We'll have to book at Canterbury soon, then, darling." She turned to Caleb. "Have you met Harper?"

"Actually, I have. She seems . . . interesting."

I scowled. What did that mean?

"Oh, very. You'll know the story of how she and Ava met, then?"

"Actually," I butted in, "I haven't told Caleb that story."

"Why ever not? It's a wonderful story. Tell him. I want to hear it again."

"Patrice," Danby muttered.

She glanced between me and her husband, confused. "Oh, it's not as if it's terribly personal. I've heard Ava tell practical strangers this story, and Caleb isn't a stranger."

Patrice wasn't lying. Now, however, I was just scared of Caleb knowing anything real about me. I didn't want him to feel like I was forcing that part of myself on him.

Yet Patrice's gaze was sharpening as it flicked between Caleb and me, and I felt her beginning to unravel our secret. Or at least realize there really was something going on between us.

"Oh, fine." I shrugged like it was no big deal. "I just don't want to bore our guest."

"It's not a boring story."

I composed myself and turned to him to find him already staring at me expectantly. "It was almost seven years ago. I'd recently arrived in Boston and I was trying to get an interior design business off the ground. My uncle lives here and he had set up an appointment for me with one of his clients who had an apartment on Beacon Street. I didn't have much money at the time and didn't want to accept outright charity from my uncle, so I was living out in this poky little apartment near Boston College. The client worked late and she had me over at her apartment to almost midnight. I had to hurry to get the last train at Park Street. It was a weeknight." I sighed, feeling naive all over again. "And, unfortunately, when I got there, there was no one else around. I was standing alone waiting on the train when this guy in a hoodie appeared out of nowhere. He had a knife and—" I shook my head, seeing Caleb's eyes narrow. "Well." My tone turned bitter. "You can imagine he wanted more than just my purse, though he wanted that too. However, I barely had time to think about what I was going to do when suddenly glass shattered over his head and he just collapsed at my feet. And there, standing in front of me with a broken bottle in her hand, was a nineteen-year-old Harper glaring at me." I smiled fondly at the memory. "'Lady, are you stupid?' she said to me. 'You can't walk around alone at this time of night.' I was shaken by what had happened, but I took one look at her and said, 'You're alone.' She just shrugged and said, 'Do I look like I can't take care of myself?'

"Anyway, I called the police, even though Harper didn't want me to, but I assured her my uncle would get it all sorted out. Which he did. The creep got arrested and Harper didn't. But there was something about her. It was more than just feeling like I owed her, you know." It wasn't my place to go into Harper's background, so I glossed over it. "Anyway, she wasn't in the greatest situation and I kind of forced her to move in with me and I found out that the girl could cook. Especially desserts. And they were so imaginative and creative. She dreamed of working as a chef and I knew my uncle was friends with Jason Luton at Canterbury. He pulled some strings, got her an audition, and Jason thought she had potential. Harper has worked her way up over the years to become his pastry chef."

"I love that story," Patrice said. "Don't you just love that story?"

Caleb's expression had turned thoughtful, intense. "Harper sounds like my kind of person."

A flare of unexpected jealousy shot through me.

"Oh, Harper's a doll. Very talented. And I'm sure she would agree that she owes everything to Ava's generosity."

"No," I said sharply, upset that Patrice would think so. "Harper would have found success no matter what."

"Fiercely loyal." Patrice reached over to squeeze my arm in affection, and then she threw Caleb a meaningful look. "I swear, this woman has no faults. I'm extremely lucky to have her as a friend and a designer."

"Everyone has faults, Patrice. Now, if you don't stop complimenting me, I'm going to die of embarrassment." I softened my words with a pleading smile. "Can we please change the subject?"

She chuckled. "Of course, dear." She turned to Caleb. "Tell us more about you, darling. We hardly know a thing."

Caleb sat up in his seat. "Actually, Patrice, I dinnae mean tae be rude, but I have a very early morning tomorrow and need tae excuse myself."

I felt relief that the conversational torture was over, but our disappointed host pouted. "Oh, well, what a shame. But of course."

"I'm tired also," I said, pushing back from the table. "I hope you understand."

And just like that the disappointment slid right off Patrice's face, her eyes bright with hope. "Of course, of course. Caleb, you must see Ava home."

I almost rolled my eyes.

But Caleb just nodded. "Of course."

We said good night to the Danbys and thanked them for dinner, and I tried to avoid Patrice's wide-eyed *Get in there* look as she kissed me on the cheek good-bye.

Once we'd escaped the matchmaker and her husband, and I'd grabbed my coat from the cloakroom, I forced myself to look up at Caleb. "I am so sorry. She is the most obvious matchmaker in the entire world. Please don't take her seriously."

He flicked me a glance. "Dinnae fash yourself. I took it all with a pinch of salt."

His refusal to meet my eyes made me uneasy and I found myself still needing to reassure him. "Good. I've never wanted to duck under a table before. Tonight was a first for me. What does 'fash' mean?"

Caleb didn't even crack a smile but his hand came to rest on the small of my back as he led me out of the building onto the busy lamplit street. The Marquess was a mere five-minute walk from the Four Seasons. "It means dinnae worry yourself."

"Oh."

Tension crept up between us as we left the chatter of people on the sidewalks, and the hum of traffic made the silence between us more pronounced. I didn't know if the tension belonged to anticipation of the night ahead or if it was because of the newfound personal discoveries we'd made about each other.

We turned onto Arlington Street. The tall streetlights placed evenly between the trees, along with the headlights of the cars passing us, lit the street so brightly you'd have to look up at the dark sky to even realize it was evening. As the silence between us stretched out, uncertainty filled me, and I felt the chill of the spring evening rush around my bare legs and seep under my light coat, when it had barely touched me moments before.

Something was wrong.

"I wasn't lying," Caleb suddenly said, his tone sounding distant and faraway. "I have an early morning. I should have put you in a cab back at the club. We'll get you one at the hotel."

He didn't want me tonight?

Hurt immediately suffused me.

Or maybe the jetlag and our late nights had finally caught up with him . . . but I suspected that wasn't why he was rejecting my company. Had we crossed some invisible line Caleb had drawn between us and now he wanted nothing to do with me? Had something Patrice said about me turned him off?

I felt a flare of pain in my chest that horrified me, and so with a carefully impassive expression, I said, "I can walk. I'm just across the Common."

"I'm not letting you walk alone at this time of night."

Silence fell between us again, and this time I didn't just feel the chill; I felt cold through and through. Goose bumps prickled down my spine, and not the good kind. The more we walked, the less angry I became at his rejection and the more concerned I grew.

He'd hurt my feelings.

Hurt me.

I raised a trembling hand to brush hair that had come loose from my braid back from my face, and I used the moment to eye him surreptitiously. He was staring determinedly ahead, his expression hard and remote as his long strides quickened, making it harder for me to keep up.

His aloofness not only hurt me; it troubled me.

Somehow, impossibly, I'd developed *feelings* for my Bastard Scot.

Feelings plus sex?

Bad idea.

As we walked down Boylston Street, the dark red brick of the hotel building coming into view, I attempted to convince myself that Caleb's rejection was a good thing.

That was easier said than done.

Caleb approached one of the doormen and asked for a cab, slipping him a tip. A sharp whistle rent the air and two seconds later a cab pulled into the hotel driveway.

I knew I should say good night, that I should let him know I understood and that this was for the best. However, I didn't understand. I didn't know what had happened back at the Marquess to chill his regard toward me, and frankly it was worrying that he had this control over my emotions.

Without saying a word to him as he opened the cab door for me, I got in and told the driver my address.

Finally, I looked up at Caleb. He frowned down at me, indecision in his expression.

Was he regretting his rejection?

"Good-bye, Caleb." I grabbed the door handle and jerked it out of his hold, slamming it shut. "Let's go," I said to the driver, not once glancing back as we drove away.

Fourteen

I couldn't sleep.

My sheets were wrinkled and abused from my tossing and turning the night before. I'd gotten up in the early daylight hours, changed into my running gear, and tried to sweat the unease and fatigue out of me. But running didn't work like it usually did. By the time I walked into the office that morning I'd had three coffees in the hopes that I wouldn't pass out from exhaustion later.

Beneath my elegant chignon, my tailored pencil skirt, pale pink silk blouse, and carefully applied makeup, were dark circles and a tired body. Worse, a confused heart.

I'd lost count of the times I'd reached for my phone to check for messages from him.

Not a peep.

I stared blankly at my computer screen, feeling blindsided, not only by my emotions, but by the way things had ended with Caleb. They'd ended in a whimper. There was no feeling of closure as I'd assumed there would be when he headed back to Scotland. Nor had it ended in an explosive argument, which, considering how things had started between us, I was almost sure would happen.

No, it ended because something had caused Caleb to climb too deep into his thoughts. But what?

Stop thinking about him.

My cell rang, making me jolt in surprise. It was Harper.

"Hey," I answered, hoping she couldn't hear the weariness in my voice.

"Still banging the Scot?"

I'd already informed Harper about my discussion with Caleb outside the restroom at Canterbury. Her reply was that I was a big girl, I could do what I wanted, but to just be careful. I should have heeded her words.

"I don't think so," I said, trying to infuse a wry *I don't care* note into my voice.

"Oh?"

"We had dinner last night with Patrice. She tried to play matchmaker and ended up making us cross these lines we'd drawn. You know . . . like not talking about personal stuff. I went home alone."

"You don't sound that bothered by it."

Huh, guess I was better at pretending than I thought. "It was just sex, Harp."

"Yeah, but great sex. I'd be sad if I had to give up great sex."

A pang of longing burned in my chest. "It was *fantastic*. And I'm not going to lie, I'm going to miss it. But it's for the best. He's leaving in a week anyway. I really shouldn't let myself get used to it." Or him, or my inexplicable feelings for him. Like my jealousy. "Oh, by the way. Patrice made me tell the story of how you and I met, and Caleb said, and I quote, 'She sounds like my kind of person.'"

Harper grunted. "Am I supposed to swoon at the honor?"

I laughed, feeling stupid that I'd mentioned it. Harper wasn't me. She wasn't looking for a stamp of approval from the guy, and for not the first time I wished I was more like my best friend.

"Anyway, I was just checking in, babe, and wanted to ask if you were free on Saturday to come and see Vince play. Jason is letting me take the night off and giving Lou a shot at handling the section." Lou was a junior chef Harper was training.

"Of course. I'll be there."

"Okay, but you need to buy a pair of jeans."

"C'mon. Can't I just be me?"

"It's an indie punk rock bar, so no. A pair of jeans won't kill you, Ava." At my silence, she sighed. "Look at it this way. You, Ava Breevort—the woman who refuses to get in a relationship because it would mean giving control over to someone else—have had some wild times with a practical stranger. You had a breakthrough. Keep it going. Wearing jeans does not mean you aren't civilized."

I heard the snicker in her voice and shook my head. I knew my obsession with looking perfect all the time was bordering on ridiculous, but this was the first time Harper had really called me out for it. "Jeans?"

"Skinny ones that will make your ass look fantastic."

I thought of my parents and how they hadn't called to see how I was doing after Gem's funeral. How they didn't have my back as our circle of friends glared at me with accusation in their eyes. How they'd forced me to that damn dinner the night before the funeral even though they should have known how horrible it was going to be for me. How they never had my back when I needed them.

And how I was still letting them control me in the most silly, indirect ways. "Skinny jeans," I said, suddenly feeling the absolute urge to buy them. "Maybe more than one pair."

Harper laughed. "Just take your time having your emotional breakthroughs."

I rolled my eyes. "You're lucky I love you because I don't put up with that kind of cheek from just anyone."

"I know. Love you too. I'll text you closer to the time about Saturday."

We hung up and I stared broodingly at my phone, thinking about Harper, my parents, and Caleb.

The bell for the front desk rang in my office. I had just pushed back my chair to go see who it was when I heard heels clack across the reception floor. The murmur of voices assured me that whoever it was was already being dealt with, so I turned back to my computer, trying to remember what the hell I was in the middle of doing.

Not even a minute later Stella's voice drew my head up from my computer screen. "There is a Mr. Caleb Scott here to see you. You didn't mention you had an appointment this morning, so I just wanted to double-check it was okay to send him in?"

Astonishment froze me in place for a second.

What the hell was Caleb doing here?

A flurry of mixed feelings overwhelmed me. Surprise, annoyance, and—worst of all—relief.

"Ava?"

"Uh, send him in."

"Are you sure?" She frowned at me.

"He's . . . a friend."

Stella's frown instantly turned into a knowing smile and then she mouthed, *Nice*, before disappearing.

I sighed. Great. Now my boss would grill me once Caleb left. In the entire six years I'd worked for her, not once had she *seen* me with a guy. She'd set me up on dates, which I'd dutifully gone to, but I never let any of them past first base. Over time, my reluctance to form any kind of a romantic connection with the opposite sex had become clear to Stella and she'd stopped trying to set me up.

My thoughts on the matter immediately halted at the sight of Caleb dwarfing the doorway to my office. He was delicious in the suit I'd seen him wearing at Canterbury days ago and he was also staring at me in a way that could be construed as pensive. Or it could have been a glare. Sometimes it was hard to tell with my broody Scotsman. What the hell was he doing here?

He stepped into the office and closed my door behind him. He locked it.

That brought me to my feet, my heartbeat falling out of its normal rhythm. "What are you doing here?"

Caleb crossed the room to stand at the opposite side of my desk. "We need tae talk."

Something inside me shuddered uneasily at his tone. "I thought you were busy planning a way to deal with your fellow CFO?"

"Aye, I am. Dinnae worry yourself on that account." He threw me a sardonic look as he began to round the desk.

I backed up a little, stumbling against my chair as he stopped beside me and then planted his big body on my desk. The action brought us face-to-face and his familiar scent triggered a wave of intense longing and need.

Seriously, I was officially addicted to him.

However, he wasn't looking at me like a man who planned to seduce me in my office, which frankly relieved me, because that kind of unprofessional behavior was the exact kind of thing my parents would have done. Not me.

"So talk." I crossed my arms over my chest, pretending I was unaffected by his presence.

Caleb studied me a little longer until I was almost squirming, and then he said, "Sometimes in my work, honesty is a commodity you can't afford. I try my best tae be vague rather than downright dishonest, but I do what I have tae for the good of the company as long as the white lies dinnae hurt anybody."

I frowned at this surprising lead. "Okay."

His gaze sharpened, those ice eyes holding me captive. "But I dinnae like it. You said something last night . . . about how we all have flaws. How *you* have flaws. You just admitted it, no big deal. Some people can't admit their shortcomings, you know that."

I snorted. "Yeah, I'm aware of that, believe me."

"I can. But honesty isn't one of them. I've been told I can be honest tae a fault."

I believed it. "You can be pretty blunt sometimes, yes."

"Aye." He seemed to deliberate for a second and then sighed. "I'm not used tae being around one woman long enough for honesty tae become a problem. I'm up front from the start that it's just sex. We have sex. One of us goes home, end of story."

A sharp, burning tightness spread across my chest in a flash of horrible intensity and I fought to mask the bolt of jealousy I felt. I apparently did not like the thought of Caleb with other women.

Wonderful.

"You're telling me this why?"

Caleb's expression softened a little. "This is just physical, like we agreed."

I nodded because I couldn't bring myself to outright lie to him.

"And I know not too long ago we didn't like each other much."

Whatever this conversation was, I wanted it to end because I had a feeling he was going to hurt me again. "Caleb, if this is about last night and Patrice offering up information about me—"

"I like you," he cut me off. The words were sweet but said in an annoyed growl.

"Oh." Something like hope began to blossom inside of me. And that confused the hell out of me—since when did I want anything meaningful with a guy?

"There's a lot tae like, Ava. From what I can see so far, you aren't at all what I expected."

I smiled. "Thank you, I think."

Caleb didn't smile. "I think maybe you like me a little bit too."

If he could be honest, then so could I. "I do."

"But this is still just sex."

His words cut right through my hope and I did my damn best to hide it. "I—I never said it wasn't."

"Last night I sent you home when I wanted you in my bed. I worried we were crossing a line at dinner."

"I was worried about that too. But I never thought anything had changed between us."

"Good. Here's the thing . . . I enjoy you. I want tae enjoy you for the next week, and I'd quite like tae be able tae do it freely without worrying that if we have an actual conversation that I'm sending you the wrong message."

Understanding dawned and I clarified, "You want us to just enjoy each other but doing so fully understanding what this is."

"Exactly." He stood up, towering over me, and I had to tilt my head to keep a hold of his gaze. "I dinnae believe in mind games or keeping a woman guessing where my head is at. That isn't me. So this is where my head is at. Even if there wasn't an actual ocean between us, I'm not a relationship kind of guy. I never will be. But I genuinely like you, and I dinnae mind us having a friendship between us if you dinnae. As long as we both know that is all this is."

His honesty was startling. The words coming out of his mouth were both reassuring and horrifying because they only made what I was beginning to feel for him more intense.

Caleb made me feel safe.

I felt like I might be able to trust him in a way I'd never dared to hope I could trust a guy again.

And he was telling me that he just wanted to be friends with benefits.

What the hell was I supposed to do now?

If I didn't agree, he'd walk out of here and I'd never see him again. But I'd be in control of my life again.

Yet . . . wouldn't I look back on my life and regret that decision?

Wasn't it better to enjoy what we had now while we could? Life was short after all. And Harper was right. I was never really in control of my life. I was letting my parents and the past dictate and control my decisions every time I tried to keep my life safe and conservative and restrained.

I stared up into Caleb's rugged face, at those lips that made me feel things no man ever had. And I couldn't imagine not having at least one more taste. "It sounds good to me," I whispered, feeling my body begin to light up.

He bent his head toward me. Our kiss was slow, deep, sexy, and I felt I could rest easy knowing this man would miss this when he returned to Scotland.

The sound of a phone ringing ruined the moment, breaking our kiss.

I clasped his prickly cheek in hand. "You should go."

"Tonight," he said.

"Tonight," was my answer.

Caleb nodded, satisfied. "Same time."

"I'll be there."

With one last searing look, Caleb crossed the room, unlocked the door, and let himself out. I could only stare after him.

With him gone, reality came crashing back in and stayed there.

A miracle had happened.

I found myself feeling something for a guy. Actually, maybe, wanting to try out something real with him.

And he just happened to be the most brutally honest, commitment-phobic man I'd ever met.

Fifteen

Several days later I found myself standing on a checkered floor in a dark bar in Allston, wondering if inviting Caleb to come hear Vince's band play was such a good idea after all.

The bar we were in was called Great Scott.

"I didn't know," I'd said to Caleb as we'd approached the building with the black awning over the front that had the words "Great Scott" in bold letters.

But Caleb had surprised me by halting, turning around, and capturing a selfie of himself with the awning in the background. I'd merely stood there beside a chuckling Harper, bemused by the uncharacteristic action. He'd shrugged when noting my bafflement. "For my wee sister. She'll think it's hilarious."

"You have a sister?" Harper had asked as we strode inside the already busy bar.

From there Harper had grilled him a little about his family, and I now knew that he had brothers as well as sisters. His brother next to him in age was Jamie, thirty years old and a mixed-media artist who had found quite a bit of fame through social media (note to self to check out his social media accounts). Then there was Quinn. Caleb's features strained as he clipped out the name, his gaze hardening. He divulged nothing about Quinn before moving on to their sister Fallon. She was twenty-eight and worked for the forestry commission. I didn't know what that meant—I wanted to know, yet daren't ask. I also wanted to know more about Quinn, but everything about Caleb screamed *back off* at the mere mention of him. After Fallon came Skye, a twenty-one-year-old junior whom Caleb sent the selfie to.

Now, as we drank beer and waited for Vince's band to come onstage, Harper continued to ask questions, making me fidget with discomfort. I was worried Caleb would think I'd put her up to it.

"Were your parents young when they had you?" she said to him.

He nodded. "My mum was only eighteen. My dad was twenty-one."

"What do they do for a living if they had you so young? They couldn't have had time for an education, popping out all those kids, right?"

I groaned inwardly. When Harper was curious about someone, her questions became blunt and almost interrogative.

To my relief, Caleb seemed merely amused by her. "My dad's father owned a farm just outside of Linlithgow. The farm goes back four generations. My parents lived and worked there with my grandparents and when my grandfather passed away my dad took over the farm. It isn't an easy life but it's a good one. We learned tae work hard from a young age but we also had a very nice childhood."

There he went surprising me again. Never would I have imagined that Caleb Scott had grown up on a working farm.

"And your parents are still there?"

"Aye. As is my gran. All still working away. Feeling the empty nest now that Skye's off tae uni."

"Well, Ava and I are envious as hell," Harper said, speaking for us both, which might sound forward to some people, but I was used to it. And in this case, she was right. "It sounds idyllic growing up on a farm with four brothers and sisters, and parents that give a shit."

I was mildly uncomfortable about how much she gave away in that one sentence, but Caleb had already been given an inkling of my unhappy family life from Patrice, so I decided to not let it bother me. Even as he skewered both of us with a questioning look. I nudged Harper discreetly, silently telling her to shut up.

Thankfully, she did. "Another beer?" she asked.

Caleb said he was fine but I asked for another and stood in silence by his side while Harper wandered over to the bar. Unfortunately, all the tables were already taken when we'd arrived, but somehow I didn't think even having a table between us would have made this less awkward.

The rest of the week with Caleb had gone on in much the same way as the days before it. Nights spent together in his hotel room and me leaving for my own place once we were done. However, on Friday he'd asked me if I was free for lunch and we'd met at his hotel and dined at the Bristol Lounge. Trying to keep things not awkward or too personal, I invited conversation about his work and he vented to me more about the CFO that concerned him.

It turned out, after speaking with his own boss, that Caleb wasn't just in Boston as part of a networking trip. The big guys in Tokyo were concerned about the North American division's performance. They decided they wanted someone to take a look into the division's finances and overall situation, and so Caleb's boss in Glasgow had offered up Caleb, knowing if there was a problem he'd spot it.

So now Caleb's job while he was in Boston was to interview staff members and collect necessary information and data. He was basically a CFO turned investigator and auditor. And he wasn't exactly comfortable with the position or his boss's subterfuge on the matter, but he was doing it anyway.

Letting Caleb vent was easy, and the guards we both had up seemed to have temporarily dropped since our honest conversation in my office. When he'd asked if I was free Saturday night and I wasn't, I disliked the idea of him being alone in Boston and had impulsively asked him to come with us to the bar.

He had easily accepted the invitation, surprising me somewhat. But actually being in a "normal, datelike" situation with him was a little more awkward than I'd been expecting. It was perhaps hanging out around my friend that made me feel like we'd crossed a line into territory we weren't supposed to.

"Have I mentioned how sexy you look in those jeans?" Caleb said, still looking around the bar and not at me.

My belly fluttered at the compliment. Taking Harper's advice, I had gone out that week and purchased a pair of dark blue skinny jeans. I'd paired them with a tight-fit plain black T-shirt and a cropped leather jacket. Unable to completely abandon *me*, I was also wearing platform red stilettos, put my usual waves through my hair with my straight iron, and gone to town on my makeup with dramatic smoky eyes.

"Thank you." I smiled. "They're new. Harper made me buy them."

"Then I'll thank Harper." He shot me a quizzical look. "You don't wear jeans usually?"

"Not in years."

"Shame." His gaze smoldered. "Your ass and legs look fantastic in them."

My lips twitched as smug pleasure moved through me. "I'm going to wear them more. But not because you think I look good in them. But because *I* think I look good in them." And I did. Walking out of the apartment tonight, I'd felt free in a way I hadn't in a long time. For so long I'd been confined by the rules I'd set myself in the hopes of not becoming like my parents. But over time the rules had become pedantic and bordering on ridiculous. I just hadn't realized how much until recently. Maybe it was the trip back to Arcadia, seeing my parents, and realizing I could never be like them no matter what. Or perhaps it was Gem's death—a cold reminder that some moments in life can suddenly be lost to us forever. And maybe that was the real reason I was letting go of some of my control to have an affair with this gorgeous, sexy Scotsman who made me question what irresponsibility really meant. Because being with him didn't feel irresponsible. It felt like an adventure.

Whatever this change was that had come over me, I liked it. I liked striding out of my apartment in jeans and high heels, feeling young and stripped free of my skirt suits and silk blouses that suddenly felt like armor I'd created for myself.

I'd liked the look on Caleb's face when he saw me walk toward him and his borrowed Maserati. And I liked even more the whoop of delight Harper let out when we met her outside of the bar and she saw how I was dressed.

Maybe it sounded silly. After all, it was just clothes, right? But not to me. The jeans symbolized the last few weeks of me pecking at the lock on my cage until it finally sprang open, letting me fly free. Did that sound melodramatic? Over the top?

Good . . . because that was how powerful the feeling was.

Caleb's sharp gaze roamed my face. "How long do we need tae be here?"

I shook my head, laughter in my eyes. "Feeling impatient?"

"Ava, I can't imagine a day ever coming when I stop being impatient for you."

Pleasure fizzled in my chest. "Back at you. However, I promised Harper we'd stay for the whole set and have a drink with Vince. His band is only playing four songs before the next band comes on. And thankfully, he's first up."

He nodded and looked away, his gaze roaming the place as he drank his beer. I allowed myself to study him. Tonight he wore what he was wearing when we first met—a henley that showed off his muscled physique, dark jeans, and biker boots. He'd pushed back the sleeves of his shirt, showing off his tattooed arm. Caleb fit in perfectly here. When we approached the venue, Harper not only whooped in delight at my outfit, but had stared a little wide-eyed and flushed at Caleb. She'd given me a secret look that said, *Whoa, mama.*

Even in my casual outfit I stood out in the crowd. I could do jeans, but I couldn't do biker chick, or rock chick. Or punk rock chick even. Harper was dressed in a tight black skirt, her long legs bare, loosely laced scuffed biker boots, and a slouchy, thin purple sweater covered in sequins that caught the light when she moved. It fell off one shoulder, baring her delicate collarbone. Her platinum hair was styled in a spiky quiff and she had all of her earrings and jewelry on tonight. With such classically pretty features, she was like a glam-punk princess. I noted guys—even those with girls—watching her as she smiled and chatted with the bartender, who was clearly flirting with her.

"You two dinnae make sense on paper," Caleb suddenly said, and I jerked my gaze from Harper to see him staring at my best friend. "But you're obviously close."

"She's my family."

"Because neither of you have a good one?" he asked. I was taken aback by his curiosity.

I nodded, but was unable to give him any more than a confirmation. Not because I didn't trust him with the information, but because I felt like if I started to confide in him, it would make my feelings for him deepen.

A small frown appeared between his brows but he didn't push the subject. Thankfully, activity on the stage and the murmurings of the crowd distracted us. People surged in front of us toward the stage as the band appeared, but Caleb and I stayed where we were.

Harper approached as Vince sauntered onto stage. I could just make him out over the heads of the people in front of us.

Harper handed me my beer, her eyes toward her boyfriend. "Do you want to get closer?" I asked.

"No, we're cool here. You know I don't like feeling cramped in."

I nodded, watching her as she stared at Vince, something like pride filling her expression as he pulled on his guitar. Vince McFarlane, a sexy Irish-American boy with an even sexier Southie accent, had risen from the depressing pits of foster care after being orphaned at twelve years old. Harper admired his ambition and talent, and I felt pleased for her that she'd finally found a guy who didn't seem to begrudge her her own ambition.

"Hey—" The mic crackled as Vince's gravelly voice echoed around us. "Thanks for coming tonight. If you don't already know, we're called State of Play." Then he strummed his guitar and the lights went down as his band began to play. I quite liked Vince's music. It was more indie rock, their sound reminding me a little of Kings of Leon. Vince had the same kind of coarse sexy vocals as Caleb Followill, and it was easy to see how Harper had fallen under his spell the night they'd met. She'd been at a bar in Cambridge with some fellow music-lover friends when she saw Vince's band play for the first time. She told me it had been instalust like she'd never felt before. He saw her in the crowd, they'd had some seriously hot eye contact, and when he'd finished his set he'd pushed through the crowd and walked right up to her and asked her if he could buy her a drink.

The rest was history.

I was delighted for my friend, but I was also a little jealous that she was brave enough to throw herself into a relationship. Harper had gone through worse than I could imagine and yet she was less restrained by her past than I was.

I envied her courage.

"They're good," Caleb said loudly, not hiding his surprise.

"Yeah, they are." Harper grinned. "My guy is going places!"

"How long have they been at this?" Caleb asked her, shouting over the music to be heard.

"About a year!" she yelled back. "Vince has been in a couple of bands, but these guys really gel together. Vince is the songwriter. Considering his age, the music blows me away."

"His age?"

"Yeah, he's younger than me. He's only twenty-two."

When Harper first told me her boyfriend's age, I'd been skeptical. Men were immature as it was, so I wasn't too keen on the idea of her dating a guy who'd only legally been able to drink for a year. But she'd assured me that Vince's time in foster care, the situations he'd been through, had given him a maturity beyond his years. He was the first guy she'd ever confided her traumatic past to, feeling he more than anyone would understand.

I was beginning to suspect my friend was falling in love for the first time.

Caleb just nodded at the information and continued to listen to State of Play. We all did. By the time they'd finished their set, my ears were buzzing, I was too hot, and my feet were starting to hurt in my stilettos. There really was a reason most of the women were wearing boots, like Harper.

Not surprisingly, after a sweaty Vince managed to make his way through a congratulating crowd toward us, he managed to charm up a free table for us. He introduced us to his three band members, who looked so alike I forgot who was who seconds after the introductions. They left us to go talk to some girls who were eager to meet them. Vince wrapped his arm around Harper and drew her into his side as he sipped at a beer across the table from me and Caleb.

"So, Caleb, where in Scotland are you from?" Vince asked.

"I live in Glasgow. I enjoyed your music, by the way."

Vince grinned. "Hey, thanks. Means a lot."

I shared a look with Harper, knowing she was thinking what I was thinking. That we could sit and listen to these two hot guys with their hot accents all night. I almost laughed at us being so profoundly girly.

Our conversation was easy despite the four of us coming from different walks of life. We talked music and Glasgow versus Boston for a while, only to be rudely interrupted by a tall girl in a tight black dress with lots of red hair and lots of cleavage. She put her hand on the table and leaned in toward Vince, giving him an eyeful of her impressive chest. "Hey, Vince, when are you coming over to catch up with me and Sarah? It's been a while."

Irritation made me tense, my gaze moving to Harper, who shocked me by merely staring dully at the table in front of her.

Vince's hand tightened on Harper's shoulder and he gave the redhead a polite smile. "Just hanging with my girl and her friends right now, Lisa."

"We can't stay long. Come hang out. You know you always have a *good* time with us." Her voice was thick with innuendo. I scowled at her brazen rudeness.

Still, Harper didn't look up from the table.

What the hell?

"Hey." I snapped my fingers in the redhead's face, forcing her up off the table. "Vince is hanging with his *girlfriend* right now—" I waved my hand at her. "So shoo."

She shot me a dark look but backed up and stalked away.

Wondering why I was the one dealing with the intrusive groupie, I gave Harper a sharp look of confusion, which she ignored.

"Sorry." Vince shrugged. "It happens."

Irritated that he didn't seem that bothered by it and that Harper was uncharacteristically quiet, I clamped my lips shut and allowed him and Caleb to carry the conversation.

They had been talking about the great music scene in Glasgow and that led to them talking about bars, then somehow onto restaurants. "There are amazing places tae eat in Glasgow," Caleb informed us. "Though Canterbury gives them a run for their money," he said to Harper. "The food is fantastic."

She grinned, a little of her cocky self finally shining through. "I told you."

"Yeah." Vince snorted. "They just work her to the bone for a goddamn dessert, but the food is fantastic."

My eyes widened at the snarky comment, a fresh tension falling over the table. Harper cut him a mystified look. "Vince?"

I watched a muscle in his jaw flex. "C'mon, I can't be the only one that thinks the hours you work are ridiculous. Right, Ava?"

I narrowed my eyes. Wasn't this guy supposed to be supportive? All evidence tonight had been to the contrary. "I think if you want to be great at anything, it takes a lot of hard work and dedication. I think Harper is only twenty-six years old and a top pastry chef in a Michelin-star restaurant. And I think that if Harper is happy to put in a lot of hours to be at the top in her industry, then I'm happy to support her."

Hearing the warning in my voice, Vince shifted uncomfortably, an expression I could only describe as petulant entering his gaze. I suddenly felt the eight-year age gap between us, and it seemed massive.

As soon as I got Harper alone, she was in for a grilling, because this Vince was not at all the Vince I'd met before or had been led to believe she was dating. He was supposed to support her career, not be like every other whining idiot who wanted her to put them before her career. And suddenly, I was done for the night. Harper wasn't acting like herself and it was pissing me off.

"You know, I have a headache." I turned to Caleb. "Would you mind if we go now?"

He immediately nodded. "Sure, babe."

We got out of our seats and I walked around the table to hug Harper good night. She stared up at me but I couldn't read her expression as I leaned down to give her a half hug and a kiss on the cheek. "We'll talk," I murmured in her ear.

My friend just nodded and bid me a quiet good night.

"Night, Vince," I said, barely looking at him as I turned away.

Caleb held out his hand to me, and I was momentarily taken aback before I reached for it, enjoying the feel of his warm hand curling tightly around my smaller one. He led me through the crowd and out of the bar, the chill night air rushing over us.

We strolled in silence down the street to where he'd parked his borrowed Maserati. He let go of my hand to open the door for me and I got in, relaxing immediately into the seat.

Nope. Great Scott was definitely not my scene, and watching Harper being cowed by a groupie and then berated by her boyfriend was *definitely* not my scene.

As soon as Caleb got into the car and drove off, I sighed. "I'm sorry. That was awkward."

"You seem worried about Harper. Do you not like this guy? We can go back and get her if you want."

Gratitude and something else I didn't want to analyze moved through me warm and swift at his offer. "No, she's a big girl. I just hope she knows what she's doing. It isn't like her to allow some catty girl to pretend like she doesn't exist. Or to allow a guy to come down on her about how hard she works. She told me Vince was different. *I* thought Vince was different."

Caleb kept his eyes on the dark road but smirked as he said, "Well, you took care of the catty girl for her."

I grinned. "Were you entertained?"

"Aye." He flashed me a wicked smile. "Aye, you entertain me."

Feeling something I didn't want to admit to but at the same time

I couldn't ignore, I found myself longing to take Caleb home. To wake up in my bed and see him sleeping there. To drink coffee with him in my kitchen.

They were dangerous thoughts, but they were also persistent. "Why don't I entertain you at my place tonight? You could . . . stay."

His hands tightened around the steering wheel, his amusement dying a quick death. "Ava . . ."

"Don't make more out of it than there is," I hurried to say, suddenly deeply aggravated by his commitment phobia. "It's still just sex but this time neither of us has to get out of bed in the middle of the night. If you fall asleep beside me I'm going to take it to mean you're tired, not that you want to fall asleep beside me forever. Okay?" I hoped I sounded dry and blithe enough for him.

His hands relaxed. "Okay."

Wanting to dispel the sudden tension between us, I mused, "I've never had sex in my bed, you know."

Just as I'd hoped, despite his misgivings, the idea that he would be the first guy in my current bed appealed to his inner alpha.

The car jolted forward, moving faster toward town and my bed.

Sixteen

t would be an understatement to say we were both eager to get back to my apartment. Several times I had to ask Caleb to slow down on our short drive back into the city. He muttered expletives under his breath but did as I asked. I was almost laughing with giddiness as he drove down Mount Vernon Street.

"This is where you live?" he asked.

"Yeah."

"Hmm."

I didn't know what the "hmm" meant, so I looked for a parking space instead. "There's a space." I pointed to an empty spot a minute walk from my place. "We can walk to the apartment." It was a miracle to get a parking spot on my street, so we'd need to take what we could get.

Once he'd parked, Caleb got out and hurried around to the passenger side to help me out. His grip on my hand tightened and I found myself being practically hauled over onto the tree-lined sidewalk as Caleb pressed the key fob to lock the Maserati.

"Where is your apartment?" he demanded.

I giggled. "Keep walking. I'll let you know when we're there."

He grunted and proceeded to drag me.

"Caleb." I laughed. "I'm in heels."

And just like that he abruptly stopped, came at me, and—before I could blink—swung me up into his arms like a groom would hold his bride to carry her across the threshold. I let out a girlish noise of shock, looping my arms around his neck as he began striding down the street like I weighed nothing.

"You are such a Neanderthal." I laughed.

He grinned at me, a flash of white teeth in the dimly lit street. "You love it."

"I'm not going to lie—this is hot. You're very strong," I purred, reaching over to bite his earlobe.

His grip on me tightened and his pace quickened. "You're five foot nothing. You weigh nothing."

That was nice but such a lie. "I have an ass and boobs. I weigh something."

He ignored me and kept walking. "Where is this bloody place?"

Smiling at his impatience, I let go of his neck to wave at my front stoop, when the sight of a dark figure standing up on the steps made me falter. "Caleb."

My tone made him slow.

"Do you know that person?"

The dark figure became clearer as he began walking toward us slowly.

My heart rate suddenly accelerated, and as if he felt it, Caleb asked in concern, "Ava?"

"Put me down," I whispered. "Caleb, put me down."

He immediately and gently lowered me to my feet.

And suddenly I was face-to-face with my past, feeling so cold it iced the sexual heat right out of me. "What are you doing here?"

The man stepped under a streetlamp, illuminating his scowl as his gaze bounced between me and Caleb. "I needed to see you."

"Ava?" Caleb asked me, his hand resting on my lower back, reminding me he was there if I needed him.

I leaned into his touch. "Caleb, this is Nick. Nick, this is Caleb."

"Nick?" he said, his tone suggesting he remembered me telling him about Nick.

"What do you want?"

"I . . ." Nick ran a hand through his hair, clearly agitated. "I got your address from your mom. I, uh . . . I came to apologize. To talk. In private."

"No," I said, my tone harsh. "Go home, Nick." I grabbed Caleb's hand and began leading him away from the blast from my past.

"Ava." Nick grabbed my arm. "Please."

Suddenly Caleb was between us, his hand on Nick's chest. He seemed to tower over him even though he was only an inch or two taller than my ex. "She said, go home."

Nick took a wary step back. "I'll leave you be. But I'm not going home. We *need* to talk."

Before I could reply Nick strode away, his hands in his pockets, his shoulders hunched at his ears.

Shaken, angry, confused, I twisted away and hurried up my stoop. When Caleb didn't follow, I called back to him. "Are you coming or not?"

He moved toward me, tailing me up to the front door and inside, our footsteps echoing on the stairs as I led him up to the first floor to my apartment. As soon as we were inside, I locked the door and grabbed fistfuls of his shirt in my hand, pulling him toward the back of the apartment, to my bedroom. I pulled him down into my kiss, not expecting him to push me away, his face flushed with anger, not passion.

"This might just be sex, babe, but it's supposed tae be sex between just you and me. If you think we're doing this when your mind is on another man, you've got another thing coming."

Shocked that he'd think that, I shook my head in denial. "I don't want him like that. It's been a long time since I ever wanted him like that. But seeing him brings up a lot of pain that I don't want to deal with right now. I don't want to think about the fact that he and Gem were the only people that kept me sane growing up with parents who neglected me to the point of putting me in harm's way. *They* protected me, not my mom and dad. Nick protected me. He said he loved me. We all went to college together. He proposed to me when we graduated. It was supposed to be forever and it wasn't. So I don't want to think about how the two people I trusted most in my life—my fiancé and my best friend— told me a year after he'd proposed that they'd been cheating on me for months and then promptly ran off together to get married. And I don't want to think about how I never forgave them and how now I can never forgive her because she's dead. And I don't want to think about why that man is in my city now when I never wanted to see him again.

"I just want you, Caleb. The one man I've ever met who hasn't lied to me. Who hasn't made promises he can't keep and that I don't want him to keep." And I didn't, I realized with a blast of cold reality. These past few days Caleb had confused me. The passion between us confused me. But Nick was a swift and much needed reminder that this kind of love just hurt too damn much and never seemed to be worth it in the end. I didn't want to feel anything beyond desire for Caleb. And I wouldn't. "You're right. This, between us, will only ever be about sex. But it is just between you and me. I am never thinking about anyone else but you when we're together. How could I?" I whispered, hoping he saw how much I wanted him. "And right now I need you to make me forget that tomorrow I have to wake up knowing that asshole is in my city."

Apparently, I didn't need to ask him twice.

Perhaps it was only the light warmth of the morning sun tickling my face that woke me up the next day. It certainly felt like it as consciousness seeped in, rescuing me from a dream where I was chasing Gem through Phoenix while Nick chased me. I'd felt terror that I'd never catch her and fear that he *would* catch me.

However, when I opened my eyes slowly, blinking against the light flooding the room, the first thing that came into focus was Caleb's pale blue eyes staring at me with unmasked curiosity.

The evening before came rushing back and as I shifted under the covers I felt our physical activities in the slight ache in my muscles.

I had attacked the poor guy last night.

Not that he'd been complaining. He gave as good as he got.

If I was being honest with myself, I'd half expected to wake up and find him gone since he'd been so uncomfortable with the idea of sleeping over in the first place, but you wouldn't think it of him with his casual, at-ease pose, lying on his side on my bed gazing at me. I suddenly wondered if it was his eyes on my face that had woken me rather than the morning sun.

"Hey," I said, my voice hoarse with sleep.

"Morning." He reached out and brushed my hair off my face in a tender action that made me snuggle deeper into my pillow. It felt nice, but my resolve from last night hadn't deserted me just because I'd woken up to Mr. Sexy brushing my hair off my face.

"What time is it?"

"Just after nine."

"Hmm. Give me a sec and I'll get up, make you coffee. Breakfast, if you like."

"Sounds good. Take your time." He braced his head on the palm of his hand, his elbow bent into the pillow beneath him. "Tell me about your parents. About Nick and Gemma."

My breath stuttered at the sudden demand. "Caleb—"

"You said some things that concern me, Ava. Put my mind at ease."

I frowned, taken aback by the fact that he was worried about me.

He must have seen the confusion in my expression. "We've both made it clear that this is just a physical relationship, and after last night I am more convinced than ever that you're not one of these women who tells you she's happy with it just being sex but is angling for more. I get that now. Which means when we talked about being friends, we both meant that too. We can handle it. So I made up my mind that you're my friend, Ava. And I'm worried about my friend."

Affection for this man suffused me and I sat up, mirroring his pose, and reached out with my free hand to stroke his chest tenderly. "I'm good, I promise."

"You aren't going tae tell me, are you?" He scowled, like he couldn't believe he wasn't getting his way.

My amusement over how adorable that was made me pause as I began to ask myself why I couldn't tell Caleb. Before Nick's arrival I knew I didn't want to tell Caleb anything personal because I was afraid revealing myself to him would only deepen my feelings for him. But I was now absolute in my decision to keep things on a friends-with-benefits level. And honestly, after last night, seeing Nick out of the blue like that, it might be nice to vent.

I stared into his searching eyes. "So I can tell you things now without you worrying it means I'm falling for you?"

"Aye."

"Then I must tell you, Mr. Scott, that you have the most beautiful eyes I've ever seen."

His lips twitched. "That wasn't the kind of thing I was talking about."

"Wolf eyes."

"Ava."

I chuckled, but the sound slowly died when I saw he was serious. Fine. "I really am okay. Nothing happened to me when I was a kid, if that's what you're worried about. It came close, but I escaped relatively unscathed."

"Tell me about it."

I sighed. "My parents are wannabe hippies. They love material things too much to be true hippies. My great-grandfather was an industrial giant and each generation since has taken care of that inheritance very well. My father has a hefty trust fund and impressive investment portfolio. It allowed us to live in a nice house in a nice neighborhood, and for my parents to not have to work," I said, hearing the bitterness in my voice. "Growing up with them was exhausting. They were irresponsible about everything but money.

"I didn't have it so bad. I know that now. I know that there are people out there who had it so much worse growing up. But my parents never treated me like I was their child. I got the same affection and attention that anybody did from them, and it was scarce because they were always living in their own little world. I took care of myself from before I could remember. Learned to make my own breakfast, got myself to school, made dinner when they were too high to make it for me. As I got older they started to have these wild parties at the house. It never even crossed their minds that they were putting their kid in danger by inviting strangers into our home." I thought back to the night it all got scary.

"I was fourteen when shit got real. One night they had a party and I was in my bedroom, kept awake by the music and laughter. I was sitting by my patio door instead of in my bed when my bedroom door opened and a man appeared.

"I'd sat frozen in fear as he searched the bed for me, his eyes darting around the room until he found me. Then slowly he closed my bedroom door and locked it. I didn't recognize him. I just knew what he wanted as soon as he started unbuckling his belt."

I felt Caleb tense and gave him a reassuring but wobbly smile. "I launched myself out the patio doors so fast. Our house was all on one level—a huge sprawling bungalow. I'd used that door many times growing up and I just fled in my pajamas, running through the neighborhood until I got to Nick's house. He wanted to tell his parents."

"You should have," Caleb bit out angrily.

"I wasn't as scared about being taken away from my parents as I was scared about being taken away from Gem and Nick. They were my family. That became even more apparent when I confronted my parents about what happened and they insisted I must have been mistaken. They didn't want to hear it. They never wanted to hear anything that would kill their buzz. Anyway, I convinced Nick and Gem not to tell anyone, but Nick was furious. He made me promise that I would stay with either one of them on the nights we knew my parents were having one of their parties. For the most part we could plan ahead and I only had to use that door as an escape a couple more times before I left for college."

"Only?" Caleb snapped. "For Christ's sake, Ava, don't play it down. Your parents were . . . are negligent arseholes."

I flinched but I couldn't argue with him. "Yeah."

Caleb flopped onto his back, heaving an exasperated sigh. "So what happened with Nick and Gemma?"

"We were all just friends until that night I escaped from the stranger in my room. Nick became my protector. Suddenly he wasn't just Nick, the boy I grew up with. He was the really cute boy who seemed to care about me best in the world. I had developed an impossible crush on him but hadn't realized how badly until that night. He was a year older, girls liked him, and I never thought he'd return my feelings. But that night when I'd snuck into his bedroom to stay with him, he told me he loved me." I almost smiled at the bittersweet memory. "I told him I loved him too and he kissed me. For the first time in a long time I felt safe. But telling Gem was awkward because I didn't want her to feel like a third wheel. She wasn't too happy at first, worried about the same thing I thought, but Nick and I never left her out if we could help it.

"It got a little messier as we got older and Nick and I started having sex, something in retrospect we probably did when I was too young. But sex didn't seem like such a big deal to me."

"How young?"

"My fifteenth birthday. I know that probably doesn't sound young to a guy, but I think it's young."

He turned his head on his pillow, his expression tender. "It is young. I'd lose my mind if I even thought my sisters had lost their virginity at that age."

I shrugged sadly. "It was Nick. I thought he was my forever."

"And Gemma?"

"Was pissed. She definitely felt left out after that. In fact, she promptly went out with the shadiest guy in school and lost her virginity to him in the back of his pickup." I felt despondent at the memory. "At least with Nick I'd felt loved at the time. I think she secretly blamed me for that decision." I pushed up into a sitting position, drawing my knees into my chest as I looked down into Caleb's sympathetic gaze. Not once, when we'd first been on those flights together, would I have ever thought he'd look at me with such tender patience. "Things seemed to normalize, though. We grew close again, and she went back to being my family, like always. Gem more than anyone was my family. I think I always knew in the back of my mind that if something happened between me and Nick I'd still always have her, so I gave her more of me than I gave to anyone." Tears filled my eyes.

"Ava." I felt his hand on my knee, reassuring me.

I sucked back the tears, still feeling that pain deep in my chest, like a knife wound no one could heal. "But unbeknownst to me she was in love with Nick. She finally confessed it to him after he proposed to me, realizing that if she didn't it would soon be too late. She told me later that he admitted that he loved her too; he just hadn't thought she loved him back in that way. So they started their affair, too afraid at first to tell me."

Tears slipped down my cheeks before I could stop them. I looked away from Caleb, staring at the window as I struggled to control my emotions. "When I found out, I told her she should have confided in me years ago. That I'd always loved her more than I ever loved Nick when we were kids and if I'd known back then I would have stepped aside before it was too late, before I'd given him everything." I wiped at the tears running down my face. "She cried so hard when I told her that, but I couldn't see her pain back then. All I saw was her betrayal. Even if they'd just told me right away, you know, rather than having an affair behind my back. It would have hurt but not nearly so much." I turned to Caleb, to find his expression dark, fierce. "I always wondered if she knew he'd sleep with me after being with her. Or did he tell her that he wasn't sleeping with me? Because our sex life never waned in those months they were cheating." My upper lip curled in disgust. "In fact, I remember afterward, after overanalyzing every little thing about that time, that he seemed insatiable in those months. I thought it was because we were engaged. He couldn't keep his hands off me. Now I know that he was getting off on it—on having two women. Two best friends.

"Do you know what *he* said when he told me about the affair? When I asked him if he'd loved Gem the whole time, why he was with me? He said that I was the one he wanted when he was just a horny kid." Anger besieged me at the reminder. "That I was so beautiful that he couldn't help but want me. That he probably would always want me that way. But that was all I was. A pretty face. He said

I was boring and uptight and I cared too much about the way I looked and what people thought of me. Gem wasn't like that. She wasn't vain. She was warm, he said. And while my beauty would fade, Gem would always be beautiful on the inside."

Silence, heavy and still, fell over the room.

And through it I could feel Caleb's anger, and it was gratifying.

"Do you want to know the sickest part? I believed him. Maybe I did care about my looks too much, of what people thought of me. After all, the only compliments my parents ever gave me growing up were on my looks. They made it seem like being attractive was my most powerful and positive quality.

"I drove myself crazy trying to think back and find evidence that Nick was right. It took me a long time afterward to realize that he wasn't right. That what he said wasn't true. I have my faults, but those weren't it. He just wanted it all to be true because he needed *not* to be the bad guy in the situation. They both did. So somehow the blame fell on me. That all these years I'd stolen Nick from Gem and kept them apart. My parents just told me to get over it. Just get over it! The only people I'd ever trusted betrayed me, and I was just supposed to get over it.

"The one person who seemed to be on my side was my uncle. He flew me out to Boston and helped me find a place to start over."

When Caleb spoke, his voice was gruff. "And then you had tae fly home for Gemma's funeral."

I let out a shaky breath. "All of our old friends just stared at me in disgust the whole time, murmuring behind my back that they couldn't believe I'd had the audacity to show up. That was hard enough as it was . . . but Nick decided to humiliate me at the wake and direct all his rage and grief at me."

"What did he do?"

"I was turning a corner in their house and I bumped into him by accident, spilling the drinks in his hand on the cream carpet. And it just set him off. He just started yelling at me, asking me why I was there. He told me that Gem died still thinking the affair was all her fault. That she'd never forgiven herself even though it wasn't just her fault. He said that he and I were to blame too. But that I couldn't let it go. I couldn't forgive her. I was too filled with hate and self-absorption. And he said that I could live the rest of my life knowing that *he* would never forgive *me*."

Caleb shot up to a sitting position, his eyes blazing at me. "You didn't actually swallow that bullshit, did you?"

I scoffed. "Of course not. But everyone else there did. I was practically shoved out of there with pitchforks while my parents watched on in embarrassment, not doing anything to have my back. I am not the woman I was back then, Caleb. Yes, I feel guilty that she died without my having forgiven her because I can forgive knowing that she felt responsible for destroying the future I had planned. But him? Never once could he admit that he was the guilty party. He always tried to make me the bad guy because it made him feel better. He's a coward." I shook my head in wonder. "I look back and I try to see it—I try to see how I could have missed what a piece of shit he is deep down."

Caleb reached over and slid his big, warm hand under my hair, cupping the nape of my neck in a firm, reassuring grip. His eyes bore into mine, capturing me in place. "Dinnae do that tae yourself. People can be masters of deception because they are so complicated. You aren't the first tae have not seen a person's true character. And frankly, Ava, when you first started dating him he was just a boy. People can be nice kids and for whatever reason grow up tae be selfish wee shits. So dinnae put that on yourself."

I nodded at his soft command and then gave him a wry smile to cover the fact that I wanted to burst into fresh tears. "Still glad you asked to hear about it?"

"Aye," he replied firmly. "Because I can tell you now knowing the facts that I think you should talk tae Nick."

Shocked, I jerked away from his touch. "Why would you even suggest that? Do you see this?" I pulled away, reaching over to my nightstand where I laid my jewelry. I picked up the tennis bracelet Nick had given me. "He bought me this. For my eighteenth birthday. I wear it to look good for my clients and I can't afford to spend money on a freaking diamond tennis bracelet to replace it. I hate wearing it because it always reminds me of him. But I wear it anyway. And it's as close as I ever want to get to him again."

Caleb scowled at the bracelet, a dark look that melted away when he looked into my eyes. "Ava, you need tae tell him what you told me. Even if he is here tae apologize, he needs tae know before he says a damn word that you dinnae care what he thinks. That you know you aren't the one in the wrong here and that he can live the rest of his life not forgiving you if he bloody well wants . . . because as far as you're concerned he's just a memory you dinnae care enough about tae offer forgiveness."

My breath caught at his fierceness and the realization that Caleb's advice was spot-on. Nick did need to know that he didn't have power over me. Not anymore. I nodded slowly. "You're right. You're so right." I grabbed his hand and placed a grateful kiss to his big knuckles. He'd been so kind, so generous, listening to me like that and not judging. But I thought about what I knew of his family and I wondered just how crazy he must think mine was. My thoughts blurted out before I could stop them. "You must think my family is insane. Yours sounds so perfect."

Hearing the melancholy tone in my voice caused Caleb's eyes to dim with sorrow. "Nobody's family is perfect, Ava."

I tensed, realizing the sorrow wasn't for me but . . . my God, for him. "Caleb?"

He shook his head. "No matter. Breakfast?"

I refused to let go of his hand. "What happened to your family?" His hesitation made my heart pound. "You can tell me. After what I just told you, you must know you can tell me anything. Friends tell each other stuff."

"It's not a happy story." Caleb refused to meet my eyes and it made my heart pound.

"What happened to you, Caleb?"

"Not me." He shook his head. "Well, to me, aye. But to us all." Finally he looked at me, his eyes bright with grief that made me squeeze his hand tight. "Quinn, my brother I mentioned earlier . . ."

"Yes?"

"He died, Ava. He died when he was eighteen. He was high. Got behind the wheel of a car."

I wanted to wrap my arms around him so tight but I knew somehow that kind of physical comfort wouldn't be welcome. "I am so sorry, Caleb."

"Aye, well." He gently eased his hand from my grip only to rub it through his hair in discomfort.

I didn't know what else to say. Caleb felt far away somehow. He always did in a way, a bitterness underlying in his gaze, his demeanor, that I didn't understand until now. It was grief.

Knowing what he needed now more than ever was for me to defuse the weighted moment between us, I forced out a cheeky smile. "Well . . . I should thank you for your advice about Nick. Pancakes?" I threw off the duvet and hopped out of bed, feeling his gaze on my naked body as I crossed the room to my dresser for some clean underwear.

"If there's a prize for good advice giving, I should at least get tae choose it, no?" he said, sounding relieved.

I glanced over my shoulder at him as I pulled up my underwear. "Sure."

His eyes smoldered. "Then lose the knickers, Ava, and get back in bed."

I shivered at that look, my body anticipating the goodness that look led to. Curling my fingers into my lacy underwear, I shimmied them back down my legs. "You know, it was such good advice," I said, kicking the underwear off my feet, "that I think it calls for an orgasm *and* pancakes." I leisurely crossed the room and got on the bed on all fours, crawling over toward him.

Caleb bestowed on me a slow, wicked smile. "Did anyone ever tell you that you are a very good friend tae have, Miss Breevort?"

I smiled back. "When I'm done with you this morning, Mr. Scott, I'll be the *best* friend you ever had."

His answering chuckle was swallowed in my kiss, and the sadness of our past histories abated for a while.

Seventeen

'm a little surprised you agreed to meet with me, but glad," Nick said as soon as Paul led him into my office.

I nodded my thanks at Paul, who quickly dismissed himself. Then I got up out of my chair, gesturing for Nick to take the seat in front of my desk.

He did so, glancing around the office, curiously taking it all in. I hadn't noticed it on Saturday night, but Nick had lost weight. Enough so that his cheekbones were sharp on his once boyish face. When we were growing up, all the girls wanted to date Nick because he had irresistible pretty-boy good looks with an edge. Dark hair, soulful dark eyes, long lashes, and olive skin. Tall—almost as tall as Caleb—Nick had a lanky, wiry build. When he'd walk toward me in the school corridor with that swagger of his, I'd thought with the shallowness of youth how lucky I was that Nick had chosen me to love.

But he hadn't loved me.

He'd been in lust with me.

When I looked back on it, he never complimented me on anything but my face and body. He never told me I was smart or funny or kind. He'd always just whispered in my ear about how beautiful and sexy I was, how he loved my eyes, my smile, my legs, my ass.

You get the picture.

I'd just been so eager for the affection that I'd never noticed his preoccupation with my appearance.

It was another reminder that what me and Caleb had was just sex too. Caleb only ever complimented me on my body and how I made his body feel. But he was honest about it, which made him a hundred times more trustworthy than this shadow of my ex-fiancé sitting in front of me.

Gaunt, exhausted-looking, he turned back to me and opened his mouth to speak.

I put up a hand to stop him as I leaned against my desk looking down at him. "I agreed to meet with you, Nick, for one reason only. You mentioned on Saturday you wanted to apologize and I need to tell you that I don't want your apology. When you first cheated on me with Gem, I temporarily allowed myself to believe all the terrible things you said about me being vain and generally not a very nice person. But I soon realized that you said all that because you needed to believe I was the bad guy so you didn't have to feel guilty. And somehow you managed to convince everyone back in Arcadia of the same with that good-boy charm of yours. But I don't believe it. I know the truth because I was there." I wanted to rage against him about how I hated him for stealing Gem from me, but the genuine grief in his eyes for his wife stopped me.

"You cheated instead of coming to me and telling me the truth. Would it have hurt? Yes. But at least the two of you wouldn't have betrayed me. And if you would just have apologized, accepted the fact that you were in the wrong, then I could have forgiven you. I'd have had the chance to forgive Gem. Because the truth is, Nick, I couldn't give a shit about you now. All I care about is that I lost my friend and the chance to forgive *her*." Tears brightened my eyes as he stared up at me, watching as his expression darkened. "As for you, I don't feel anything. You're just a blip on my radar. So go home and take an apology I don't need or want with you."

He got to his feet, staring at me incredulously. "I lost my wife and you can't give me this? And you say you're not self-absorbed."

Indignation suffused me, pushing me to be ugly, but somehow I controlled the feeling. "Go home, Nick."

"No." He stepped into my space, his legs touching my knees, and I felt a moment of panic at his nearness. "You need to hear what I have to say. You have to give me that, Ava. I've lost too much already. I need to say this to someone who knew Gem better than anyone."

Sympathy I didn't want to feel for the bastard cut through my anger. "Then speak and leave."

"You're right." He raised a shaky hand to push back his overlong hair. "I was a coward. Gem and I, we talked about it a lot once you were gone. We argued about it. I was the one who convinced her not to tell you right away, delaying it by saying I needed time. But she started to work out the truth the longer we were together." Nick's dark eyes blazed at me. "The truth was, I didn't know how to choose between you. I loved you both."

"I don't believe that," I snapped. "You don't treat someone the way you treated me when you love them."

"You always saw everything in black and white, Ava." He shook his head sadly. "People are more complicated than that. You . . . you always felt like you were seconds from slipping through my hands. Like something better would come along and you'd be gone. I never really had you. I had your body and Gem had your trust."

"You both had my trust."

"But you let her in in a way you didn't let me in."

I couldn't argue with that, because it was true, but she was my friend and he was my lover. I let them both in, in different ways. "Maybe deep down I always knew you would betray me and that's why."

"No. You just didn't love me the way I loved you."

Bullshit! I had been so in love with him, he blinded me. "Oh, so this is your new way of justifying your actions?" I asked calmly, crossing my arms over my chest like I was merely amused by the turn in the conversation rather than furious.

"Gem loved me, Ava. She loved me in a way I knew you could never love me. I just couldn't admit it out loud so I twisted everything in my head and I said some awful things to you. When Gem accused me of still being in love with you, I told her all the things I said when you and I broke up, and she was so mad at me. She didn't know I'd put the blame on you. We didn't talk for weeks. She thought about getting in touch with you a lot," he told me softly. "She just never felt brave enough to do it."

"Nick." I sighed, feeling a tightness in my chest, an uneasiness in my belly. "What is the purpose of this?"

His expression turned fierce. "I don't have a second chance to tell Gem I was sorry for all the stupid things I did. But I can tell you. I never stopped loving you, Ava. I loved you too much. When we were kids, I felt like you needed me. I felt like your protector and it made me feel good. But as we got older, you stopped needing me. You became untouchable. Maybe that's what I loved." He laughed bitterly. "Maybe it was the mystery of you that kept me dangling on your hook for so long. I lost my shit at you at the funeral because I was grieving for Gem while at the same time feeling things I shouldn't be feeling when I saw you."

That uneasiness turned to a chill, and I slid out from where he was leaning into me to round my desk, wondering if I was crazy to even think that my grieving ex-fiancé might be coming on to me. "Nick," I warned.

"I cheated on her," he blurted out.

I froze, staring at him in outrage.

"I was always looking for something when you left. I did love my wife, Ava. She made mistakes with you but we both know that she was so good and kind and loving. She loved me like no one has ever loved me and it made her betray you. She never got over it."

"So you rewarded her by cheating on her?"

"I loved her . . ." He shrugged, his features strained with guilt. "But there was no excitement like there was with you."

"Wore off, huh, once you two became legit and weren't sneaking off behind my back?"

He blanched and I felt a wave of revulsion toward him because I'd hit the nail on the head. "It just wasn't the same. Even you have to admit, Ava, sex between you and me is off the charts."

Was this seriously happening right now? Was my ex-fiancé actually standing in my office talking about missing sex with me weeks after his wife had died in childbirth? I gaped at him, wondering how on earth I had been so blind to what a weak, selfish man he was for so long. I wanted to hurt him and not because he hurt me but because he hurt Gem. He stole us from each other and he didn't even love her the way she deserved to be loved.

"The man you saw me with on Saturday?"

Nick winced. "Yeah?"

"He's the best sex I've ever had, Nick. He made what you and I had in bed look like an inexperienced fumble in the dark. And even if I didn't currently have that man in my bed, *you* would never be welcome back in it. So if you came here looking to satiate some need that has driven you for years to cheat on a woman who deserved better, then you can go to hell."

He paled. "That's not why I'm here."

"Then why are you standing in my office talking to me about how you miss sex with me when your wife has just died?"

"I don't know," he moaned. "I'm saying it wrong."

"Do you want me to forgive you on Gem's behalf? Is that it?"

"You knew her best. What would she say?"

"Did she know, Nick? Did she know about this other woman?"

"Wom*en*," he whispered. "They looked like you."

I suddenly felt queasy as understanding began to dawn. Nick thought he loved me but it wasn't love. It was an infatuation he'd never been able to rid himself of. He'd self-destructed over and over again, searching for something that didn't exist. And he'd pulled Gem right down with him. Along with the queasiness, I felt an unbearable sadness for my lost friend, and an impatient need to get her widowed husband out of my sight. "She would have forgiven you," I whispered back. "She gave up a lot for you and Gem would have needed to believe that you were worth it."

"She wanted a baby so badly. She thought it would bring us closer together. I killed her." He suddenly sobbed.

I flinched, looking down at my desk, the ache in my chest for Gem almost more than I could handle. "She loved you. Just hold on to that."

"Say you understand, Ava, please. Say you get it now. That you know I really did love you. I think I still—"

"Don't." I glared over at him. "Get this through your head now, Nick, and then leave and don't come back. You don't know me. You never knew me. Forget about me and move on with your life. Go home and grieve for a woman who I have to believe in your own weak way you loved. And then forget about the past. I have, Nick. I'm not saying this to be cruel. I'm saying it for your own good—I don't love you. I don't even like you. A part of me wants to be angry at you for Gem's sake. But you don't deserve to have that from me. So now, as soon as you walk out that door, you'll be just a memory."

For a moment he stood there staring at me, like he couldn't quite believe this was how it was ending. Was he honestly so delusional he thought it would end differently?

"Your mom thought . . ."

"My mom thought what?" I asked wearily.

He shook his head, his smile bitter. "She thought you were still in love with me."

"You do remember my mother doesn't know anything about me, right?"

Nick gave me a sad, pathetic smirk. "It's coming back to me now."

"Good-bye, Nick."

He stared at me for so long I gestured to the door.

Finally, he nodded. "Good-bye, Ava."

And as he disappeared out of my office, his footsteps fading away, I felt a peace settle over me that I hadn't felt in a long time. Two days ago I never would have imagined being brave enough to have this discussion with Nick, but Caleb was right. I had needed to do that.

I thought about calling Caleb to confide in him about the disturbing and woeful conversation I'd just had with my ex, but that felt too much like something a girlfriend would do. Instead I called Harper.

"Harp, you won't believe what just happened to me," I said on her voice mail. "Call me so I can tell you all about it." I hung up, hoping she would return my call. I'd spent much of yesterday rolling around in bed with Caleb, but during a breather I'd called Harper and she hadn't picked up. Not sure if she was mad at me or avoiding the questions she knew I had about Vince, I was a little worried.

But if I knew my best friend like I knew I did, she wouldn't be able to ignore me if she thought I needed her. And right now I needed to tell someone about Nick, because part of me couldn't even believe that had just happened.

Harper had texted me to grab a quick lunch with her at the restaurant so we could talk. I was hurrying toward Canterbury when my cell rang. Seeing it was Roxanne Sutton, my hard-to-please client, I groaned, but answered the call as I turned left on Milk Street.

"Roxanne, how are you?"

"How am I?" Her high-pitched voice screeched through the phone and I winced. "I've just seen the chaise for the master bedroom. Who approved that fabric choice? Because it was not me!"

Irritation made my skin flush hot, but as always I kept my feelings on the inside where they belonged when dealing with a client. "Roxanne, you did approve it. I sent you samples over a week ago that you approved. My upholsterer got to work straightaway and the chaise is the first completed piece for the master suite."

"I did not choose that fabric," she insisted. "And frankly, I am appalled by your lack of commitment to this project. Stella assured me that you were just as good as Paul, but I am having serious doubts."

Irate as I found myself marching down Pearl Street toward Canterbury, I did my best to mask it. "I'm truly sorry you feel that way because I certainly have been giving my all to the project."

"Not your all. Now . . ." She took a deep breath. "I am willing to give you a second chance because I have seen the work you've done on previous projects that I found satisfactory—"

High praise indeed.

"So I insist that you meet me at the summerhouse again, on Wednesday, so I can remind you of what it is that I'm looking for in this redesign. Hopefully the visit will help you recommit to the project."

Dismay filled me, my immediate thought of Caleb and how he

was only here for a few more days and I would lose them if I went to Nantucket. "I'm afraid that's a little short notice, Roxanne. I do have other projects—"

"Are you saying my money isn't important to you, Miss Breevort?"

I stumbled to a stop, disappointment filling me as I realized I would have to do this. "No, of course not. I'd be happy to meet you at the summerhouse. But I can only be there Wednesday. I have to return to the office on Thursday."

"Well, we'll just need to see about that. I can't let you leave until I'm assured you truly understand my vision. I expect you at the house at ten a.m. sharp." And then she hung up on me.

Deflated, annoyed, and generally wishing I hadn't gotten out of bed that morning, I made my way into Canterbury in desperate need of my friend's shoulder, pronto.

As I wandered over to the hostess's podium, I caught sight of Jason Luton, the owner and head chef. He was conversing with his bar manager and lifted his head to acknowledge me as I walked in. He said something to his staff and then began making his way over to me. Jason was average height for a guy, with a slim, athletic build, concealed at the moment by his chef whites. He smiled at me and despite my bad mood I couldn't help but smile back. Jason was a very handsome man in his mid-forties. His hair was gray but it did nothing to detract from his crinkly, sexy, twinkly blue eyes or charmingly lopsided smile. He had the kind of charisma that made your belly flutter.

He was also happily married and father to two daughters.

"Ava," he said, bending down to kiss my cheek. "It's been a while." And did I mention the attractive British accent?

"How have you been?"

"The same." He shrugged, looking around proudly at his restaurant. "Tired but happy."

"And how are Gillian and the girls?" I asked after his wife and kids.

"Brilliant as always." He gestured for me to walk with him and so I did. "Here to see Harper?"

"Yeah, she suggested we have lunch together."

"She's just working on a new concoction I'm sure the critics are going to rave about." His eyes brightened at the thought. "I'll send her out." He pulled out a chair at a private table near the fireplace. "Lunch is on me."

"Oh, you don't have to," I tried to protest, but he waved me off and sauntered away, disappearing into the kitchen.

As I waited, I stewed over the fact that I was going to Nantucket instead of spending time with Caleb. It shouldn't have bothered me so much, but it did.

"I'm sorry." Harper came hurrying out of the kitchen toward me. She practically fell into the seat opposite me. Her cheeks were flushed and her eyes had this bright kind of madness to them that I recognized. She was in a creative mood and high on it.

"Hey, I can leave," I said, not wanting to interrupt her flow. "If you need to get back in there."

"Nah." She shook her head. "Everything I can do right now is done. What do you need to tell me?"

Before I could open my mouth, the kitchen doors swung open and a guy I didn't recognize in chef whites appeared. He was carrying two plates of food, which he brought over to us. "From Jason. Enjoy." And he disappeared just as quickly.

I stared down at a beautiful plate of pan-fried hake, heritage potatoes, mussels, and a saffron butter sauce. It was one of my favorite dishes on the current menu. "Oh, yum. Who was the guy?" I asked, digging in, not one to lose my appetite when I was anxious or nervous.

"Denny, new sous chef." She shrugged, picking up her fork and knife.

"Oh, what happened to Kevin?"

"New job. I didn't tell you?"

"Nope."

She looked up from her plate. "We're not here to talk about our staffing situation. What happened this morning?"

And that's how over the best lunch I'd had in a while I told Harper everything about Nick on Saturday night, then coming to a real understanding with Caleb, him advising me to talk to Nick, and finally what Nick actually had to say.

When I was done, Harper slumped back in her chair, looking exhausted for me. "Babe."

"Right."

"God, it never ceases to amaze me how messed up people are."

My smile was sad. "I know."

She narrowed her eyes on me. "So . . . you're not even a little gratified?"

"About what?"

"That all this time the bastard has been so hung up on you that he screwed up his whole life."

"You know me better than that."

"You're sad for Gemma." She sighed and nodded. "I get that."

"I'm even a little sad for him," I whispered, hating to admit it. "He screwed up his marriage over something that wasn't even real. I was only ever an infatuation. He didn't know me like I thought he knew me, and I definitely didn't know him. Plus, you don't cheat on someone you apparently adore, right? I don't even think it was our relationship he was holding on to either. I think he just . . . he didn't want to grow up. He always seemed to be the one in control when we were kids, the protector, the one Gem and I could rely on. After high school he just seemed so lost. I remember how the thought of the future scared the shit out of him. He preferred living in the past."

"Right." She dropped her fork and knife on her empty plate. "But after all this time, with everyone thinking you got the raw deal, that you were the victim, it turns out you were the one who escaped."

I nodded, having thought the same myself. "I know. I realized that as he left my office this morning. I finally realized that I was the lucky one. As heartbroken as I am for Gem, I can't tell you how much peace it gives me knowing my life is better for the fact that he left me."

Harper reached across the table and squeezed my hand. "I'm glad."

I covered her hand with mine and then took a deep breath to prompt, "Speaking of relationships." She immediately tried to pull her hand away but I held on. "I'm not judging, Harp. I just . . . I'm just a little concerned."

She wouldn't meet my eyes. "There's nothing to be concerned about."

"Vince doesn't seem so happy and supportive anymore about your job. And you just sat there letting that groupie flirt with him right in front of you. Not Harper-like behavior."

Harper yanked her hand free, glaring at me. "*I* was being classy."

"Oh, unlike me?"

Her lips twitched, amusement cutting through the chill in her eyes. "No, it was funny when you shooed her away."

"So why didn't *you*?"

"I promised Vince I wouldn't react to the girls. He warned me that they get a bit much and he's had problems with girlfriends before not reacting well to it. I know that it's just part of the industry he wants to be in and so I have to learn to let it go."

"The same way he's letting the fact that you work long hours go?"

Harper stared at me, clearly deciding between being pissed at me for asking and being grateful I cared enough to. Thankfully she decided on the latter. "He'd never mentioned it before. Saturday night was the first night he ever said something negative about it. We talked yesterday and he admitted that my hours do bother him, but not for him, for me. He's worried I'm burning myself out."

That I could understand. "And what did you say?"

She sucked in a breath. "I'm not going to lie, Ava. I worry about it too sometimes. That if I'm going to be working this hard, then surely it should be for myself."

"You want to open your own restaurant?"

"Dessert bar." She smiled shyly. "Eventually. Not yet, anyway. I convinced him that I'm good and he seemed to accept it."

There was something in her tone that was off. She sounded placating, and that wasn't Harper. She did what *she* wanted, no matter what anyone else said. "Okay. As long as you're happy."

"Very. Now, what about you?" She sought to change the subject. "And Mr. Scott?"

The reminder that I didn't have him for long crashed over me. "It looks like we'll be finishing things up sooner that I'd thought. The Shrew called. This time on Wednesday I'll be in goddamn Nantucket."

Eighteen

While Caleb vented about his day at the office, I tried my best not to be distracted by the longing in my chest, that harsh pang of feeling I got anytime I remembered tonight would be the last night we spent together.

When we met at my favorite Italian restaurant in Back Bay, one of the first things I wanted to ask him was when he was leaving. It seemed even more crucial to know since he'd been unable to meet me the night before. Things at the office had exploded and Caleb was up to his neck in the disaster. He video-called me from the office to show me him standing in the North American division CFO's office surrounded by piles and piles of files.

That meant that if he was leaving sooner than expected, tonight was all we had. However, I didn't want to seem desperate or upset when the guy was clearly stressed out.

"Long story short," he said, sipping at the Scotch he'd ordered, "the bastard was not only lazy—he was using company money for private investments. Savvy investments too. If only he'd used that savvy tae do his job right, I wouldn't be sitting here having not slept for thirty-six hours. Anyway, I presented my findings tae the CEO.

He took it tae our bosses in Tokyo. A few hours later we dragged the sleekit wee bastard into a conference call and he was fired."

"My God, what an idiot." I shook my head, thinking about all the people who would kill for a chance at a six-figure salary.

"Aye, well, they wanted me tae stick around and interview new candidates for the position, but I'm needed back in the Glasgow office." He stifled a yawn with his fist as my heart began to thump hard in my chest.

"When do you leave?"

Caleb's gaze suddenly intensified as he leaned back in his seat. "Thursday morning. I dinnae think I'll be much use tae you tonight, but that still gives us Wednesday."

I winced. "Actually, it doesn't."

He scowled. "Why?"

"Do you remember when I mentioned the difficult client I have right now?" At his nod, I continued, "She's demanding I head back out to the house on Nantucket tomorrow. I won't be back until Thursday."

The frown lines between his brows deepened. "Nantucket isn't far."

"It's about a four-hour trip from here. I have to be there at ten a.m. tomorrow morning, so I'll leave around five thirty."

"And you'll not be back tomorrow evening?"

"If it was anyone other than Roxanne Sutton, I'd say yes, but that woman will trap me there for as long as she legally can." I let my frustration show. "I'm sorry. I thought we'd at least have one last night together."

"And we will."

"But you're tired."

"Ava." His eyes narrowed. "I'm not leaving Boston without another taste of you." He glanced around, missing my cheeks flush with arousal, and spotted a waiter. Waving the man over, Caleb ordered, "A pot of black coffee."

I snickered as the waiter hurried off to do his bidding. "The things a man will do for sex."

Caleb grinned. "Not just any sex."

Pleasure shifted through me at the compliment.

"Let's make this meal a quick one, eh?"

I nodded my agreement. "That sounds like a plan."

"So . . ." He leaned back in his chair. "You promised me last night you'd tell me how it went with Nick."

Unwilling to spend our last few hours together discussing my ex, I gave Caleb a quick summary of events, watching his features harden with anger as the story went on. "But thankfully he's gone now and I don't really want to spend any more time talking about the asshole."

"What a prick," Caleb said vehemently, just as his coffee arrived. The waiter's eyes rounded at the aggression in Caleb's voice as he placed the coffee on the table, but my companion didn't even notice. He was too focused on me. I gave the waiter a reassuring smile and he hurried away.

"It's done. Let's talk about something else."

His expression said he wanted to call Nick a few more names first, but he poured himself a coffee and made an effort to look relaxed. "What do you want tae talk about?"

On a rush of sentimentality I shouldn't be feeling, I blurted out, "I want you to know I've had a lot of fun with you these past few weeks. I'm glad we decided to be friends."

"With benefits," he teased.

I smiled. "Yes, definitely. It's been far more pleasurable than the usual friendship."

He lowered his gaze to his coffee, shielding his thoughts from me. "You know, I was thinking that at some point I'll be back in Boston again. Probably near the end of the year."

My pulse raced at the thought of seeing him again. "Oh?"

"If you're not attached, I'd quite like us tae do this again when I'm in town."

"I'd like that."

Caleb's eyes finally found mine. "Aye?"

"Yes." I nodded, serious. "I'm going to miss you in my bed, Caleb Scott. And in a hotel bed. And against the wall. And in the shower."

He grinned, wicked and full of want. "Don't miss me just yet. We've still got tonight."

Nineteen

SIX WEEKS LATER

can't believe you dragged me to Faneuil Hall on my day off," Harper grumbled after the third tourist in five minutes bumped into her.

I hid a smile, heading toward my target. "It's raining, it's miserable, and you know what that means."

"Clam chowder, yeah, yeah."

"Not just any clam chowder. The best clam chowder."

"That's a matter of opinion."

"Hey, don't let the fact that it's produced in a heavily populated tourist area sway your judgment." I threw her a mock look of annoyance as we wandered into the Irish pub I'd been heading for since the moment I stepped out of my apartment that morning. "This right here is the best clam *chowdah* in Boston."

"Yeah, apparently everyone else thinks so too." Harper gestured to the busy pub.

Damn.

No seats.

Disappointment hit me much harder than it should have considering this quest was merely about food. But lately, when anything went marginally wrong, I seemed to take it dramatically badly. "Oh man!"

"We're just leaving." A woman sitting at the bar called to us, her accent drawing my attention.

"Aye, ye can have oor stools," the man next to her said as we slowly made our way over.

Scottish.

A pang of longing hit me dead center of my chest and then spread out like a burn across the entire area.

"Hey, thanks," Harper said as we watched them pull on their jackets and get up off the stools.

"No problem. The clam chowder is bloody amazing." The woman gave us a cheery smile.

"You're from Scotland?"

She nodded. "Aye. Glasgow. Just here on a wee anniversary trip."

"Oh?" I wanted her to keep talking. "How long have you been married?"

"Thirty years," her husband announced proudly, either because it was an impressive amount of time or because he'd actually remembered.

"Wow." Harper shared a wide-eyed look with me. "Uh, congrats. That is awesome."

"Yeah, congratulations."

"Oh, thank ye," they said in unison.

"Here ye go." The woman stepped aside, patting the stool at the bar. "Enjoy."

Disappointment flooded me anew to realize they were leaving. "Oh, okay. Have a wonderful trip."

"Thank ye," they said as they left.

Harper practically had to haul me onto a stool before someone else could take it, because I was busy staring after the Scottish couple, pining.

It had been six weeks since I'd heard the accent.

Six weeks since I'd heard his voice.

*W*ell, I best be off," Caleb said suddenly.

We were lying in my bed, staring up at the ceiling, taking time to catch our breaths after enjoying a couple of rounds of our usual epic sex. There had been no soft kisses or sweet touches this time, as if we were both mindful that we had to keep this as it should be or it might feel like a tender good-bye.

"Yeah," I answered, even though there was still a part of me that wanted to reach across the bed and ask him to stay. I squashed that part, reminding myself exactly why that was a bad idea. Plus, I didn't really know Caleb. Not well enough to feel any real kind of attachment.

Liar.

The ache in my chest as he got out of bed and began to dress was entirely misplaced and it was making me angry.

He finally looked at me once he was done lacing his boots. His expression revealed nothing of his emotions. "I'll call you, then, when I visit again?"

"Sure. I'd like that."

Caleb suddenly frowned, hesitating, seeming almost unsure. Then finally he bent over, putting his hands to the mattress, and he kissed me. It was soft, sweet. Filled with affection.

And I had to force away the sudden burn of tears in the back of my eyes.

He brushed his mouth over mine one last time and then pulled back to stare into my eyes. I couldn't read his searching gaze, enigmatic as always. I did my best to keep my expression neutral.

"Good-bye, Ava," he said, his voice low and hoarse.

Once more I fought those goddamn tears, masking them with a smile I hoped was both cheeky and affectionate. "Bye, my Bastard Scot."

He grinned, kissed the tip of my nose, and pushed away from the bed. I made to move, to see him out, but he waved me back down. "Stay. Sleep. You're up early."

Thinking he was probably right, I lowered my back to the bed. "Safe travels."

He nodded, reached down to switch off my bedside lamp, and then I watched the shadow of his figure leave my bedroom.

There was a minute of no noise and then I heard my apartment door shut with a loud click that told me he'd put the lock (or the snib, as he so cutely called it) on.

I tried to sleep knowing it was too early to get up.

However, my mind wouldn't let me. Instead it just kept replaying every moment with Caleb Scott over and over again. Every kiss, every wicked smile, and the fierce tenderness in his gaze when I told him about Nick and Gem.

Even though I felt betrayed by the tears, like my heart was a traitor to my mind, I couldn't stop myself from crying. That night my heart won a battle.

But when my alarm went off and I got up to get ready for my trip to Nantucket, my mind sought control again and was triumphant.

Caleb Scott was just a fun memory and he'd remain that way. There was no way I would make our dalliance out to be more than it was. Resolved, ignoring the disquiet and unease that sat in the pit of my stomach, I strolled out into my living area to make coffee and was startled at the sight of what had been placed next to the coffee machine.

There was a velvet box sitting next to it, along with a note. My hands shook as I reached for the note first.

In Caleb's big, masculine scrawl were the words:

You deserve only good memories. Caleb.

Heart pounding, I dropped the note and picked up the velvet box. Prying it open, I let out a little gasp at the item that sparkled and winked under my kitchen lights. Lying on black velvet was the most beautiful diamond tennis bracelet. The one Nick had given me was demure, the diamonds small in a traditional square-cut claw. Caleb's platinum tennis bracelet was more modern, with larger round-cut diamonds. Okay, wow.

I could barely breathe, I was so overwhelmed by the gift. I picked up his note again.

You deserve only good memories. Caleb.

I couldn't believe he remembered the detail about that damn tennis bracelet. It was so thoughtful. So romantic.

So not what we were.

It didn't make sense.

I turned, slumping back against my counter as I tried to interpret what the gift meant.

And then something horrible occurred to me.

What if this was like . . . payment? What if Caleb was basically saying, Hey, thanks for the great sex—have some diamonds on me? *I glowered down at the bracelet. That bastard.*

"Argh." I huffed. That didn't seem like Caleb either.

". . . I genuinely like you, and I dinnae mind us having a friendship between us if you dinnae. As long as we both know that is all this is."

The memory of his words came flooding back.

". . . when we talked about being friends, we both meant that too. We can handle it. So I made up my mind that you're my friend, Ava. And I'm worried about my friend."

I was Caleb's friend. He really meant that. I looked down at the bracelet and decided that was what I'd see in this expensive gift. A friend giving me something beautiful to replace a bad memory.

And just like that, my mind had to battle harder than ever to win the war my heart wanted to wage.

"Babe. Ava, babe." Harper shoved me suddenly and I had to grip on to the bar in front of me to keep myself on the stool.

I shot her a dirty look and she returned it with a worried one of her own. "The guy has been asking you for your order for about five minutes." She gestured in front of us, where a bartender stood, staring back at me in what I could only guess was impatient amusement. "Well?"

"You could have ordered for me." I turned to the bartender. "Clam chowder, please."

He disappeared, leaving us to sit in silence, surrounded by the noisy chatter of the crowded bar.

"It was the accent, wasn't it?" Harper said. "Made you think of him."

I glanced down at the bracelet on my wrist. "It's bound to, right?" I shrugged, like it was no big deal.

"Sure, of course. But I don't think it's the first time you've thought of the guy in the six weeks since he left. I pretty much know you're thinking about him all the time."

My eyebrows drew together. "Not all the time. And when I do, it's just because I miss the sex."

"Why are you lying to yourself?"

We stared at each other, my best friend's expression fierce with irritation. I studied her face and saw the one person—other than my uncle—who I could trust. "Because . . . I don't want to get hurt again."

Harper took a minute to process that, and then her gaze softened with understanding. "Okay."

"Okay?"

"Okay."

I reached over and squeezed her hand in gratitude and then let it go to mutter sardonically, "So how 'bout them Red Sox?"

She chuckled and nudged me with her shoulder. "I have a better awkward-conversation breaker than that."

"Yeah?"

"Yeah. I'm thinking about breaking up with Vince."

I let out a little sound of surprise and Harper gave me a wobbly smile. "I think he's taking drugs."

"Oh no."

"I'm not one hundred percent sure, because I know he's never high when he's with me. That's a fact. I know what high looks like. But I know his band members are into recreational drug use and he acts cagey sometimes, like he's hiding something. I can't put up with that crap, Ava." She shook her head, and I saw tears glisten in her eyes.

"I'm so sorry, Harper."

She laughed but the sound was hollow. "I knew it was too good to be true."

"You don't know for sure, though, right?"

"I'm confronting him tonight. I can tell when someone is lying, so one way or another I'll know the truth."

"Why didn't you say anything about this sooner?"

"I was . . . I'm irritated that I've fallen for a guy who, if my suspicions prove correct, is not at all who I thought he was. I'm pissed that I've told him things about myself—personal, private things. And I'm . . . ashamed that I really, really want to wish the truth away and bury my head in the sand." She stared at the bar counter, her jaw locked with gritted teeth as she refused to meet my eyes.

"Hey." I placed a comforting hand on her small shoulder. "One, you don't know it's the truth just yet. And two, even if it is, you have nothing to be ashamed of. We can't help who we fall for, but we are in control of our actions. Don't blame yourself for caring about Vince, Harp. He's not a bad guy. But if he's taking drugs, he's a good guy into bad things, and you know what you need to do in that situation."

She covered my hand with hers and looked up at me, tears in her beautiful gray-blue eyes. "You won't judge me for being a typical girl with a broken heart?"

"You already know the answer to that."

Her lips trembled. "I really, really want to be wrong."

Hurting for her, I had to blink back my own tears. "I really, really hope you are."

"Clam chowdah!" The bartender rudely burst into our moment by dumping two big bowls in front of us.

Harper's lips twitched and that set me off.

We both burst into laughter, hysterical, rib-hurting laughter, over our bowls of clam chowder. Not because the interruption was really that funny, but because we both needed to laugh.

It was either that or cry.

Twenty

The month of May was one of my favorites in Boston. The weather began to turn a little warmer, to pleasant mid-sixties during the day, so I could walk around without a jacket. And so far the weather, other than the rainfall last weekend, had been sunny and bright, like the city was trying to lift its inhabitants' spirits.

However, at night the temperatures dropped to upper forties. So while I was enjoying a beautiful Wednesday afternoon on a long lunch date with a man Stella had set me up with, I was surprised to get a text from Patrice inviting me onto her boat on Saturday night.

She was having a boat party.

That was going to be a chilly event.

"Everything okay?"

I stopped licking my ice cream and glanced up from my phone.

Leo Morgan was licking his own ice cream and staring at me quizzically. The sight should have really done more to me in my excitable areas. After Caleb left, Stella took the fact that I'd been seeing him as a green light to start setting me up again. When she first mentioned Leo Morgan, an acquaintance's son who was getting back into the dating game after the end of a youthful marriage, I'd said no. Stella didn't take no for an answer. She started telling me about how he was a successful corporate lawyer, about all the charities he worked with, and blah blah blah. It was only when she finally shoved his photo in my face and I saw him that I paused. He looked awfully young.

Turned out Leo Morgan was a very, very handsome twenty-six-year-old.

And I started to rethink the idea.

Not out of shallowness, but pragmatism.

Perhaps the only way to get over Caleb was to get under someone new. Yet I didn't want to get into a relationship with any man. A casual arrangement, however, didn't sound like such a bad plan. And before I saw Leo's photo, I knew he was a divorcé—which meant he was way too capable of commitment—a lawyer, and a philanthropist. Something about him didn't say casual date. But the cheeky twinkle in his eye and the fact that he was only twenty-six made me wonder. Maybe Leo Morgan got married too young and maybe Leo Morgan would like something that was mere fun this time around.

Moreover, he was way more my type than Caleb ever was. He had thick, light brown hair that was brushed back off his forehead in a natural silky wave, glittering dark eyes a woman could drown in, beautiful lips, a perfect nose, and an angular jaw. He was about six feet tall with a possible swimmer's build underneath his shirt, tie, and suit pants. His shirtsleeves were currently rolled up to his elbows, revealing corded forearms and more of that tan skin. No tattoos in sight.

He would have been almost too perfect if it weren't for his smile. Although he had the most beautiful, straight, gleaming white teeth, there was a crookedness to his smile that chipped the perfection. It was a boyish, wicked smile that suggested that, underneath his good intentions, he was actually up to no good.

A man that hot, licking ice cream, should have affected me more than it did. I definitely felt a fizzle of something. But there was no great, rolling wave of lust that a certain other person managed to elicit. Damn him.

But I wasn't giving up on the idea of casual sex with this guy. If anything, I was more determined than ever to find someone who could make sex with Caleb look like a clumsy fumble in the dark.

Presently I was walking through the Public Garden with a very cute man on our lunch break, hoping he could still be that one. I really liked that Leo was happy to meet this way for the first time. Casual, relaxed, no pressure.

"Uh—" I glanced back at the text from Patrice.

Patrice: Darling, having party on the boat this Saturday. Anniversary thing. Will call to explain later. Just wanted you to RSVP now. Kisses.

"A friend is having a party on a boat," I explained as I quickly typed an RSVP reply with one hand while trying to lick my melting ice cream and talk at the same time. "That's going to be cold."

He chuckled. "Will anyone turn up?"

To a Danby event? Yes. "Yeah. And she knows it. She's probably doing it to deliberately torture us."

Leo grinned. "She sounds fun."

"She is." I tucked my phone back in my suit jacket pocket. I'd unbuttoned it and rolled my own sleeves up, but I was still too hot.

"So . . ." He threw me that boyish smile of his. "How do you think this is going?"

Quite well, actually. So far we'd talked about work and living in Boston. We were both out-of-towners who had been adopted by the city, but we seemed to share a similar love for it.

Still, I decided to be honest. "Good, but—"

"Damn, there's a but?" He stopped, having finished off his ice cream, and gestured to me. "Hit me with it. It's the hair, isn't it? It's too perfect."

I laughed, shaking my head.

Leo gave me a wide, comical grimace and pointed to his teeth. "These?"

Giggling now at his antics, I shook my head again.

"Hmm. Stella told you I play One Direction when my boss's kid visits the office, didn't she? It's just for my boss's kid." He raised his hands defensively. "I don't secretly listen to them when I'm soaking in the tub with a glass of wine after a long, hard day. That definitely . . . doesn't happen."

Grinning so hard, my cheeks were hurting, I shook my head again. "None of the above. All of which is hugely endearing."

Leo crossed his arms over his chest, his expression turning mildly more serious. "Okay. Honestly, hit me with it."

I sucked in a breath and exhaled it slowly. "I don't know how to say this without coming across as someone I'm not. I'm not someone who sleeps around. At all. I assure you." I winced. This was coming out wrong. "But I, um . . . I'm not looking for anything serious right now. If this"—I gestured between us—"was to go any further after today it would have to be totally casual."

He stared at me with a little frown line between his brows, and for so long I wondered anxiously if he now did think I was promiscuous. Oh God.

Then he dropped his arms to place his hands on his hips and he grinned. "Are you for real?"

"I take it that means you're okay with casual?"

"Ava," he said, starting to walk again, approaching Lagoon Bridge. "I got married when I was twenty-one years old. All was great for the first year, and then the next three years were an absolute hell of disappointed expectations, pressure, misery, and resentment. The last year of divorce proceedings hasn't exactly been a picnic either. A casual relationship with a beautiful, sexy, smart woman who laughs at my jokes sounds like heaven right now."

Although relieved to find us on the exact same page, I was curious about something. "Stella gave me the impression you were looking for your next big romance—that's why I was reluctant to meet you."

He shook his head, smiling wryly. "Stella is friends with my mother. And my mother is determined to have grandchildren. She forgets that I'm only twenty-six and have time for that stuff. Anyway, she's the one filling Stella's head, and I'm sure other would-be matchmakers' heads, with this idea that I'm looking for wife number two."

"But you're not."

He stopped on the middle of the bridge and leaned his elbows on the railing, turning his head to look at me. I settled next to him, feeling his eyes move over me in a way he'd been too polite to allow before. Soon, possibly, Leo Morgan could make me forget about my Bastard Scot. And why shouldn't he? He was far more personable than Caleb.

"I'm definitely not. And obviously you're not looking for a husband. Since this is going to be casual, I'm not going to ask why. I'm curious"—he flashed me a grin—"but I won't ask."

I nodded in approval. "You might actually be good at this casual thing."

"Yet . . . it's not something you do a lot?" He raised an eyebrow. At my pointed look, he chuckled. "Hey, I said I was curious."

I merely shrugged, my gaze drifting over to the couple in a swan boat as it neared the bridge. "It wasn't something I thought much about. I didn't want anything serious, so I didn't date. Then, a while back, I kind of accidentally fell into something casual. It worked for me."

"But it ended?"

"It was very short-lived."

"And you and I, if we end up having the right chemistry . . . would there be expectations for duration? The relationship," he hurried to add. "Not the sex. I can confirm that I have fantastic endurance."

I burst out laughing at his roguishness. This could work. So far, I liked him. He made me laugh. He gave me the tingle. And we were on the same page. "That's the beauty of a casual relationship. One of us can end it at any time without any hurt feelings."

"This feels surreal," Leo suddenly said. "I've just met you and we're standing on a bridge, discussing casual sex and the rules. I did not expect that this would be my afternoon while I was brushing my teeth this morning."

Realizing it was weird and hoping it wasn't sleazy, I bit my lip. "I'm not suggesting we jump into anything. I thought we could just go on a few casual dates, see if we like each other enough to enjoy the other benefits of a casual relationship."

"I got you," he reassured me. "You don't cross me as the type of woman who has sex with a guy she met an hour ago."

No, not an hour ago.

"I'm still trying to figure out if you're real." He reached out and gently pinched my arm, making me laugh and smack his hand away. "Okay, you're real."

I shimmied a little closer to him in appreciation of his playfulness and saw his eyes darken as our gazes locked. Tension immediately fell between us and a rush of exultation swooped over me. There was definite chemistry here. And that meant, *Good-bye, Caleb Scott.* No longer would the bastard plague my thoughts and inspire such longing.

"Sunday?" I asked softly. "Casual dinner?"

Leo's eyes dropped to my mouth. "Not Saturday, right, because that's a typical date night."

"And I have my chilly boat party."

"Right." He reluctantly dragged his eyes up to mine. "Sunday. Sounds good."

I offered him a grin. "Great."

"Am I allowed to compliment you?"

It was an adorable question. "Yes."

"Then can I just say you are the most beautiful woman I've ever met and I feel like the luckiest son of a bitch in Boston right now."

It was a grand compliment. A lovely one. However, I couldn't tell this guy that I was inured to compliments on my physical appearance. That they made me uncomfortable. Instead, I lowered my gaze, as though he'd embarrassed me, and thanked him.

"Modest too. You are perfect."

My eyes flashed back to his. "No one's perfect. That's the beauty of a casual relationship. We don't have to be."

Leo's expression sobered as he processed what I'd said. Then he nodded and said, in the most serious tone he'd used since we'd met, "Then I think this is definitely what I've been looking for."

Twenty-one

For Patrice and Danby, the boat party on Saturday evening was an impromptu event, just for the hell of it, to celebrate life and good times with their nearest and dearest friends.

For me, the party was a celebration of moving forward. I'd finally finished Roxanne Sutton's summerhouse project, much to my relief. Moreover, tomorrow would be the next step in putting Caleb Scott behind me. Leo had texted to tell me he'd booked us a table at a little Italian place in Cambridge. I thought it was a great choice because we were less likely to be spotted in Cambridge, and neither of us wanted to draw attention to the fact that we were on a date and give people the wrong idea. I'd told Stella that we'd decided not to pursue each other, much to her disappointment.

In general, I was feeling good. Whatever lingering melancholy I might have felt, I buried it.

"I can't believe you let me come to this party alone," I said to Harper, clutching my cell to my ear as the taxi let me out at the marina.

"I'm sorry. We're busy."

She didn't sound sorry, and renewed uneasiness niggled me at whom she was busy with. "You're sure about this?"

Harper gave me an irritable sigh. "I told you I believed him when he said he doesn't need the drugs. It was recreational. He knows how I feel and he loves me enough to not touch the stuff."

I shook my head, realizing love did really make you crazy, insensible, and irrational if it could do this to my friend. "I'm worried about you."

"Don't be. Look, I need to go."

"Harper—"

But she'd already hung up on me.

Great.

By the time I found Patrice's boat on the marina (I just followed the loud chatter and music), I was already feeling the chill in my little red dress, and I was sullen over the situation with Harper. Not exactly in the party spirit. All I'd brought with me was a silk wrap, a decision I was now regretting as security took my name before letting me on the boat. I ventured onto the unsheltered area of the lower deck, waving away a waiter's offer of champagne. There were a few people lingering, but I could hear from the level of noise above me that the party was taking place on the two upper decks. As I considered getting off the boat to find a restroom, my savior arrived in the shape of Patrice Danby herself.

"Darling, there you are." She floated down the spiral staircase from the upper deck. She wore an elegant pantsuit, and I envied her jacket. She grabbed my shoulders and kissed both my cheeks. "Stunning as always. Come, come. There's someone I want you to meet."

"Patrice—" I hadn't even had the chance to say hello yet. "I . . . um . . . do you think I could use your restroom?"

"Oh, no need to look embarrassed, darling. I have a small bladder too." She reached into her suit pocket and pulled out a key card. "It opens the master bedroom suite." She pointed to the sliding doors that led inside before handing the card to me. "Meet me on the top deck when you're done."

I thanked her and slipped inside the lower deck, the sounds of her politely moving the guests who were lingering there back upstairs fading as I closed the door behind me.

There was no one inside, because obviously it was out of bounds for the party. Although I doubted once people started getting drunk that they'd care to respect anyone's privacy. I passed through the small living room and bar area, decked out in rich walnuts and expensive leathers and plush fabrics, marveling at the fact that I had a friend who owned a luxury yacht. Beside the wall where a large flat-screen television was mounted was a narrow door with a key card lock. I slipped the card into it, watching the red light turn green, and pushed down on the handle.

I gasped as I stepped inside.

As an interior designer, I'd seen beautiful and awe-inspiring homes. I'd never designed the interior of a boat, however, and had no idea one could look this opulent. Standing on thick-pile carpet, I gazed around at the semicircular room. The walls were made of glass, with two sets of French doors on either side. The only part of the wall that wasn't glass was the nose of the semicircle, directly across from a magnificent super-king-sized bed. That wall was a frame for a beautiful gas fire that was currently lit, despite the fact that there was no one in here. There were two gorgeous velvet armchairs on either side of it.

Beyond, through the glare of the light against the glass, I could see the control deck. As I stood there gaping at such luxury, the blinds suddenly started to lower over all the windows, startling me. Confused, I looked around and found a familiar panel on the wall near the door.

The blinds were on a timer. I'd had a similar system fitted into Patrice's guesthouse. As the blinds lowered, the lighting in the room also dimmed, giving it a romantic, intimate vibe. Very nice.

Remembering my current needs, I stopped ogling and strode

toward the open doorway to my left that led into a small, Roman-esque marble bathroom. When I let myself out of the room, making sure it was locked behind me, I hurried to make it onto the upper deck to give Patrice her key card back.

I didn't get the chance, however. As soon as I stepped up onto the deck crowded with guests, waitstaff, a bar, buffet, and a small orchestra, the hostess zeroed in on me. "Come, come. I have a sur-prise." She grabbed my hand, pulling me and gently pushing people out of her way as she moved us through the crowd.

God, it was breezy up here. I threw people apologetic smiles as we bumped them out of our way and noted that many women were either huddled into their date's sides or had their wraps practically covering their entire upper body.

Only Patrice would get people out on a yacht in May.

"The fireworks are about to start and I want you to see your sur-prise first," Patrice called back to me. "Here you go." She tugged me harder, almost swinging me around, so that I tottered on my high heels and stumbled right into my surprise.

My surprise gripped hold of my biceps to steady me and the breath was expelled from my body.

I didn't know what hit me first.

The familiar cologne, the heat that was all his, or the unforget-table feel of his large hands on my body.

"Caleb?"

He stared down at me, his expression almost frighteningly fierce; then his grip tightened to near bruising. My first thought was that he'd recently shaved his short beard, because it was now merely stubble.

My second thought, whatever it might have been, was inter-rupted by an intense punch of physical longing deep in my belly as I took in his familiar blue eyes and the way his suit stretched over his biceps as he held me. He always looked handsome but kind of rough and uncivilized in a suit. It was so sexy it was almost unbearable to look at him.

I did have thoughts, questions. *Why is he here? How long is he here for?*

But those weren't a priority.

Right then my desires were the priority. The need to feel his skin against mine, to taste his lips, to touch him, to have him touch me, felt like a basic, necessary requirement to breathe.

My face was level with his strong chest as I leaned into him. As always, just standing there, he made me feel small, fragile, feminine, and I wondered how I could have possibly thought anyone could ever make me feel the way he made me feel.

I suspected I was glaring at him in a mixture of frustration, resentment, and utter longing. He glowered right back at me.

Vaguely, I was aware of Patrice excusing herself, but everything was muted around us. The music, the people. And I no longer felt the chill, because a fire had erupted inside of me.

Without saying a word, I reached up and took one of his hands off my bicep and curled mine around it. I turned, his hand dropping from my other arm. He didn't let go of my hand as I began to slowly—far more sedately than I inwardly felt—lead him through the crowd of the upper deck.

My hand tightened on his and he squeezed it back as I tentatively walked down the spiral staircase in my heels. There was no one on the lower deck. I led him to the patio doors, inside the small living space, to the master bedroom.

I didn't consider my friend's privacy, or how irresponsible I was acting. In that moment I was selfishly aware of only two things.

Caleb Scott.

And my lust for him.

I took out Patrice's key card and led us into the private master bedroom. I dropped Caleb's hand to turn to face him as he closed and locked the door behind us.

We stared at each other a moment, my chest rising and falling visibly as I struggled to catch my breath.

I opened my mouth to say something, although I wasn't sure what, and instead let out a little gasp as I found myself jerked against him.

He immediately picked me up like I weighed nothing and I wrapped my legs around his waist, my dress riding up, as he spun and held me up against the wall. His mouth claimed mine and I sighed into him in what I could only name utter relief.

Our harsh breathing filled the bedroom as he broke the greedy kiss to stare at me in longing that matched my own.

My breath stuttered as his fingers slipped beneath my underwear. Caleb's eyes darkened at finding me so aroused, his features growing taut with restraint . . . and then whatever control he'd exerted over himself snapped.

"Inside my jacket. Wallet," he demanded.

I slipped my hand under his lapel and found the wallet tucked in the inside pocket. My hands shook as I withdrew it and removed a condom. I put his wallet back as I tore the condom wrapper open with my teeth. Caleb took it from me impatiently.

He unzipped his trousers and I gasped at the heat of him throbbing between my legs before I felt him lean all of his body weight against me to hold me against the door. My thighs tightened around his hips as he used both hands to roll on the condom. Then he had a hand back under my ass, holding me up, as his other one slid up my waist to rest possessively over my right breast. I watched his gaze turn triumphant as he nudged aside my underwear and thrust into me. The slight discomfort I felt dissipated, replaced with pleasure that tingled down my spine, through my legs, rippling in my belly as he rocked inside me.

Our breaths puffed against each other's lips and I gripped his waist, urging him closer, harder. It was as though I couldn't get him deep enough, close enough. As though I needed him to lock some piece of me back into place, a piece of me I'd lost when he left.

As if Caleb felt my urgency, or shared it, he picked up his pace. My head flew back against the door but only for seconds before his hand slid behind my nape and forced it back up.

His eyes blazed into mine and without saying a word I understood his demand.

Look at me.

See me.

This is us. No one else.

I nodded.

Caleb's hold on me tightened and he slammed his hips against mine.

It was hard, fast, desperate.

Six weeks without him felt like an eternity and it barely took any time for the tension inside of me to tighten to the breaking point. With one more hard drive, Caleb shattered me.

A cry—almost a scream—tore out of me as wave after wave of deep, hard pleasure rolled through me. His long, guttural groan sounded in my ear and his grip on my thigh tightened to biting and painful as he found his own release.

Caleb held me pinned against the door as we both tried to catch our breath. I felt every inch of him inside me, on me. The familiar smell of his cologne flooded through me and almost brought tears of sweet relief to my eyes.

My throat was tight with emotion I did not want to identify.

"It's not enough," Caleb said, lifting his head to look at me. I didn't give him my eyes this time, afraid of what he'd find in them. Thankfully, he let me have my privacy. "We need tae get out of here. I need you again."

This brought my gaze up. "I have questions."

"Aye, I'm sure you do. But I doubt you want tae get caught in here."

Remembering what we'd just done in my friend's private bedroom, I flushed. "Right. Well . . . you better let me down."

"Pity," he murmured.

We had exchanged very few words by the time we left Patrice's party. Seeing my embarrassment at the idea of handing Patrice her room key back after our obvious absence, Caleb told me to wait on the lower deck while he returned it to her and made our excuses.

After a quiet cab ride to my apartment, I stared at the big Scotsman sitting on my small sofa, his suit jacket strewn across the back of it, with a coffee in his hand. I couldn't believe how much I wanted to crawl all over him again. But there were questions to be asked and answers to be had.

"You want tae know what I'm doing back in Boston?" he said, staring up at me from under his lids in a way that told me he'd rather be rolling around in bed right now too.

Somehow I'd forgotten, in his absence, how intense our sexual connection was. I'd only ever read about this kind of attraction in books and seen it in movies. But here it was. Real. And it had an unhappy side effect of making me confuse lust for something else.

Or did it?

I couldn't stop staring at him and it wasn't just because I wanted to wrap my body around his.

I'd missed him.

I'd missed that sardonic smirk, his fierceness, his surprising gentleness, his honesty. He didn't say a lot, but it made you pay attention when he did, and, moreover, most everything he said made sense. There was a blunt kindness to Caleb that I appreciated and respected. He wasn't perfect—definitely not. Because there was also a blunt meanness to him too. He could be rude and abrupt and sometimes cuttingly honest. In saying that, I knew this wasn't infatuation. When you were infatuated with someone, you failed to see their imperfections. When it was more than a fixation, you still cared about them in spite of their flaws. You saw past their flaws.

I saw past Caleb's faults.

I'd never been around a man who at once made me feel emotionally secure and insecure. I would never have to guess how Caleb felt about me, because he was up front about that, no matter if his feelings disappointed me or, worse, had the ability to hurt me. And I would never have to guess if Caleb listened to me when I spoke, because I knew with one hundred percent certainty that he did listen to me. He didn't always agree with me, but he always listened.

I liked him. A lot.

Tell him to leave, Ava, I suddenly thought to myself, as goose bumps prickled across the tops of my shoulders, as though my body sensed danger.

Yet I couldn't open my mouth to tell him to leave, even though somehow, despite what Nick had put me through, I found myself back here again with Caleb. With my heart making too much ground against the battle with my mind.

"You're staring," he murmured.

"You're staring too."

Caleb's mouth curved into that smirk I loved and loathed so much and he gave me a little nod of acquiescence. "True."

Deciding I almost looked combative standing over him, I settled down on the sofa opposite him with my coffee and tucked my feet under me. "So why *are* you in Boston?"

"They offered me the CFO position in the Boston office."

I'm sure I didn't do a very good job of hiding my astonishment, but I hoped like hell I hid the awful rush of hope that swooped through me. "The guy that got fired? They offered you his job?"

"Aye. Almost as soon as I left Boston. They weren't impressed with the other candidates and I won their trust during my time here."

Ignoring the delighted butterflies fluttering around my belly and how confusing they were, I was glad that my voice sounded so calm, neutral when I replied, "And you said yes?"

"The North American division is the company's biggest division, Ava. The CFO position here is a far more complicated job and as such they are offering double the wage I get back in Glasgow. It may sound like the same position, but it's a promotion. A massive promotion and I couldn't turn down this opportunity."

"Your family?" How would a family that had already lost one son feel about another moving so far away?

Caleb lowered his gaze to the floor. "Aye, I'll miss them. But I'll be back and forth for work a lot, so I'll get tae see them. Plus, they all want tae visit. My brother Jamie's here already. He's planning tae stay with me awhile, do some new work here."

Jamie was the social media artist. I'd checked him out online. He shared no pictures of himself, just his work, and it was pretty impressive. I could see why he was so successful. His aesthetic was just different enough to catch the eye, but had a wide commercial appeal. He was a mixed-media artist and he did a lot of semiabstract portraits and landscapes.

I began to wonder if I'd get to meet Caleb's brother and I immediately threw the thought away because it was hazardous thinking. It was overtaken, however, by an even more perilous thought.

Or feeling, rather.

A prickle of hurt.

"You've known you were coming back for weeks?"

A person unfamiliar with Caleb Scott might think he was unaffected by my question or the slight accusatory tone to it, but I was starting to know him. I recognized the abruptly blank expression for what it was.

Irritation.

Still, I couldn't help but push, knowing he'd be honest, even if I didn't like what he had to say. "You didn't tell me because you weren't sure you wanted to start things back up again?"

He shifted in his seat and drank the rest of his coffee before finally meeting my eyes.

My heart had started to race, wondering when I had become such a masochist, daring a man who could hurt me to be his usual bitingly honest self.

"There wasn't much time tae tell you. And anyway, I quite liked the idea of surprising you. And as it turned out"—his ice eyes turned smoky with want—"it was a brilliant idea."

Relief flooded me and I almost hated him a little for having this kind of control over my emotions and body. "It was a nice surprise."

"That's not how I would describe it. And I'm guessing from that reunion that you are more than happy tae start this up again."

The reminder of how I'd acted on the boat, that unleashing of my savage desire, almost made me blush. Instead, I offered him a self-deprecating laugh, feeling a weird mixture of fear and giddiness that I no longer had to miss and long for him. He was right here and he wasn't going anywhere anytime soon.

Quite abruptly Caleb stood up and reached over, taking the mug of coffee out of my hand. I watched him, my eyes lingering on his ass as he strode over to the kitchen. His shirt was hastily tucked back into his suit pants, the aforementioned spectacularly fitting ones showcasing that strong, muscular ass in a way that made my nipples pebble against my bra.

He put the coffee mugs into the sink and casually returned to me. But what he did next was anything but casual. He got on his knees before me and pulled my legs apart, forcing me to open them and sit up. His big hands smoothed over the tops of my thighs, shoving the hem of my dress up as he leaned into me, his gaze on my lips.

"I've missed this mouth," he whispered before capturing said mouth in a kiss that brought tears to my eyes. Tears I valiantly forced back.

It was the best kiss of my life.

It was like he was drinking from me, a deep, slow, mesmerizing kiss that made my heart slam hard against my chest. It was the kind of sweet, sexy, thorough kiss that confused a woman, because it said I meant more to him than just sex.

It said he hadn't just missed my mouth.

He'd missed me.

My hands caught his stubbled, prickly cheeks to hold him to me, not wanting that kiss to end anytime soon. Between the thorough seduction of his mouth and the way his thumbs caressed the inner skin of my thigh, I could feel my body melting, sweet and pliant and ready for him.

His right hand abandoned my thigh to take hold of my left wrist. I instinctively knew his intention was to put my hand where he wanted to feel it most because he was never shy in telling me what he needed from me, but he froze as his fingers brushed the bracelet on my wrist.

To my disappointment, he broke the delicious kiss to turn his head and look at the object.

Caleb's eyes lingered on the diamond tennis bracelet for a second or two before returning to meet mine. There was a rare smile in that cool gaze and it made my breath catch. "You like it, then?"

I jerked my eyes from his to the bracelet, afraid that if I continued to let him see me, he'd see *into* me. He'd see the truth that I was struggling so hard to deny now that he was back.

"Very much," I whispered.

I felt his gaze burning into my face, but I kept mine on the bracelet.

Then he was kissing me again, this time more fiercely, the tenderness gone, replaced by what felt like a need to claim. It was a ferocious, ravaging, possessive kiss, and while it thrilled me a little, it also pissed me off.

Did he think he'd won something by putting that bracelet on me? Did he think that I was his? Because no woman could truly belong to a man unless she knew he belonged to her in return. And Caleb Scott did not belong to me.

So I fought his claiming; I turned the kiss into a battle for supremacy.

I couldn't say which one of us tormented and teased the other more as our kisses, our caresses caught fire. All I knew as the night wore on was that I felt like a warrior equal to him, that I could set him ablaze just as much as he made me mindless with passion. In bed Caleb *did* belong to me and I belonged to him.

It was a battle with no clear winner. An impasse.

My feelings were most definitely engaged, but I buried that truth, knowing if I let those feelings reign it would lead to an inevitable war between us. A war for Caleb Scott's heart.

A war I knew I would lose.

Twenty-two

The sound of rustling woke me up, and when I felt the mattress bounce slightly, I sleepily rolled over and blinked my eyes open. After wincing against the morning light for a second or two, I finally took in the sight of Caleb pulling on his pants.

"Morning," I mumbled.

"Morning, babe," he replied quietly, giving me a little satisfied smile as he shrugged on his shirt.

As cognizance returned to me, I looked back at my alarm clock and saw it was only after nine in the morning. "You're leaving? You don't want breakfast?"

"I promised Jamie we'd do the tourist thing together today. I need tae get back."

I stopped myself from telling him how sweet it was that he wanted to spend time with his younger brother and instead just let myself think it. Evidence so far suggested Caleb was a good brother.

"Let's do dinner, though," he said, sitting down on the bed to put his socks and shoes back on.

About to agree, I stopped in my tracks as I remembered I had a date that night.

Leo.

Oh no.

Should I tell Caleb the truth or just—

He glanced over his shoulder in question and I knew I couldn't ever lie to him. Not even a little white lie. He wouldn't lie to me. "I, um . . . well, I actually have a date tonight." And I wasn't sure I wanted to cancel it. Yes, I was addicted to Caleb. But Leo was charming and a much safer option for my heart than Caleb Scott.

I wasn't sure I wanted to relinquish that option.

Caleb turned away to concentrate on lacing up his shoes. His voice was flat as he asked, "I'm going tae assume it's not serious yet."

I hated the dull quality of his tone. It made my skin prickle in warning. "You assume correctly. This is technically our first date tonight. Moreover, Leo and I agreed we're not looking for anything serious."

He looked over his shoulder again, one eyebrow impressively raised in what I'd soon realize was disbelief. "So you're telling me I'm not enough tae satisfy you?"

I rolled my eyes. "You know that's not true. But I wasn't expecting to see you so soon . . . or at all. I made plans and he's a nice guy."

"Quick work," Caleb muttered, standing up off the bed, his back to me again.

Realizing that the warning prickle I'd felt earlier was in recognition of Caleb's rapidly changing mood, I lay stunned. It was as if he was upset by this information. Which totally pissed me off, because I'd been trying for the last six weeks not to think about the plethora of women he'd probably already been with. And he was pissed I had a date? I seethed but kept it hidden behind a sardonic, "Are you saying you've been celibate for the last six weeks?"

I watched him, his back still to me, as he began to button his shirt. "I've been uprooting my life for the last six weeks. There wasn't time tae find a woman."

This surprised and warmed me. But I hated the relief that shuddered through me and I wanted him to turn around and look at me.

Instead he bit out, "I take it that means you've fucked other men while I've been gone?"

"Oh yeah." I glared at him. "Because that sounds like me."

His hands fell to his sides and still he didn't turn to me. Finally, after a few tense seconds of silence, he spoke in that dull, horribly flat tone again. "Well, call me when you have time tae fit me into your busy schedule." He turned ever so slightly, so I could just see his profile and the brittle clench of his jawline. "And if we're both now good tae see other people, we'll need tae get tested regularly."

And on that rather unromantic and alarming announcement, he walked out before I could respond.

I flinched at the sound of my apartment door slamming shut. It wouldn't surprise me to find the plasterwork cracked around the frame.

His last words reverberated around my head like a scream, and bitter tears filled my eyes. I didn't want Caleb sleeping with other women! But I would have no right to demand that of him if I started sleeping with Leo.

Suddenly I couldn't even picture the idea of having sex with Leo Morgan. How could I think he was even an option now that Caleb was back? I was in serious, serious denial about the state of my relationship with Caleb—I knew that. But after his cold reaction, I didn't think I was the only one.

Groaning, I got out of bed, pulled on a robe, and wandered out to the living room, where my shoes and underwear lay on the ground. My purse with my cell was on the coffee table. Not looking forward to the task ahead, I found Leo's number and called him.

T he compulsion to speak to Caleb, to tell him I had no intention of sleeping with anyone but him in the foreseeable future, was too strong. Throughout the day, I attempted to distract myself from my mess of confused emotions. First I went for a long run. Then I texted Harper to see if she was free, but she was working since she hadn't worked Saturday night. With that option out the window, I grabbed my sketchbook and walked to the Public Garden. I hadn't had time to just relax and sketch in months.

Unlike Caleb's brother Jamie, I wasn't a painter, but I loved drawing. I'd been sketching the world around me since I was a kid, and one of my favorite things to do since moving to Boston was to find an empty bench in the gardens and lose myself in a subject. Sometimes it was the gardens themselves, but mostly I'd find a person or people who captured my attention and I'd draw them. Sometimes it was a loved-up couple whose closeness fascinated me, or a young woman sitting by the pond lost in thought. I liked to be able to soak up whatever emotion I found in them and bleed it back out through my pencil.

There was a small kind of accomplishment I enjoyed in being able to successfully transfer that emotion to the page. Plus, it relaxed me. When I was sketching, I didn't think about anything else.

Unfortunately, I just couldn't find a subject I felt like drawing. After an hour of wandering around, starting sketches only to scrap them minutes later, I gave up and went home.

Back at my apartment, I tried to read several different books, I cleaned the place from top to bottom, I did some grocery shopping, I cleared out clothes and shoes from my closet that I hadn't worn in a while to donate to Goodwill. Moreover, I searched the Internet looking for a lamp I had in mind for my latest project with a young divorcée who was using part of her settlement money to redesign her new apartment in Jamaica Plains.

Eventually I found the lamp.

I did not find peace of mind.

Which was probably why I shot off a message to Caleb before I could get control of the compulsion. I asked him if we could meet. Thankfully, before I could regret sending the message, Caleb responded with an address on Northern Avenue. The text was terse and he only gave me thirty minutes to get there. A cab could get me there in about ten, fifteen minutes depending on traffic, but I still had to throw something on and call a cab.

Even though I was the one who had requested the meet, I bristled at his demanding bossiness and texted him back that I would be there in forty-five minutes.

He didn't reply, so I assumed that was okay.

Throwing on the skinny jeans I liked so much along with a slouchy, off-the-shoulder sweater, I had just enough time to fix my makeup and hair before my cabdriver rang to let me know he was outside. I had stupid butterflies in my belly as I hurried out of the apartment.

It was clear to me that Caleb was pissed at the idea of me seeing other men, and I was definitely not amenable to him seeing other women. I didn't know what that meant for us, or if either of us really wanted to analyze it too much. Quite willing to bury my head in the sand and just keep enjoying my time with the brooding Scot, I could only hope that whatever Caleb was feeling didn't spook him out of *any* kind of relationship with me.

The address he'd given me was a luxury apartment complex by the water. It seemed to be made up entirely of glass, all the lights from neighboring buildings and traffic bouncing off it in the dark.

When I stepped inside, there was a woman at reception and a

security guy standing near a bank of elevators. The main lobby was huge, with two separate sitting areas on either side of the reception desk.

"Good evening. Can I help you?" The receptionist smiled at me.

My step faltered, wondering if Caleb had called down to let them know I'd be visiting him. I had to assume this was his new place and wondered just how much this was cutting into that nice new salary of his. "Um . . . hi. Ava Breevort visiting Mr. Scott in apartment 16A."

"Of course. Mr. Scott let us know you were on your way." She turned and pointed to the elevators. "Go right on up. Floor sixteen."

I nodded my thanks, smiled congenially at the security guy when he lifted his chin in greeting as I passed. The receptionist's voice could be heard behind me saying, "Mr. Scott, it's Angela at reception. Your guest is on her way up."

Hmm. Swanky indeed.

The whole place smelled new and shiny, and if memory served me correctly, these apartments had only come on the market a little while ago. Stella had been interested in landing the account for the interior decoration, but they'd gone with a firm in New York. If the reception area was anything to go by, with its rich woods, touches of marble, and muted, modern pieces of furniture brought to life with pops of bright colors in the soft furnishings, our competition had done a good job. It was the kind of comfortable, modern aesthetic that had a commercial appeal.

Thinking about the interior of the apartment building took my mind off telling Caleb I wanted to be exclusive friends with benefits. For about thirty seconds.

The butterflies returned in force as the elevator drew to a smooth halt on the sixteenth floor. *Ping* went the doors, opening out onto a bright, expansive hallway with shiny white floor tiles and soft blue walls. My heels squeaked annoyingly on the floor as I strolled down the hall, and I was grateful to come to a halt in the middle of it at the sight of the dark blue door on my left. Two brass numbers and a letter told me I'd found Caleb's apartment. That, and he'd left the door ajar for me.

I knocked and pushed it open, my eyes drinking in the space. To my left was the kitchen with an island. The cupboards were dark walnut with white-and-gray-marble countertops. The kitchen blended seamlessly against the walnut flooring that ran into the open-plan living space up ahead. From my position, frozen in the hall/kitchen, I could see a large gray corner suite and coffee table. But what really grabbed my attention was the floor-to-ceiling windows that made up the back wall. One of the windows was actually a door that led out onto a balcony that sat above the water. You could see Boston Harbor across the way.

Very nice.

To my right was a closed door, and up ahead to the left was another closed door.

There was no sign of Caleb.

"Hello?" I called. "Caleb?"

Two seconds later the door up ahead to the left opened and Caleb sauntered out. I was vaguely aware that he had emerged from a room with a bed in it, but only vaguely aware because he was walking toward me wearing nothing but a worn pair of jeans and a scowl.

"Did you fuck him?" he asked, his voice harsh as he came toward me. I took a wary step back, hitting the front door and inadvertently causing it to shut behind me.

The fact that he'd so easily intimidated me pissed me off. With a scowl, I pushed off the door and marched around him, giving him a wide berth. I felt his glare on my back as I strode into the living room. The sofa was facing a large flat-screen TV mounted on the wall opposite the windows. On the wall adjacent was an open door that revealed another bedroom. The wall opposite that, the one next to what I was now assuming was the master bedroom, since Caleb had emerged from it, had fitted floating shelves. They mostly contained books. Another surprise.

Ignoring his seething anger, I looked out over the water, envious of the view, before coming to a stop at the bookshelves. The man was a reader. From what I could tell, he enjoyed crime novels, thrillers, classic and modern sci-fi.

"Nice place," I finally said, turning toward him. He was standing in the middle of the room, still glaring at me. His greeting echoed in my head. *Did you fuck him?*

Why do you care?

I stifled a heavy sigh. "I didn't sleep with Leo. We didn't even go on a date. I called him just after you left to cancel. FYI, you're officially a Neanderthal."

The glare softened into a look of neutrality but not before I saw the flicker of something that revealed a truth that equal parts terrified and thrilled me.

I saw relief.

It was there in his eyes for just a second.

Moreover, I now knew Caleb well enough to know that he only ever slipped on that damn blank mask of his when he was determined to hide the depth of the emotions he was feeling. "I don't want to sleep with other people. I'd like whatever this is to be exclusive."

He didn't say a word.

He didn't have to.

One minute I was standing by his bookshelves; the next I was bent over the arm of his sofa, the breath knocked out of me as he fumbled for the zip on my jeans. As he yanked the jeans and underwear down my legs, cool air hitting me in all my vulnerable areas, I gasped, shocked by the deep, tugging wave of desire in my belly—I felt like I should have been upset instead of turned on.

"Caleb?" His name came out on a harsh breath that didn't sound like me. My heart rate had shot off into the stratosphere and with it my breathing.

I curled my fingers into the back of the sofa to keep me steady. The sound of his zipper lowering made me shudder in need, and then he gripped my hair in his fist to hold me, while his other hand caressed my ass.

His fingers trailed a teasing path down the curve of my bottom to between my legs, and my excitement escalated.

"I'm clean."

Understanding what he meant, I could only nod, too confused to be thinking completely clearly.

A mere second later he pushed into me and I cried out at the swift invasion. But as he moved in me, an uneasiness triumphed over my lust. We'd never had sex without a condom, but we'd had sex like this before and I'd enjoyed it. Yet right then, not being able to see his face—being faceless to him—felt wrong. It felt like he was making a point to cover up his earlier jealousy.

It felt like he was telling me I was just a body.

And all the heat leaked out of me.

Tears pricked my eyes before I could stop them.

It shouldn't have shocked me that Caleb sensed the change in me immediately, but it did. I suspected most guys would have been too blinded by their own pleasure-seeking to notice. Instead he was so attuned to me, he knew instantly the moment I stopped enjoying myself. He withdrew from me completely. He let go of my hair to grip my hips with both hands. "Ava?"

I shook my head, afraid if I spoke I'd start to cry.

"Shit," he bit out. "Ava?"

When I continued to remain silent, he cursed again, and then I heard the sound of the zipper on his jeans. This was followed by him inexplicably removing my shoes and then my jeans and underwear from around my ankles.

I glanced down over my shoulder to protest, but the words were halted when he suddenly stood and swung me up into his arms. Instinctively, I wrapped my arms around his neck, but I couldn't look at him. I felt his eyes on my face and I wondered if he could feel how fast my heart was beating. Wearing nothing but my sweater, I found myself carried into the large master bedroom, noting wearily that the floor-to-ceiling windows continued in here, as did the balcony.

"Caleb," I whispered.

He laid me gently on the bed but didn't give me space. At all. He settled over me, between my legs, his body braced above me by his hands at either side of my head. And he frowned down at me, his eyes studying me with an intensity that made me breathless.

"What just happened? Was it because I didn't want tae wear a condom? You're on the pill, right? I've seen you take it."

Determined to be as honest as I could with him while still protecting myself, I attempted to keep the hurt out of my voice as I replied, "No. I mean, yes, I'm on the pill, but it's not about the condom or lack thereof. It just . . . that felt a little too much like sex between strangers."

His brows pulled together. "Explain."

"I was never going to overanalyze the fact that you didn't want me sleeping with Leo. Okay. You don't like to share. Great. Got it. I don't like to share either—that's why I called it off with Leo. But—" I sucked in a breath, forcing the tears away, the emotion, so he wouldn't know how much he could toy with my feelings. "That didn't feel like how it normally feels. It felt like you were proving a point. Like . . . I could be anybody. That I was just a body to use."

Anger suffused his features. Caleb was Pissed with a capital *P*. I wanted to sink into the mattress to melt out of his sight range.

"No matter what is going on between us," he bit out, "I would never treat you like you were just a body to be used."

I flinched. "Then what was that out there? Why did it feel different?"

Caleb pushed up off me so that he was kneeling between my spread legs and scrubbed his hands over his beard, letting out a grunt of frustration.

"Caleb, I'm always honest with you."

He glowered at me and didn't respond for what felt like ages. Then finally . . . "I was jealous. You're right. I just . . . I wanted tae wipe any thought of that arsehole out of your head. It wasn't anything more than that."

"I make you feel more than you want to."

"Jesus Christ, do you just say everything you're thinking, Ava?"

I couldn't tell if he was mad at my honesty or in awe of it. I think maybe a bit of both. "You can feel possessive of someone without it having to mean anything serious," I answered, attempting to reassure us both. "We have a great sexual connection. It makes sense that we'd be covetous of it."

He seemed to process this for a second, and then he leaned over me again, bracing himself above me. His mouth hovered over mine and he said softly, "I'm sorry I made you feel like you were being used. You're the last person I want tae hurt, wee yin."

Warmth flooded me, soothing my earlier fears. "Wee yin?"

"Aye, wee yin. Wee one."

I bit my lip to stop a cheesy smile from taking over my face. "I like that better than 'babe.'"

He kissed me in answer, a soft, sweet, gentle kiss filled with a quiet yearning that made my heart catch and words tumble out of my mouth before I could stop them as he pulled back. "Make love to me."

Caleb's gaze sharpened as his whole body locked above me with tension. "Ava—"

"It won't mean that you love me or that I love you," I whispered. "But I'm still a *woman*, Caleb. I just . . . I need to feel like you want *me*. I need to feel that you see me."

This whole conversation, our entire interaction since I'd walked into his apartment, was breaking our unspoken rules, but I couldn't help myself. If he ended things, he ended things, but at least I would know I hadn't let myself be treated like a mere means of satisfaction.

"I *do* see you, wee yin," he said, the words gruff, hoarse, as if discussing any kind of emotion was so rare the words came out all rusty from disuse. "I didn't touch another woman back home and it wasn't because there wasn't an opportunity tae. I *do* see you."

More than pleased by that response, my heart fluttering wildly in my chest, I sat up, forcing him back a little so I could whip my sweater off. My bra soon followed it to the floor and I wrapped my arms around his broad shoulders to press my breasts to his hard naked chest. My kiss was fierce, yearning, and he immediately got swept up in my desire. His strong arms banded around me, crushing me against him, and we kissed and kissed until we were panting for breath.

When his mouth left mine, it was so he could kiss me all over. I felt his tender kisses on my chest, my breasts, trailing a path down my body, to my center. He kissed me there until I exploded in relief, and while I was coming down from my climax, he removed his jeans and rejoined me on the bed.

This time when he pressed inside it was a slow, thick glide as he returned his mouth to my mouth. We kissed and gasped against each other's lips. I wrapped him up, my thighs pressed against his hips, my arms around his back, holding him to me.

In that moment this man was my entire world and the orgasm he gave me was world-shattering. He tensed, his groan filling my mouth, and I kissed him, capturing his release inside me in every way I could.

When he finally lifted his head and our eyes met, I saw something that chased the pleasure away.

I saw his fear.

And I hated it.

Lowering my gaze, I forced a smile. "Multiple orgasms. Someone is in fine form tonight," I joked, trying to break the sudden tension.

I prepared myself for his cold withdrawal. Instead, he grinned and I knew he'd fought back the fear. We would be okay. We would find our way back to a safe place where it was just great sex between two friends who trusted each other.

We would.

We had to.

W e were still lying in bed when we heard a male voice, remarkably similar to Caleb's, call out, "I know you told me tae bugger off, but it started tae piss down out there and I'm bored!"

Caleb threw the duvet over me, hiding me, as he jumped out of bed to shut the bedroom door. "I'll be out in a second!" he yelled back.

Amused, I watched as he hurried back into his jeans and threw my sweater and bra at me. "Your brother, I presume," I said as I got out of bed and pulled my clothes on.

"Aye." His eyes glazed over a little at the sight of my half-nakedness. "Where are your knickers and jeans?"

"Out there. Where you took them off."

He didn't seem as entertained by this as I was. "Stay here."

"Oh, like I have every intention of wandering out there naked in front of your little brother."

He scowled at the thought before turning his back on me to get a T-shirt out of his built-in wardrobe. When he opened the bedroom door, it was just enough so he could slip out and his brother wouldn't be able to see in. Once it was closed, I tiptoed over to it, but I couldn't make out their conversation, just the sound of their voices.

Then Caleb returned, the door forcing me back into the room. He handed me my jeans, underwear, and shoes, appearing almost grim faced.

"I take it he had something to say about these." I tried not to snicker as I pulled on my clothes.

"He's a cheeky arse, that's what he is."

Chuckling, I stepped into my heels and gestured to myself. "All good?" I strolled over to him, where he was still blocking the door. "Are you going to let me out of this room?"

He scowled at my head. "You have sex hair."

"That's because we just had sex."

"You're in a good mood."

"Because of the aforementioned pleasurable physical activity."

When he still didn't move, I sighed. "Do you not want me to meet your brother or something?"

He made a face at me like what I'd said was ridiculous and finally opened the door to let me out.

The man who switched the TV to mute and got up off the couch at my appearance made me draw to an abrupt halt, causing Caleb to collide into the back of me. He gripped my arms to stop me stumbling forward.

Oh my goodness.

There were two of them.

Ice blue eyes traveled over me with an intensity that felt unsettlingly familiar. The eyes belonged to a younger version of Caleb.

"Ava, this is Jamie. Jamie, this is Ava," Caleb introduced us.

At first I was too busy cataloging the brothers' similarities to notice Jamie's countenance. All I saw was the same dark blond hair, the same scruff, and the same taste in clothing. Then I saw that his features were slightly softer than Caleb's, more handsome in a traditional sense, and although he was extremely tall—a good two inches taller than Caleb at least—he was of a slimmer build. He was still muscular, but lean.

He also didn't have any tattoos that I could see.

And finally, as I stopped my appraisal and looked into his face to smile a greeting, I caught the way he was looking at me.

Perturbed was a nice way of putting it.

Unimpressed was more accurate.

Jamie's gaze flew over my head to his brother. "Thought you learnt that lesson." He gestured rudely to me.

As I flinched in confusion, I felt Caleb tense behind me. "Watch it," he warned dangerously.

His tension leaked into me and I stepped aside, glancing from brother to brother, wondering what the hell was being said between them in their silent glaring match. And why did Jamie seem pissed off by the mere sight of me when he didn't even know me?

After what felt like a really long time but was probably only seconds, Jamie sighed and turned to me. He appeared defeated. "Nice tae meet you, Ava." But it didn't sound like it was nice to meet me at all, and I had no idea why.

"Um . . . you too?"

My response made him snort.

"Bedroom. Now." Caleb pointed to the guest room.

Jamie rolled his eyes but did as his brother commanded. Caleb cut me a look. "Stay."

As he followed his brother into the room, I replied, "Would you like a 'sit' or a 'roll over' with that?"

He threw me an amused smile over his shoulder but didn't

respond. The door closed behind him and his brother, and I silently crept over to eavesdrop.

I know, I know! Not cool. But I was so confused! I needed answers and I knew Caleb, Mr. Stoic and Brooding, would not provide them for me.

". . . aye, but you have tae admit she's like a short version of Carissa," I heard Jamie say.

Who was Carissa? And I wasn't that short!

Okay, I was that short, but still. I frowned at my legs. No need to point it out like it was a bad thing.

"She is not," Caleb snapped. "They look nothing alike. They *are* nothing alike."

"Coloring, aye, different. But . . . they've both got that shiny, immaculate, fresh-coat-of-paint look about them. You know, the high-maintenance type that's only after one thing. Carissa should have taught you that lesson. We all thought it did."

Who the hell was Carissa and what did she do?!

"Ava is definitely not Carrie. And what I'm doing with her is definitely not your business, but I'm going tae tell you anyway so you'll shut up. Ava and I are just friends. Neither of us is looking for anything serious."

I scowled at the doorway, wondering why that pissed me off when only a few short weeks ago it had reassured me.

"A woman like that is always looking for something serious. As in serious money."

"You don't know the first thing about her and what's she been through. Trust me, she doesn't do serious. As for money, she has her own and plenty of it."

My irritation with his brother was eased by Caleb's defense of me. Although the altercation only drove home the similarities between the two of them, because hadn't Caleb treated me with the same condescension at first? He judged me before he knew me. Apparently the brothers were *very* alike.

"Okay," Jamie finally said. "I just dinnae want you making the same mistake twice."

What mistake?

"Learned that lesson the hard way, brother."

What lesson? WHAT LESSON?!

I hurried silently over to the other side of the room and was pretending to peruse his bookshelves again when the brothers emerged. I turned on my heel, keeping my eyes on Caleb, since I wasn't comfortable with his judgy little brother. "Is the powwow over? Did you decide on nail polish color and which unfortunate hanger-on gets to run your errands tomorrow at school?"

Caleb smirked at me. "Funny."

"That was semi-amusing." Jamie shot me a perplexed look as he wandered by me heading for the kitchen.

"Semi-amusing, pfft. I'm funny," I called after him, and added pointedly, "I'm freaking awesome."

Caleb startled me, coming up behind me and wrapping his arms around my waist so he could nuzzle my neck. "Fancy ordering some takeout?"

I looked up at him. "I should probably get home."

He squeezed me. "Stay. I'm not finished with you yet."

Unbelievably, I felt my body tingle to life at the thought of a round three. "Okay," I answered immediately. "Do you have an extra toothbrush?"

"Aye."

I cocked my head to the side in thought. "Did you buy it just for me?"

He shook his head, smiling. "I'll never tell."

I grinned at his playfulness, about to say something when I

thought I heard Jamie mutter as he passed us with a beer, "Just friends, my arse."

There was a possibility I heard right because Caleb growled at him. "Shut it or I'll shut it for you."

Unperturbed, Jamie settled onto the couch and switched the mute button off the television, the sound of *The Big Bang Theory* filling the apartment.

"You have a TV in your room," Caleb said, still holding on to me.

"Aye, so do you," his brother said, as if to say, *Your point being?*

Instead of arguing with him over the television, Caleb grabbed my hand and led me back into his bedroom.

I didn't see Jamie again that night because his big brother kept me all to himself. I was okay with that. Things were confusing enough without having to deal with his judgmental not-so-little brother.

Around one o'clock in the morning, after Thai takeout, some television, and a round of playful sex, Caleb spooned me.

I felt him start to drift to sleep, but my mind refused to shut down. All I could hear was Jamie saying the name Carissa over and over again. Who the hell was she? And why was she a lesson Caleb had to learn from? It didn't make sense that there could be a woman of that kind of importance in Caleb's life, because he'd told me he'd never gotten serious with a woman. And Caleb never lied to me . . . right?

"Caleb?" I whispered.

"Mmm," he murmured sleepily against my hair.

Knowing he was already halfway into dream world, I did something I shouldn't have. I deliberately used his half-consciousness against him.

"Did you miss me?" I whispered, already tensing up in anticipation for his reply.

"Mmm, aye, missed you, wee yin," he mumbled. "Sleep."

And then he was out, his soft, even breathing filling my ears.

An ache spread out across my chest, the claws of it burrowing deep to my heart. What were we doing?

"I missed you too."

Twenty-three

ONE MONTH LATER

S urprised?"

I quirked an eyebrow at Caleb, a smile prodding at my lips. "Not in any way."

He grinned and turned back to the television.

We were at his apartment, and he'd told me that he would surprise me with his movie choice for the night. What was now flickering across his huge flat screen was in no way shocking.

Goodfellas.

I shook my head. "You could have at least tried to be original."

"It's a great movie," he argued, throwing popcorn into his mouth.

"It is," I agreed honestly. "But if you'd asked me to guess what movie you would choose, it would have been a toss-up between this and *The Godfather.*"

"Let's watch that next."

"Are we not having sex tonight?"

He gave me "a look." *Of course* we were having sex tonight. After all, we were friends with benefits. However, since he arrived back in Boston a month ago, Caleb had really been embracing the friends part. In truth, he was so busy in his new role at work, and I was so busy with new clients, that finding time to see each other had become a little trying at times. I felt like we were both frustrated by it, but neither of us would admit it.

"Then I don't think we have time for *The Godfather* on top of *Goodfellas*," I said. "Plus, if we watch *The Godfather* we'll want to watch *The Godfather: Part II* and even though it's not my favorite you can't watch parts one and two without watching part three. And we definitely don't have time for a *Godfather* marathon on top of *Goodfellas*."

"Is it wrong that the fact that you enjoy mafia movies turns me on a wee bit?" He grinned, one filled with wicked boyishness.

My chest fluttered with too much feeling. Over the last month I felt like I was getting to see the real Caleb. The relaxed, nice, down-to-earth Caleb. I didn't know if it was having Jamie around or if it was us settling into a real friendship, but I liked this side of him either way.

"It's a little wrong," Jamie answered for me, striding out of his bedroom, covered in flecks of paint. I hadn't seen inside his room, but Caleb told me he had let his brother turn the guest room into a bedroom/art studio.

"I wasn't asking you." Caleb threw a piece of popcorn at him.

"And yet here I am sharing my opinion for free. I'm such a good brother." Jamie sighed dramatically as he passed us.

"If you're heading into the kitchen for a beer, you'll be an even better one if you bring us one too."

"I'm working," Jamie called to us, having disappeared out of sight. "So I'm on water."

I glanced at the open doorway of his room, but all I could see was the head of a bed and a nightstand. Curiosity was compelling me to get up and have a wander into the room, but my good manners quelled the compulsion.

"He won't let me in either," Caleb said quietly, having noted my interest. "He keeps his work private until it's finished."

"He has a huge social media following," I said, as if that explained my curiosity.

"I do." Jamie appeared from out of the kitchen. "And I have great hearing." He handed us beers and kept hold of the bottle of water in his hand. He pinned me to the sofa with his ice blue gaze. I found it remarkable that two brothers could have identical beautiful eyes and yet only one of them made my heart flutter when he focused on me.

"You been stalking me, Miss Breevort?" Jamie teased.

The upside to hanging out with Caleb as a friend was that Jamie was around in the background during most of those times and he'd gotten to spend a little time with me. Although I still sensed his hesitancy with me, for whatever weird reason (Carissa?), he was at least congenial enough now.

And on that Carissa note, I still had no idea who she was or what lesson she'd taught Caleb.

"I was curious." I shrugged. "And you have over half a million Instagram followers. That's pretty impressive."

"Plus, Ava sketches," Caleb offered. I'd left my sketchbook out on the coffee table a week ago and nosy Caleb had taken a peek. Admittedly, I'd flushed with pleasure at his praise for my drawings. "She's good. You should check them out."

I tried to ignore the warmth his words caused in my chest. "They're nothing like your paintings. I just . . . doodle."

"They're more than doodles."

"I didn't know you were into art." Jamie studied me curiously.

I stopped myself from responding that he didn't know anything about me because he refused to ask. Instead I said, "I went to art school. Interior design."

"Oh, right, of course. *I* dropped out of art school."

"Not that it did him any harm. Jamie's got an exhibit coming up in New York," Caleb said, smirking at his brother, but it was a proud smirk. I could tell. And it made my insides mushy.

Jamie flicked his brother an amused but pleased look. "What can I say . . . I'm a genius."

Caleb chuckled, shaking his head at him. And with one last look at me, Jamie wandered back to his room.

"And modest too." I turned to his big brother. "A self-portrait next, I think. Titled *Genius*."

Caleb grunted, his lips quirking up at the corners.

"I heard that," Jamie grumbled before slamming the door shut behind him.

"Just when he was starting to like me." I took a swig of my beer as I felt a hand on my naked thigh. We were having an extremely warm June and so I was still in the shorts and T-shirt I'd put on to wander around Back Bay in the sun earlier that day. I followed the length of his arm all the way up to its owner's face.

Mirth danced in Caleb's gaze. "Do you really want tae watch the movie?"

"I thought you wanted to watch the movie?"

His big hand caressed my skin, his fingers disappearing under the hem of my shorts. "You're being cute. So now I dinnae want tae watch the movie," he whispered, the amusement giving away to heat.

"I wasn't being cute." I leaned toward him. "You just have a one-track—" My phone began to vibrate on the coffee table, cutting me off.

Harper's name flashed on the screen.

Caleb saw. "Call her back later."

But I couldn't.

These last four weeks had been strained between me and my best friend. My uncertainty over her boyfriend meant she was avoiding me, and I didn't know how to make things right. I felt like I was forcing her to have lunch or drinks with me because when we were together she barely laughed and she seemed on edge, afraid, I think, that I'd ask about Vince.

I didn't ask about Vince because I just wanted my best friend back. This was the first time in weeks that Harper had initiated contact.

Caleb knew all this because I'd confessed my concerns. He saw the look on my face. "You better answer it, then."

I grabbed the phone and answered it on a breathless "Hey." My heart had started racing a little with relief.

"Ava?"

My blood chilled instantly at the garbled way Harper said my name.

"Harper?"

"Ava," her voice croaked. "I'm . . . I'm in trouble." And then I heard the soft whimpers of her crying, and fear slammed into me.

My eyes flew to Caleb, whose gaze turned questioning. "Harper, where are you? What's going on?" He leaned toward me at the urgency in my voice.

"I'm in my apartment." She sobbed and then coughed, spluttering in a way that made me feel sick as I seemed to intuit what she was about to tell me. "Vince attacked me. He's barricaded me in my bedroom. I managed to grab my phone and hide it on me before he threw me in here. He's out in the living room. He's . . ." She started to cry, soft, heartbreaking cries that brought tears to my own eyes. "He's high on something."

"I'm on my way. When I get off the phone, call the police."

"No," she said, her voice sharp. "Please, Ava, no police. Please. You can't. Please."

I looked up at Caleb. "Okay, no police."

His expression darkened. *What's going on?* he mouthed.

"I'll be there soon. Just hold tight."

"Okay," she whispered and hung up.

"Vince attacked her," I said, my hands shaking as I got up and reached for my purse on the coffee table. "He's got her barricaded in her bedroom and she won't let me call the police. She says he's on something."

"You're not going there alone," Caleb bit out angrily, pushing up off the sofa to stride past me and across the room. He pounded on Jamie's door and then threw it open without permission.

"What the fu—?"

"Ava's friend is in trouble," Caleb cut him off. "Get your shoes."

Somewhere in my fear-soaked brain I processed that Jamie followed Caleb out of the room without asking for more of an explanation, and I thought that said a lot of good things about Jamie Scott. It was only when we were all in the elevator together, Caleb holding my hand tight because I couldn't stop trembling, that Caleb asked me to tell them everything Harper had said on the phone.

I repeated our conversation.

"How far away is she?" Jamie asked as we hurried across the underground parking garage to Caleb's car. We piled into the Range Rover Sport he'd bought when he first moved to Boston, and I gave Caleb instructions on how to get to her place. She lived in a tiny one-bedroom in Charlestown just off Bunker Hill Street, so it was a mere ten minutes up Route 93.

That ten minutes felt like a goddamn lifetime.

I was jittery with adrenaline, my teeth chattering together and my left knee bouncing constantly.

Caleb reached over and placed a gentle hand on said knee as he was driving. "We'll get tae her and she'll be okay," he promised, so steady. I looked over at him, his profile stern and his gaze focused and determined on the road. He was strong and capable and protective.

I still felt sick, but Caleb's reassurance and his brother's presence— their support—calmed me a little. In a perfect world I would be strong enough physically to march into Harper's apartment and save her from Vince myself. But I was a tiny five foot three and I ran to keep fit. I didn't lift weights. Vince could overpower me as easily as he'd overpowered Harper, and then where would we be?

It was a sad truth that weeks ago this would have made me feel bitter and frustrated. I was still frustrated, but I didn't feel bitter that I had to lean on Caleb for help. Perhaps if I didn't trust him, I would feel resentment that I had to rely on a man for support. But I didn't see this as having to rely on a *man*. I saw this as relying on a *friend*.

He was my friend.

And I'd never been more grateful for him than I was in that moment.

"Here—" I pointed to a small parking lot between her building and the next and then fumbled in my purse for my keys. I had a spare to Harper's apartment as she had for mine.

Caleb swung into a free spot and I jumped out of the car before he'd stopped moving. I ran toward the modern redbrick building, driven by the need to get to my friend. Seconds from the building door, I suddenly felt the breath knocked out of me as a strong arm encircled my waist. I found myself hauled back against Caleb and he growled in my ear, "Dinnae you jump out of a moving car again." He shook me a little and I pressed against his arms in an attempt to rush ahead.

"Caleb," I bit out in warning.

He released me slowly and I turned to match him glare for glare. He held out his hands. "Keys. Stay behind me and Jamie the whole time. You hear?"

Arguing would only have wasted time, so I handed the keys over and fell back behind the two brothers. "Second floor," I said.

They took the stairs two at a time and I hurried up after them, out of breath from panic and distress by the time we reached her apartment. I pointed to her door and Caleb unlocked it, but when he opened it, it caught on the chain.

He cursed and looked at Jamie and then at me.

I read his silent question. "Break it in."

Taking a few steps back, Caleb seemed to brace and then he punched a long, strong leg out with more force than I knew he was capable of. The door flew open, the chain snapping off, and wood in the center panel cracked and splintered.

I didn't care.

I rushed in behind Caleb and Jamie to find Vince standing up from the sofa in her small living room. In my head I'd imagined the apartment wrecked from a violent struggle, but it was mostly intact except for a smashed vase in the corner by the window.

The retro fridge, however, was no longer in her tiny kitchen but barricading her bedroom door.

Son of a bitch!

Before I could launch myself at him, he raised his hands in defense against a menacing Jamie and Caleb, who were approaching him slowly, predatorily.

I finally noted that Vince's face was splotchy and his eyes watery and red-rimmed. He'd been crying. He still was. And his hair was all over the place, like he'd been tugging it in vexation.

"I didn't mean it." He shook his head, blubbering. Spit dribbled down his chin and he wiped it, sobbing harder. "I didn't mean it." His eyes flew to me and he started toward me. "Ava, I didn't mean it."

Caleb lunged between us and shoved Vince hard enough to send him sprawling to the hardwood floor. "You stay the hell away from her," he warned. "Jamie, watch him while I help Ava get Harper."

Jamie nodded. "He isn't going anywhere."

Pulling my eyes away from Vince, holding back my desire to physically attack him, I hurried over to the fridge with Caleb and together we hauled it out of the way. Hands shaking, afraid of what I'd find beyond the door, I hesitated just a second before I threw it open.

I heard Vince behind me whimpering. "I just didn't want her to leave me. I'm sorry. I just didn't want her to leave me." The sound of a struggle brought my head back around to the living room and I watched as Vince tried to get past Jamie to the bedroom.

With a grunt of annoyance, Jamie let him go for a millisecond before knocking Vince out with a right hook.

Vince crumpled to the ground and Jamie stepped over him, hurrying across the room to us.

With Vince unconscious and no longer sobbing and pleading, I finally heard her whimpers and groans.

Heart squeezing in alarm, I hurried into the bedroom, my eyes searching the small space, and panicking when I couldn't see her. Relief flooded me as I caught sight of her head behind the far side of the bed.

Rounding it, feeling the brothers' presence at my back, I stumbled to a stop at the scene that greeted me.

My best friend was slumped on the floor cradling her wrist. She sensed me and lifted her head slowly. Her left eye was swollen shut, her nose was bloodied, there was a cut on her lower lip, and her T-shirt was torn with splatters of blood on it.

I felt my knees tremble so hard they nearly took me to the ground, and I had to stifle the sob that rose in my throat.

My hands and legs shook as they took me toward her.

"Where's Vince?" Harper slurred.

"He's in the living room. He's out." I lowered to my knees, reaching for her, my hands hovering over her because I was afraid to touch her and hurt her more. "Sweetie, we need to get you to the hospital."

"No, no." She shook her head and I finally saw the matted, blooded hair near her temple. Her slurred words made sense and fear took hold of me.

"We have to, baby. You might have a concussion. Hospital and police."

"No, no," she kept repeating.

"Let me, wee yin," Caleb said, gently pulling me up out of the way. And then he was even more gentle as he lifted Harper into his arms. She cried out, a shrill sound that made my stomach sink.

Caleb's gaze flew to me, his countenance grim. "Her ribs," he surmised.

"Broken?"

"Maybe just bruised." He looked ready to kill Vince.

I was right there with him.

"Ava, please, no." Harper began to cry pitifully as Caleb carried her out of the room. Jamie held the door for them and I hurried at Caleb's back only to hear her whisper mournfully, "I'm so ashamed."

Tears filled my eyes as my gaze connected with Jamie's.

Empathy shone out of his eyes and he touched Harper's arm, drawing Caleb to a stop. "You have nothing tae be ashamed of," he said to her.

"Who are you?" she whispered.

"My brother Jamie," Caleb answered. "Now let's get going."

"Hospital, police," I repeated.

"I'll call the police and wait here for them," Jamie said. "I'll make sure the bastard doesn't get away before they get here."

"I'm surprised someone hasn't already called the police," Caleb muttered.

I gave the room one last sweep. Everything was in its place except for that vase—and Vince's sprawled body on the floor. "There's not a lot of damage, so maybe not a lot of noise." And if Harper had fought back, made noise, a neighbor would surely have called the police. Which means my friend had taken this beating without a fight.

I knew her history.

I knew her.

She blamed herself for staying with him. I feared she'd taken his beating as a punishment—a thought that made me feel sick. If that was true, we had bigger problems than bruised ribs and a concussion.

I squeezed Jamie's shoulder as I passed him. "Thank you."

He gave me a tight smile and nodded.

"Ava, keep talking tae her," Caleb said as we hurried out of the apartment.

"What's going on?" A belligerent voice stopped me on the landing while Caleb kept hurrying down the stairs.

I jerked around at the sight of Harper's elderly neighbor, Mr. Haggerty, standing in his doorway scowling. "Mr. Haggerty, Harper's hurt. We're taking her to the hospital."

"I'm calling the police." He glowered at us.

"My friend already has," I assured him. I didn't have time to stick around, though, so I gave him a nod and rushed down the stairs after Caleb and Harper.

The entire drive to the hospital I made my friend recite recipes to keep her awake. When we got there and handed her over to the nurses, it took everything within me to hold it together.

Harper Lee Smith was my only true family and I had let her down. If I had just kept on at her about Vince—damn the consequences— there was a huge possibility we wouldn't be at a hospital and Caleb wouldn't have my friend's blood on his T-shirt.

Twenty-four

The wait to hear how Harper was doing was excruciating. I just wanted to be by her side. Images of her before she met Vince, of her laughing, full of attitude, filled my head and I was terrified that those images would remain memories, that after all she'd been through this horrible end to a bad relationship would be the thing that broke her.

I clung to hope that if Harper was tough enough to make it out of her past, she was strong enough to eventually realize that what happened tonight had not been her fault.

Sensing that I was deeply buried in my own thoughts and concerns, Caleb was a silent support at my side as we sat in the waiting room of the ER. We were surrounded by people, yet every single one of them faded out of existence as I stewed in anxiety. That is . . . every single one except Caleb. I still felt him there. His strength and warmth beside me anchored me even if it seemed to the outside like I'd floated away from him.

"Harper Smith's family?"

Her name jolted me out of myself and I rose to my feet, as Caleb stood up at my back. "Yes?"

The doctor, a young brunette with kind eyes, gestured to us and we marched over to her. "You're Harper's relatives?"

"She doesn't have any blood relatives," I answered. "I'm her best friend. I'm her only family. I'm her emergency contact on her insurance. Ava Breevort."

"Okay. I'm Dr. Hunter." The doctor lifted her hand in a calming gesture, sensing my building anxiety at the thought of being barred from Harper. "Ava, I can tell you that Harper is going to be all right. She's got a fractured rib and a broken wrist. The wrist we've put in a cast, but unfortunately there's not a lot we can do about her rib except administer pain relief while it heals. Thankfully her nose isn't broken, but a deep cut on her eyebrow and left temple required stitches. Which brings me to what I am concerned about. Harper threw up while we were treating her and is feeling very disoriented. I've ruled out any serious brain injuries but I always ask that patients suffering from concussion have someone stay with them for at least forty-eight hours. This is just a precaution to make sure there aren't any concerning changes in Harper's behavior."

"I can do that," I said instantly. "She can stay with me."

"Good. Now, I've given Harper some painkillers, but she'll need bed rest and plenty of fluids. We'll be a little while longer discharging her, but the nurse will let you know as soon as she's ready to be taken home. Oh, and—" Dr. Hunter lowered her voice even further. "Harper has asked us not to call the police, however—"

"We called the police," Caleb cut her off. "They're on their way."

I looked at him questioningly. He gave me a reassuring nod. "Jamie texted. The police took Vince into custody and Jamie's on his way here. The police will be here shortly tae take a statement from everybody. Including Harper."

"Right," Dr. Hunter said. "Then Harper stays until the police have asked their questions." She seemed appeased and left us to return to her duties.

As soon as she was out of sight, I just began to walk forward.

My feet slapped hard in my flats against the hospital linoleum floor as I rushed away from the waiting room.

I heard Caleb calling my name, but I only stopped when I reached an empty corridor with a vending machine in it. And then I bent over, my hands on my knees, and began to sob.

He could have killed her.

The bastard could have killed her.

Caleb pulled me up and crushed me to him, my arms automatically winding around his back to hold on tight as every feeling and fear I'd gone through that night spilled out of me with absolutely no control.

"I could have stopped this." I sobbed, the words garbled. "I should have. If I'd just—"

"No." He shushed me, stroking my hair. "You dinnae get tae blame this on yourself, wee yin. I won't allow it."

I did blame myself for not pushing Harper harder. But I heard the steel in Caleb's voice and shut up. Eventually the hard sobs that racked my body calmed to silent tears that didn't seem to want to stop leaking out of my eyes.

"Harper okay?" Jamie's voice brought me out of my Caleb cocoon, but I didn't lift my face from where it was pressed against his chest.

"Harper's going tae be fine," Caleb said, giving me a squeeze. "He messed her up pretty good, though."

I tabulated her injuries in my head and felt my fear melt to wrath almost instantly. I lifted my head but didn't pull out of Caleb's embrace as I turned to Jamie.

His eyes searched my face and I knew I looked a mess but I didn't care. Jamie informed me, "The police have Vince in custody. He still hasn't fully come down from whatever drug he's on and he pretty much admitted tae them that he beat Harper because she wanted tae break up with him. The police are on their way here tae take a statement from you two and Harper."

Reality of daily life after abuse was nothing new for Harper. But this was different. I felt it in my bones. It made me cold with stifled panic. "How do I get her through this? She'll blame herself. She'll see it like she allowed him to do this to her."

Caleb turned me to face him and said sternly, "You just keep telling her that this wasn't her fault. Every day for as long as it takes tae sink in."

"You don't understand . . . her history . . . this . . . she doesn't deserve any more pain. She's been through enough." Tears spilled down my cheeks again as a feeling of powerlessness overwhelmed me.

"Hey." Jamie's hand came down on my shoulder and I looked up at him through blurry vision. "You did well back at the flat when we found her. You kept it together even though it was awful for you tae see her like that. You find that strength you had in that moment and hold on to it tae be there for her again."

Jamie's advice would stick with me over the next few days. Somewhere I'd find the strength to be what Harper needed, but worried constantly that it wasn't enough.

I went in alone to be with Harper while the police interviewed her and took photos of her injuries. Although she told them everything that had happened (and I had to shut out the visuals her description produced because they made me nauseous), she was angry with me for calling the cops.

"I told you not to," she hissed as they left us in the hospital room.

I slipped my arm around her waist to help her up off the bed. "Well, I did. Vince needs to face charges for this and you know it."

"Yeah, so his defense team can drag up my history and twist it around on me to make it my fault. That I'm out looking for this kind of shit."

I glared at her. "You do not. This is not your fault and you have absolutely nothing to be ashamed of."

She looked away, tears burning in the eye that wasn't swollen shut.

"Harper . . ." I ducked my head so she couldn't avoid my gaze. "Do you think for one second that I would have let him anywhere near you if I thought he was capable of this?" Then an awful thought occurred to me. "He hadn't . . . he didn't hit you before this, right?"

Her gray-blue eye blazed with ire at the suggestion. "No."

"Then how can you blame yourself for something you didn't even know he was capable of? He was high and messed up. This is not your fault."

"We both know that once he started saying negative things about my work and once I started to suspect he was on drugs that I should have walked away."

"You had hope." I squeezed her arm. "You wanted to believe he could change. There is nothing wrong with that. And when you realized he wasn't going to change, you made the choice to leave him. It isn't your fault that he attacked you for that decision. Do you hear me?"

Harper nodded, but the dull expression on her face told me she still wasn't ready to forgive herself.

While Caleb got us a cab to my place, Jamie had taken the Range Rover back to Harper's to collect some clothes and toiletries for her. I had to hope she'd forgive me for the invasion of her privacy, but I didn't want to let her out of my sight long enough to get her clean clothes and pajamas. By the time we got to my apartment, Jamie had arrived with her things.

She'd barely acknowledged him or Caleb, and sensing her distress that they had paid witness to all of this, I settled her in my bed and ushered the two big Scotsmen out into the living room.

"I would offer you a coffee—Strike that. I would offer you a freaking kidney for what you both have done tonight." I gave them a teary, grateful smile. "But she's not doing great and—"

"You need us tae go," Caleb cut me off, giving me a reassuring nod. "We get it. We'll leave you be. But call me if you need anything." He pressed a sweet, tender kiss to my forehead and I pressed my hand over his heart in thanks.

Jamie surprised me by wrapping me up in a big hug, but I quickly recovered, hugged him back, and whispered a thank you to him.

Once they'd left, with Caleb gone, I felt an emptiness I couldn't explain. It was an emptiness that frightened me almost as much as the woman lying broken in my bed.

Only able to deal with one thing at a time, I shoved Caleb to the back of my mind and got down to the business of watching over Harper. That night I slept on the armchair in my bedroom, waking every hour or so to check that Harper was okay. She slept deeply, thankfully, exhausted by her ordeal.

The next morning, however, she woke in pain and I forced some food down her throat so she could chase it with painkillers. Harper was a terrible patient. Partly because she still hadn't forgiven me yet for calling the police, and partly because she spent her life constantly on her feet. Her energy was admirable, but trying to keep her in bed when she needed bed rest was exhausting.

Despite her protests, I called Jason. She knew her boss had to be informed because she had a broken wrist and wouldn't be able to work for a while until it healed. Jason and his wife, Gillian, appeared at my apartment less than two hours after I called to tell him what happened.

He walked in seeming to have been struck haggard by the news. Gillian, a tall, striking woman who took a long sabbatical from professional tennis to be a full-time mom—a fact visible in her broad shoulders and muscular arms—had kind hazel eyes that were filled with horror when she took in the sight of Harper in my bed.

Jason went from haggard to enraged. "I'm going to kill him," he announced.

"I'll help," Gillian muttered.

Harper appeared ready to sink under the covers. "Stop glaring at me like that."

"She thinks it's her fault," I said.

If looks could have killed, I would have been dead. "Screw you, Ava."

I flinched, the undeniable pain piercing me even though I knew she was just humiliated and taking it out on me.

"Watch it," Jason snapped, rounding the bed. "You don't talk to her like that."

Harper just glowered at him. "You better not be here to tell me I can't work."

He pointed to her wrist. "How the hell do you plan on working with that?"

"I'm going back to work. Tomorrow."

"Like hell you are."

"I am."

"Harper—"

"Jason—" Her voice broke on his name, her lips trembling. "Please."

His expression softened and he looked over at Gillian. Whatever he saw in his wife's face made him curse under his breath. "You can't work with a broken wrist, Harper. But"—he cut off her coming protest—"after a few more days' bed rest you can come back to work and help where you can, as long as you don't become a frustrated nuisance in there."

"I want to come back tomorrow—"

"No." He lifted a hand to cut off whatever she'd say next. "That's final."

She stared at him in irritation for a few seconds and then slumped back against the pillows. "Fine."

"You can't stay here either." Gillian shook her head and gave me an apologetic look. "Sorry, Ava, but you don't have the room. You can't sleep on the couch for an indefinite amount of time."

"I don't mind," I said, feeling panic build at the direction the conversation was taking.

"Gillian's right." Jason shook his head. "And you have work. Gillian's at home. Harper will stay with us for a week or so until she's okay to go back to her apartment."

"A week or so? No way. I'm going home today."

"No, you're not," all three of us said in unison. And then I stepped farther into the room. "Look, Gillian, Jason, I appreciate the offer, but I can take time off work to look after Harper."

"I'm not a child," she bit out. "Ava, stop treating me like I'm made of goddamn porcelain."

That was all it took to make my temper snap. Suddenly I was braced over her on the bed and she was leaning back in shock at my abrupt, fast movement. "You have people who love you," I said, my voice hoarse, harsh. "Deal with it and stop acting like a brat."

She studied my face, her swollen eye marginally better today because we'd iced it through the night. "Good. You've stopped tiptoeing around me. That's all I wanted."

I rolled my eyes and sat down on the bed. "Whether you like it or not, you need to stay in bed for a few more days and you need someone watching over you for the next twenty-four hours, per the doctor's instructions. Being a little shit to me isn't going to change that."

"Well, here's the plan," Gillian announced. "Harper stays with Ava for another night while Jason and I get our guest room ready for her. Harper, you can stay with us for however long you like."

"I don't need to stay with anyone. I'll stay here another night but then I'm going home."

"No, you're not, and that's an order from your boss," Jason decreed. "Gillian and I will be back tomorrow to collect you." He put his hand out to me. "Do you have her keys so Gillian can pack a bag for her?"

"Hello, I'm right here, stop talking about me like I'm not."

Jason ignored her and I hesitated. I feared the idea of letting Harper out of my sight. As if he intuitively understood this, he said softly, "We'll take good care of her."

"But the kids?"

"Our guest suite is on the other side of the house. We'll make sure the kids don't bother her."

"The kids can bother me if they want," Harper announced.

"It's up to Harper." I turned to her. "Do you want to stay here or with Jason? And no, your apartment is not an option right now."

After a moment of scowling at us all, she sighed. "Fine. I'll stay with you guys—" She gestured to Jason and Gillian and my heart fell.

I knew it was ridiculous to feel hurt by her decision, but I did. I hadn't been able to protect her from Vince, but I had hoped to make it up to her in a small way by being there to take care of her.

Fighting the silly urge to cry, I got up off the bed. "Anyone want tea? Coffee?" I asked, my voice sounding flat even to my own ears.

To my relief, Jason and Gillian decided not to stay. They took Harper's keys and left to get ready for her arrival.

I set myself up with a book on the armchair in the bedroom, giving Harper my tablet so she could watch a TV show she liked on Netflix. She fell asleep before the first episode was even finished and I switched the device off, placing it on the nightstand.

For a while I couldn't concentrate on anything but my best friend. In truth, she had always felt more like my little sister, and I'd never felt that more than I did watching her sleep. For the rest of the day we barely spoke. I made her eat and drink lots of water and orange juice, but beyond that our interactions were minimal.

Her anger toward me hurt, but I suffered through it, clinging to the hope that her resentment was temporary. That she needed someone to be livid at other than herself. Someone she knew would take it and still be there for her in the end.

Later the next day, despite my disappointment and agitation that I wouldn't be able to hover over her every five seconds, I was actually a little relieved when she left with Jason. Despite my rational understanding of her motivations, I was injured by her grievance with me.

When I hugged her gently, she didn't hug me back. After all I'd been through that weekend, being her emotional punching bag bruised worse than I'd expected.

It wasn't until after she'd left that I realized how drained I'd felt in her presence.

Still, I'd only let her leave under the vow that she pick up her cell when I called. Jason gave me a look that promised me he'd keep me updated even if Harper didn't.

"I'll be out tomorrow evening to the house to check on you."

She'd ignored that but once again Jason nodded, thanked me, and bid me good-bye.

Then I cried when they left.

There was so much to cry over the tears took a long time to stop. When they did, I was no longer stunned by the realization that the one person I wanted to comfort me was Caleb. I knew if I called him, he'd come. He'd already called and texted me several times over the last two days. He and Jamie were eager for an update on Harper and even suggested he come over. And although I wanted him there, I knew Harper was embarrassed that the two brothers had witnessed Vince's abuse, so I didn't allow it.

Now I wished he would call again.

But he didn't.

And for some reason that made me want to cry more.

Instead, I gave myself a stern talking-to and spent the rest of the evening cleaning the apartment and keeping myself busy so I didn't have time to think.

Twenty-five

The next morning, I was barely able to concentrate at work between thinking about Harper and the Scotsman who had swept into my life and turned it upside down. Harper hadn't replied to my texts, so I had to call Jason for an update, which pissed me off.

"She's fine," Jason assured me.

"Good. I have to get back to work. I'll be over tonight around seven, if that's okay?"

"I'll be at the restaurant, but Gillian wants you to stay for dinner."

"I can do that. Thanks."

We got off the phone, and the urge to call Caleb and tell him how hurt I was by Harper's misdirected wrath was strong. But calling him wouldn't be enough for me.

Before I could rethink it, I texted him.

You free for lunch?

His reply was gratifyingly speedy.

Caleb: A quick one, aye. Can you meet me at my office? 12:30 p.m.?

I smiled and texted him that I'd be there.

Not long later I walked into the tall granite building in the Financial District that housed a number of different companies, including Koto Tech. Walking over to reception, I told them who I was there to see and they called up to Caleb's office.

The receptionist handed me a temporary security pass. "Tenth floor." She gestured to a bank of elevators.

I flashed my pass at security before I got on the busy elevator that let me off on the tenth floor. I was greeted by a large reception area with a huge reception desk in its center. On the curved wall behind the desk hung engraved silver letters that read "Koto Technologies." There was a half-moon-shaped gray couch situated around a glass coffee table. A woman in a tailored suit was waiting there, her laptop open on her lap, her fingers moving with super speed over the keys.

A young man sitting behind the reception desk wearing an earpiece stared at me, so I moved toward him, my high heels clicking on the shiny black tiled flooring.

"Ava Breevort." I smiled. "Here to see Caleb Scott."

The young man nodded. "You're expected."

"Miss Breevort?"

I glanced to my left to find a woman of indeterminate age staring at me. She was dressed in a light gray pantsuit with a soft pink blouse underneath. Her ash brown hair was cut short in tight spirals and she was immaculate from top to toe, from her smooth, wrinkle-free umber skin to her pearls and Prada loafers.

"Yes?"

"I'm Elizabeth." She held out her a manicured hand. "Mr. Scott's personal assistant."

I shook it. "Nice to meet you."

"The meeting he's in is running a little late, but I have coffee for you while you wait." She gave me a small smile before turning around to walk down the corridor beyond us.

I followed as we stepped from tiled flooring onto carpet. The whole place still smelled like fresh paint. We wound our way past individual offices until we came out into an open space that housed a desk and a waiting area. Behind the desk was a large office door with a silver plate on it that read "Caleb Scott, CFO."

I couldn't help but feel more than a prickle of pride for him and his success.

Elizabeth walked over to a table by the seats in the waiting area where there was a coffee machine. "How do you take it?"

But before I could answer, Caleb's office door opened and something fluttered in my chest at the sight of him. He had the door braced open with one hand and was looking down at the individual who was currently standing half in, half out of his office.

When that individual's hand suddenly rested on his chest, I dragged my gaze from Caleb to her. I tensed.

An attractive, very tall platinum blonde was smiling up at him flirtatiously. She was dressed in a suit much like my own, except she was all model-like lines and legs that went on forever. "Well, my offer still stands," I heard her say in a throaty voice. "If you need someone to show you around Boston, I'm born and bred."

Caleb nodded, thankfully not breaking a smile. "I'll keep that in mind. For now, I just need you tae get your team tae where *you* are. If not, then you'll need tae clean house, Jen. You have two more weeks and any deadweight still remaining needs tae go."

She dropped her hand but that smirky little smile of hers didn't leave her face. "It won't come to that."

"Good." He glanced over at me, apparently having sensed me there already if his lack of surprise was anything to go by, and I more than liked the subtle softening of his expression. "My lunch date is here. This meeting is over."

I smiled at him and flicked a look at "Jen." She drew her suspicious gaze over the entire length of me and muttered, "Of course," before walking away. I didn't bother to see if she looked back at us. I was too busy forcing myself not to run at Caleb and throw my arms around him.

"Hey."

He gave me that little half-smile I loved as he closed his office door behind him. "Hey yourself."

Kiss me.

As if he heard my silent plea, he leaned down when I reached him and brushed the softest kiss across my lips. They tingled as if telling me they wanted more.

"Liz," he said over my head as he slid an arm around my waist. "I'll be back within the hour."

"You have a meeting in forty minutes," she said, grimacing apologetically. "Your meeting with Miss Granton ran over a little."

He sighed. "Fine. I'll be back in forty minutes."

While he led me back the way I'd come, his hand resting possessively on my lower back, I tried to stifle the urge to ask about Miss Jen Granton and found I couldn't. I kept my voice light as I asked, "Who is the platinum blonde?"

Caleb hesitated a second before he answered, "The head of marketing."

"She wants to sleep with you," I told him, as if he didn't already know that.

"Aye, well, she can want." His hand pressed deeper against my back. "I dinnae shit where I eat."

It took everything within me not to stiffen at his comment, which should have been, *I dinnae want tae have sex with anyone but you.*

"You aren't jealous, are you?" he asked, a hum of amusement in his tone as we stepped onto the elevator.

It was thankfully empty, so I could retort, "Kiss my ass."

"With pleasure," he murmured in my ear.

Still irritated, both at him and at myself for my jealousy, I stared stonily ahead and attempted to ignore his roaming hand.

Caleb sighed and stepped away from me as the elevator stopped and more people got on. It wasn't until we hit the ground floor that he returned his hand to my back and gently led me forward.

"You have no need tae be jealous," he said conversationally, holding the exit door open for me. Our eyes met as I moved to go ahead of him and I was halted by his next words. "You're all I need."

And even though it was what I wanted to hear, I couldn't help the melancholy that swelled over me, because what he didn't add at the end of the sentence were the words "for now." Yet those words hung between us anyway, and I scooted out past him, forcing my gaze away so he couldn't see the turmoil in it.

"How is Harper?" Caleb sought to change the subject as we joined the crowd on the sidewalk. It was a hot day, the sun beaming fiercely against my head, and I felt envious of the businessman in front of me wearing a fedora. I wished hats were more fashionable with female business attire. It would be cute—very 1940s—and serve the purpose of protecting my scalp from burning during the summer.

"Harper?"

I'd wanted to talk about this with him, so why was I stalling? Was it the reminder that he wasn't going to be my permanent shoulder to lean on?

Sighing, I shrugged. "She won't talk to me."

At the hollowness in my voice, he took my hand in his, drawing my eyes up to his face. "She'll come around. She knows you love her, Ava."

"I'd do anything for her."

His grip on my hand tightened and something flashed in his gaze that I didn't quite understand. "Aye, she knows that too. You're the only one she'll talk tae and she needs tae talk about it. I know you dinnae want tae push but you need tae at least try tae feel her out about what happened. She'll get mad at anyone who tries, but you're the only one who might actually succeed in getting her tae open up."

His words of advice settled over me and I decided he was right. As much as the thought of confronting her about her emotions frightened me because I didn't want to push her away, I knew she needed to do it before she buried what she felt. Burying it would only mean the distinct possibility of it being unearthed sometime in the future. Still, I had to ask, "I did the right thing?"

"You know you did. Stop beating yourself up about this."

"How would you feel if it happened to one of your sisters? You can't tell me you wouldn't blame yourself for not having stepped in sooner. I know you, Caleb."

He nodded, his eyes turning to ice chips at the thought. "You're right. I would. But I'd like tae think my friend Ava would tell me that the blame didn't lie with me."

I smiled softly at his reply, the warmth of his words easing some of my tension. I squeezed his hand. "I would. Thanks. Not just for saying that, but for everything you did for me and Harper on Saturday. You and Jamie."

"You dinnae need tae thank me for that." He let go of my hand but only to slide his arm around my shoulder and tuck me into his side as we made our way to the café.

I felt safe tucked into him.

Dangerously safe.

The Lutons lived in a midcentury ranch house in Winthrop, a mere thirty minutes from the city. The shingles were a saltwater taffy blue, and I knew from Harper that they'd put a lot of work into restoring the large detached family home.

I'd decided against dinner at seven and called Gillian to ask her if I could visit that afternoon instead, squaring it away with Stella that I'd catch up with work after my trip out there to see Harper. The idea of trying to talk to her, to get her to open up to me, while surrounded by the Lutons and their kids sounded impossible—because it would be impossible.

I parked in their drive at the side of their house, feeling ridiculous that my heart was slamming against my rib cage. After my quick lunch with Caleb, I still hadn't relaxed and I knew I wouldn't until Harper and I had an honest conversation. Something I felt we could do now that she'd rested up a bit.

"Hi, Ava." Gillian stepped out of the front door onto the porch as I made my way around the garden to the front stoop.

"Hey. How are you?" I asked as I climbed the steps.

She gave me a tired smile, surprising me. On all occasions that we'd spent time together there was a constant bronze glow to Gillian's skin and a brightness in her hazel eyes that matched this irrepressible aura of energy that athletes seemed to have. Today both her skin and gaze seemed dull. She looked exhausted. "I have three kids and a belligerent houseguest who has quite frankly made me terrified of my kids becoming teenagers. Other than that, I'm fine."

I passed her, walking into the beautiful entrance to their home. Ahead of me was an expansive oak staircase with a light gray carpet runner up the center. To my left was a formal living room with a baby grand piano in the corner. To my right a larger family room, with a lived-in corner sofa, armchair and stool, coffee table, television center, and lots of knickknacks. Both rooms had a central feature modern glass-box gas fireplace, neither of which was lit since it was June.

"She's just restless," I replied to Gillian's comment. "She doesn't mean to be exhausting."

"I know." Gillian nodded. "Jason has agreed to let her back in the kitchen tomorrow."

"It's probably for the best."

"I agree."

"Kids at school?"

"Yeah, I'm actually just heading out to pick them up. I'll show you to Harper's room first. We put her in the guest suite at the back of the house." She led me past the staircase into a sprawling kitchen and dining room. A set of French doors in front of us led out onto the back garden. I admired the modern twist on the country kitchen. They had pale green Shaker-style cupboards, a thick woodblock countertop, a Belfast sink, and a matching island. Built in between cupboards was a large black ceramic range cooker that seemed to have all the bells and whistles. The freestanding combined refrigerator and freezer was one of the biggest I'd ever seen. It was a huge kitchen, accented with copper accessories and copper pans hanging from a rack on the far wall.

"Love." I gestured to kitchen.

"Thanks." She grinned. "Our pride and joy. Most of our budget went into it."

With Jason being a chef, I had no doubt.

Double doors to our right took us into a fully stocked pantry. A door at the back of the pantry led us out into a small corridor. Gillian drew us to a halt and pointed to the door at the bottom of the hall. "Guest suite."

"Thank you."

"I hope . . ." She lowered her voice. "I hope you can get her to talk to you. She can't keep what happened to her bottled up."

I nodded. "I know."

As soon as Gillian left, I knocked on the door.

"Gillian, I said I don't need anything," Harper grumbled from the other side.

So I turned the handle and pushed the door open.

Harper was sitting curled up on an armchair in the corner of a lovely room. There was a four-poster bed in the center of it, a TV cabinet opposite the bed, and a door next to the cabinet that led into an en suite bathroom. Behind the armchair were French doors that led out onto the side garden.

Sunlight cast a halo over my best friend's head as she looked up from the book she was reading and let out a dramatic sigh. Her broken wrist lay on her lap, and the sight of the small cast caused me to wince. "I thought you weren't coming until later?"

I shut the door behind me and dropped my purse on the bed before rounding it to stand in front of her. Her left eye was much better now, although the bruising had turned dark and brutal around it. The swelling had gone down in her nose, and the stitches on her temple and eyebrow were small, clean, and neat. The cut on her lip didn't look so bad either. Still, my stomach roiled at the visual evidence of what she'd gone through. "We need to talk."

"I don't want to talk," she answered stubbornly.

"You're going to. *We* are going to." I lowered myself to my knees, tucking my skirt in neatly around them. "I'll start." I began by exhaling shakily and saw Harper frown at the sign of my nervousness. "I feel guilty for not pressuring you more to dump Vince. And I feel guilty that I even pressured you at all because I'm worried that my doubts about him are only intensifying your own guilt. And I'm terrified that you feel guilty at all because you're not the one to blame in this situation. We have all trusted the wrong person at one time or another in our lives, Harp. It happens. It's shit, but it happens and we've got to learn to give ourselves a free pass every now and then."

Harper stared at me sullenly. "Wow. You just dived right into the good stuff, huh?"

"Don't." I reached for her good hand, pulling it away from the edges of her book. "This is me. Ava. Don't think you can hide behind snark and that I won't see right through it. Be honest with me."

She glanced sharply away, grinding her teeth for a second. And then I felt her squeeze my hand ever so gently. "I . . ."

I waited patiently and not so patiently for her to continue.

Harper swallowed and finally, slowly dragged her eyes back to mine. "I can't believe I let someone do this to me. Again."

"This is very different," I said immediately. "*I* didn't know Vince was capable of this. I just thought he was an unsupportive wannabe rock star who wasn't good enough for you. And I know you didn't know he was capable of this, Harp. Did you stick around and tell yourself that it was a one-off, that he was high? No. Did you listen to him when he pleaded with you that he didn't mean to hurt you? No. You called me to come and get you out of there. Do you want to go back to him?"

"God no," she spat, jerking her hand out of mine. "What kind of question is that?"

"The kind of question I needed to ask so you can see that you're not trapped in an emotionally and physically abusive relationship with this guy. He showed what he was capable of and you have unequivocally walked away."

"I didn't want to call the police. What does that say about me?"

"It says you didn't want strangers dragging up ugly memories from your past. It says you just wanted to walk away and move on."

"And let him do this to someone else," she muttered, self-hatred gleaming from her eyes.

"You weren't thinking about that then, sweetie. And no one can blame you for it."

"You should. I've been treating you like crap for just doing the right thing." Tears started to spill down her cheeks.

I moved forward and rested my arms on her knees before placing my chin on them. "Yeah, and that lasted all of two days. And anyway, you know I'll be your emotional punching bag anytime you need me to. That's what family is for. To be good to each other, to be kind and loving for ninety-nine percent of the time, and to forgive each other the one percent of occasional shittiness."

She wiped at her cheeks but the tears kept falling. "I let him, Ava," she whispered. "I was in so much shock I didn't even fight back. And then . . . all I could think about was if someone called the police and people found out what I'd let happen to me. So I stayed quiet and took the beating. I've never once not fought back in my entire life. I fight! So why did I just lay there like a coward? I'm a coward!"

"No." I lifted myself up to grip her by the shoulders, forcing her to look me in the eye. "You are not a coward. You are one of the strongest people I know." My vision turned blurry with my own tears. "This bad thing happened to you. You didn't *make* it happen to you. Don't let this change you, Harp. Please."

"How can I not?" She shrugged sadly. "I've tried so hard to stay open with people despite everything. And look where it got me." Her shoulders shook beneath my hands as she started to sob harder. "Only you, Ava. I've only got you. You're the only one I trust."

I grabbed her to me, feeling her tears against my skin as she sobbed into my neck. I held her tight, when what I longed to do was break down right along with her. Because I was afraid for her. I was afraid too much ugliness was going to turn her bitter.

"Shh," I hushed, stroking her hair. "You have more than me. Look at where you are, Harp. Jason and Gillian are here for you too. And you are still an amazing and successful pastry chef. No one can take us or that from you."

After a while she calmed down and pulled away. I got up to grab some tissues from the bathroom so she could wipe her nose. Her smile was small and shaky. "What a baby, right?"

"Babe, you mean," I joked, sitting down on the edge of the bed.

She rolled her eyes. "Oh yeah, I've never looked hotter."

"Well, you've never looked more badass."

Thankfully she chuckled, throwing me a grateful look. "This is what I need from you. I need you—everyone—to not treat me like I'm fragile or like I might break at any second. I just want to be treated like Harper. Not like Harper, the chick who got her ass kicked by her druggy musician ex-boyfriend."

"Okay." I nodded. "I can do that. And so in that spirit I'm going to ask you if you've heard from Vince since he got out on bail?"

My friend glowered, but it wasn't at me. "Yeah, he's been calling. I finally answered the phone last night and told him that if he didn't stop calling I'd file harassment charges to go along with the assault charges. And then I hung up. He hasn't called again."

"Good."

Her sudden soft contemplation of me confused me. "What?" I asked.

She shrugged. "I just . . . I used to wonder about you. And Nick. After everything you told me about him, how much you used to love him, I could never really wrap my head around how you could just walk away from him even if he did cheat with Gemma. I never got it. How could you just stop loving someone because he made a mistake? I sometimes wondered if at first you were in denial about that . . . whether distance was really what made you get over him. I didn't get it because there's a part of me that still loves my mom." Her eyes filled with fresh tears. "Not the mom I left behind but the mom of my childhood, you know. The one who loved me more than anything. I can't make myself stop loving that mom. So I didn't get it. You and Nick. But now I get it. His betrayal was a punch to the heart while Vince's was literally a punch to the face. A moment so big that it kills every good feeling you ever had for them."

"Yes," I whispered.

"Shouldn't I feel that about my mom too?" She wiped angrily at her tears. "Is there something wrong with me?"

"No, there isn't." I moved back to her, needing to touch her, comfort her, my heart breaking because hers was. "It's like you said . . . it's Greta you love." I referred to her mother by name. "It's your childhood mom. And as far as I'm concerned, she is a different person from the woman you left behind." I rubbed her back, trying to soothe her, and when her breathing seemed to even out again, I said as gently as possible, "Maybe you should think about talking to someone."

Harper stiffened beneath my touch. "A shrink?"

"A therapist. Someone who can give you an unbiased, rational sense of perspective so you can stop blaming yourself for feelings that are only natural."

She was silent so long I wondered if I'd made a very bad move by bringing up the subject.

But then she gradually relaxed against my touch and whispered, "Would you come with me? I know they won't let you in but . . . you could wait outside for me?"

Tears of gratitude blurred my vision and I leaned down to kiss her forehead, the tears spilling over with the movement. "Anything, Harp. I'd do anything."

"Love you, Ava," she whispered, her voice hoarse with emotion.

"I love you too."

Twenty-six

Once a few days had passed, Jason and I moved Harper back to her apartment, and I stayed with her the first night. While she'd been at Jason's, I'd had someone replace her door with one even sturdier than the last. However, I also suggested she find a new place so she didn't have to worry about the possibility of Vince dropping by. The suggestion was met with approval and we'd already toured two apartments she liked, including a studio in Caleb's building. I didn't tell her it was Caleb's building because I was worried she wouldn't move in if she was embarrassed by what he'd witnessed. But I liked the idea of her in that building with its tight security. Plus, I would just feel safer knowing Caleb was there if she ever needed his help.

Being busy with Harper meant I didn't see Caleb for four days. We stayed in contact and I heard his frustration the last time he called. There was a part of me that could no longer deny that I hoped his frustration was more emotional than sexual—or at least both.

Harper was back at Canterbury, and with each passing day she worked more and more hours. She basically, according to Jason, oversaw the kitchen and unnecessarily bossed people around. But in her own words it made her feel human again, so Jason was allowing it, as long as it didn't interfere with service.

Finally, Caleb and I agreed I'd come over to his apartment on Friday after work.

Caleb: Don't wear any underwear. I've no patience for it tonight.

I'd laughed at that text, assuming he was joking. But then I began to wonder.

That was a joke. Right?

Twenty minutes later I'd received:

Caleb: Since when do I tell jokes?

I'm wearing underwear. Deal with it.

Caleb: Then wear cheap underwear.

I don't own cheap underwear. And why?

Caleb: Because I'm going to rip it off.

Then . . .

Caleb: I'm supposed to go into a meeting in five minutes and I'm hard thinking about tonight.

A thrill of lust shot through me.

See you tonight.

Caleb: I hope you don't have any plans tomorrow.

Why?

Caleb: Because I'm not letting you out of my bed for the next 48 hours.

Desire consumed me, making my cheeks hot.

Then I guess I do have plans. Very sexy plans with a hot Scot.

Caleb: Good. See you soon.

However, when Caleb's apartment door opened later that evening, I wasn't greeted by the hot Scot I was most looking forward to greeting.

Jamie let me into the apartment, giving me an apologetic smile. "Caleb's running late. I said I'd wait around tae let you into the apartment."

His usual uniform of T-shirt and jeans had been replaced by a dark navy shirt and suit trousers. I gave myself permission to acknowledge that Jamie was sexy as hell.

"Hot date?" I asked, following him into the living room.

He shrugged. "Just some bird I met at the gym. Said I'd meet her for drinks."

Bird? Charming.

It almost made me not want to thank him, but he ultimately deserved my gratitude. "I don't know if I said this before, but thank you for your help last weekend."

Jamie grabbed his watch off the coffee table, and as he put it on he studied me beneath his lashes. When the watch was on, he straightened, sliding his hands into his trouser pockets and cocking

his head in contemplation. "You thanked me already. You know . . .
I misjudged you, Ava. I'm sorry."

Remembering our first meeting, I nodded and crossed my arms
in an unconscious defensive maneuver. "Why *did* you get all judgy
with me when we met?"

"Because you reminded me of Carissa. Caleb's ex-fiancée was just
like you. Or so I thought. Well put together. Designer clothes. Into
her looks and material shit that doesn't matter. Everyone could see
it but Caleb. He thought she had hidden depths, but the woman was
a bloody kiddie pool."

There was no way to describe what I felt in that moment.
"Stunned" didn't quite cut it. Neither did "hurt." Or "angry" or "bitter." I was all those things as Jamie continued talking as if he hadn't
delivered the epic, discombobulating news that Caleb Scott had
once been engaged to be married.

"Carrie messed Caleb up. She really did. And there is something
about you that reminds me of her."

"Gee. Thanks."

He held his hands up in defense. "I dinnae mean—Look, you just
have that same quality about your physical appearance. But that's
where the similarities end. I saw that for real on Saturday night. You
really care about your friend. And I think you really care about Caleb
too. I dinnae think Carrie ever cared about anyone but herself."

Ex-fiancée.

Carissa.

Carrie.

WHAT?!

"Anyway, I best get going. Make yourself at home. Caleb
shouldn't be long."

I was barely aware of him leaving, my mind in chaos over the
information bomb that had just exploded about my supposedly
commitment-phobic friend with benefits.

Not even ten seconds after Jamie departed, the door opened again. I marched across the living room into sight of the door as Caleb shut it behind him and threw his keys into a bowl at the end of the kitchen counter. His lips started to turn up at the corners at the sight of me.

Then he saw my expression.

Caleb drew to an abrupt halt. "What's happened now?"

I glared at him even as I was desperate for some explanation that would mean that the only man who I'd trusted to be completely honest with me hadn't goddamn lied to me this whole time! "Carissa." The name was supposed to come out in an angry huff. But I just sounded sad and confused.

His eyes flattened, his features slackened, and he gave me that blank look I hated as he began to loosen his tie. "What about her?"

Indignation fired through me. "What about her? What about her?! How about the fact that she was your fiancée, Caleb? Mr. I've Never Been in a Serious Relationship with Anyone. You lied to me!"

Whipping the tie off, he kept his blank expression all of five seconds. Caleb started toward me, a flush of anger in his cheeks, his eyes intimidatingly cold. "I didn't lie."

"You told me you'd never been serious with anyone before," I retorted as he strode right by me and into his bedroom.

I followed, ignoring the fact that he was shrugging out of his suit jacket. "Well?"

"I never said that," he bit out. "I said I didn't do serious relationships, not that I never had."

Furious that he was trying to get out of this on a technicality, I yelled, "You implied otherwise!"

"Do you want tae keep your voice down," he growled at me as he marched by me in just his shirtsleeves and trousers.

Where the hell was he going now?

The thought was answered instantly as he delved into the liquor cabinet in his kitchen and poured himself a whiskey. I wanted to throw it in his face! "You said you would never lie to me. And I stupidly trusted you."

Caleb turned to face me. "I didn't lie tae you, Ava."

How could he be so calm? "Yeah? It was a lie by omission."

"I'm not talking about this. You can either march that sweet arse back into the bedroom and take off your clothes or you can get out."

I flinched like he'd slapped me. I was barely aware of the instant remorse in his eyes as I grabbed my purse and began to make my way to the door.

His strong hand circled my left bicep and jerked me around with enough force to bring me colliding against his chest. Once there, Caleb wrapped his arms around me, trapping me. "I'm sorry for saying that," he apologized, his voice hoarse. "But I'm not a liar, Ava, and I won't let you say I am."

"We're supposed to be friends," I whispered, letting my feelings show in my gaze as I looked up into his. "You know everything about me. You know about my parents, about Nick and Gem. And now I realize I don't know anything about you."

"That's not true." He gave me a little shake, his gaze accusatory. "You know more than most."

I immediately thought of Quinn. Confiding in me about his brother's death couldn't have been easy and I felt ashamed for momentarily forgetting that he had. Still, it didn't erase my anger. "Then why didn't you tell me about Carissa?"

Like I'd suddenly turned scorching hot in his arms, he pushed me away and turned around. I watched in confusion as he walked into the living room, running a hand through his hair in seeming frustration.

"I dinnae want tae talk about her."

"Well, I do!"

He spun around and yelled, "Tough shit!"

I winced, frozen to the spot, because he was more than a little intimidating. I'd never seen him so furious and I began to dread knowing the truth about his ex-fiancée. It cut me deeply that she could elicit this kind of emotion from him. "Caleb . . . you're still in love with her, aren't you?"

Instantly, his features arranged themselves into a harsh mask of revulsion. "I *hate* the bitch."

Shock parted my lips at the dark vitriol in his words. Now I really wanted to know. "Tell me what she did."

"Why?" He strode toward me, his chest heaving with emotion. "Why are you doing this tae me?"

As I saw the desperation in him, my motivations changed in an instant. It was no longer about me and my feelings, but about him. For as long as we'd known each other, there had been this quiet anger simmering within him. I hadn't acknowledged it before, always putting it down to whatever was happening in the moment. But it didn't just surface in moments of frustration like our first meeting or my announcement that I was going on a date with someone else. It was *always* there. "Because whatever happened to you is slowly eating you up inside."

He stopped, his body inches from mine, and stared at me with such pain I wanted to reach out and soothe him. What had she done to him?

"Ava . . ." My name sounded like it had been dragged out of him. It was a plea.

"You told me that Harper needed to talk about what happened to her. It's time to take your own advice."

Caleb exhaled a shuddering breath, and to my horror I watched his eyes fill with tears. "She killed my baby, Ava. She killed my baby."

Just the sight of him, this big, strong man who made me feel so safe, in tears, in agony, so vulnerable, was enough to bring tears to my own eyes. And his words caused a sharp streak of pain through my chest. "Caleb."

His whole body seemed to sag and he stumbled back toward the couch and dropped into it. Resting his arms on his knees, he bowed his head, breaking eye contact. "Carrie . . . We dated four years ago. We were together a year when she fell pregnant." His voice was so hoarse, the words like sandpaper against rock. "I was happy. Thought she was. I proposed even though my family told me they had doubts about her. She was twelve weeks pregnant, and a day after saying yes tae marrying me, she went behind my back and had an abortion. I was dreaming of holding that wee person in my arms one day, of watching him or her grow up, being part of a big family like I had been. And she decided she didn't want tae be a mum."

He looked up at me now and the tears he'd been holding at bay spilled down his cheeks. "The worst part? She said she'd lost the baby when she was out shopping with a friend. She pretended tae be devastated for about two weeks, until her friend decided I had the right tae know the truth. When I confronted her, Carrie tried tae deny it at first . . . until she couldn't keep the lie up any longer. I asked her why. Why did she do it behind my back? And she told me it was because she was afraid of what it would do tae her physically and emotionally. She said she still wanted tae have kids but later, when we were older, and even then she wanted tae get a surrogate and employ a nanny. Have you ever heard anything like it? That someone could be so vain, so selfish, so cowardly, she'd kill the life inside of her without talking tae me about her fears. She would take my child from me, knowing I'd already lost my wee brother, she would add tae my grief. And then think I'd still want her. How the hell did I not see it?"

"I'm sorry," I whispered as I approached him. I kneeled at his feet and grabbed his hands in mine, needing to touch him. Suddenly I understood that the bitter grief I saw in the back of Caleb's eyes sometimes wasn't just about losing Quinn. It was about losing his child. "I'm so sorry."

His pain was unbearable and in that moment I felt every stab of it myself. I felt like my heart was breaking. I wanted to hunt his ex down and destroy her for what she'd done to him.

"Wee yin," he whispered, letting go of one of my hands to brush his thumb down my cheek. "Dinnae cry."

I stiffened because I hadn't realize I was, but at his words I felt the wetness on my cheeks.

And it hit me like a hammer to my chest.

I loved him.

His pain was my pain.

I was in love with him.

"How could she do that?" I wondered out loud. "How could she?"

Caleb didn't answer. He stared at me, the tears having dried on his cheeks. He looked calmer. Finally he asked contemplatively, "Did you ever think about having kids? Before Nick and Gemma . . ."

This time the tears that spilled down my cheek were for me, because I'd let Nick and Gem take so much and now here I was, in love with a man who was afraid to love anyone. "I gave up on that dream a while ago."

"Aye," he whispered, holding on to my hands tightly. "Me too."

Twenty-seven

There are many different kinds of love in this world. I knew that. Silly me, however, to think I could control my complex heart by telling it what kind of love it was allowed to feel.

You're not allowed to love a man romantically, I told it.

I'll do what I want, it eventually replied.

Reeling by how heartbroken I felt for Caleb and the obvious conclusion that I had fallen in love with him, I was the perfect companion for him that evening. Lost in the emotions I'd forced him to face, we sat together with the TV on but neither of us really watched the movie. We were handling our own feelings but with a reassuring presence beside us.

Moreover, he didn't ask me to leave and I didn't tell him I was going to. Instead we got into bed together and for the first time we just held each other until we fell asleep.

I thought it was beautiful.

The beginning of something.

Little did I know it was the biggest mistake I'd made with Caleb thus far.

When I woke up in his bed the next morning, I was alone. I

quickly washed in the bathroom and put on the wrinkled clothes I'd worn yesterday. I wandered out into the apartment only to be greeted by a pajama-clad Jamie eating a bowl of cereal. He swallowed his food at the sight of me.

"Morning, Ava."

"Good morning." I searched the apartment but there was absolutely no sign of Caleb. "Where's your brother?"

Jamie frowned and stared determinedly ahead at the television as he replied, "Oh, he asked me tae tell you that he got called into the office. Some emergency."

There was something off about the way he said it, but I didn't know him well enough to know if he was lying. Still, my heart began to pound and a queasy, uneasy feeling began to roil in my stomach. "Will he be gone all morning?"

"All day."

"Oh." What the hell was going on? "Right. I'll get going. See you later."

"Bye, Ava."

There was something in his tone that made me look back at him. As if he was really saying good-bye. But he was still watching the TV like nothing out of the ordinary was happening, so I shoved away the thought, assuming I was paranoid.

As it turned out . . . I was not at all paranoid.

SATURDAY, JUNE 2, 4:43 P.M.

Ava: Hope everything is okay at work? Are you free tonight?

Caleb: In middle of crisis. Looks like I'll be working well into the night to fix it.

Ava: Okay. I could swing by the office with food and coffee if you need it?

Caleb: No, we're fine.

SUNDAY, JUNE 3, 2:23 P.M.

Ava: Crisis averted?

Caleb: Getting there.

Ava: Call me when you're free.

TUESDAY, JUNE 5, 7:36 A.M.

Ava: Free for lunch?

Caleb: Not today.

FRIDAY, JUNE 8, 9:32 P.M.

Ava: I'm at the bar at Canterbury, hanging with Harper. Come meet us.

Caleb: Busy. Sorry.

Ava: We need to talk.

Caleb: I'll call you tomorrow.

SUNDAY, JUNE 10, 10:01 A.M.

Ava: You didn't call.

Caleb: Busy week. I'll call you later.

I stared at my phone, my friend's chatter with the real estate agent background noise to my growing anger and frustration. That was putting it mildly. The last week of Caleb avoiding me had filled me with such anxiety and outrage it was a wonder I was able to focus on work at all. He made me feel like a clingy girlfriend.

I just wanted him to be honest, even if that honesty was going to break my heart.

The studio apartment we were standing in was the one in Caleb's building. It was on the second floor, had a view of the water from the windows in the kitchen/living room/bedroom, and the entire thing could probably fit into Caleb's living room on the sixteenth floor.

For its steep rental price, it was a tiny 460 square feet, but it was thirteen hundred dollars a month cheaper than my rent and it came with security personnel and access to an indoor and outdoor pool, sauna, and gym.

"I'd feel safe here," Harper said, spinning slowly around in the space.

It was our third viewing of the apartment, and because I sensed Harper was on the verge of choosing this place I decided I needed to fess up to her.

"Could you give us a minute?" I asked the real estate agent.

He nodded. "I'll be outside."

I waited until the apartment door closed behind him and turned to an expectant Harper.

"What's up?"

Although her wrist was still in a cast and her ribs still hurt, she was looking a million times better. I was glad. It was hard to look at her all bruised and battered and not want to kill someone. "Confession time."

She frowned. "Okay?"

"Caleb lives in this building. His brother Jamie is staying with him indefinitely too."

"Why didn't you say anything before?"

"I didn't want it to affect your decision and I liked how secure this place was. But it's not up to me and you should know that you'll probably see them around if you rent this place."

Harper nodded, the excitement dimming from her eyes as she surveyed the space again. I waited as she walked slowly over to the window and stared out across the water at Boston Harbor. "What must they think of me?"

"Not at all what you're thinking they think," I said instantly. "They were angry *for* you, Harper, not at you."

"Then I shouldn't be afraid to face them." Her shoulders straightened and she turned to me, looking determined. "I can't let other people's opinions sway my decisions. And I can't let Vince win that way, you know. Time to be brave."

I nodded in agreement.

"I feel safe here. I'm taking it."

"I'm glad." I gave her a relieved smile.

"And you"—she stepped toward me, her expression sober—"you need to be brave too, Ava. No more letting Nick win. Because that's what you'll be doing if you don't tell Caleb the truth. You need to tell him that you love him."

I couldn't even pretend to be surprised that she'd worked it out, probably long before I did. "How did you know?"

"The way you talk about him. Especially now, after how he was with me that night . . . it changed things for you. You love him. And I know not seeing him all week has you paranoid and upset. Go work it out."

Emotion choked me, so all I could do was nod.

Harper smiled a real smile for the first time in weeks. "He loves you too, Ava. I know it. Make him admit it. Please. One of us needs to get a happily ever after." When she just continued to stare at me, I fully comprehended her meaning.

"What? Now?"

"He lives in this building, right?" She smiled.

My pulse instantly sped up at the thought of just showing up at Caleb's place. There was no denying he was giving me the brush-off this week and I knew that it was because of everything he'd told me about Carissa. He had made himself vulnerable to me and I was pretty sure it had spooked him.

However, I knew Harper was right. I couldn't go on pretending I didn't love him and I definitely wanted to stop running away from my feelings.

"Okay."

Harper grinned and grabbed me by the shoulders. "You can do this. Go. I'll get all the paperwork signed for this place, and if you and Caleb work things out, text me and I'll just head back to the apartment."

"Are you sure?" An angry swarm of butterflies suddenly erupted in my belly. "Oh, I feel a little sick."

"That's because this matters." She turned me around to face the door and then slapped my ass. "Go get him, tiger."

I rolled my eyes but released a nervous little laugh that made me feel marginally better.

By the time the elevator took me up to the sixteenth floor, however, my heart was racing so fast I thought I might pass out. Breathing in and out slowly as I stood outside his apartment door, I fought for calm, and reminded myself that, no matter what, this was Caleb. I could trust him to be totally honest with me and I'd have closure, one way or another.

I rang the doorbell and felt flutters in my throat at the sound of footsteps coming toward me on the other side of the wall.

Caleb pulled open the door and froze at the sight of me.

He was wearing a plain black T-shirt and worn blue jeans. Last week his beard was starting to become an actual beard—not that I'd minded—but he'd trimmed it. Maybe even that morning. His hair was wet, as if he'd only recently gotten out of the shower.

My eyes finally found his after perusing him hungrily.

Caleb wasn't looking at me hungrily in return. He looked pissed. "What are you doing here?"

Without giving him a chance to shut the door on me, I stepped inside and walked toward the living room, seeing it was empty. "Are we alone?"

"Jamie's out. And I repeat, what are you doing here?"

I turned to face him, unhappiness and anger piercing me at the way he was staring at me. Like I was a mere acquaintance who had decided to inconvenience him on a Sunday morning. "Harper is interested in a studio in your building. We were here anyway, and you've been avoiding me, so I thought I'd drop by and ask why." Thankfully, I sounded much calmer than I felt.

His expression turned almost pitying and I think I loathed him as much as I loved him in that moment. "You know why, Ava."

Inwardly, I flinched, feeling a painful crack down the middle of my chest. "Too much of a coward to just come out and say it?" I whispered.

"We aren't in a relationship. We dinnae need tae offer each other explanations or owe each other a conversation. I thought my lack of communication spoke for itself. I no longer want tae sleep with you." His eyes were hard, flat, his features carefully lacking in expression.

And I knew with soul-deep certainty that Caleb Scott was lying to me.

"Liar," I whispered.

His eyes narrowed as he walked toward me. "I never took you for the clingy type. You knew what this was and you were good with it."

I wanted to smack the unemotional look right off his face and shake the flatness out of his voice. "We both know that it changed. And we both know why you're running scared now."

Caleb shrugged. "I'm not running scared. I'm just done."

"You're in love with me." I couldn't hold back my emotion anymore.

He just stared at me. Giving me nothing.

So I wrenched the words out, hoping that he'd crack knowing what they cost me. "And I'm so in love with you," I whispered. Sadly. My heart breaking because those words should be whispered in elation. Not in sorrow and regret.

Because he was making me regret them with every second that passed.

Especially when his eyes turned pitying again. "I dinnae. And I'm not going tae feel bad, because we agreed this was casual."

"What happened to our friendship?" I seethed now. "Or is this the way you treat your friends?"

"I think we both knew that as soon as one of us lost interest in sex with the other that the friendship would die."

So matter of fact.

So cold.

"I don't believe you."

His eyes lit with anger and I almost rejoiced at the sign of emotion. "Then believe this. I've got *someone* coming tae the apartment this morning."

I felt like I might throw up. "Someone?"

"Aye. Someone, Ava. Someone who is going tae stick tae the rules."

Liar.

"And who is this someone?"

"Jen." He answered immediately.

Jen Granton? Yeah. He was lying. My nausea eased. "That's a little pathetic, Caleb."

Still, the thought that he might have started sleeping with anyone already made tears prick my eyes. I hated him for it. "You were just going to start sleeping with someone else without telling me this was over?"

For a moment he was silent and then he looked away, as if he couldn't bear to stare at me any longer.

"Stop lying," I said. "Jen isn't on her way over."

"If she was, it would be none of your business," he snapped, striding toward me suddenly, looking furious, masking what I knew with certainty was panic. "We're no longer each other's business."

I shook my head, frustrated that he wouldn't just admit the truth. Caleb was usually so brutally honest that I didn't know how to handle him like this. I had to make him admit that he loved me, but how? "Why would you want me to think you're with her?"

"Maybe because I am."

"Nah. You've developed champagne tastes, Caleb. You can't go back to cheap wine."

Something like admiration flickered in his gaze and he smirked. "Arrogance doesn't become you, Ava."

"Yes, it does." I stepped into his personal space and watched him tense and glower instantly. "You want me right now."

He put his hands on my shoulders and gently pushed me away from him, dropping his hands like I'd scalded him. "I dinnae know how tae make this any clearer. We're done. You've forced the conversation so here it is. I dinnae want you anymore because you broke the rules. You think I didn't know how you were starting tae feel after your tantrum about Carissa?"

"Tantrum?" I sucked in a breath at the word. "Screw you, Caleb."

"You've done that." He moved away, walking toward the window, his tone cold and sardonic. "Now find someone new tae do it with."

"Stop this," I demanded. "Just . . . stop! I know you're scared. *I'm* scared. But we've found something amazing here. Don't throw it away because of what she did. If I'm willing to be brave enough to give something real between us a shot, then shouldn't you be too?"

He glanced over his shoulder at me, his expression shadowed by the glare of daylight from the window. Then he fully turned, strode back toward me, and his voice was as icy as his eyes. "I've tried tae be as diplomatic as I'm capable of here. Since it's not working, here's the truth. I could never love you, Ava. Is that clear enough? *Never.*"

Each word was like a knife slice through my skin, every inch of me seeming to burn from the pain. Some small spark of hope that was clinging to the belief that it was his fear talking died as Caleb drew his gaze down my body and back up again.

There was something in the way that he looked at me. Disdain he was trying hard not to reveal.

It reminded me of the way Nick had looked at me when he told me he could never love me like he'd loved Gem.

And that was when realization hit me with so much force I honestly couldn't breathe for a second or two. Survival kicked in and I gulped in a huge gasp of air, not aware of Caleb taking a step toward me, only aware of the sudden glaring truth.

"You don't see me as anything but a piece of ass," I said softly, not seeing him, not seeing anything. "Just a pretty face."

When he didn't say anything, when he didn't disagree, I tried to make him.

"Your jealousy? Your possessiveness? They meant nothing?"

"That isn't love. It's lust. Pure and simple. You're beautiful and you know I'm attracted tae you. Aye, it made me possessive of you.

But that isn't love. Not like you want. And that's why this needs tae end."

He couldn't have said anything worse. He couldn't have killed the hope inside me any more proficiently. And in that moment my love turned to hate as quickly as a match striking tinder.

I hated him more than I had ever hated anyone.

Finally I dragged my gaze up to meet his, feeling lost and sick, and wondering how I was going to put myself back together again. Why was I so unlovable? "What was it Nick said? That I'm empty? Nothing to see here but a beautiful face." My voice hardened with the bitterness rising up inside of me.

All I saw was my pain and rage. I didn't see the way Caleb paled at my words. "Ava."

I turned, needing to get out of there, to find someplace to lick my wounds. Someplace where I could find the strength one more time to not let Nick's or Caleb's treatment of me turn me into something cold and filled with self-loathing.

That wasn't here.

I needed to be as far away from this man, whom I had trusted more than any man—I hated him!

"Ava." I heard his footsteps behind me and I picked up my pace, throwing his apartment door open. "Ava!"

Instinct made me run to the elevator, my hands shaking as I hit the button. Thankfully, it binged right open.

"Ava!" I heard Caleb roar, but I wouldn't look up.

"Shut the door, shut the door, shut the door," I muttered in prayer.

It shut before he could reach it.

I heard the muffled shout of my name once more as the elevator descended.

I was in so much pain I was almost numb from it. Like my brain had frozen my pain receptors because it knew my body, my heart, couldn't handle it.

The elevator doors opened and I walked out into the reception in a daze. Harper was waiting for me, sitting on one of the reception chairs, reading a magazine. Her head lifted at the sight of me and she stood, her smile faltering at my expression.

An overwhelming rush of love for her broke through the numbness and tears began spilling down my cheeks before I could stop them. Not wanting to have a public meltdown, I grabbed her good arm when she came toward me. "I need to go home," I whispered.

Concern and fury fought for dominance in her eyes but she controlled both, taking hold of me to lead me out of the building. "What happened?" she asked as she searched the street for a cab.

"He said just because I was beautiful didn't mean he could love me. It was Nick all over again." I wiped angrily at my tears. "Why do men want me to feel worthless? What is that?" I laughed harshly.

"I'm going to kill him," Harper growled with such menace I thought she might actually mean it.

Thankfully, a cab appeared before she could, and she waved it down. Just as I was getting in it, someone shouted my name.

Not someone.

Him.

I glanced back over my shoulder to see Caleb standing outside the building, his chest heaving like he was out of breath.

"Get in." Harper practically pushed me into the cab. Then she yelled, "Burn in hell, dickwad!" before sliding into the cab beside me. "Mount Vernon Street. Now," she ordered the driver.

He pulled away and I kept my eyes straight ahead, determined not to look back.

"He's a liar and a coward, Ava." Harper wrapped her arms around me as she spoke. "He loves you, I know it. But he doesn't deserve you. A man who knows what you've been through, who knows what saying that to you would do to you, doesn't deserve you. He chose to protect himself over protecting you and that is not okay. Do you understand? It's not okay and you need to let him go."

I nodded, feeling so dazed, it was a little like being drugged. I think I might have been in shock. "You're right."

"You are the smartest, bravest, kindest, funniest woman I know. No one can take that from you." She gripped my hand tight. "You told me you were afraid I'd lose myself after what Vince did, and I'm trying really hard not to. And now you have to do the same. You can't let Caleb shatter all the pieces of yourself you put back together after Nick and Gemma's betrayal. Okay?"

I glanced up from our hands to hold her gaze. "Okay."

"Promise?"

"I promise." I took strength from her strength.

"We have each other. That's more than some people ever get."

"Damn straight."

Our eyes were mirrors, reflecting back pain that we were determined to obliterate with our silent solidarity and gratitude for each other.

Twenty-eight

Caleb called.

Five minutes after the cab pulled away, my phone rang. Harper saw the gut-punch look on my face and promptly took the phone from me and blocked Caleb's number. She then proceeded to give the cabdriver her address, in case the Scot decided to pay me an immediate visit.

I felt exhausted as we climbed the stairs to Harper's place. My limbs were heavy, my eyes felt swollen, and all of my insides felt like they'd just suffered through an internal earthquake. It almost felt like the time when I was fifteen in the car with my mother when someone slammed into us in an intersection. For a while afterward my body still shook from the impact. That's how I felt now.

My phone rang again in my purse and Harper shook her head at my wide-eyed look of panic. "It can't be," she said. "I blocked him."

Fumbling for my phone, I winced when I saw it was Stella. I was not in the mood to take a work call, but I was also incapable of ignoring calls from my boss. "Stella?" I said, hoping I sounded normal.

"Emergency," Stella clipped. "Gabe is supposed to be going to New York this weekend to get the specs on that Fifth Avenue penthouse he's been bragging about."

I liked Gabe. But he was a bragger and, yes, he had not shut up about that penthouse for the last week, not just because it was on Fifth Avenue, but because it was owned by a famous actress. "Okay?"

"He has the flu. And did not tell me but proceeded to get ready to leave for New York only to faint at the top of a flight of stairs in his apartment building. Now he's in the hospital and his fiancée is blaming me for putting too much pressure on him."

"It's not your fault," I said immediately. "And is he okay?"

"He has a concussion, and of course the flu. As sorry as I am for that, if he'd just told me, he would not currently be hospitalized and I would not be panicking about losing this client. A Hollywood A-lister, Ava. We haven't had one of those in a while. If she likes what we do, she will tell her friends."

Realization hit me and my exhaustion actually doubled. "You want me to go to New York."

"Yes. First swing by the office. I'm here and have all of Gabe's notes, so you're going in prepared."

"I'll be right there."

We hung up and I stared dully at Harper, who was scowling. "Guess I'm going to New York."

My friend's hands flew to her hips. "You just had your heart broken. You should have told her that."

"Well, Gabe has the flu and a concussion, which kind of trumps broken heart at the moment."

"Do you hear yourself? Your voice is all flat and sad. Not the greatest impression to make on a client."

"I'll pull it together. In fact, this is just what I need. A distraction." I began making my way back down her apartment building steps. "I'd better call another cab."

"Maybe I should come with you," Harper suggested.

I threw her a grateful smile over my shoulder, one I knew didn't quite make it to my eyes. "Hey, I'll be fine."

She did not look convinced. "Call me when you land."

I hugged her. "Thank you."

As it turned out, the trip to New York was exactly what I'd needed. It forced me to stop myself from crumpling up into a ball in my bed and sobbing until there was no water left in my body. Anytime my thoughts turned to Caleb and our confrontation, my throat seemed to thicken with too much emotion. I felt like I was choking on it.

So I buried my head in the client file Stella had given me.

Once I was in New York, I got to my hotel and could barely eat, but I had a couple of glasses of wine knowing it would make me sleepy. It worked and I thankfully slept, my alarm waking me early. On Monday I was much too busy taking specs at the penthouse to dwell on anything else. Just as I assumed would happen, I didn't meet with the actress, but with her personal assistant. We spoke at length about the design and she hovered over me the entire time I was taking measurements with my laser distance meter. It was a smart little tool that worked out lengths, heights, and area volume. After I'd taken copious amounts of photos of the space, the PA and I talked even more. I spent a total of six hours with her, leaving just in time to catch my evening flight back to Boston. The entire time on the flight I worked on the project, jotting and sketching ideas.

I updated Stella in the taxi ride back to my apartment, and I did it with the same calm I'd approached the entire weekend. Somehow, I'd even managed to convince myself that I was okay.

So when I stepped into my empty apartment and closed the door behind me, I was taken aback by the overwhelming pain that squeezed my chest like a vise, forcing out the first sob.

My ass hit the floor and I cried like I'd never cried before in my life. Big-hiccupping, can't-breathe-properly, might-throw-up-all-over-my-deep-pile-carpet crying.

When the tears eventually stopped, I was left with the horrific unease in my gut and tightness in my chest. Panic. Panic and loneliness.

"No," I whispered to myself, shaking my head, seeing images of him everywhere. Lounging on my armchair, staring at me with that distinctive, brooding intensity. Leaning on my kitchen counter drinking a cup of coffee and smirking at me like he thought I was funny and cute.

My head rolled to the side and I looked through the doorway to my bedroom.

I closed my eyes against the memories I found in there.

Loss.

The feeling . . . that terrifying, incapacitating feeling that was creeping over my body like a phantom pain that couldn't be explained . . . it was loss.

The next morning I dragged my butt out of bed and got ready for work. I prepared myself for the day like it was any other day, faltering only when I looked at the jewelry on my nightstand. The watch I put on, the earrings too. But the diamond tennis bracelet I'd loved so much only yesterday was a beautiful dagger to the heart today. I clutched it tight in my hand, feeling its sharp edges bite into my skin, and I promptly found an old shoe box buried at the back of my wardrobe. I stuffed it in there, where I wouldn't have to look at it.

Where Nick's bracelet had chafed with the memories, Caleb's wounded me too deep to pretend otherwise. It would stay in the box, image be damned.

The rest of my preparation went as well as could be expected.

Makeup was a wonderful thing. I didn't know what I would have done without it, because the puffy dark circles under my eyes from all the crying and lack of sleep were no longer visible under my magic makeup.

I still looked a little tired, but that could be explained away by traveling, and not the result of a broken heart. I didn't want Stella to know about Caleb. I didn't want anyone to know.

But that was not to be, because as I walked to work that morning I got a call from my uncle David. We'd kept in touch during his travels. However, my gut instinct told me somehow he'd found out. Not somehow, actually. My gut told me Harper had called him.

"Hey, you," I greeted, trying to sound like I wasn't dreading him asking me how I was.

"Hey, sweetheart," he said, and I flinched at the underlying sympathy and concern in just those two words.

"I'm fine," I said, wincing at how agitated I sounded.

"Hmm. Harper called."

"Yeah, I guessed that." I was going to kill her.

"She's worried about you."

"I'm fine."

"You don't sound fine."

"I'm hurrying to work, that's why."

"Sure."

"Uncle David." I blew out an exasperated sigh. "How are you?"

"I'm good. We're good. How are you since some asshole broke your heart?"

"I'd rather not talk about it."

"Fearne and I were thinking about coming home a little early and—"

"Nope," I said immediately, attempting not to feel anger but only gratitude that he cared that much. "Do not come home early because of me. I am a grown woman and a nonrelationship relationship I was in, unsurprisingly, did not work out. I am not going to wallow. And having my uncle, whom I love dearly for thinking so much of me, cut his travel plans short to come home and hold my hand is the equivalent of wallowing."

He was quiet a moment and then he sighed heavily. "No wallowing."

"No wallowing."

"It's just . . . Harper was worried that something this man said may have caused serious emotional harm."

Harper's concerns for me were similar to my concerns about how she would recover from Vince's assault. I didn't want him to change her. And she didn't want Caleb to change me. Yet that was inevitable. However, as I stood frozen on the corner of Walnut Street and Beacon, I was hit with powerful determination.

"No." I shook my head, staring dazedly around me. "I'm not going to let what he said undo all the good he did. He . . . my time with him . . . it woke me up, Uncle David. Nick made me afraid to trust people—he made me afraid to think about settling down with someone worthy and starting a family. But I want those things. As scary as it is to try to reach for them, as frightened as I am of someone hurting me *again*, I have to believe that there's someone out there who will love me. I've seen it. I see it in you and Fearne, Jason and Gillian, Patrice and Michael, Stella and Iain—hell, even in Mom and Dad in their own weird way."

"I'm glad to hear this," my uncle said softly. "I worry about you being alone."

I didn't want to be alone anymore.

It hurt that the person I wanted to be with didn't want me, and I could feel my throat tightening painfully with the emotion, but I breathed through it, searching for calm.

"Ava?"

"I'm okay," I croaked out. "Or I will be. Eventually."

He was quiet so long I thought we'd disconnected, but then he told me, "We're all afraid of something, sweetheart. It's up to us whether we stay and fight that fear . . . or whether we run and hide from it. I'm glad you're not going to hide anymore. You have to *promise* not to hide anymore."

"I promise." I swiped at a tear that escaped, ducking my head, embarrassed I was getting emotional on a street corner.

He cleared his throat, as though uncomfortable with all the emotion. "Well, good. I know . . . I know I'm gone a lot, but you know I'm still *here*, don't you?"

In all honesty, I'd let myself forget.

But I wouldn't again. "I know. I love you."

"I love you too. Fearne and I will be home in three weeks. We'll arrange a dinner."

"I'd like that."

We hung up and I continued on to work, shaking a little with my epiphany. It was too much not to share with Harper, so I called her while she was in the middle of bossing a junior chef around at Canterbury. As I stepped into our building on Beacon Street, Harper left the kitchen to hear me.

"You're mad I called David?" she asked, sounding confused.

"No, but a little heads-up would have been nice."

"I just wanted to remind you that you had more than me who loves you. Like you reminded me that I have more than you."

"I know and I get that. Actually, it was a good conversation." I waved to Stella as I passed her office and headed for my own. "I realized something. I'm not giving up."

Harper went silent. And then I could hear the glower in her tone, "On Caleb?"

"No." I flinched at his name. "That's over. You were right. Even if he does care about me, I couldn't be with someone who would choose to inflict that kind of pain on me just to protect himself.

No . . . I'm not giving up on love." I paused, wrinkling my nose. "That sounded less cheesy in my head."

Harper chuckled. "What does that mean exactly?"

"It means I don't want to be alone for the rest of my life. I want a family. It's time to get back out there, no matter how frightening it is to make myself vulnerable to someone again. It's time to start fighting for what I really want."

My friend went quiet.

"Harper?"

"When . . . you get all that—and I know you will because you're amazing and there are plenty of guys out there who will see that—so when you get him and you start popping out little mini versions of yourself . . . you won't forget me, right?" She laughed, like it was a joke, but I heard the pain underlying the question.

"Of course I won't. But you know you'll be too busy with your own guy and little mini versions of yourself too."

"I'm not there, Ava. I don't know if I'll ever be."

I thought of the therapist, a Dr. Ren, Harper got an appointment with at the end of the week. It was during my lunch hour so I could go with her as a silent support in the waiting room. "We'll see."

I could practically feel her rolling her eyes. "I don't know how I feel about this optimistic version of you."

"I don't know how to feel about it either. She scares me." I laughed.

Harper didn't. Instead she brought tears to my eyes when she said, "I think she's brave."

Twenty-nine

F red Russo was in the middle of showing me new curtain fabric that he'd ordered, and I was oohing and aahing over the beautiful shimmering silk taffeta, when my cell rang.

"Stella," I told Fred, giving him an apologetic look before walking to the other end of the storeroom for some privacy.

"Stella, I'm at Fred's," I said as a greeting. "Is everything okay?"

"Ask him for an update on my order for Lola Perera."

"I will."

"I'm just calling to let you know your handsome *friend* popped by the office five minutes ago, seeming very anxious to see you. In fact, he was under the impression I was lying about you not being here. Trouble in paradise?"

Caleb had come by the office? During his workday?

My stomach churned at the thought of facing him. What did he want?

"He said since he can't get you on your phone, he's left a message on your office phone and would you please do him the courtesy of returning his call."

"Thank you," I said, my voice flat even to my ears. "I really better get back to Fred."

"Ava—"

But I rudely told her I had to go and blew out a shaky breath. I stared at my cell for a minute or two, trying to decide if I was ready to hear his voice. Since I'd spent the entire morning convincing myself that I was ready to face my fears, I really had no option but to dial into my office voice mail.

"You have three new messages."

I impatiently waded through the first two messages from clients and then it felt like my heart stopped at the sound of his deep voice. He sounded *pissed*.

"Ava, where have you been? I stopped around your flat on Saturday and *Sunday . . . We need tae talk. Call me immediately."*

I replayed Caleb's message. I didn't know it was possible to feel so much from just hearing someone's voice. Guessing at why Caleb wanted to see me was too dangerous a game to play, so I refused to allow my mind to go there.

I did, however, play the voice mail a second and third time, rubbing at the ache in my chest as his voice rumbled in my ear.

"Everything okay?" Fred called to me.

No, I thought. *No, it's not okay.*

But one day it would be.

I snapped my phone shut.

It had to be. Because the alternative was not an option.

Despite my best efforts, I could not get Caleb's voice out of my head, and I agonized over whether calling him back was a good idea or not. Even as I sat in a quiet café with a client, I wasn't fully focused on discussing the redesign of his bijou apartment. Part of me was pondering the Caleb problem. Did I meet with him, let him say whatever he needed to say, so I could move on? Or did I decide he didn't deserve that chance and cut him out of my life entirely?

Since both options made me feel sick with uncertainty, it was proving a very difficult decision.

After the client meeting it was lunchtime. Nervous about heading back to the office in case Caleb turned up again (and also because I didn't want to answer Stella's inevitable questions), I stopped at the Earl of Sandwich in the Common and grabbed a tuna melt and iced tea to go.

I hadn't eaten much the last few days, but I was determined to nibble through the wave of nausea that had clung to me since my conversation with Caleb. Lost in my thoughts as I strolled from the Common toward the Public Garden, I was jolted back to my surroundings when a man blocked my way.

"Ava?"

Blinking in surprise, I needed a moment before recognizing him. And honestly, I didn't know how to feel when I did. "Leo?"

He gave me that handsome boyish grin and waved a half-eaten sub at me. "I'm on the go too. Where you off to?"

I gestured toward the Charles Street entrance into the gardens. "Just walking. Eating."

"Can I join you?"

Something about the interest in his eyes made me exclaim, "I'm no longer looking for just sex. You should know that."

Leo, thankfully, laughed good-naturedly at my embarrassing too-much-information declaration. "Well, I just thought we'd walk and eat and talk. If that's okay?"

I blushed and nodded as he fell into step beside me. "How have you been?"

"Good." He bit into his sandwich and waited to speak until he'd eaten the bite. "After we discussed the whole casual relationship thing, I decided it was the right move for me and I've just been . . . you know . . . having fun."

I grinned. In other words, he was slutting himself up all over Boston. "Having fun. Right."

"Obviously, things have changed for you."

Despite my weird announcement to him, I really didn't want to explain it to Leo. "I decided casual relationships aren't for me after all."

"I knew it was too good to be true." He chuckled.

"What do you mean?"

Leo shrugged as if it was obvious. "You're the kind of woman a man marries. You're not the kind of woman he casually sleeps with."

"Can I ask what the hell that means?"

"There are women you want to marry and women you just want to have sex with."

"What's the difference between them?"

If he heard the agitation and growing annoyance in my voice, he pretended not to notice. "Smart, successful, witty, and beautiful and doesn't need your money. You know, if she falls in love with you, she's actually fallen in love with *you* and not the kind of lifestyle you can provide for her. Dumb or pretends to be dumb because she thinks it makes you feel like more of a man, focused a lot on her looks, and not interested in anything but stroking your ego and other sensitive manly areas, then she's just a casual sex partner."

"You know, before you said all that I was actually feeling pretty good about being your best buddy." I scowled at him.

"What?" He shrugged before wolfing down the last of his sandwich.

"That's chauvinistic crap."

Leo wiped his mouth with his napkin and gestured to a bench on our right. I reluctantly followed him, hoping he was going to save himself. We settled onto the bench and I continued to nibble at my tuna melt, waiting for a response.

"It's not crap. I wish it were. But there are a lot of women out there like that in my experience. Some guys see her as the marrying kind because that's all they want. Someone to stroke their ego, etc. But men like me, if we're smart, we learn from that lesson and move on."

Understanding dawned. "Your first wife?"

"Interested in nothing but my family money."

"I'm sorry."

"Yeah, well, now I know better. If I'd done it the right way the first time, the thought of marriage wouldn't make my balls jump back up inside my body."

I'd just taken a sip of my iced tea and it promptly exploded out of my mouth in my shocked amusement. Leo threw his head back in a rich, deep laughter, and I coughed and laughed along with him. As our hilarity faded to gentle mirth, Leo handed me a clean napkin so I could wipe the iced tea off my chin.

It was as we were sharing a smile that I felt the burn on the side of my face.

I knew that sensation.

Tense, I followed it, and my breath stuttered at the sight of Caleb standing in the middle of the path. I didn't have to wonder how long he'd been there, because the furious glower on his face told me it was long enough to have witnessed my camaraderie with Leo.

"Caleb." My voice came out in a surprised croak. I cleared it and stood up, sensing Leo stand too. He shifted his body, almost protectively, close to mine. "Uh, what are you doing here?"

"Stella told me you take your lunch in the gardens when the weather is nice."

Damn Stella.

His glacial stare suddenly fixed on Leo.

"Uh . . . this is my friend Leo. Leo this is my . . . this is Caleb."

Caleb's nostrils flared at the introduction and I cursed myself for forgetting that I'd told him Leo was the guy I was going to date when I thought he wasn't returning from Scotland.

"Nice to meet you." Leo stepped forward and stuck out his hand.

Caleb stared at his hand like it was a piece of dung.

I winced.

Leo, however, cool as you please, just dropped his hand. "Or not." He shrugged, like he didn't care, and I decided I liked him all the more for it.

"We need tae talk," Caleb said. I knew it was directed at me, but he was still staring at Leo like he wanted to rip his head off.

I shouldn't have cared.

But I did.

I felt a smug, soothing satisfaction that I could still make him jealous. It meant he cared. And although it didn't change what he'd done, it was a small kind of balm to my pain.

"Leo." I turned to my companion with an apologetic smile. "I should . . ." I gestured to Caleb. "But it was really nice to see you again."

"Let's do lunch. Properly." He leaned down to kiss my cheek and whispered so only I could hear, "Best bud." When he pulled back, he winked at me and I knew that all he was asking for was friendship. However, he was deliberately provoking Caleb.

I shook my head, biting back my nervous laughter at his mischievousness, and gave him a little wave as he walked away.

Caleb's gaze followed him and I swear he looked ready to stalk Leo and murder him.

Ignoring the zing of dangerous thrill at being in his presence again, I started to walk away. "So talk."

"Where have you been?" he demanded as he caught up with me,

grabbing hold of my arm to stop me on the bridge. A young girl passed us, giving us a quizzical look, and Caleb sighed, easing his hold on me.

My arm tingled and I had to force myself from taking the last step that would bring us chest to chest. Instead I looked up into his face, feeling too many emotions—anger, grief, loss, love, hate—to choose one. Anger, however, autonomously decided to trump them all. I yanked my arm away. "Not that it is any of your business anymore, but I had to go to New York to meet a new client."

"Did you block my number?"

"Yes."

He ground his teeth together, the muscle in his jaw flexing. "If you had just given me a second tae explain . . ."

"I'm giving it to you now."

With a clipped nod, Caleb took hold of my arm again and started walking me off the bridge. We took a right just before the George Washington statue and Caleb stopped us at the end of the path, under the shade of a tree.

"I can see you better here," he explained, his voice gruff as his eyes seemed to drink in every aspect of my face.

The intensity of his stare made me shiver in awareness and I had to pull my gaze away from his. "Talk, Caleb."

"I think you're wonderful."

Astonished, I felt my gaze fly to his face to determine the seriousness of this statement. He looked at once fierce and sorry.

"I can't let you think you're anything else. I tried tae tell you that, but you ran out of my place before I could get the chance. As soon as I realized you thought I was . . . I'm not Nick. I dinnae think like Nick. No man in his right mind would, Ava. I am sorry for how I acted. I felt ambushed. I wasn't expecting you tae turn up, let alone force that conversation. I honestly thought if I stopped calling you, you would just protect yourself and move on without ever confronting me. Bringing up nonsense about another woman . . . I acted like a child. And I'm sorry."

Before I could even get over the monumental moment of alpha guy Caleb Scott apologizing and admitting to acting like a child, he reached for me, his palms on my neck, his thumbs stroking my cheeks. I knew he could probably feel my pulse racing beneath his hold. "You are the smartest, funniest, most caring, loyal, determined woman I have ever met. Having a beautiful face and a beautiful body doesn't make you any less of those things and it doesn't make you more attractive. Who you are makes you beautiful, Ava. When I met you, I thought you were sexy, aye, but the more I got tae know you the more beautiful you became. You are a find, wee yin. A precious find." He pulled me closer, and I gasped at the frustration and pain in his eyes. "If it could be anyone . . . it would be you, Ava Breevort. In a heartbeat. But I just . . ." He sighed, a shuddering, harsh sigh, and I felt the hopes he'd just built up crash as he let me go and stepped back. "I dinnae have that left tae give. *She* killed it when she—" Caleb cut off, his voice breaking, and he glanced around the gardens as if seeking something.

When he didn't find it, he stared off into the distance and whispered, "I need you tae be a good memory." He wrenched his eyes to me again. "I could handle almost anyone else in my life turning into a regret. But not you. I can't have what we had together going bad. I was an arse for trying tae make it that way. So we end it now the right way. In honesty and kindness. Because I can't regret you."

His words were agony. Tears of exasperation filled my eyes. "You know it would have been better if you never tried to explain. Better for me to think of you as a bastard than—"

"Than what?" he bit out impatiently.

I shook my head. "Caleb, don't you see? You changed me. You made me brave enough to fight against what I was most afraid of and admit that I'm in love with you. I wish I could make you feel brave too. But that's not going to happen apparently." I swiped at my tears but refused to break eye contact. He needed to understand the reality of what he was doing to us. "Just because you've decided I'm not worth the risk doesn't mean that I'm not willing to take it again. So I have to thank you for that. Because it might take weeks, months, but I will fight to get over you. I will fight to find someone who loves me and wants to make a future with me. I will move on."

The look on his face . . . it nearly crippled me.

Caleb didn't hide behind his usual blank mask. No. He looked furious and tortured and resentful of my words all at once.

I placed a hand on his chest, over his heart, hating to hurt him like he had hurt me but knowing it was necessary to get through to him. "Does that hurt, Caleb? To think of me with someone else?"

His answering expression was almost menacing and it said it all.

"Then don't you see? If you don't fight for me, if you let me go . . . there is no if or maybe about it. You *will* regret me." I reluctantly dropped my hand from his chest, waiting for him to answer. To wake the hell up!

All he did was stare at me, so visibly conflicted I had to fight not to comfort him. Instead I turned to my disappointment and my resentment of him because they were the emotions that bolstered me. They stiffened my spine and gave me the strength to walk away from the man I loved.

For good.

Thirty

What's that song that guy sings? You know, the one with those lyrics . . .

I'm only human after all.

Well, I am only human after all, and that's why, after saying that I wouldn't, I gave myself permission to wallow.

I told Harper I was allowing myself a week and then she had to drag me out of my gloom.

It didn't quite work out like that. After seeing Caleb, I couldn't return to the office; instead, I called in sick and asked Stella to explain to any clients who called that I'd be back in the office the next day. I went back to my apartment, curled up on my bed, and cried until I passed out from exhaustion.

Harper woke me later that evening calling to check on me, and that was when I told her about my confrontation with Caleb and how I was probably going to need a week to get over him. She acted like she thought it made sense, but I'd soon realize she was just appeasing me.

Although I dragged myself to work the next day and the day after that, the pain didn't lessen. In fact, I had to retreat to this numb place where I didn't let any kind of emotion in, in order to block out my grief. I was a black cloud of heartbreak, depressing everyone I met.

I was vaguely aware that Stella was quietly losing her mind over my passionless interaction with the clients and Harper kept subtly suggesting I should see her therapist.

By the end of week two I was not getting any better.

When I turned up to work on that Friday I was surprised to find Patrice waiting for me in my office. "Stella called me. She's worried about you." Patrice's gaze drifted over me and she threw up her hands. "What are you wearing?"

I glanced down at myself.

I had on the skinny jeans I loved so much.

But that wasn't really the problem.

I was wearing a white T-shirt with a giant coffee stain on it. Oops.

Patrice hurried at me, her eyes searching my face and growing wider by the second. "You're not wearing any makeup. And your hair—" She gestured to me.

I patted my head where I'd tied my hair up into a messy bun.

"When did you last wash it?"

Oh, and I might not have washed it in a while.

My friend sighed. Heavily. Then she grabbed her purse off my desk, and then came back to me. Taking hold of my arm, she led me out of the building, calling good-bye to Stella before I could say anything.

"Where are we going?" I asked, totally confused.

"Back to your apartment."

I didn't need to ask why.

"Sorry," I mumbled.

"What has gotten into you? This isn't like you."

I'm wallowing. I gave myself permission to wallow. "A month tops," I suddenly said.

"What?" Patrice frowned at me as she marched down Beacon Street.

"It was supposed to be a week of wallowing. Allowing myself to grieve for the bastard. You know . . . get it out of my system before I move on to bigger and better things. But I'm thinking—" I glanced down at my stained T-shirt and my unmanicured fingernails as they clutched at the T-shirt. "A month tops."

"I'm thinking neither. It stops. Today."

I glared at her as she marched ahead.

You couldn't just tell your heart to stop wallowing! And I never allowed myself to wallow over Nick, probably because he wasn't worth the time. But it was my right now to wallow over he who shall not be named!

Pain constricted my throat as I rushed after Patrice.

By the time we got to my apartment I was beginning to panic that she might actually force me to stop my pity party before I was ready.

"Keys," she demanded when we reached my place.

I handed them over and then, like a sullen teenager, followed her in and up to my apartment. When she opened the door, she gasped with all the melodrama of someone walking onto a murder scene.

As she stared dispassionately around at my space, I realized in a way it was. A murder of neat freak Ava Breevort.

Every inch of the place was covered. In dirty clothes, food wrappers, soda cans, takeout cartons, and the kitchen sink was overflowing with dirty dishes.

What?

I was wallowing.

"Oh my God." Patrice gaped at everything. "This is not your apartment." She took a sharp inhale of breath at finding a curry stain on my cream carpet. "Have you seen this?"

I shrugged.

Her eyes widened in horror and she reached out to grab me by the upper arms. "Ava, are you in there?"

I rolled my eyes. "Patrice."

"The Ava Breevort I know would die at seeing her apartment like this. There is never an inch of you or your apartment out of place. This . . . Oh my God, what is going on?"

Seeing mold gathering on my dishes for the first time, I began to feel a niggle of shame. "I should clean."

"Yes, you should. But more importantly, why aren't you losing your mind over the state of your apartment?"

Now it was my turn to be disbelieving. "Really, Patrice? Really?" Tears burned my nose and my lips shook as I waved at the place. "I should care about a stain when I feel like my insides have been torn out!"

The words echoed around the room and I bit my lip, wishing I could pull them back because they'd acted like a huge sledgehammer against my comfortable numbness.

Patrice's eyes shone bright with sympathy. "Darling . . . I'm so sorry I ever thought matchmaking you with Caleb was a good idea. Still, I never thought I'd see the day when nothing else would matter to you but a man."

Not sure if I was being reprimanded, I stared her down. "I'm allowed to be heartbroken. It doesn't make me weak."

"I never meant that." She stepped over a pile of laundry to take hold of my hand. "I just don't want you to lose yourself."

I nodded, wrinkling my nose as I saw the apartment from her perspective, and repeated, "I should clean."

"Yes."

"But I don't think it's a bad thing to stop caring about the things that don't really matter. So much of my life felt out of my control that I became obsessed with the little things I could control. Like my apartment and my appearance. I wouldn't even buy a pair of skinny jeans, for God's sake."

"Uh . . . you're wearing a pair of jeans."

"Yes. I am. And I intend to wear more. I'm going to clean my apartment and I'm going to wash my hair . . . but after I wash it I might just throw it back up in a messy bun. And I might not wear mascara if I don't feel like it. Or high heels."

Patrice seemed unsure. "To work? Events?"

I laughed softly, the act of it a relief. "Don't worry, Patrice. I'll be my immaculate self for work and to any of your wonderful events. I just might give myself a break on the weekends if I feel like it. And I'm changing my carpet because there's a stain on it and I live my life tiptoeing around my own apartment, worrying about my guests leaving stains on the carpet with their footwear and following them around with coasters. It's exhausting and I'd rather spend my time on things that matter." I gazed at the floor. "I think I'll put down hardwood and a nice big rug."

"Oak." Patrice nodded, tapping her mouth in thought. "It'll warm the room up. And I'd get rid of your white sofa."

"I hate that sofa," I agreed. "It looks pretty but I can't eat cheese puffs on it."

"Then it should go."

I locked eyes with my very understanding friend. "I'll stop wallowing."

"Good. You can be as heartbroken as you want for as long as you want. There is no magic number of days or weeks or months, my darling. But wallowing makes you look and sound just awful."

I cracked a smile at her bluntness. "I'll jump in the shower."

"And I'll . . ." She made a face at the kitchen. "Call my cleaner."

"I can clean my own apartment," I said as I made my way into my bedroom.

"Yes, but Stella said she needs you at the office. Hello, Anne-Marie? Yes. I have an emergency . . . right now . . . I'll pay you double . . ."

I rolled my eyes as she talked on the phone presumably to her cleaner. But I did as she asked. I stripped and got in the shower.

And as soon as the water poured over me, I let go of my numbness and let the pain back in again. I muffled my sobs, squeezing my arms around my chest to try to stop the harsh racking of my body.

I missed him.

So much.

Knowing I'd never touch him again or feel him smile against my skin while he was kissing me all over.

Knowing I would never be able to turn to him again when I needed him the most, that he would never be a strong, supportive presence to help bear the weight of future burdens.

One day I'd have that again with someone, but it wouldn't be the same. I couldn't imagine anyone ever making me feel as safe as he did. And I'd lost him before I ever really had him.

I never knew anything could feel so unbearable.

Finally, the sobs slowed to tears and I wiped them away, still shaking but feeling calmer. And I promised myself that that would be my last meltdown.

I had to let him go.

I just . . . I had to.

Not wanting a serious relationship because of Vince isn't healthy," I said the following night.

I was doing my best to act like I was moving on by sharing a celebratory drink with my best friend. Harper's cast had come off, much to her relief. Not only could she return to work in a full capacity, but she said the cast coming off was the last physical reminder of what had happened to her. She still had Vince's trial to deal with, and it wouldn't be for months, but for now she could move on.

We were in a down-to-earth dive bar on Pearl Street. I was wearing new skinny jeans and a Ralph Lauren tee I got on sale, and my hair was washed. Moreover, I was wearing strappy sandals, because some things didn't change. I liked my heels.

Harper looked gorgeous as always, her bruises gone, and the dark marks from the cuts that had needed stitches covered up with makeup. However, having been informed that she planned on only having casual physical relationships from now on, I felt an uneasy sense of déjà vu.

"My therapist says it's okay if that's what I want."

"Are you going to try to win every discussion with, 'My therapist thinks it's okay'? Because I may regret asking you to make an appointment with the shrink."

Harper gave me her best dirty look, but her quivering lips gave away her amusement. "Now I am."

I leaned across the tall round table where we sat on our high stools. "Seriously, learn from my mistakes. You're not built for casual sex."

"Right now I am. Look, I'm only twenty-six. I'm not saying that from here on out I just want to do casual. Who knows what the future holds? I am, however, saying that right now and for the foreseeable future there is no part of me that feels like handing over the kind of trust you need to give a guy to be in a real relationship with him."

Since that all sounded reasonable and rational, I nodded at her in support.

"What about you?"

That made me scowl, as I didn't particularly want to *talk* about moving on while I was still figuring out how to *pretend* to move on. "What about me?"

"You look better. You've even gained back a few of the pounds you lost with all that sex, and you look great."

I flinched at the reminder I was no longer having sex with Caleb. Harper winced.

"I'm sorry. Sometimes my mouth opens before it engages with my brain."

"It's okay." I glared at my drink. "He just ruined the entire act for me, but it's fine."

"You'll find someone just as good."

At my brittle silence, Harper leaned toward me. "Don't answer if it pisses you off . . . but . . . was he seriously that good?"

I looked up at her with all the pain of my loss shining in my eyes. "*He* wasn't good. *We* were phenomenal. It was like we were made for each other in that respect. It'll never be like that with someone else. That's a once-in-a-lifetime thing. *Now* can we change the subject?"

"Another beer?" Harper replied in answer.

I nodded and watched her hop gracefully off the stool to make her way through the busy room to the bar. Peeling at the label on my now empty beer bottle, I studied her as she edged her way through the crowd around the bar. Only a few months ago she would have bulldozed her way in, grinning at the people she was pissing off, her adorable dimpled smile giving her a free pass. She would lean across the bar and flirt until the bartender served her next.

She wasn't doing that now. Although she was still blunt and straightforward, there was a tentativeness about her that wasn't there before. I could only hope time would take care of it.

"Ava?"

Caleb?

My heart stopped.

I whipped my head around, only somewhat relieved the voice belonged to Jamie Scott and not his older brother. He stood just off to my side, a pint of beer in his hand, eyeing me uncertainly.

"How are you?"

"I'm okay," I said, my voice stiff. "You?"

"Not bad." He took a step toward me, his eyes moving across the room. "Is that Harper with you?"

Realizing he'd only seen Harper beat up, I nodded. "The one and only."

He scrutinized her, but not in the way a guy usually scrutinizes a girl. There was definite curiosity, but I wasn't sure it was sexual. Still, as he continued to stare at her, I felt the need to say, "She's off-limits."

Jamie swung his gaze back to me. "Caleb says she lives in our building. I haven't seen her."

"Jamie," I warned.

He held up his hands in a defensive gesture. "It's not like that. I just . . ." His attention returned to my friend. "She's striking. Do you . . . do you think she'd let me paint her?"

"I don't see how that's any different."

Jamie's brows pulled together. "It's completely different. I never sleep with my models. The art is too important."

There was so much sincerity and passion in his tone that I decided to believe him. "I . . . You would have to ask her but . . ." If Harper was even slightly interested in being an artist's model, it would mean I'd inadvertently be connected to Caleb again. It was bad enough I couldn't visit my friend at her apartment . . . "Maybe not now."

Seeming to understand, Jamie nodded and I sank down into my stool in relief.

Awkward silence fell between us and I kind of wished he'd just leave. "Are you here alone?" I hinted.

His gaze sharpened in sympathy. "Caleb's here."

My heart rate, which had increased already in Jamie's presence, instantly took off like a rocket. I searched the bar.

When I found him, I wished I hadn't. He was sitting in the corner with a bunch of people, including Jen from his office, who was pressed up beside him on a bench. Whatever she was saying, Caleb was nodding.

I felt sick.

I was going to be sick.

Jamie cursed. "It's not what you think, Ava."

But I was already off my stool. "Tell Harper I'm outside. Don't tell your brother I'm here." Before he could argue, I was weaving my way through the crowd, trying to leave inconspicuously.

Then I waited nervously across the street behind one of the granite pillars of an office building. When Harper appeared a minute later, looking left and right with concern etched over her pretty face, I stopped hiding like an idiot.

"Harp!" I called.

She caught sight of me, waited for a gap in traffic, and jogged across the street. She immediately slung her arm over my shoulder and didn't say anything as we began to hurry away together.

We were a couple of blocks away when she finally said, "You are *way* smarter than her."

A surprised laugh burst out of me as I realized she must have seen Jen next to Caleb. If I didn't laugh, I'd cry, and I'd already promised myself no more crying. "How could you tell?"

"He looked bored out of his mind."

"Really?" I hadn't noticed that. To be fair, I hadn't noticed much in all my panicking.

"Oh, God yeah. When you were in the room, he watched you like a hawk. He looked at you like everything you said was fascinating. He was barely looking at her at all."

Although this information hurt, I also craved it. "He looked at me like that?"

Harper nodded at me sadly. "He loves you. He might be too

messed up in the head to do something about it, but I can't hate the guy for loving you."

That familiar burn started in my chest and I needed it to go away. "Can you hate him for not loving me *enough*? Because I can't, Harper. I can't hate him. You need to do it for me so I don't look back on my life and regret him. Because if my best friend hates him, then he isn't worth my regret."

"I hate him," she answered instantly and seriously. "He's quinoa to me."

Harper detested quinoa. Like, more than she hated most things. "I love you."

"I love you back. Another beer? In a bar where there's no quinoa in sight."

"Yeah." I nodded, clinging to my strength. "This city is big enough for the both of us."

"It belongs more to you, though. He's an intruder. He should really leave."

My heart ached at the thought even though I wouldn't be in this situation if he'd just stayed in Scotland. "He should. He can have Scotland. I want Massachusetts. I don't think I'm asking for a lot."

"Yeah," Harper agreed enthusiastically. "He should go and take his little Mini-Me with him so you can visit my apartment."

"Jamie wants to paint you," I blurted.

Harper appeared stunned by this news. "What? Paint me?"

"You know he's an artist?"

"Yeah?"

"He thinks you're interesting."

"Meaning he wants to get into my pants," she scoffed.

"No, I actually think he really means he wants to paint you. Apparently he doesn't sleep with the models because his art is more important to him than sex. From what I've gleaned about him, I think that's true."

"Well, whatever." Harper shook her head, seeming a little dazed by the idea. "I don't have time to be some guy's model. Doesn't he know I am a very important person?"

"I don't think he got that memo."

"I'll slip it under his door. 'Hey, weird Scottish dude. I make very important art too. And mine tastes better than yours so I win. Find another muse, Mini-Quinoa.'"

I burst out laughing, my love and affection for my friend pushing away the pain I felt at seeing Caleb. "I don't know what I'd do without you."

"Lucky for you, that's something you'll never have to know." She stuck her tongue out at me playfully and skipped ahead. "Now let's find a bar. There are many sorrows to be drowned!"

Isn't that the truth, I thought as I hurried to catch up with her in my strappy heels.

Thirty-one

My carry-on suitcase bumped along behind me as I walked down the Jetway to the plane. The nice thing about flying first class—besides the more spacious seats and complimentary dining—was getting on the plane first. There were very few things I disliked more than waiting at a gate to board a plane. At least once you were on the plane you could get settled and crack open a book or put on a movie.

Not that I had been expecting to be getting on a plane at all. This was the second time in as many weeks that Stella had put me on one at the last minute.

The Monday after I saw Caleb with Jen Granton at the bar, I'd walked into the office to start my day only to be interrupted by Stella. She'd perched her pert ass on my desk and announced, "You need a distraction."

I wasn't going to lie. A distraction would be wonderful. "What kind of distraction are we talking about?"

"Chicago."

"Chicago? The musical?"

Stella smirked. "No. The city." She handed me a slim portfolio. "Calum Scotia. Banker. Divorced. Looking for a design overhaul on his penthouse apartment in the River North area. East North Water Street." Her smile was smug. "Quite the property and quite the find."

"How did he find out about us?" I asked, reading through the information Stella had collected on the potential client and what he was looking for.

"He's friends with one of our Boston clients. She recommended us."

"And you want me to go out there?" I felt my excitement build as I looked over the photographs of the property's current condition. The design was about fifteen years out of date and very feminine. But the duplex had extraordinary views and stunning high ceilings and vast spaces. There was a lot of fun to be had with it.

"Yes. Tomorrow."

I raised an eyebrow. "Why such late notice?"

She shrugged. "He gave us late notice. He has a few other designers coming out to give him their pitch. I don't want to lose out on this. We haven't had work in the Chicago area in a few years."

"Fine," I agreed. In fact, it was more than fine. This was just what I needed right now. Although, I said, "I don't know if I'll be able to handle this design on top of everything else."

"You'll make it work." Stella patted my hand reassuringly as she hopped off my desk to leave. "The best thing for you right now, sweet Ava, is to throw yourself into your career."

I studied the portfolio again. This place would be worth the stress. "Okay."

"I've booked you on a first-class flight leaving tomorrow morning at nine fifteen. Oh, and a suite at the Sheraton Grand. It's not far from Mr. Scotia's apartment."

"That was presumptuous!" I called after her.

"I knew you'd say yes!"

And my boss is always right, I mused as I boarded the plane. I had a window seat, and whoever was sitting in the aisle hadn't shown up yet, so I managed to get my luggage into the overhead bin without knocking anyone on the head. I winced at the memory and threw it away.

This business trip was a distraction, I reminded myself.

Settling into my seat, I pulled down my tray table and placed the portfolio with the photos and info about the client on it, along with a sketchpad. Keeping my brain occupied was of the utmost importance, and although I usually waited to sketch until I'd seen a space in real life, I decided to get a head start on my ideas.

Soon I was so lost in my drawings that I forgot where I was. The slight jolt of my chair filtered into my awareness and I realized the person sitting in the aisle seat had arrived. I didn't bother to look up, but I felt their heat. As I sketched ideas for the kitchen, however, the tantalizing scent of a familiar cologne began to invade my senses and my pencil scratched to a halt on the page.

No.

Not possible.

Slowly, I think because I feared it was him, and feared that it wasn't, I turned my head to the right and felt the breath knocked out of me at the sight of Caleb Scott sitting beside me. He stared at me with such tenderness and affection my lungs tightened with the ache of seeing it. Caleb wore his usual uniform of T-shirt and jeans, so all his tattoos were on display. I preferred him like this, I decided finally. The suits were hot. But this was the Caleb I first met, and the biker guy look suited him better than Armani. All the longing and loss I'd felt became so acute now that he was in front of me. Strangely, it hurt more than it did when I couldn't see him.

"How?" I whispered, not knowing what else to say. I was so confused.

What was he doing here?

The corner of his mouth tilted up attractively. "I know a guy."

I let out a noise of disbelief. "You know a guy?"

"I know a guy."

That didn't clear up my confusion. Caleb was here. Sitting in the seat next to mine. And I had no idea how he'd managed it. But more important for me to know was his reason for being here.

"Why?"

He reached out and took my hand in his, his thumb caressing my knuckles. "Because I can't regret you for the rest of my life. I won't."

Shock, elation, fear, bafflement . . . I didn't know what to feel. "What does that mean?"

"It means there is no Calum Scotia in Chicago." He gestured to my sketches. "Just a *Caleb Scott*."

"Oh my God . . ." I shook my head and squeezed his hand, cursing myself for not having worked that one out.

He grinned unrepentantly.

"Stella?"

Caleb nodded. "I didn't know how tae do this. I was worried that if I even tried, you wouldn't give me the time of day. So I remembered the last time I had you trapped." He chuckled. "You couldn't escape me on our flights. And Jamie has an exhibition in Chicago this week. I called Stella tae see if she'd help me and she agreed. She gave me your identification details and I booked us on the flight together. She came up with the Calum Scotia stuff."

"I'm going to kill her." I thought my heart might pound right out of my chest.

He tugged on my hand, his eyes darkening. "Does that mean you aren't willing tae give me another chance?"

Hope began to build, swelling inside of me until I felt uncomfortably stretched by it. It was at once a wonderful and horrifying feeling. "Is this real?"

Turning toward me, Caleb took hold of my other hand and

brought them both to his chest. I could feel his heart banging hard and fast against my palm. "I want tae be with you, Ava. Do you still want tae be with me?"

There was a part of me that whispered I should leave him hanging after the weeks of hell he'd put me through, but staring into his face—a face I loved—I couldn't. "No more running away?"

"No more running away, wee yin. Never from you. And I am sorry I ever did."

Recognizing the sincerity in his voice, I slid my hand up to cup his face, to feel the familiar prickle of his stubble beneath my palm, and I reached for him.

He reached back.

Our kiss was deep, tender, and filled with such longing.

It was also entirely inappropriate for the plane, but I didn't care.

When we broke apart, we panted softly against each other's mouths, and I felt tears of joy sting my eyes. "Is this really happening?"

"It's really happening."

"You hate flying," I murmured randomly.

"Aye. But I have you tae distract me."

Despite the euphoria and relief flooding me, my insides still felt shaky with uncertainty. Caleb seemed to sense it, pressing soft kisses along my jaw until he reached my ear, where he whispered, "You're mine forever now, wee yin."

I fought back the tears his words incited and tightened my hold on him. "And you're mine."

He drew back to look me deep in the eye and he nodded.

He was mine.

I smiled. Big and happy and I was rewarded with his grin. I touched my fingers to his lips and whispered, "You should do that more."

"I have a feeling I'll be doing it a lot more from now on."

We gazed at each other, taking in every little detail of each other's face, but the moment was broken when the flight attendant asked us if we'd like a drink. I asked for two glasses of champagne and made Caleb clink glass to glass. "We're celebrating."

"I can think of a better way tae celebrate than this."

"Oh?" I knew that look on his face. He was going to say something dirty and I was going to pretend to be appalled all while he made my girly parts tingle.

His gaze smoldered. "We could join the mile high club."

I glanced over at the curtain that hid the bathroom and galley. "Are you kidding?"

"Not even a little bit."

"We can't." Everyone would hear us.

"Who is going tae know," he whispered. "Hidden behind the curtain, everyone will think I'm just waiting in line for the loo. Instead I'll be inside it with you. While you come very, very hard but very, very quietly."

He reached out to put his hand on my knee and he caressed it, his palm pushing the hem of my skirt up slightly.

"I need you, Ava."

All cheekiness had faded from his voice, leaving just raw, serious need.

"We shouldn't."

Hearing the change from "can't" to "shouldn't," Caleb's expression tightened. "We should." His fingers slid between the gap between my knees, caressing my inner thigh, and my belly tightened.

"Caleb," I whispered.

He leaned over to whisper in my ear, "One way or another I need you. Here or in there?"

I pushed away his hand, even though it was the last thing I wanted to do. "In there," I said shakily, my pulse rocketing at the idea of having sex in the bathroom of an airplane. I didn't think the mile-high club was actually a thing!

Not too long later the flight attendant took away our glasses and the announcement came over that we were readying for takeoff.

Seeing Caleb tense, I reached for his hand again, bringing his attention back to me and not the plane. "I saw you with Jen," I said, knowing the controversial subject would definitely take his mind off everything but us.

Sure enough, he scowled. "Jamie told me. And I told you that there's nothing between me and Jen. There was a whole bunch of us from the office in that bar. Jen just . . ."

"She squeezed her way in beside you, huh?" I tried to suppress my grin at his agitated expression.

"She's a pain in the arse."

I chuckled. "I'm sorry I got jealous."

"I'm not." His gazed moved lovingly over my face. "I wanted you back as soon as you walked away from me in the park. But I thought I didn't deserve you for making you feel like you weren't worth the risk. I fought with myself for two weeks and then when Jamie told me how you reacted tae seeing me, I knew it was now or never. There was a window between you loving me and resenting me and I couldn't miss it."

"Leo is just a friend," I replied, thinking it best to clear that up too. "We bumped into each other that day at the park. That's all that was."

The muscle in his jaw popped as he clenched his teeth, his hold on my hand tightening a little too much. I squeezed it and he loosened his grip. "I dinnae like the way he looks at you."

"Just friends," I repeated. Then I laughed, suddenly remembering our first time on a plane together. "I never would have imagined us being here right now that first time flying from Arizona to Chicago."

"No, me neither. But I was thinking about getting you into bed."

"I never would have guessed that. You were so mean."

"Hey, you were mean back." His lips twitched, eyes dancing with mirth. "It only made me want you more. When you got up to go to the bathroom, I imagined following you in there." His lips brushed my ear again as he said in that low, sexy voice of his, "I imagined you pressed up against the sink, your back tae me."

My breath stuttered. "Is that what you're going to do to me?"

I felt him shake his head before he drew back to look deep into my eyes. "I need tae look at you when we're in there. You're not just some sexy stranger now. You're Ava."

Suddenly the beep of the seat belt sign drew us out of our bubble and we realized we were up in the air. We shared a smile.

"You're so very good at distracting me, wee yin." He caressed my lower lip with his thumb.

I discreetly swiped at it with my tongue and then pulled away, grinning at the hot look he gave me. "I think you were the one who did the distracting this time."

He nodded and then gestured to the aisle. "I think you might need tae use the facilities, no?"

My belly flipped. "Now?"

"Aye," Caleb practically growled. "Now."

And that was how, on trembling legs, I got up out of my seat, readying myself to join the mile high club. I felt his hand caress my ass as I squeezed by him and I shivered, unable to fully comprehend the reality of what I was planning to do because all I really cared about was getting him inside me.

It felt like I hadn't had him inside me in years.

And I never thought I'd get to love him like this again.

I pushed the curtain aside, giving the flight attendant a weak smile, before I let myself into the bathroom with shaky fingers. I locked it. And waited.

Less than a minute passed before I heard a knock. "It's me."

Lust tugged deep in my belly as I unlocked it and stumbled back in the tiny space to let Caleb in. We were crammed together, our bodies touching, as he locked the door behind us.

"I keep forgetting how tall you are," I whispered, my head tilted back to look up at him.

His answer was to lift me up and my legs automatically wound around his hips, my skirt bunching up around my waist as he propped me on the edge of the small countertop.

"Only you," he suddenly whispered.

I looked into his eyes, questioning the hoarse, painful quality in his voice.

He rested his forehead against mine, holding me tight. "You have the power tae hurt me. Only you."

Understanding caused a rush of emotion within me, tears stinging my nose. "When you hurt, Caleb, I hurt." My voice broke as I promised, "I'll never hurt you."

"I love you," Caleb choked out abruptly, the words coarse and dragging, as if they cost him his soul to say it.

Relief, bliss, and sweet, painful connection made me smile in sympathy. "It'll get easier."

"Tae say it?"

"No." I placed my hand over his heart. "To feel it."

His answer to that was a kiss so hungry and deep I miraculously forgot where I was. I forgot everything but the need to be with him.

Epilogue

THREE WEEKS LATER

A nod's as guid as a wink tae a blind horse."

Lying facing Caleb in bed, I felt my lips twitch in amusement. "I have no idea."

We were playing the "let Ava guess what Scottish words and sayings mean" game and I was having no such luck in guessing correctly so far.

"It means, 'Explain yourself more clearly.'"

"Yeah, I was never getting that. What?" I shoved him playfully. "You're making stuff up now."

Caleb grinned and shook his head as much as he could since it was propped up by his hand, elbow bent to his pillow. "Another?"

"Yes. I am going to get one eventually."

"Is the cat deid?"

"Is the cat dead?" I translated.

"Aye. But it's a saying."

Bewildered and wondering if he really was just making phrases up now, I announced, "How the hell am I supposed to know what that means?"

He chuckled. "You would say it to someone to mean, 'Your trousers or your hem is too short.'"

"You're lying."

"Am not."

"Why would you ask if 'the cat is deid' for that?"

"If your hemline is too short it's like a flag flying at half mast."

Understanding dawned and I felt a snicker rise in my throat. "Like when someone dies."

"Exactly."

I threw my head back in laughter, tears of mirth drenching my eyes, and I heard Caleb's soft, husky laughter join mine. "Okay, that's funny." I giggled. "Completely bonkers, but funny."

"We've got tons of sayings like that."

"And you all grow up saying them?"

"Nah." He shook his head. "Most of them are from generations past. I only know them because my gran still says them."

I thought of the last three weeks of bliss together and how although Caleb hadn't repeated that he loved me; he showed it in his every action. At his brother's art show in Chicago, he barely let me out of his sight, and Jamie looked genuinely pleased to see us together. Since arriving back home in Boston, we hadn't spent a night without each other. The bathroom cabinet in my place was overflowing because of the toiletries Caleb kept there, and I had my own products littering the bathroom in his apartment. Although we were both busy with work, Caleb wanted us to come home to each other at the end of the day and I was not complaining. Not a bit.

In fact, we felt so much like a couple, I wondered if he would introduce me to his gran and the rest of his family during one of their Skype calls. I was nervous about their reaction to me after Jamie's presumption that I was just like Caleb's deplorable ex.

Sweeping the thought from my mind to concentrate on my guy, I smiled and leaned closer to him. It was a Saturday morning, we both had nothing to do but laze around with each other, and so far it was tremendous. "Tell me another one. One I might actually guess this time."

"Whit's fur ye'll no go by ye," he answered, reaching out a hand to draw his finger in a soft caress from the top of my shoulder down my outer arm.

I translated its literal meaning in my head and melted into his touch, realizing this wasn't just another saying for me to guess, but one with significance for us. "What's for you will not go by you."

"Meaning?"

I thought of a similar saying here. "What's meant to happen will happen."

Caleb nodded, our gazes locked, and I felt a little breathless at the shine of love in his eyes. "See, you guessed one correctly."

"We were meant to meet at O'Hare," I whispered, feeling emotional because although I'd thought it at the time, I hadn't dwelled on the fact that we had kept weirdly bumping into each other everywhere. "Meant to sit next to each other on that plane. It wasn't just coincidence. You knowing Patrice, staying with her, her being my client, my friend, and then us meeting in Canterbury just when I was contemplating ending things. It was all meant to be."

He pushed up off the pillow and moved over me, pressing me gently down on my back to brace himself above me. I opened my legs, caressing the back of his calf with my foot and feeling more than a spark of lust ignite through my body. "You really think that?"

"I never believed in fate until you," I answered honestly.

Caleb studied me thoughtfully, seeming to drink in every facet of my face. "I dinnae know if I believe it was fate."

I frowned. "No?"

"Maybe the flights, aye, and I suppose it was quite the coincidence about Patrice. But when she said your name, I could have just ignored that she knew you and went about my business. I didn't. I pursued you. From that point on we've been in charge of this, Ava. When one of us stopped fighting, the other didn't. And I know you think you fought harder than me for us, and I'm not saying that isn't true—although you know I plan tae make that up tae you from now on—but even if my mind battled against wanting you, it didn't always win."

"I know that," I said. I did. Otherwise we wouldn't be lying in bed together.

"No." Caleb shook his head. "I'm talking about when I left for Scotland. When I got offered the job in Boston. I talked it over with my family tae see how they'd feel about it. I knew they weren't too keen on me leaving, but they wanted me tae do what was best for my career. And it was best for my career . . . but it wasn't the only reason I accepted the job."

My breath caught as I began to understand his meaning.

He nodded and gave me a rueful, boyish smile at odds with his ruggedness. "I couldn't even admit it tae myself at the time . . . but I was addicted tae you, wee yin. And you swayed my decision tae get on that plane and come back here."

Tears pricked my eyes as my heart filled with too much emotion, too much need and love. And guilt. "And I mentioned Leo the first night we were together again."

"You didn't know. Hell, I didn't even know really. I just knew I wanted tae tear off his head and I didn't even know him." He lifted a hand from beside my head and followed it with his eyes as he trailed his fingertips down my collarbone, across my naked breast, and down my ribs. I sucked in a breath as desire flushed through me. "All I knew was that the thought of any other man touching you drove me crazy. Still does." His eyes came back to mine. "You're the first person I've ever wanted tae belong tae, Ava. The first person I ever wanted tae belong tae me."

"I never thought I'd ever want that," I admitted on a hitched breath. "But you have a habit of changing my perspective."

He stared down into my eyes, his fierce with love and mine reflecting the intense emotion back at him.

I'd never felt more cherished, more loved, more wanted or needed as Caleb made gentle, sweet love to me that morning.

We kissed, sweet, luscious kisses that made me feel drowsy and satisfied, and then Caleb lifted his head from my lips and said, voice hoarse with vehemence, "I love you, Ava Breevort."

I tightened my hold on him, anchored to him.

Safe with him.

Home with him.

"I love you too, Caleb Scott."

This time his kiss was more savage, needful, and when he eventually broke it, he nuzzled his lips against my neck, rolling so I was lying sprawled across the top of him. We lay in sweet silence for a while. A silence he ended when he whispered, "You're right."

"About what?"

"You make it easier tae feel it every day."

I held on to him tighter and was just dozing off when his body jerked beneath me. "What is it?" I raised my head to stare at him in concern.

He was frowning. "What time is it?"

"I don't know. Why?" I clambered off him to reach over to the nightstand where my phone was charging. I flipped it open. "Just past ten fifteen." I glanced back at him, watching curiously as he relaxed against the pillows.

He reached out to me. "That's fine. Come back."

I did, but as I crawled over him, I asked, "Why?"

"I forgot, I have a Skype call with the family at two o'clock."

"Oh, you've got plenty of time," I assured him.

"They're looking forward tae meeting you."

I tensed, my voice involuntarily high-pitched as I replied, "Today?"

His arms tightened around me. "That a problem?"

Glaring at him incredulously, I didn't see any concern etched between his brows. "You could give a girl some warning."

"You dinnae want tae meet them?"

"Of course I do!" I slapped his chest. "But meeting your family is a big deal and I haven't even—Look at my hair!"

Relief flooded his features and he began to shake with laughter. "You have plenty of time tae do your hair, wee yin."

A thought occurred to me and I sat up, still straddling him. "Maybe I shouldn't. I don't want them to think I'm like your ex the way Jamie did. He said we both had that shiny, polished look. Maybe I should leave off the makeup and not style my hair so they don't think—" The rest of my sentence was muffled against his big hand clamped over my mouth.

He didn't look amused anymore. "You'll wear what you want. You'll be Ava and no one else for them. I've already told them loads about you and they're happy you make me happy. That's all they care about."

I slumped against his hold and he released my mouth. "You're sure? I want them to like me."

He gripped my waist and gave it a squeeze. "I love that you care so much about them liking you, but I dinnae want you working yourself into a worry about it. My family will love you but all that matters is that I love you and you love me. Right?"

And just like that I melted and my anxiety momentarily fled. "Right."

"And you already know Jamie likes you. That's one down."

I did know that. Jamie had made it clear over the last few weeks that he was grateful to me for making Caleb happy again. For giving him back hope for the future. Funnily enough, however, now that Caleb's simmering anger had abated, I saw clearly for the first time that the similarity I'd noted between the two brothers had nothing to do with physical appearance really.

They both had this underlying bitterness in their ice blue eyes.

"He doesn't seem happy," I whispered all of a sudden.

Caleb's grip on me tightened in response. "Quinn," he replied, his voice like sandpaper against the name. "He was Jamie's twin. Jamie was in the car with him when Quinn lost control of the car."

His words pierced my heart and suddenly that bitterness in Jamie's eyes made so much sense.

Although Caleb would never truly get over what Carissa did—and it hurt that I couldn't repair that damage—the bitterness in his eyes had dissipated. Every day it got chipped away at by our love. Sound cheesy? Maybe. But it was beautiful and it was true.

Jamie's bitterness, however, was still there and now I knew why.

"I wish there was something we could do for him," I said, heart aching for his brother.

"Well . . . we can only hope one day he meets his Ava."

Love broke through the empathetic ache in my chest. I was no longer astonished by Caleb's romantic side. He showed me it more and more each day—the man he had been before Carissa. The man he was becoming again. "We're staying in this bed until one o'clock." I kissed him, pressing my lower body to his.

"Again?"

I kissed along his jaw, his stubble prickling and tickling my lips. "I'm going to wring you dry, Caleb Scott," I purred, biting his earlobe.

"Do with me what you will, wee yin." He wrapped his arms tight around me, binding me to him as he whispered in my ear, "Every inch of me is yours."

Acknowledgments

First, I have to thank Amy Jennings for coming up with the title of this book. I asked all the amazing folks in my Facebook readers group "Sam's Clan McBookish" for help in choosing a title for this manuscript. I gave you all hardly anything to go on, and yet, Amy, you somehow produced the most fitting title. Thank you!

Moreover, thank you to all the readers in my Facebook Clan who show me love and support and so much enthusiasm on a daily basis. I'd be lost without you!

I want to also say a massive thank you to the team of people around me who, whether directly or indirectly, help make each book develop into the best story it can be: my fantastic agent, Lauren Abramo; my wonderful editor, Kerry Donovan; the brilliant team at Berkley; my fabulous publicist, KP Simmon; my "can't live without you" PA, Ashleen Walker; my awesome friends and family; and my supportive author buds.

All of you encourage me and challenge me in the best way possible. You find ways to make my life easier, and I'm grateful for you.

And finally, the biggest thank you of all to my tremendous readers. What are words without someone to read them? Thank you.

Don't miss the first book in
Samantha Young's Hart's Boardwalk series,

The One Real Thing

Available now.
Turn the page for a special excerpt.

One of my favorite feelings in the whole world is that moment I step inside a hot shower after having been caught outside in cold, lashing rain. The transformation from clothes-soaked-to-the-skin misery to soothing warmth is unlike any other. I love the resultant goose bumps and the way my whole body relaxes under the stream of warm water. In that pure, simple moment all accumulated worries just wash away with the rain.

The moment I met Cooper Lawson felt exactly like that hot shower after a very long, cold storm.

The day hadn't started out all sunshine and clear skies. It was a little gray outside and there were definite clouds, but I still hadn't been prepared for the sudden deluge of rain that flooded from the heavens as I was walking along the boardwalk in the seaside city of Hartwell.

My eyes darted for the closest available shelter and I dashed toward it—a closed bar that had an awning. Soaked within seconds, blinded by rain, and irritated by the icky feeling of my clothes sticking to my skin, I wasn't really paying much attention to anything else but getting to the awning. That was why I ran smack into a hard, masculine body.

If the man's arms hadn't reached out to catch me I would have bounced right onto my ass.

I pushed my soaked hair out of my eyes and looked up in apology at the person I had so rudely collided with.

Warm blue eyes met mine. Blue, blue eyes. Like the Aegean Sea that surrounded Santorini. I'd vacationed there a few years back and the water there was the bluest I'd ever seen.

Once I was able to drag my gaze from the startling color of those eyes, I took in the face they were set upon. Rugged, masculine.

My eyes drifted over his broad shoulders and my head tipped back to take in his face because the guy was well over six feet tall. The hands that were still on my biceps, steadying me, were big, long fingered, and callused against my bare skin.

Despite the cold, I felt my body flush with the heat of awareness and I stepped out of the stranger's hold.

"Sorry," I said, slicking my wet hair back, grinning apologetically. "That rain came out of nowhere."

He gave a brief nod as he pushed his wet dark hair back from his forehead. The blue flannel shirt he wore over a white T-shirt was soaked through, too, and I suddenly found myself staring at the way the T-shirt clung to his torso.

There wasn't an ounce of fat on him.

I thought I heard a chortle of laughter and my eyes flew to his face, startled—and horrified at the thought of being caught ogling. There was no smirk or smile on his lips, however, although there was definitely amusement in those magnificent eyes of his. Without saying a word he reached out for the door to the quaint building and pushed. The door swung open and he stepped inside what was an empty and decidedly closed bar.

Oh.

Okay for some, I thought, staring glumly out at the way the rain pounded the boardwalk, turning the boards slick and slippery. I wondered how long I'd be stuck there.

"You can wait out there if you want. Or not."

The deep voice brought my head back around. The blue-eyed, rugged, flannel guy was staring at me.

I peered past him at the empty bar, unsure if he was allowed to be in there. "Are you sure it's alright?"

He merely nodded, not giving me the explanation I sought for why it was alright.

I stared back at the rain and then back into the dry bar.

Stay out here shivering in the rain or step inside an empty bar with a strange man?

The stranger noted my indecision and somehow he managed to laugh at me without moving his mouth.

It was the laughter-filled eyes that decided me.

I nodded and strode past him. Water dripped onto the hardwood floors, but since there was already a puddle forming around the blue-eyed, rugged, flannel guy's feet I didn't let it bother me too much.

His boots squeaked and squished on the floor as he passed me; the momentary flare of heat from his body as he brushed by caused a delicious shiver to ripple down my spine.

"Tea? Coffee? Hot cocoa?" he called out without looking back.

He was about to disappear through a door that had *Staff Only* written on it, giving me little time to decide. "Hot cocoa," I blurted out.

I took a seat at a nearby table, grimacing at the squish of my clothes as I sat. I was definitely going to leave a butt-shaped puddle there when I stood up.

The door behind me banged open again and I turned around to see BRF (blue-eyed, rugged, flannel) Guy coming toward me with a white towel in his hand. He handed it to me without a word.

"Thanks," I said, bemused when he just nodded and headed back through the Staff Only door. "A man of few words," I murmured.

His monosyllabic nature was kind of refreshing, actually. I knew a lot of men who loved the sound of their own voice.

I wrapped the towel around the ends of my blond hair and squeezed the water out of it. Once I had wrung as much of the water from my hair as I could, I swiped the towel over my cheeks, only to gasp in horror at the black stains left on it.

Fumbling through my purse for my compact, I flushed with embarrassment when I saw my reflection. I had scary black-smeared eyes and mascara streaks down my cheeks.

No wonder BRF Guy had been laughing at me.

I used the towel to scrub off the mascara, then, completely mortified, I slammed my compact shut. I now had no makeup on, I was flushed red like a teenager, and my hair was flat and wet.

The bar guy wasn't exactly my type. Still, he was definitely attractive in his rough-around-the-edges way and, well, it was just never nice to feel like a sloppy mess in front of a man with eyes that piercing.

The door behind me banged open again and BRF Guy strode in with two steaming mugs in his hands.

As soon as he put one into mine, goose bumps rose up my arm at the delicious rush of heat against my chilled skin. "Thank you."

He nodded and slipped into the seat across from me. I studied him as he braced an ankle over his knee and sipped at his coffee. He was casual, completely relaxed, despite the fact that his clothes were wet. And like me he was wearing jeans. Wet denim felt nasty against bare skin—a man-made chafe monster.

"Do you work here?" I said after a really long few minutes of silence passed between us.

He didn't seem bothered by the silence. In fact, he seemed completely at ease in the company of a stranger.

He nodded.

"You're a bartender here?"

"I own the place."

I looked around at the bar. It was traditional décor with dark walnut everywhere—the long bar, the tables and chairs, even the floor. The lights of three large brass chandeliers broke up the darkness, while wall-mounted green library lamps along the back wall gave the booths there a cozy, almost romantic vibe. There was a small stage near the front door and just across from the booths were three stairs that led up onto a raised dais where two pool tables sat. Two huge flat-screen televisions, one above the bar and one above the pool tables, made me think it was part sports bar.

There was a large jukebox, beside the stage, that was currently silent.

"Nice place."

BRF Guy nodded.

"What's the bar called?"

"Cooper's."

"Are you Cooper?"

His eyes smiled. "Are you a detective?"

"A doctor, actually."

I was pretty sure I saw a flicker of interest. "Really?"

"Really."

"Smart lady."

"I'd hope so." I grinned.

Laughter danced in his eyes as he raised his mug for another sip.

Weirdly, I found myself settling into a comfortable silence with him. We sipped at our hot drinks as a lovely easiness fell between us. I couldn't remember the last time I'd felt that kind of calm contentedness with anyone, let alone a stranger.

A little slice of peace.

Finally, as I came to the end of my cocoa, BRF Guy / possibly Cooper spoke. "You're not from Hartwell."

"No, I'm not."

"What brings you to Hart's Boardwalk, Doc?"

I realized then how much I liked the sound of his voice. It was deep with a little huskiness in it.

I thought about his question before responding. What had brought me there was complicated.

"At the moment the rain brought me *here*," I said coyly. "I'm kind of glad it did."

He put his mug down on the table and stared at me for a long beat. I returned his perusal, my cheeks warming under the heat of his regard. Suddenly he reached across the table, offering me his hand. "Cooper Lawson."

I smiled and placed my small hand in his. "Jessica Huntington."

"Nice to meet you, Doc."

Photo by Mark Archibald

Samantha Young is the *New York Times* and *USA Today* bestselling author of the On Dublin Street series, the Hart's Boardwalk series, and the stand-alone novel *Hero*. She resides in Scotland.

Ready to find
your next great read?

Let us help.

Visit prh.com/nextread

Penguin
Random
House

P9-ELT-086

E A R L Y

S P R I N G

by Tove Ditlevsen
translated by Tiina Nunnally

The Bean Trees —
Barbara Kingsolver

The Seal Press 𝕊

English translation copyright © 1985 Tiina Nunnally
All rights reserved. No part of this book may be reproduced in any form, except for brief reviews, without the written permission of the publishers.

Originally published as *Barndom* (1967) and *Ungdom* (1967) by Steen Hasselbalchs Forlag, Copenhagen, Denmark; published in one volume as *Det tidlige forår* (1976). Copyright © 1967, 1971 by Tove Ditlevsen. Published by arrangement with Gyldendal Dansk Forlag.

The cover photograph shows Tove Ditlevsen at a young age. Our thanks to Forum København, the publishers of *Om Tove Ditlevsen* (1976). The back cover photograph is reproduced courtesy of the Royal Library in Copenhagen.

Early Spring was published with the help of the Danish Ministry of Cultural Affairs and the National Endowment for the Arts.

Cover design by Deborah Brown
Text design by Barbara Wilson and Sally Brunsman
Typeset by Accent & Alphabet, Seattle
Printed by Braun-Brumfield
Published by The Seal Press, 312 S. Washington, Seattle WA 98104

Library of Congress Cataloging in Publication Data

Ditlevsen, Tove Irma Margit, 1918–1976.
 Early spring.

Translation of: Det tidlige forår.
 1. Ditlevsen, Tove Irma Margit, 1918–1976 — Biography —
Youth. 2. Authors, Danish — 20th century — Biography.
I. Title.
PT8175.D5Z47513   1985   839.8′187209 [B]   85-2091
ISBN 0-931188-29-6
ISBN 0-931188-28-8 (pbk.)

First edition, May, 1985
10 9 8 7 6 5 4 3 2 1

Printed in the United States of America

Acknowledgments

I would like to thank the staff of The Seal Press for their patience and encouragement. I am particularly grateful to Barbara Wilson for her support and enthusiasm—and for her skill and tenacity in finding rhymes for the poems in the book! Special thanks to Susan Wright, Melissa Lowe Shogren, Steve Murray, and Anne Beicher Becker.

Introduction

Two years ago I picked up a copy of the second volume of Tove Ditlevsen's memoirs, *Ungdom* (*Youth*), at a local Seattle library. I had read several of Ditlevsen's novels and some of her poetry; still, I was not prepared to be so taken by her memoirs. I read the book in one sitting. I was fascinated by her account of growing up in Vesterbro, a working class neighborhood in Copenhagen, during the 1930s. And I was attracted by her natural, direct style of narrative, her vivid descriptions, and her wry sense of humor.

Several weeks later I found the first volume, *Barndom* (*Childhood*), in the University of Washington library. Again, I raced through the book. I felt myself drawn to this young girl whose dream of becoming a writer was her one hope of escaping the narrow confines of her childhood home. Her determination to write set her apart from the other children, but it also protected her from the common female fate: early pregnancy, marriage to a "stable, skilled worker," and a lifetime inextricably bound to the Vesterbro milieu.

I liked this first volume so much that I felt compelled to translate several chapters. I started with Chapter 6, which begins: "Childhood is long and narrow like a coffin...." And for the next two years I spent much of my free time working on both volumes.

Translating is rather like taking a house apart, brick by brick, and then rebuilding it. You must examine every sentence, turn over each word. But the translated version

i

will never be exactly the same as the original. It is a reconstruction. The translator hopes that it will be as sturdy and well-built as the original. The translating process reveals a great deal about the writing skill and talent of the author. I learned to appreciate Ditlevsen's careful choice of words and her keen sense of irony. Her writing style is natural, fluid, colloquial, and deceptively simple. It was a difficult task to transform her lyricism, her wit, and the easy flow of her words into English.

I was surprised to discover that only a few of Ditlevsen's stories had previously appeared in English (*Complete Freedom and Other Stories*, translated by Jack Brondum, Curbstone Press, 1982), although many of her books have been translated into other languages, including German and Japanese. Tove Ditlevsen is one of Denmark's best loved and most read authors. She enjoyed enormous popularity, from the time of her debut with a collection of poems, published when she was eighteen, until her death in 1976. She was a prolific writer, producing over thirty works — including poetry, short stories, and novels — as well as numerous newspaper articles. She also wrote an advice column for a Copenhagen newspaper for twenty years.

Tove Ditlevsen drew heavily on autobiographical material for her fiction. Her memoirs often seem more like novels, just as her fiction and poetry are full of her own personal experiences as a woman and a writer. The first two volumes of her memoirs, *Childhood* and *Youth,* appeared separately in Denmark in 1967, and as one volume, *Det tidlige forår (Early Spring)*, in 1976. A third volume, *Gift (Married)*, which details the personal tragedies that were to shadow Ditlevsen's later life, was published in 1971.

In an article published in 1972 in the Danish newspaper

Politiken, Ditlevsen told the story behind the memoirs. They were written during a period of great depression; she had been unable to write for three years. Suddenly one evening, "six little words rose up from the depths of my soul like the first feeble beginnings of something — what it was, I didn't know. Or why they appeared when I was close to death. But I had them; they were mine. Had I ever owned anything other than the chains of words that I put together? The words were: 'In the morning there was hope!' Burning with desire to continue, I rushed for my typewriter and for the first time in three cursed years I wrote something that was good."

Childhood and *Youth* tell the story of a working class girl who longs to be a writer despite the complete lack of support or interest from nearly everyone around her. Perhaps by retelling that story at a time when she felt blocked as a writer, Ditlevsen found a way to recapture both the scenes of her childhood and the youthful creativity that had made her persist and even thrive. As author Klaus Rifbjerg said in reviewing *Childhood* in *Politiken,* "The romantic who lives so strongly in Tove Ditlevsen . . . has been shaped in protest against a way of life that, in a sense, did its best to annihilate her. She survived and became what she had always dreamed of becoming: an artist."

Tove Ditlevsen's background was not just a destructive force, however. It also gave her determination, courage, and a wealth of stories. She may have written the memoirs with the same hope she describes at the end of *Youth* after the publication of her first collection of poetry — hope that a child might find her book in the library, a child "who in all secrecy is fond of poetry, who will someday find it there, read the poems and feel something from them, something that people around her don't understand."

Tove Ditlevsen is a writer of strength and hope; this is her story.

Tiina Nunnally
Seattle, Washington
February 1985

Translator's notes have been included in the form of footnotes where they are necessary to the understanding of the text. Notes on books, writers, and historical events will be found at the end of Early Spring.

EARLY SPRING

CHILDHOOD

I

In the morning there was hope. It sat like a fleeting gleam of light in my mother's smooth black hair that I never dared touch; it lay on my tongue with the sugar and the lukewarm oatmeal I was slowly eating while I looked at my mother's slender, folded hands that lay motionless on the newspaper, on top of the reports of Spanish flu and the Treaty of Versailles. My father had left for work and my brother was in school. So my mother was alone, even though I was there, and if I was absolutely still and didn't say a word, the remote calm in her inscrutable heart would last until the morning had grown old and she had to go out to do the shopping in Istedgade like ordinary housewives.

The sun broke over the gypsy wagon, as if it came from inside it, and Scabie Hans came out with bare chest and a wash basin in his hands. When he had poured the water over himself, he put out his hand for a towel and Pretty Lili gave it to him. They didn't say a word to each other; they were like pictures in a book when you quickly turn the pages. Like my mother, they would change in a few hours. Scabie Hans was a Salvation Army soldier and Pretty Lili was his sweetheart. In the summer, they packed a bunch of little children into the green wagon and drove into the country with them. Parents paid one krone a day for this. I had gone myself when I was three years old and my brother was seven. Now I was five and the only thing I could remember from the trip was that Pretty Lili once set me out of the wagon, down in the warm sand in what I thought was a desert. Then the green wagon drove away from me and got smaller and smaller and inside of it sat my brother and I was never going to see him or my mother again. When the children came back home, they all had scabies. That's how Scabie Hans got his name. But Pretty Lili was not pretty. My mother was, though, on those strange and happy mornings when I would leave her completely in peace. Beautiful, untouchable, lonely, and full of secret thoughts I would never know. Behind her on the flowered wallpaper, the tatters pasted together by my father with brown tape, hung a picture of a woman staring out the window. On the floor behind her was a cradle with a little child. Below the picture it said, "Woman awaiting her husband home from the sea." Sometimes my mother would suddenly catch sight of me and follow my glance up to the picture I found so tender and sad. But my mother burst out laughing and it sounded like dozens of paper bags filled with air exploding all at once. My heart pounded with anguish and sorrow because the silence in the world was now broken, but I laughed with her because my mother expected me to, and because I was seized by the same cruel mirth as she was. She shoved the chair aside, got up and stood in front of the picture in her wrinkled nightgown, her hands on her hips. Then, with a clear and defiant little-girl voice that didn't belong to her in the same way as her voice did later in the day when she'd start haggling about prices with the shopkeepers, she sang:

> Can't I sing
> Whatever I wish for my Tulle?
> Visselulle, visselulle, visselulle.
> Go away from the window, my friend,

Come back another time.
Frost and cold have brought
The old beggar home again.

I didn't like the song, but I had to laugh loudly because my mother sang it to amuse me. It was my own fault, though, because if I hadn't looked at the picture, she wouldn't have noticed me. Then she would have stayed sitting there with calmly folded hands and harsh, beautiful eyes fixed on the no-man's-land between us. And my heart could have still whispered "Mother" for a long time and known that in a mysterious way she heard it. I would have left her alone for a long time so that without words she would have said my name and known we were connected to each other. Then something like love would have filled the whole world, and Scabie Hans and Pretty Lili would have felt it and continued to be colored pictures in a book. As it was, right after the end of the song, they began to fight and yell and pull each other by the hair. And right away, angry voices from the stairwell began to push into the living room, and I promised myself that tomorrow I would pretend the wretched picture on the wall wasn't even there.

When hope had been crushed like that, my mother would get dressed with violent and irritated movements, as if every piece of clothing were an insult to her. I had to get dressed too, and the world was cold and dangerous and ominous because my mother's dark anger always ended in her slapping my face or pushing me against the stove. She was foreign and strange, and I thought that I had been exchanged at birth and she wasn't my mother at all. When she was dressed, she stood in front of the mirror in the bedroom, spit on a piece of pink tissue paper, and rubbed it hard across her cheeks. I carried the cups out to the kitchen, and

5

inside of me long, mysterious words began to crawl across my soul like a protective membrane. A song, a poem, something soothing and rhythmic and immensely pensive, but never distressing or sad, as I knew the rest of my day would be distressing and sad. When these light waves of words streamed through me, I knew that my mother couldn't do anything else to me because she had stopped being important to me. My mother knew it, too, and her eyes would fill with cold hostility. She never hit me when my soul was moved in this way, but she didn't talk to me, either. From then on, until the following morning, it was only our bodies that were close to each other. And, in spite of the cramped space, they avoided even the slightest contact with each other. The sailor's wife on the wall still watched longingly for her husband, but my mother and I didn't need men or boys in our world. Our peculiar and infinitely fragile happiness thrived only when we were alone together; and when I stopped being a little child, it never really came back except in rare, occasional glimpses that have become even more dear to me now that my mother is dead and there is no one to tell her story as it really was.

2

DOWN IN THE BOTTOM OF MY CHILDHOOD MY FATHER
stands laughing. He's big and black and old like the stove,
but there is nothing about him that I'm afraid of. Everything that I know about him I'm allowed to know, and if I
want to know anything else, I just have to ask. He doesn't
talk to me on his own because he doesn't know what he
should say to little girls. Once in a while he pats me on the
head and says, "Heh, heh." Then my mother pinches her
lips together and he quickly takes his hand away. My father
has certain privileges because he's a man and provides for all
of us. My mother has to accept that but she doesn't do it
without protest. "You could sit up like the rest of us, you
know," she says when he lies down on the sofa. And when
he reads a book, she says, "People turn strange from
reading. Everything written in books is a lie." On Sundays,
my father drinks a beer and my mother says, "That costs
twenty-six øre. If you keep at it like this, we'll end up
in Sundholm." Even though I know Sundholm is a place
where you sleep on straw and get salt herring three times a
day, the name goes into the verses I make up when I'm
scared or alone, because it's beautiful like the picture in one
of my father's books that I'm so fond of. It's called "Worker
family on a picnic," and it shows a father and mother and
their two children. They're sitting on some green grass and
all of them are laughing while they eat from the picnic
basket lying between them. All four of them are looking up
at a flag stuck into the grass near the father's head. The flag

is solid red. I always look at the picture upside down since I only get a chance to see it when my father is reading the book. Then my mother turns on the light and draws the yellow curtains even though it's not dark yet. "My father was a scoundrel and a drunkard," she says, "but at least he wasn't a socialist." My father keeps on reading calmly because he's slightly deaf, and that's no secret, either. My brother Edvin sits and pounds nails into a board and afterwards pulls them out with pliers. He's going to be a skilled worker. That's something very special. Skilled workers have real tablecloths on the table instead of newspaper and they eat with a knife and fork. They're never unemployed and they're not socialists. Edvin is handsome and I'm ugly. Edvin is smart and I'm stupid. Those are eternal truths like the printed white letters on the baker's roof down the street. It says, "*Politiken* is the best newspaper." Once I asked my father why he read *Social-Demokraten* instead, but he just wrinkled his brow and cleared his throat while my mother and Edvin burst into their paper-laughter because I was so incredibly stupid.

The living room is an island of light and warmth for many thousands of evenings — the four of us are always there, like the paper dolls up on the wall behind the pillars in the puppet theater my father made from a model in *Familie Journalen*. It's always winter, and out in the world it's ice cold like in the bedroom and the kitchen. The living room sails through time and space, and the fire roars in the stove. Even though Edvin makes lots of noise with his hammer, it seems like an even louder sound when my father turns a page in the forbidden book. After he has turned many pages, Edvin looks at my mother with his big brown eyes and puts the hammer down. "Won't Mother sing something?" he says. "All right," says my mother, smiling at him, and at once my father puts the book down on his stomach and looks at me as if he'd like to say something to me. But what my father and I want to say to each other will never be said. Edvin jumps up and hands my mother the only book she owns and cares about. It's a book of war songs. He stands bending over her while she leafs through it, and though of course they don't touch each other, they're together in a way that excludes my father and me. As soon as my mother starts to sing, my father falls asleep with his hands folded over the forbidden book. My mother sings loudly and shrilly, as if dissociating herself from the words she sings:

> Mother — is it Mother?
> I see that you have wept.
> You have walked far, you have not slept.
> I am happy now. Don't cry, Mother.
> Thank you for coming, despite all this horror.

There are many verses to all of my mother's songs, and before she reaches the end of the first one, Edvin starts hammering again and my father is snoring loudly. Edvin has asked her to sing in order to avert her rage over my father's reading. He is a boy and boys don't care for songs that make you cry if you listen to them. My mother doesn't like me to cry, either, so I just sit there with a lump in my throat and look sideways down at the book, at the picture of the battlefield where the dying soldier stretches his hand up toward the luminous spirit of his mother, who I know isn't there in reality. All of the songs in the book have a similar theme, and while my mother is singing them I can do whatever I want because she's so completely absorbed in her own world that nothing from outside can disturb her. She doesn't

9

even hear it when they start to fight and argue downstairs. That's where Rapunzel with the long golden braid lives with her parents who haven't yet sold her to the witch for a bunch of bluebells. My brother is the prince and he doesn't know that soon he'll be blind after his fall from the tower. He pounds nails into his board and is the family's pride and joy. That's what boys are, while girls just get married and have children. They have to be supported and they can't hope for or expect anything else. Rapunzel's father and mother work at Carlsberg, and they each drink fifty beers a day. They keep on drinking in the evening after they've come home, and a little before my bedtime they start yelling and beating Rapunzel with a thick stick. She always goes to school with bruises on her face or legs. When they get tired of beating her, they attack each other with bottles and broken chair legs and the police often come to get one of them — and then quiet finally falls over the building. Neither my mother nor my father likes the police. They think Rapunzel's parents should be allowed to kill each other in peace if they want to. "They're doing the big shots' work," my father says about the police, and my mother has often talked about the time the police came and got her father and put him in jail. She'll never forget it. My father doesn't drink and he's never been in jail, either. My parents don't fight and things are much better for me than for them when they were children. But a dark edge of fear still invades all my thoughts when things have gotten quiet downstairs and I have to go to bed. "Good night," says my mother and closes the door, and goes into the warm living room again. Then I take off my dress, my woolen petticoat and bodice, and the long black stockings I get as a Christmas present every year. I pull my nightgown over my head and sit down on the windowsill for a minute. I look into the dark courtyard way down below and at the front building's wall that's always crying as if it has just rained. There are hardly ever lights in any of the windows because those are the bedrooms, and decent people don't sleep with the light on. Between the walls I can see a little square scrap of sky, where a single star sometimes shines. I call it the evening star and think about it with all my might when my mother has been in to turn off the light, and I lie in my bed watching the pile of clothes behind the door change into long crooked arms trying to twist around my throat. I try to scream, but manage only a feeble whisper, and when the scream finally comes, the whole bed and I are both sopping wet with sweat. My father stands in the doorway and the light is on. "You just had a nightmare," he says. "I suffered from them a lot when I was a child, too. But those were different times." He looks at me speculatively, and seems to be thinking that a child who has such a good life shouldn't be having nightmares. I smile at him shyly and apologetically, as if the scream were just a foolish whim. I pull the comforter all the way up to my chin because a man shouldn't see a girl in her nightgown. "Well, well," he says, turning off the light and leaving again, and in some way or other he takes my fear with him, for now I calmly fall asleep, and the clothes behind the door are only a pile of old rags. I sleep to escape the night that trails past the window with its train of terror and evil and danger. Over on Istedgade, which is so light and festive during the day, police cars and ambulances wail while I lie securely hidden under the comforter. Drunken men lie in the gutter with broken, bloody heads, and if you go into Café Charles, you'll be killed. That's what my brother says, and everything he says is true.

11

3

I AM BARELY SIX YEARS OLD AND SOON I'LL BE ENROLLED IN school, because I can read and write. My mother proudly tells this to everyone who bothers listening to her. She says, "Poor people's children can have brains too." So maybe she loves me after all? My relationship with her is close, painful, and shaky, and I always have to keep searching for a sign of love. Everything I do, I do to please her, to make her smile, to ward off her fury. This work is extremely exhausting because at the same time I have to hide so many things from her. Some of the things I get from eavesdropping, others I read about in my father's books, and still others my brother tells me. When my mother was in the hospital recently, we were both sent to Aunt Agnete's and Uncle Peter's. That's my mother's sister and her rich husband. They told me that my mother had a bad stomach, but Edvin just laughed and later explained to me that mother had "ambortated." A baby had been in her stomach, but it had died in there. So they had cut her open from her navel down and removed the baby. It was mysterious and terrible. When she came home from the hospital, the bucket under the sink was full of blood every day. Every time I think about it, I see a picture in front of me. It's in Zacharias Nielsen's short stories and depicts a very beautiful woman in a long red dress. She's holding a slim white hand under her breast and saying to an elegantly dressed gentleman, "I'm carrying a child under my heart." In books, such things are beautiful and un-bloody, and it reassures and comforts me. Edvin says that

I'll get lots of spankings in school because I'm so odd. I'm odd because I read books, like my father, and because I don't understand how to play. Even so, I'm not afraid when, holding my mother's hand, I go in through the red doorway of Enghavevej School, because lately my mother has given me the completely new feeling of being something unique. She has on her new coat, with the fur collar up around her ears and belt around her hips. Her cheeks are red from the tissue paper, her lips too, and her eyebrows are painted so that they look like two little fish flicking their tails out toward her temples. I'm convinced that none of the other children has such a beautiful mother. I myself am dressed in Edvin's made-over clothes, but no one can tell because Aunt Rosalia did it. She's a seamstress, and she loves my brother and me as if we were her own children. She doesn't have any herself.

When we enter the building, which seems completely empty, a sharp smell strikes my nose. I recognize it and my heart stiffens because it's the already well-known smell of fear. My mother notices it, too, because she releases my hand as we go up the stairs. In the principal's office, we're received by a woman who looks like a witch. Her greenish hair perches like a bird's nest on top of her head. She only has glasses for one eye, so I guess the other lens was broken. It seems to me that she has no lips — they're pressed so tightly together — and over them a big porous nose juts out, its tip glowing red. "Hmm," she says without introduction, "so your name is Tove?" "Yes," says my mother, to whom she has hardly cast a glance, let alone offered a chair, "and she can read and write without mistakes." The woman gives me a look as if I were something she had found under a rock. "That's too bad," she says coldly. "We have our own method for teaching that to children, you know." The blush of shame floods my cheeks, as always when I've been the cause of my mother suffering insult. Gone is my pride, destroyed is my short-lived joy at being unique. My mother moves a little bit away from me and says faintly, "She learned it by herself, it's not our fault." I look up at her and understand many things at once. She is smaller than other adult women, younger than other mothers, and there's a world outside my street that she fears. And whenever we both fear it together, she will stab me in the back. As we stand there in front of the witch, I also notice that my mother's hands smell of dish soap. I despise that smell, and as we leave the school again in utter silence, my heart fills with the chaos of anger, sorrow, and compassion that my mother will always awaken in me from that moment on, throughout my life.

4

In the meantime, there exist certain facts. They are stiff and immovable, like the lampposts in the street, but at least they change in the evening when the lamplighter has touched them with his magic wand. Then they light up like big soft sunflowers in the narrow borderland between night and day, when all the people move so quietly and slowly, as if they were walking on the bottom of the green ocean. Facts never light up and they can't soften hearts like *Ditte menneskebarn*, which is one of the first books that I read. "It's a social novel," says my father pedantically, and that probably is a fact, but it doesn't tell me anything, and I have no use for it. "Nonsense," says my mother, who doesn't care for facts, either, but can more easily ignore them than I can. Whenever my father, on rare occasions, gets really mad at her, he says she's full of lies, but I know that's not so. I know every person has their own truth just as every child has their own childhood. My mother's truth is completely different from my father's truth, but it's just as obvious as the fact that he has brown eyes while hers are blue. Fortunately, things are set up so that you can keep quiet about the truths in your heart; but the cruel, gray facts are written in the school records and in the history of the world and in the law and in the church books. No one can change them and no one dares to try, either — not even the Lord, whose image I can't separate from Prime Minister Stauning's, even though my father says that I shouldn't believe in the Lord since the capitalists have always used Him against the poor.

15

Therefore:

I was born on December 14, 1918, in a little two-room apartment in Vesterbro in Copenhagen. We lived at Hedebygade 30A; the "A" meant it was in the back building. In the front building, from the windows of which you could look down on the street, lived the finer people. Though the apartments were exactly the same as ours, they paid two kroner more a month in rent. It was the year that the World War ended and the eight-hour day was instituted. My brother Edvin was born when the World War began and when my father worked twelve-hour days. He was a stoker and his eyes were always bloodshot from the sparks from the furnace. He was thirty-seven years old when I was born, and my mother was ten years younger. My father was born in Nykøbing Mors. He was born out of wedlock and he never knew who his father was. When he was six years old, he was sent out as a shepherd boy, and at about the same time his mother married a potter named Floutrup. She had nine children by him, but I don't know anything about all of these half brothers and half sisters because I've never met them, and my father has never talked about them. He cut off ties with everyone in his family when he went to Copenhagen at the age of sixteen. He had a dream of writing and it never really left him completely. He managed to get hired as an apprentice reporter with some newspaper or other, but, for unknown reasons, he gave it up again. I know nothing of how he spent the ten years in Copenhagen until, at twenty-six, he met my mother in a bakery on Tordenskjoldsgade. She was sixteen, a salesgirl in the front of the shop where my father was a baker's assistant. It turned out to be an abnormally long engagement that my father broke off many times when he thought my mother was cheating on him. I think that most of the time it was completely innocent.

Those two people were just so totally different, as if they each came from their own planet. My father was melancholy, serious, and unusually moralistic, while my mother, at least as a young girl, was lively and silly, irresponsible and vain. She worked as a maid at various places, and whenever something didn't suit her, she would just leave. Then my father had to go and get the servant's conduct book and the chest-of-drawers, which he would drive over on a delivery bicycle to the new place, where there would be something else that didn't suit her. She herself once confided to me that she'd never been at any job long enough to have time to boil an egg.

I was seven years old when disaster struck us. My mother had just knit me a green sweater. I put it on and thought it was pretty. Toward the end of the day we went over to pick up my father from work. He worked at Riedel & Lindegaard on Kingosgade. He had always worked there — that is, for as long as I'd been alive. We got there a little too early, and I went and kicked at the mounds of melting snow along the curb while my mother stood leaning against the green railing, waiting. Then my father strode out of the gate and my heart began to beat faster. His face was gray and funny and different. My mother quickly went up to him. "Ditlev," she said, "what's happened?" He looked down at the ground. "I've been fired," he said. I didn't know the word but understood the irreparable damage. My father had lost his job. That which could only strike others, had hit us. Riedel & Lindegaard, from which everything good had come until now — even down to my Sunday five øre that I couldn't spend — had become an evil and horrible dragon that had spewed out my father from its fiery jaws, indifferent to his fate, to us, to me and my new green sweater that he didn't even notice. None of us said a word on the

17

way home. I tried to slip my hand into my mother's, but she knocked my arm away with a violent motion. When we got into the living room my father looked at her with an expression heavy with guilt. "Well, well," he said, stroking his black mustache with two fingers, "it'll be a long time before the unemployment benefits give out." He was forty-three and too old to get a steady job anymore. Even so, I remember only one time when the union benefits ran out and welfare came under discussion. It happened in whispers and after my brother's and my bedtime, because it was an indelible shame like lice and child support. If you went on welfare, you lost your right to vote. We never starved, either, at least my stomach was always full of something, but I got to know the half-starvation you feel at the smell of dinner coming from the doors of the more well-to-do, when for days you've been living on coffee and stale pastry, which cost twenty-five øre for a whole school bag full.

I was the one who bought it. Every Sunday morning at six o'clock my mother woke me up and issued her orders while well hidden under the comforter in the marriage bed next to my father, who was still sleeping. With fingers that were already stiff from the cold before I reached the street, I grabbed my school bag and flew down the stairs that were pitch-dark at that time of day. I opened the door to the street and looked around in every direction and up at the front building's windows, because no one was supposed to see me perform this despicable task. It wasn't proper to be buying old bread, just as it wasn't proper to take part in the school meals at the Carlsbergvej School, the only social-service institution that existed in Vesterbro in the 30s. The latter, Edvin and I were not allowed to do. For that matter, it wasn't proper, either, to have a father who was unemployed, even though half of us did. So we covered up this disgrace with the craziest lies — the most common of which was that father had fallen off a scaffold and was on sick leave. Over by the bakery on Tøndergade the line of children formed a winding snake along the street. They all had bags with them and they all jabbered on about how good the bread was at that particular bakery, especially when it was freshly baked. When it was my turn, I shoved the bag up on the counter, whispered my mission and added aloud, "Preferably cream puffs." My mother had expressly told me to ask for white bread. On the way home I stuffed myself with four or five sour cream puffs, wiped my mouth on my coat sleeve, and was never discovered when my mother rummaged in the depths of the bag. I was never, or rarely, punished for the crimes I committed. My mother hit me often and hard, but as a rule it was arbitrary and unjust, and during the punishment I felt something like a secret shame or a heavy sorrow that brought the tears to my eyes and increased the painful distance between us. My father never hit me. On the contrary — he was good to me. All of my childhood books were his, and on my fifth birthday he gave me a wonderful edition of *Grimms' Fairy Tales*, without which my childhood would have been gray and dreary and impoverished. Still, I didn't hold any strong feeling for him, which I often reproached myself for when, sitting on the sofa, he would look at me with his quiet, searching glance, as if he wanted to say or do something in my direction, something that he never managed to express. I was mother's girl and Edvin was father's boy — that law of nature couldn't be changed. Once I said to him, "Lamentation — what does that mean, Father?" I had found the expression in Gorky and loved it. He considered this for a long time while he stroked the turned-up ends of his mustache. "It's a Russian term," he said then. "It means pain and misery and sorrow. Gorky was a great poet." I said happily, "I want to be a poet too!" Immediately he frowned and said severely, "Don't be a fool! A girl can't be a poet." Offended and hurt, I withdrew into myself again while my mother and Edvin laughed at the crazy idea. I vowed never to reveal my dreams to anyone again, and I kept this vow throughout my childhood.

5

It's evening and I'm sitting as usual up on the cold windowsill in the bedroom and looking down at the courtyard. It's the happiest hour of my day. The first wave of fear has subsided. My father has said good night and has gone back to the warm living room, and the clothes behind the door have stopped frightening me. I look up at my evening star that's like God's benevolent eye; it follows me vigilantly and seems closer to me than during the day. Someday I'll write down all of the words that flow through me. Someday other people will read them in a book and marvel that a girl could be a poet, after all. My father and mother will be prouder of me than of Edvin, and a sharp-sighted teacher at school (one that I haven't had yet) will say, "I saw it already when she was a child. There was something special about her!" I want so badly to write down the words, but where in the world would I hide such papers? Even my parents don't have a drawer that can be locked. I'm in the second grade and I want to write hymns because they're the most beautiful things that I know. On my first day of school we sang: "God be thanked and praised, we slept so peacefully"; and when we got to "now lively like the bird, briskly like the fish of the sea, the morning sun shines through the pane," I was so happy and moved that I burst out crying, at which all the children laughed in the same way as my mother and Edvin laugh whenever my "oddness" brings forth my tears. My classmates find me unceasingly, overwhelmingly comical, and I've gotten used to the clown role and even find a sad comfort in it, because together with my confirmed stupidity, it protects me against their peculiar meanness toward anyone who is different.

A shadow creeps out from the arched doorway like a rat from its hole. In spite of the dark, I can see that it's the pervert. When he's certain that the way is clear, he pushes his hat down on his forehead and runs over to the pissoir, leaving the door ajar. I can't see in, but I know what he's doing. The time is past when I was afraid of him, but my mother still is. A little while ago, she took me to the Svendsgade Police Station and, indignant and trembling with rage, told the officer that women and children in the building weren't safe from his filthiness. "He scared my little girl here out of her wits," she said. Then the officer asked me whether the pervert had bared himself, and I said no with great conviction. I only knew the word from the line "thus we bare our heads each time the flag is raised." He had really never taken off his hat. When we got home, my mother said to my father, "The police won't do anything. There's no law or justice left in this country."

The door opens on its screeching hinges and the laughter and songs and curses break through the solemn silence in the room and inside of me. I crane my neck to get a better look at who's coming. It's Rapunzel, her father, and Tin Snout, one of her parents' drinking companions. The girl is walking between the two men, each with an arm around her neck. Her golden hair shines as if reflecting the glow from some invisible streetlamp. Roaring, they stagger across the courtyard, and a little later I can hear their ruckus out on the stairway. Rapunzel's real name is Gerda, and she is almost grown-up, at least thirteen years old. Last summer, when she went with Scabie Hans and Pretty Lili in the gypsy wagon to mind the smallest children, my mother said,

"I guess Gerda has got herself more than just scabies on this trip." The big girls said something similar in the trash-can corner in the courtyard, where I often find myself on the outskirts. They said it in a low voice, giggling, and I didn't understand any more than that it was something shameless and dirty and obscene, something about Scabie Hans and Rapunzel. So I got up my courage and asked my mother what really had happened to Gerda. Angrily and impatiently she said, "Oh, you goose! She's not innocent anymore, that's all." And I wasn't any the wiser.

I look up at the cloudless, silken sky and open the window in order to be even closer to it. It's as if God slowly lowers His gentle face over the earth and His great heart beats softly and calmly, very close to mine. I feel very happy, and long, melancholy lines of verse pass through my soul. They separate me, unwillingly, from those I should be closest to. My parents don't like the fact that I believe in God and they don't like the language I use. On the other hand, I'm repelled by their use of language because they always employ the same vulgar, coarse words and expressions, the meanings of which never cover what they want to say. My mother starts almost all of her orders to me by saying, "God help you, if you don't. . . ." My father curses God in his Jylland dialect, which is perhaps not as bad, but not any nicer to listen to. On Christmas Eve we sing social democratic battle songs as we walk around the tree, and my heart aches with anguish and shame because we can hear the beautiful hymns being sung all around in the building, even in the most drunken and ungodly homes. You should respect your father and mother, and I tell myself that I do, but it's harder now than when I was little.

A fine, cool rain strikes my face and I close the window again. But I can still hear the soft sound of the hallway door as it's opened and closed far below. Then a lovely creature trips across the courtyard as if held upright by a delicate, transparent umbrella. It's Ketty, the beautiful, spiritlike woman from the apartment next to ours. She has on silver high-heel shoes under a long yellow silk dress. Over it she has a white fur that makes you think of Snow White. Ketty's hair is black as ebony, too. It takes only a minute before the arched doorway hides the beautiful sight that cheers my heart night after night. Ketty goes out every evening at this time, and my father says that it's scandalous when there are children around, and I don't understand what he means. My mother doesn't say anything, because during the day she and I are often over in Ketty's living room drinking coffee or hot chocolate. It's a wonderful room, where all the furniture is red plush. The lampshades are red, too, and Ketty herself is pink and white like my mother, although Ketty is younger. They laugh a lot, those two, and I laugh with them even though I seldom understand what's so funny. But whenever Ketty starts to talk to me, my mother sends me away because she doesn't approve of that. It's the same with Aunt Rosalia, who also likes to talk to me. "Women who don't have children," says my mother, "are always so busy with other people's." Afterwards she puts Ketty down because she makes her old mother live in the unheated room overlooking the courtyard and never lets her come into the living room. The mother is called Mrs. Andersen; and, according to my mother, that's "the blackest lie," since she's never been married. It's a great sin then to have a child—I know that. And when I ask my mother why Ketty treats her mother so badly, she says it's because the mother won't tell her who her father is. When you think about something that terrible, you really have to be grateful you have the proper relationships in your own family.

When Ketty has disappeared, the door to the pissoir opens cautiously, and the pervert edges sideways like a crab along the wall of the front building and out the door. I had completely forgotten about him.

6

CHILDHOOD IS LONG AND NARROW LIKE A COFFIN, AND YOU can't get out of it on your own. It's there all the time and everyone can see it just as clearly as you can see Pretty Ludvig's harelip. It's the same with him as with Pretty Lili, who's so ugly you can't imagine she ever had a mother. Everything that is ugly or unfortunate is called beautiful, and no one knows why. You can't get out of childhood, and it clings to you like a bad smell. You notice it in other children — each childhood has its own smell. You don't recognize your own and sometimes you're afraid that it's worse than others'. You're standing talking to another girl whose childhood smells of coal and ashes, and suddenly she takes a step back because she has noticed the terrible stink of your childhood. On the sly, you observe the adults whose childhood lies inside them, torn and full of holes like a used and moth-eaten rug no one thinks about anymore or has any use for. You can't tell by looking at them that they've had a childhood, and you don't dare ask how they managed to make it through without their faces getting deeply scarred and marked by it. You suspect that they've used some secret shortcut and donned their adult form many years ahead of time. They did it one day when they were home alone and their childhood lay like three bands of iron around their heart, like Iron Hans in Grimms' fairy tale, whose bands broke only when his master was freed. But if you don't know such a shortcut, childhood must be endured and trudged through hour by hour, through an absolutely interminable number of years. Only death can free you from it, so you think a lot about death, and picture it as a white-robed, friendly angel who some night will kiss your eyelids so that they never will open again. I always think that when I'm grown-up my mother will finally like me the way she likes Edvin now. Because my childhood irritates her just as much as it irritates me, and we are only happy together whenever she suddenly forgets about its existence. Then she talks to me the way she talks to her friends or to Aunt Rosalia, and I'm very careful to make my answers so short that she won't suddenly remember I'm only a child. I let go of her hand and keep a slight distance between us so she won't be able to smell my childhood, either. It almost always happens when I go shopping with her on Istedgade. She tells me how much fun she had as a young girl. She went out dancing every night and was never off the dance floor. "I had a new boyfriend every night," she says and laughs loudly, "but that had to stop when I met Ditlev." That's my father and otherwise she always calls him "Father," just as he calls her "Mother" or "Mutter." I get the impression there was a time when she was happy and different, but that it all came to an abrupt end when she met Ditlev. When she talks about him it's as if he's someone other than my father, a dark spirit who crushes and destroys everything that is beautiful and light and lively. And I wish that this Ditlev had never come into her life. When she gets to his name, she usually catches sight of my childhood and looks at it angrily and threateningly, while the dark rim around her blue iris grows even darker. This childhood then shivers with fear and despairingly tries to slip away on tip-toe, but it's still far too little and can't be discarded yet for several hundred years.

People with such a visible, flagrant childhood both inside

27

and out are called children, and you can treat them any way you like because there's nothing to fear from them. They have no weapons and no masks unless they are very cunning. I am that kind of cunning child, and my mask is stupidity, which I'm always careful not to let anyone tear away from me. I let my mouth fall open a little and make my eyes completely blank, as if they're always just staring off into the blue. Whenever it starts singing inside me, I'm especially careful not to let my mask show any holes. None of the grownups can stand the song in my heart or the garlands of words in my soul. But they know about them because bits seep out of me through a secret channel I don't recognize and therefore can't stop up. "You're not putting on airs?" they say, suspiciously, and I assure them that it wouldn't even occur to me to put on airs. In school they ask, "What are you thinking about? What was the last sentence I said?" But they never really see through me. Only the children in the courtyard or in the street do. "You're going around playing dumb," a big girl says menacingly and comes up close to me, "but you're not dumb at all." Then she starts to cross-examine me, and a lot of other girls gather silently around me, forming a circle I can't slip through until I've proved I really am stupid. At last it seems clear to them after all of my idiotic replies, and reluctantly they make a little hole in the circle so I can just squeeze through and escape to safety. "Because you shouldn't pretend to be something you're not," one of them yells after me, moralistic and admonishing.

Childhood is dark and it's always moaning like a little animal that's locked in a cellar and forgotten. It comes out of your throat like your breath in the cold, and sometimes it's too little, other times too big. It never fits exactly. It's only when it has been cast off that you can look at it calmly and talk about like an illness you've survived. Most grown-ups say that they've had a happy childhood and maybe they really believe it themselves, but I don't think so. I think they've just managed to forget it. My mother didn't have a happy childhood, and it's not as hidden away in her as it is in other people. She tells me how terrible it was when her father had the D.T.'s and they all had to stand holding up the wall so that it wouldn't fall on him. When I say that I feel sorry for him, she yells, "Sorry! It was his own fault, the drunken pig! He drank a whole bottle of schnapps every day, and in spite of everything, things were a lot better for us when he finally pulled himself together and hanged himself." She also says, "He murdered my five little brothers. He took them out of the cradle and crushed their heads against the wall." Once I ask my Aunt Rosalia, who is mother's sister, whether this is true, and she says, "Of course it's not true. They just died. Our father was an unhappy person, but your mother was only four years old when he died. She has inherited Granny's hatred of him." Granny is their mother, and even though she's old now, I can imagine that her soul can hold a lot of hatred. Granny lives on the island of Amager. Her hair is completely white and she's always dressed in black. Just as with my father and mother, I may only address her in an indirect way, which makes all conversations very difficult and full of repetitions. She makes the sign of the cross before she cuts the bread, and whenever she clips her fingernails, she burns the clippings in the stove. I ask her why she does this, but she says that she doesn't know. It was something her mother did. Like all grownups, she doesn't like it when children ask about something, so she gives short answers. Wherever you turn, you run up against your childhood and hurt yourself because it's sharp-edged and hard, and stops only when

29

it has torn you completely apart. It seems that everyone has their own and each is totally different. My brother's childhood is very noisy, for example, while mine is quiet and furtive and watchful. No one likes it and no one has any use for it. Suddenly it's much too tall and I can look into my mother's eyes when we both get up. "You grow while you're asleep," she says. Then I try to stay awake at night, but sleep overpowers me and in the morning I feel quite dizzy looking down at my feet, the distance has grown so great. "You big cow," the boys on the street yell after me, and if it keeps on like this, I'll have to go to Stormogulen where all the giants grow. Now childhood hurts. It's called growing pains and doesn't stop until you're twenty. That's what Edvin says, who knows everything — about the world and society, too — like my father, who takes him along to political meetings; my mother thinks it will end in both of them being arrested by the police. They don't listen when she says things like that because she knows as little about politics as I do. She also says that my father can't find work because he's a socialist and belongs to the union, and that Stauning, whose picture my father has hung up on the wall next to the sailor's wife, will lead us into trouble one day. I like Stauning, whom I've seen and heard many times in Fælled Park. I like him because his long beard waves so gaily in the wind and because he says "comrades" to the workers even though he's Prime Minister and could allow himself to be more stuck-up. When it comes to politics, I think my mother is wrong, but no one is interested in what girls think or don't think about such things.

One day my childhood smells of blood, and I can't avoid noticing and knowing it. "Now you can have children," says my mother. "It's much too soon, you're not even thirteen yet." I know how you have children because I sleep with my parents, and in other ways you can't help knowing it, either. But even so, somehow I still don't understand, and I imagine that at any time I can wake up with a little child beside me. Her name will be Baby Maria, because it will be a girl. I don't like boys and I'm not allowed to play with them, either. Edvin is the only one I love and admire, and he's the only one I can imagine myself marrying. But you can't marry your brother and even if you could, he wouldn't have me. He's said that often enough. Everyone loves my brother, and I often think his childhood suits him better than mine suits me. He has a custom-made childhood that expands in tune with his growth, while mine is made for a completely different girl. Whenever I think such thoughts, my mask becomes even more stupid, because you can't talk to anyone about these kinds of things, and I always dream about meeting some mysterious person who will listen to me and understand me. I know from books that such people exist, but you can't find any of them on my childhood street.

7

ISTEDGADE IS MY CHILDHOOD STREET — ITS RHYTHM WILL
always pound in my blood and its voice will always reach me
and be the same as in those distant times when we swore to
be true to each other. It's always warm and light, festive and
exciting, and it envelops me completely, as if it were created
to satisfy my personal need for self-expression. Here I
walked as a child holding my mother's hand, and learned
important things like an egg in Irma costs six øre, a pound
of margarine forty-three øre, and a pound of horse meat
fifty-eight øre. My mother haggles over everything except
food, so that the shopkeepers wring their hands in despair,
declaring she'll drive them to wrack and ruin if this keeps
up. She's so wonderfully audacious, too, that she dares to
exchange shirts that my father has worn as if they were
brand new. And she can go right in the door of a store,
stand at the end of the line and yell in a shrill voice, "Hey,
it's my turn now. I've certainly waited long enough." I have
fun with her and I admire her Copenhagen boldness and
quick-wittedness. The unemployed hang around outside
the small cafés. They whistle through their fingers at my
mother, but she doesn't give them the time of day. "They
could at least stay at home," she says, "like your father."
But it's so depressing to see him sitting idly on the sofa
whenever he's not out looking for work. In a magazine, I
read this line: "To sit and stare at two fists that our Lord has
made so magnificently skilled." It's a poem about the unemployed and it makes me think of my father.

It's only after I meet Ruth that Istedgade becomes a playground and permanent hangout for me after school until dinner time. At that time I'm nine years old and Ruth is seven. We notice each other one Sunday morning when all of the children in the building are chased out into the street to play so the parents can sleep late after the week's drudgery or dreariness. As usual, the big girls stand gossiping in the trash-can corner while the little ones play hopscotch, a game I always make a mess of because I either step on the line or touch the ground with my swinging leg. I never understand what the point is and find the game terribly boring. Somebody or other has said that I'm out, and resignedly I'm leaning against the wall. Then quick footsteps pound down the front building's kitchen stairway, which leads out into the courtyard, and a little girl emerges with red hair, green eyes, and light brown freckles across the bridge of her nose. "Hi," she says to me and grins from ear to ear, "my name is Ruth." I introduce myself shyly and awkwardly, because no one is used to new children making such a cool entrance. Everyone is staring at Ruth, who doesn't seem to notice it. "Want to run and play?" she says to me, and after a hesitating glance up at our window I follow her, as I will follow her for many years, right up until we've both finished school and our profound differences have become apparent.

Now I've got a friend and it makes me much less dependent on my mother, who of course doesn't like Ruth. "She's an adopted child and nothing good ever comes of that," my mother says darkly, but she doesn't forbid me to play with her. Ruth's parents are a pair of big, ugly people who themselves could never have brought something as lovely as Ruth into the world. The father is a waiter and drinks like a fish. The mother is obese and asthmatic and hits Ruth for the slightest reason. Ruth doesn't care. She shakes off the claws, roars down the kitchen stairs, shows all of her shining white teeth in a smile, and says gaily, "That bitch, I wish she'd go to hell." When Ruth swears it isn't ugly or offensive because her voice is so crisp and fine, like the little Billy Goat Gruff. Her mouth is red and heart-shaped with a narrow, upturned upper lip, and her expression is as strong as that of the man who knew no fear. She is everything that I'm not, and I do everything she wants me to do. She cares as little as I do for real games. She never touches her dolls and she uses her doll buggy as a springboard when we put a plank on it. But we don't do that very often because the landlady comes running after us or we're told to stop it by our watchful mothers who have much too good a view from the windows. Only on Istedgade are we away from any supervision, and that's where my criminal path begins. Ruth accepts sweetly and good-humoredly that I'm not prepared to steal. But then I have to distract the clerk's attention from her tiny, quick figure that indiscriminately grabs things while I stand there asking when they expect to get bubblegum in the store. We go into the nearest doorway and share the plunder. Sometimes we go to stores and endlessly try on shoes or dresses. We select the most expensive one and politely say that our mother will come in to pay for it if they would kindly put the goods aside for the time being. Even before we get out the door, our delighted giggles break loose.

Throughout the whole long friendship, I'm always afraid of revealing myself to Ruth. I'm afraid that she'll discover how I really am. I make myself into her echo because I love her and because she's the strongest, but deep inside I am still me. I have my dreams about a future beyond the street, but Ruth is intimately tied to it and will never be torn away from it. I feel as if I'm deceiving her by pretending that we're of the same blood. In a mysterious way I am indebted to her; together with fear and a vague guilt feeling, this burdens my heart and colors our relationship in the same way it will all close and lasting relationships later in my life.

The shoplifting comes to an abrupt end. One day Ruth has pulled a coup by swiping a whole jar of orange marmalade inside her coat. Afterwards, we eat ourselves sick on it. Completely stuffed, we throw the rest into one of the garbage cans, which is so full that it can't be closed. So we jump up and sit on the lid. Suddenly Ruth says, "Why the hell does it always have to be me?" "The receiver is as bad as the thief," I say, terrified. "Yes, but still . . ." grumbles Ruth, "you could do it once in a while." I can see the reasonableness in her demand and promise uneasily to do it next time. But I insist it has to be very far away, so on Søndre Boulevard I pick out a dairy store that looks suitably deserted. Ruth cautiously opens the door and sails in, followed by her long shadow, which could very well be her own slumbering conscience. The shop is empty and there's no window in the door out to the back room. On the counter there's a bowl full of twenty-five-øre chocolate sticks in red and green foil. I stare at them, pale with excitement and fear. I lift my hand, but it's held back by invisible powers. I shake all the way down to my feet. "Hurry up," whispers Ruth, who is keeping an eye on the back room. Then the hand-that-can't-steal reaches up to the bowl, grabs some of the red and green dancing before my eyes, and knocks the whole pile over behind the counter. "Idiot," hisses Ruth, and races off just as the back door bangs open. A pale woman comes rushing out and stops, astonished, when she sees me standing there like a pillar of salt with a piece of chocolate in one upraised hand. "What's the meaning of this?" she says. "What are you doing here? Oh, look, now the bowl is broken!" And she bends down and picks up the pieces, and I don't know what to do, since the world hasn't crashed around me after all. I wish that it would happen now, right there. All I feel is a boundless, burning shame. The excitement and the adventure are gone; I'm just an ordinary thief, caught in the act. "You could at least say you're sorry," says the woman as she goes out with the shards of glass. "Such a big, clumsy oaf."

All the way down by Enghavevej, Ruth is standing laughing so hard she has tears in her eyes. "You're such a blithering idiot," she manages to say. "Did she say anything? Why didn't you get out of there? Hey, do you still have the chocolate? Let's go to the park and eat it." "Do you really want to eat it?" I ask in disbelief. "I think we should throw it under a tree." "Are you crazy?" Ruth says. "Good chocolate?" "But Ruth," I say, "we'll never do it again, will we?" Then my little friend asks me whether I'm becoming a goody-goody, and in the park she stuffs the chocolate in her mouth right before my eyes. After that the stealing expeditions stop. Ruth doesn't want to do it alone. And whenever my mother sends me out shopping, I always barge into the store with unnecessary noise. If, after that, it still takes a while for the clerk to come, I stand far away from the counter with my eyes on the ceiling. But my cheeks still flush red when the woman appears, and I have to control myself to keep from desperately turning my pockets inside out in front of her so she can see they're not full of stolen goods. The episode increases my guilt feeling toward Ruth, and also makes me afraid of losing her prized friendship. So I show even greater daring in our other forbidden games, such as trying to be the last one to run over the tracks in front of the train under the viaduct on Enghavevej. Sometimes I'm toppled over by the air pressure from the locomotive, and I lie on the grass embankment for a long time, gasping for breath. It's reward enough when Ruth says, "Good God! That time you just about kicked the bucket!"

8

It's FALL AND THE STORM RATTLES THE BUTCHER'S SIGNS. The trees on Enghavevej have lost nearly all of their leaves, which almost cover the ground with their yellow and reddish-brown carpet that looks like my mother's hair when the sun plays in it, and you suddenly discover it's not totally black. The unemployed are freezing, but still standing erect with their hands deep in their pockets and a burned-out pipe between their teeth. The streetlamps have just been lit, and now and then the moon peeks out between racing, shifting clouds. I always think there is a mystical understanding between the moon and the street, like between two sisters who have grown old together and no longer need any language to communicate with each other. We're walking in the fleeting dusk, Ruth and I, and soon we'll have to leave the street, which makes us eager for something to happen before the day is over. When we reach Gasværksvej, where we usually turn around, Ruth says, "Let's go down and look at the whores. There are probably some who have started." A whore is a woman who does it for money, which seems to me much more understandable than to to do it for free. Ruth told me about it, and since I think the word is ugly, I've found another in a book: "Lady-of-the-evening." It sounds much nicer and more romantic. Ruth tells me everything about those kinds of things; for her, the adults have no secrets. She has also told me about Scabie Hans and Rapunzel, and I can't comprehend it, since I think Scabie Hans is a very old man. And he has Pretty Lili, besides.

I wonder whether men can love two women at once. For me the grownups' world is still just as mysterious. I always picture Istedgade as a beautiful woman who's lying on her back with her hair near Enghaveplads. At Gasværksvej, which forms the boundary between decent people and the depraved, her legs part, and sprinkled over them like freckles are the welcoming hotels and the bright, noisy taverns, where later in the night the police cars drive by to pick up their scandalously intoxicated and quarrelsome victims. That I know from Edvin, who is four years older than me, and is allowed to be out until ten o'clock at night. I admire Edvin greatly when he comes home in his blue DUI shirt and talks politics with my father. Lately they're both very outraged over Sacco and Vanzetti, whose pictures stare out from the poster displays and the newspaper. They look so handsome with their dark foreign faces, and I also think it's too bad they're going to be executed for something they didn't do. But I just can't get as excited about it as my father, who yells and pounds the table whenever he discusses it with Uncle Peter. He's a Social Democrat like my father and Edvin, but he doesn't think that Sacco and Vanzetti deserve a better fate since they're anarchists. "I don't care," yells my father furiously and pounds the table. "Miscarriage of justice is miscarriage of justice, even if it concerns a conservative!" I know that's the worst thing you can be. Recently, when I asked whether I could join the Ping Club because all the other girls in my class were members, my father looked at my mother sternly, as if I were a victim of her subversive influence in political matters, and said, "There, you see, Mutter. Now she's becoming a reactionary. It will probably end with us subscribing to *Berlingske Tidende*!"

Down by the train station life is in full swing. Drunken

39

men stagger around singing with their arms around each other's shoulders, and out of Café Charles rolls a fat man whose bald head strikes the pavement a couple of times before he lies still at our feet. Two officers come over to him and kick him emphatically in the side, which makes him get up with a pitiful howl. They pull him roughly to his feet and push him away when he once again tries to go into the den of iniquity. As they continue down the street, Ruth puts her fingers in her mouth and sends a long whistle after them, a talent I envy. Near Helgolandsgade there's a big crowd of laughing, noisy children, and when we go over there I see that it's Curly Charles, who is standing in the middle of the road, putting the steaming horse droppings in his mouth. All the while he's singing an indescribably filthy song that makes the children scream with laughter and give him shouts of encouragement in the hope he'll provide them with more entertainment. His eyes roll wildly. I find him tragic and horrifying, but pretend he amuses me because of Ruth, who laughs loudly along with the others. Of whores, however, we see only a couple of older, fat women who energetically wiggle their hips in an apparently vain attempt to attract the favors of an audience driving slowly by. This disappoints me greatly, because I thought all of them were like Ketty, whose evening errands in the city Ruth has also explained to me. On the way home, we go through Revalsgade, where once an old woman who owned a cigar store was murdered. We also stop in front of the haunted house on Matthæusgade and stare up at the fourth floor window where a little girl was murdered last year by Red Carl, a stoker my father worked with at the Ørsted Works. None of us dares go past that house alone at night. In the doorway at home, Gerda and Tin Snout are standing in such a tight embrace that you can't tell their figures apart in the dark.

40

I hold my breath until I'm out in the courtyard because there's always a rancid stench of beer and urine. I feel oppressed as I go up the stairs. The dark side of sex yawns toward me more and more, and it's becoming harder to cover it up with the unwritten, trembling words my heart is always whispering. The door next to Gerda's opens quietly as I go by, and Mrs. Poulsen signals me to come inside. According to my mother, she's "shabby-genteel," but I know that you can't be both shabby and genteel. She has a lodger who my mother contemptuously calls "a fine duke" even though he's a mailman and supports Mrs. Poulsen just as if they were married; they have no children, however. I know from Ruth that they live together as man and wife. Reluctantly, I obey the command and step into a living room exactly like ours except that there's a piano that is missing many keys. I sit down on the very edge of a chair and Mrs. Poulsen sits on the sofa with a prying look in her pale blue eyes. "Tell me something, Tove," she says ingratiatingly. "Do you know whether many gentlemen come to visit Miss Andersen?" I immediately make my eyes blank and stupid and let my jaw drop slightly. "No," I say, feigning astonishment, "I don't think so." "But you and your mother are over there so much. Think a little. Haven't you ever seen any gentlemen in her apartment? Not even in the evenings?" "No," I lie, terrified. I'm afraid of this woman who wants to harm Ketty in some way. My mother has forbidden me to visit Ketty anymore, and she only goes over there herself when my father is not around. Mrs. Poulsen gets nothing else out of me and lets me go with a certain coolness. Several days later a petition goes around in the building and because of it, my parents have a fight when they come to bed and think I'm asleep. "I'm going to sign it," says my father, "for the children's sake. You can at least

41

protect them from witnessing the worst filth." "It's those old bitches," says my mother hotly. "They're jealous because she's young and pretty and happy. They can't stand me, either." "Stop comparing yourself to a whore," snarls my father. "Even though I don't have a steady job, you've never had to earn your own living — don't forget that!" It's awful to listen to, and it seems as though the fight is about something totally different, something they don't have words for. Soon the day arrives when Ketty and her mother are sitting out on the street on top of all their plush furniture, which a policeman, pacing back and forth, is guarding. Ketty looks right through all the people, full of contempt, holding her delicate umbrella up against the rain. She smiles at me, though, and says, "Good-bye, Tove. Take care of yourself." A little later they drive away in the moving van and I never see them again.

9

SOMETHING TERRIBLE HAS HAPPENED IN MY FAMILY.
Landmands Bank has gone under and my Granny has lost
all of her money. Five hundred kroner saved over an entire
lifetime. It's a nasty business that only strikes the small
investors. "The rich pigs," my father says, "will see that
they get their money." Granny cries pitifully and dries her
red eyes with a snow-white handkerchief. Everything about
her is clean and neat and proper, and she always smells like
the cleaners. The money was supposed to be used for her
funeral, which she always seems to be thinking about. She
pays money into a funeral coffer — she never can forget that
I once thought this was the same as a coffin. It still makes
her laugh whenever she thinks of it. I'm very fond of
Granny, not at all in the same terrified way as I am of my
mother. I'm allowed to visit her by myself, because that's
what she wants and my mother doesn't dare go against her
will. She told me Granny was very angry with her when she
was expecting me because, since they'd had a boy, there was
no reason to have any more children. Now Granny doesn't
know how she's going to get a decent burial, since we don't
have any money and Aunt Rosalia with her drunken husband doesn't, either. Uncle Peter is certainly very rich, but
with his proverbial stinginess, no one dreams of him con-
tributing anything for his mother-in-law's funeral. Granny
is seventy-three years old and she herself doesn't think she
has long to live. She's even smaller than my mother, slight
as a child and always dressed in black from head to toe. Her

white, silky-soft hair is put up on her head, and she moves as nimbly as a young girl. She lives in a one-room apartment and she only has her old-age pension to live on. Whenever I visit her for coffee, I have rye bread with real butter, which I scrape back with my teeth until it's all on the last mouthful; it tastes better than anything I ever get at home. Since Edvin started his apprenticeship, he visits her every Sunday. Then she gives him a whole krone because he's the only boy in the family. My three cousins and I don't get anything. Every time I'm at Granny's, she asks me to sing in order to see whether I sing a little less off-key than last time. "That's almost right," she says encouragingly, even though I can hear that the tones coming from me don't sound like the ones I want to produce at all. You can't speak to her without being addressed first, but she herself likes to talk and I like to listen to her. She talks about her childhood, which was awful because she had a stepmother who practically beat her to death every other minute for the smallest trifles. Then she became a maid and was engaged to my grandfather, who was named Mundus and was a coach builder before he began to drink heavily. "The Bellowing Drunk" they called him in the building, and when he hanged himself, Granny had to go out as a washerwoman in order to keep the wolf from the door. "But my three little girls got a start in life," she says with understandable pride. Once I let slip that I would have liked to have known my grandfather, and she says, "Yes, he was handsome right up to the end, but a heartless scoundrel! If I wanted to, I could tell you things. . . ." Then she presses her lips tightly together over her toothless gums and won't say any more. I think about the word "heartless" and am afraid that I'm like my dreadful grandfather. I often have a nagging suspicion that I'm not capable of really feeling anything for anyone, with the exception of Ruth, of course. One day when I'm at Granny's and have to sing for her, I say, "I've learned a new song in school." And with a false and quavering voice, I sit on her bed and sing a poem I've written. It's very long and—like "Hjalmar and Hilda," "Jørgen and Hansigne," and all of my mother's ballads—it's about two people who can't have each other. But in my version, it ends less tragically with the following verse:

> Love, rich and young,
> bound them with a thousand chains.
> Does it matter that the bridal bed
> is found on country lanes?

When I've gotten this far, Granny wrinkles her forehead, stands up, and smooths down her dress as if defending herself from an unpleasant impression. "That's not a nice song, Tove," she says sternly. "Did you really learn it in school?" I answer affirmatively, heavy-hearted because I thought she would say, "That was very beautiful—who wrote it?" "One must get married in a church," says Granny mildly, "before having anything to do with each other. But you couldn't know that, of course." Oh, Granny! I know more than you think, but I'll keep quiet about it in the future. I think about a few years ago when I discovered with astonishment that my parents were married in February the same year that Edvin was born in April. I asked my mother how that could be possible, and she answered briskly, "Well, you see, you never carry the first one more than two months." Then she laughed, and Edvin and my father frowned. That's the worst thing about grownups, I think—they can never admit that just once in their lives they've acted wrongly or irresponsibly. They're so quick to

45

judge others, but they never hold Judgement Day for themselves.

I only see the rest of my family together with my parents, or at least with my mother. Aunt Rosalia lives on Amager like Granny. I've only visited her a couple of times, because Uncle Carl, whom they call The Hollow Leg, is always sitting in the living room, drinking beer and grumbling, which isn't good for children to see. The living room is like everyone else's, with a buffet along one wall, a sofa against the other, and between them a table with four high-backed chairs. On the buffet, as in our apartment, there's a brass tray with a coffee pot, sugar bowl and cream pitcher that are never used, just polished bright and shiny for all special occasions. Aunt Rosalia sews for the department store Magasin and often visits us on her way home. Over her arm, in a big alpaca wrap, she carries the clothes that she's going to sew, and she never puts it down while she's visiting us. She's only going to stay "a minute," and always keeps her hat on as if to deny she's been here several hours when she finally leaves. She and my mother always talk about events from their youth, and in that way I find out a lot that I shouldn't know. Once, for example, my mother hid a barber in the wardrobe in her room because my father unexpectedly came to visit. If my mother hadn't gotten him to leave again, the barber would have suffocated. There are lots of stories like that, and they laugh heartily at them all. Aunt Rosalia is only two years older than my mother, while Aunt Agnete is eight years older and wasn't really young with them. She and Uncle Peter often come to play cards with my parents. Aunt Agnete is pious and suffers from it whenever someone swears in her presence, which her husband does frequently just to annoy her. She is tall and wide and has a Dagmar cross resting on her bosom, which Uncle

46

Peter calls the balcony. If I were to believe my parents, he is evil and cunning incarnate, but he's always friendly to me, so I don't really believe them. He's a carpenter and never out of work. They live in a three-room apartment in Øster-bro and have an ice-cold parlor with a piano, and they only set foot in it on Christmas Eve. It's said that Uncle Peter inherited an enormous sum of money that he keeps in various bank accounts in order to fool the tax authorities. Sometimes the employees at the shop where he works are invited to visit other companies, where they are hosted free-of-charge. When he went with them to Tuborg, he drank so much that he had to be taken to the hospital and have his stomach pumped out the following day. And when he visited the Enighed Dairy, he downed so much milk he was sick for the next week. Otherwise he never drinks anything but water. My three cousins are all older than me and rather ugly. Every evening they sit around the dinner table, knitting furiously. "But they're not too bright," says my father, and there's not so much as a single book in that whole big apartment. My parents make no bones about saying we've turned out better than those girls. Uncle Peter was married once before, and from that marriage he has a daughter who's only seven or eight years younger than my mother. Her name is Ester, and she's a great hulk with a wriggling, bent-over walk. Her eyes look like they're about to pop out of her head, and whenever she visits us she talks baby-talk to me and kisses me right on the mouth, which I despise more than anything else. "Sweetie pie" she calls my mother, whom she goes out with in the evening, much to my father's dismay. One time they're going to a masquerade at Folkets Hus and I hold the mirror while they put on their make-up, and I think my mother is fantastically beautiful as "The Night Queen." Ester is a "coachman from the eighteenth century," and her arms stick out of the puff sleeves like heavy clubs. They have to hurry because my father will be arriving soon. My mother stands there in all of the black tulle, which is covered with hundreds of shiny sequins. They fall off as easily as her own frail happiness. Just as they're going out the door, my father comes home from work. He stares my mother in the face and says, "Ha, you old scarecrow." She doesn't answer, just slips past him without a word, on Ester's heels. My father knows that I heard him, and he sits down across from me with an uncertain expression in his kind, melancholy eyes. "What do you want to be when you grow up?" he asks awkwardly. "The Night Queen," I say cruelly, because here is that "Ditlev" who always has to spoil my mother's fun.

10

I'VE STARTED MIDDLE SCHOOL AND WITH THAT THE WORLD
has begun to widen. I was allowed to continue because my
parents have figured out I still won't be much more than
fourteen when I finish school, and since they're giving
Edvin training, I shouldn't be left out. At the same time,
I've finally gotten permission to use the public library on
Valdemarsgade, which has a section with children's books.
My mother thinks that I'll get even stranger from reading
books that are written for adults; and my father, who
doesn't agree, doesn't say anything since I come under my
mother's authority and in crucial matters he doesn't dare go
against world order. So for the first time I set foot in a
library, and I'm speechless with confusion at seeing so many
books collected in one place. The children's librarian is
named Helga Mollerup, and she's known and loved by
many children in the neighborhood because whenever
there's no heat or light at home, they're allowed to sit in the
reading room right up until the library closes at five o'clock
in the evening. They do their homework there or leaf
through books, and Miss Mollerup throws them out only if
they start getting noisy, because it's supposed to be completely quiet, like in a church. She asks me how old I am
and finds books she thinks are right for a ten-year-old. She
is tall and slim and pretty, with dark, lively eyes. Her hands
are big and beautiful and I regard them with a certain
respect, because it's said that she can slap harder than any
man. She's dressed like my teacher, Miss Klausen, in a

rather long, smooth skirt and a blouse with a low white collar at the neck. But, unlike Miss Klausen, she doesn't seem to suffer from an insurmountable aversion to children — on the contrary. I'm placed at a table with a children's book in front of me, the title and author of which I've fortunately forgotten. I read, " 'Father, Diana has had puppies.' With these words, a slender young girl fifteen years old came storming into the room, where, in addition to the councilman, there were..." etc. Page after page. I don't have it in me to read it. It fills me with sadness and unbearable boredom. I can't understand how language — that delicate and sensitive instrument — can be so terribly mistreated, or how such monstrous sentences can find their way into a book that gets into the library where a clever and attractive woman like Miss Mollerup actually recommends it to defenseless children to read. For now, however, I can't express these thoughts, so I have to be content with saying that the books are boring and that I would rather have something by Zacharias Nielsen or Vilhelm Bergsøe. But Miss Mollerup says that children's books are exciting if you just have patience enough to keep reading until the plot gets going. Only when I stubbornly insist on having access to the shelves with the adult books does she give in, astonished, and offer to get some books for me if I'll tell her which ones, since I can't go in there myself. "One by Victor Hugo," I say. "It's pronounced Ügó," she says, smiling, and pats me on the head. It doesn't embarrass me that she corrects my pronunciation, but when I come home with *Les Misérables* and my father says approvingly, "Victor Hugo — yes, he's good!" I say didactically and self-importantly, "It's pronounced Ügó." "I don't give a damn how it's pronounced," he says calmly. "All those kinds of names should be said the way they're spelled. Anything else is just showing off." It's

50

never any use to come home and tell my parents anything people said who don't live on our street. Once when the school dentist requested that I ask my mother to buy me a toothbrush and I was dumb enough to mention it at home, my mother snapped, "You can tell her that she can darn well buy you a toothbrush herself!" But whenever she has a toothache, she first goes around suffering for about a week, while the whole house echoes with her miserable moaning. Then, out on the landing, she asks the advice of another woman, who recommends that she pour schnapps on a wad of cotton and hold it against the infected tooth, which she spends several more days doing, with no results. Only then does she get all dressed up in her finest and venture out to Vesterbrogade, where our doctor lives. He takes his pincers and pulls out the tooth and then she has peace for a while. A dentist never comes into the picture.

In the middle school the girls are better dressed and less sniveling than in the primary school. None of them has lice or a harelip, either. My father says that now I'll be going to school with children of people who are "better off," but that that's no reason for me to look down on my own home. That's true enough. The children's fathers are mostly skilled workers, and I make my father into a "machinist," which I think sounds better than stoker. The richest girl in the class has a father who owns a barbershop on Gasværksvej. Her name is Edith Schnoor and she lisps from sheer self-importance. Our classroom teacher is named Miss Mathiassen, a small, lively woman who seems to enjoy teaching. Together with Miss Klausen, Miss Mollerup, and the principal at the old school (the one who resembled a witch), she gives me the distinct impression that women can only have influence in the working world if they're completely flat-chested. My mother is an exception; otherwise

51

all the housewives at home on my street have enormous busts that they consciously thrust out as they walk. I wonder why that is. Miss Mathiassen is the only female teacher we have. She's discovered that I like poetry, and it doesn't work to play dumb with her. I save that for the subjects that don't interest me — but there are lots of those. I only like Danish and English. Our English teacher is named Damsgaard, and he can be terribly short-tempered. Then he pounds the table and says, "Upon my word, I'll teach you!" He uses this mild oath so often that before long he's known exclusively as "Upon my word." One time he reads aloud a sentence that's supposed to be especially difficult, and he asks me to repeat it. It goes like this: "In reply to your inquiry I can particularly recommend you the boarding house at eleven Woburn Place. Some of my friends stayed there last winter and spoke highly about it." He praises my correct pronunciation, and that's the reason I can never forget that idiotic sentence.

All the girls in my class have poetry albums, and after I've nagged my mother long enough, I get one too. It's brown and it says "Poetry" on the outside in gold letters. I let some of the girls write the usual verses in it, and in between I put in some of my own poems with the date and my name underneath so that posterity will have no doubt that I was a child genius. I hide it in one of the dresser drawers in the bedroom under a stack of towels and dishcloths, where I think it will be relatively safe from profane eyes. But one evening Edvin and I are home alone because my parents are out playing cards with my aunt and uncle. Otherwise Edvin is usually out in the evening, but he's been too tired for that since he started his apprenticeship. It's a bad workplace, he says, and he often begs my father to let him find a different one. When that does no good, he starts shouting and says that he'll run off to sea and leave home and much more. Then my father shouts, too, and then when my mother interferes in the fight and takes Edvin's side, there's an uproar in the living room that almost drowns out the racket downstairs at Rapunzel's. It's Edvin's fault that nearly every evening now all peace in the living room is destroyed, and sometimes I wish that he'd follow through with his threats and leave. Now he sits sulking and withdrawn, leafing through *Social-Demokraten*, while only the ticking clock on the wall breaks the silence. I'm doing my homework, but the silence between us oppresses me. He stares at me with his dark, thoughtful eyes that are suddenly just as melancholy as my father's. Then he says, "Aren't you going to bed soon, damn it? You can never be alone in this damn house!" "You can go into the bedroom, you know," I answer, hurt. "I bloody well will, too," he mumbles, grabbing the newspaper and going out. He slams the door hard after him. A little while later, to my surprise and uneasiness, I hear a burst of laughter from in there. What can be so funny? I go inside and stiffen with horror. Edvin is sitting on my mother's bed with my poor album in his hand. He's completely doubled up with laughter. Bright red in the face with shame, I take a step toward him and put out my hand. "Give me that book," I say and stamp my foot. "You have no right to take it!" "Oh God," he gasps and doubles up with laughter, "this is hilarious. You're really full of lies. Listen to this!" Then, interrupted by fits of laughter, he reads:

> Do you remember that time we sailed
> along the still, clear stream?
> The moon was mirrored in the sea.
> Everything was like a lovely dream.

Suddenly you lay the oar to rest,
and let the boat go still.
You said nothing, but my dear —
the passion in your gaze did thrill.

You took me in your arms so strong.
Lovingly you kissed me.
Never, never will I forget
that hour spent with thee.

"Oh no! Ha ha ha!" He falls back and keeps on laughing,
and the tears stream from my eyes. "I hate you," I yell,
stamping my foot powerlessly. "I hate you, I hate you! I
wish you'd drown in a marl pit!" With those last words, I'm
just about to rush out the door, when Edvin's insane laughter takes on a new, disturbing sound. I turn around in the
doorway and look at him lying on his stomach across my
mother's striped comforter with his face hidden in the crook
of one arm. My precious book has fallen to the floor. He
sobs inconsolably and uncontrollably, and I am horrified.
Hesitantly, I approach the bed, but I don't dare touch him.
That's something we've never done. I dry my own tears
with the sleeve of my dress and say, "I didn't mean it,
Edvin, the part about the marl pit. I . . . I don't even know
what it is." He keeps sobbing without answering and suddenly turns over and gives me a hopeless look. "I hate them,
the boss and the assistants," he says. "They . . . beat me . . .
all day and I'll never learn to paint cars. I'm just sent out to
get beer for all of them. I hate Father because I can't change
workplaces. And when you come home, you can never be
alone. There's not one damn corner where you can have
anything for yourself." I look down at my poetry album and
say, "I can't have anything for myself, either, you know —

and neither can Father or Mother. They're not even alone when they... when they...." He looks at me, surprised, and finally stops crying. "No," he says sadly. "Jesus, I've never thought about that." He gets up, regretting, of course, that his sister has seen him in a moment of weakness. "Well," he says in a tough voice, "it probably all gets better when you move away from home." I agree with him about that. Then I go out and count the eggs in the pantry. I take two and move the rest around so it looks like there are more of them. "I'm going to mix us an egg schnapps," I yell toward the living room and start the preparations. At that moment, I like Edvin much better than in all the years when he was distant and wonderful, handsome and cheerful. It wasn't really human that he never seemed to feel bad about anything.

II

GERDA IS GOING TO HAVE A BABY AND TIN SNOUT HAS
vanished. Ruth says he had a wife and children, and that I
should never have anything to do with a married man.
I can't imagine I'll ever have anything to do with an unmar-
ried man either, but I keep that to myself. My mother says
I'll be thrown out if I ever come home with a child. Gerda
isn't thrown out. She has just stopped working at the factory where she earned twenty-five kroner a week, and she
stays home now with her big stomach, singing and humming all day long, so you can hear from far away that she
hasn't lost her good spirits by any means. Her golden braid
has long since been cut off, and in my heart I don't call her
Rapunzel anymore, although, as a matter of fact, the fairy-
tale girl had had twins by the time the blinded prince found
her in the desert. It sounds so nice and remote that you can
easily miss it, and when I was little, I never thought about
how it might happen. Last year the landlady's Olga had a
baby by a soldier, who also disappeared without a trace, but
she was over eighteen and she later got married to a policeman who didn't worry about who the child's father was.
Whenever I see women with a big stomach, I try my best to
stare only at their faces, where I vainly search for a sign of
transcendent happiness like in Johannes V. Jensen's poem:
"I carry in my swollen breast a sweet and anxious spring."
They don't have the kind of glorious expression in their eyes
I myself will have when I'm someday expecting a child, I'm
sure of that. I have to find poems in books of prose because

my father doesn't approve of me lugging home poetry collections from the library. "Castles in the air," he says contemptuously, "they have nothing to do with reality." I've never cared for reality and I never write about it. When I'm reading Herman Bang's *Ved vejen*, my father takes the book between two fingers and says with every sign of disgust, "You may not read anything by *him*. He wasn't normal!" I know it's terrible not to be normal, and I have my own troubles trying to pretend that I am. So it comforts me that Herman Bang wasn't either, and I finish reading the book in the reading room. I cry when I get to the end: "Under the grave's turf sleeps poor Marianne. Come, girls, weep for poor Marianne." I want to write poetry like that, that anyone and everyone can understand. My father doesn't want me to read anything by Agnes Henningsen, either, because she's a "public female" — which he doesn't bother to explain any further. If he saw the book with my poems, he would probably burn it. After Edvin found it and laughed at it, I always keep it with me — in my school bag during the day, and otherwise in my underpants, where the elastic keeps it from falling out. At night it's under my mattress. Edvin said later, by the way, that he actually thought the poems were good, if only they had been written by someone other than me. "When you know the whole thing is a lie," he says, "you just die laughing over it." I'm pleased by his praise, because the part about it being a lie doesn't bother me. I know that you sometimes have to lie in order to bring out the truth.

We've gotten new neighbors since Ketty and her mother were thrown out. It's an older couple with a daughter named Jytte. She works in a chocolate store, and in the evening she often visits us when my father is working the graveyard shift. Then she and my mother have lots of fun because my mother gets along best with women who are younger than she is. Jytte gladly brings chocolate to Edvin and me, and we eat it happily, even though my father says that it's probably stolen. As a result of Jytte's generosity, something awful happens to me. One day when I come home from school, my mother says, "Well, wasn't that a good lunch you had with you today?" I blush and stammer and don't know what she's talking about. I always throw my lunch away untouched because it's wrapped in newspaper. The others have wax paper around theirs, which my mother would never in her life give in to. "Oh yes," I say miserably, "it was great." "I wonder whether she really steals it," says my mother talkatively. "You'd think the owner would keep an eye out for that." Relieved, I understand then that there was some chocolate in my lunch packet, and I feel very happy, because that's a sign of love. It's so strange that my mother has never discovered when I'm lying. On the other hand, she almost never believes the truth. I think that much of my childhood is spent trying to figure out her personality, and yet she continues to be just as mysterious and disturbing. Practically the worst thing is that she can hold a grudge for days, consistently refusing to speak to you or listen to what you're saying, and you never find out how you've offended her. She's the same way with my father. Once, when she made fun of Edvin for playing with girls, my father said, "Oh well, girls are a kind of human being, too." "Humph . . ." said my mother, pressed her lips tight, and didn't open them again until at least a week had passed. Actually I was on her side, because of course girls and boys shouldn't play together. They can't at school, either, unless they're sister and brother. But a boy wouldn't dare be seen with his little sister either, and whenever it's absolutely necessary for Edvin and me to go down the street together, I have to walk three paces behind him and under no circumstances reveal that I know him. I'm nothing to brag about. My mother doesn't think so either, because when I'm going to the commemoration of Folkets Hus, she makes a serious effort to get me to look half-way decent. She singes my stiff, yellow hair with the curling iron, and tells me briskly to curl up my toes so that they'll fit into a pair of shoes we borrowed from Jytte. "She's pretty enough, damn it," consoles my father, who is having trouble himself with the collar on his white shirt that was bought for the occasion. Edvin is now so grown up that he's mad at having to go out with his family, so he omits his usual lovable remarks about how I'm so ugly that I'll never get married. It's a very special evening, because after making a speech to the workers, Stauning will personally present a gift to all of Vesterbro's recruiters, and among them is my father. Sunday after Sunday he trudges up and down stairs in our neighborhood to enlist members in the political club, and my mother brings him to despair by withdrawing him from it once a month whenever the membership fee of fifty øre is due. Then he mumbles a bunch of curses, grabs his old hat, and rushes after the man to sign up again. She harbors an inarticulate hatred for Stauning and the party, and now and then she hints that my father was once something almost as criminal as a Communist. She doesn't say the word out loud — she doesn't dare — but sometimes I think about the forbidden book he was always reading during my early childhood, the one with the red flag that the happy worker family is looking up at, so there's probably some truth to her insinuations.

My heart beats faster when Stauning goes up to the podium, and I'm sure that my father's does, too. Stauning speaks the way he usually does, and I understand at most half of it. But I enjoy his calm, dark voice that soothingly settles over my soul, assuring me that nothing really evil can happen to us, as long as Stauning exists. He talks about instituting the eight-hour day, even though that's a long time ago now. He talks about the unions and about the criminal scabs who should never be tolerated at any workplace. I quickly promise myself, Stauning, and our Lord that I will never be a scab. Only when he talks about the Communists, who damage and divide the party, does he raise his voice to an angry thunder, which quickly gives way, however, to a soft, almost gentle explanation of the unemployment, which my mother isn't alone in blaming him for. But no, it's due solely to the worldwide depression, he says, and I find the expression pleasant sounding and appealing. I imagine a deeply grieving world where everyone has pulled down their shades and turned off the lights, while the rain streams down from a gray and inconsolable heaven without a single star. "And now," says Stauning finally, "I have the great pleasure of presenting a prize to each of our industrious recruiters as a reward for their work for our great cause!" I blush with pride that my father is among them and look sideways at where he's sitting. He twists his mustache nervously and smiles at me, as if he knows that I share his joy. The battle over the workplace is still creating a coldness between him and Edvin, who looks as though he's about to fall asleep. Then Stauning says each name loudly and clearly, grasps each man's hand in turn, and gives each a book. Everything swims before my eyes when it's my father's turn. The book he receives is called *Vers og værktøj*,* and Stauning has written his name and some words of acknowledgement on the title page. On the

---

* *Poetry and Tools*—Trans.

way home, my father, who is still elated over the honor, says: "I'll let you read it when you're grown up. I know you like poetry." My mother and Edvin aren't with us. They're going to the dance afterwards, which doesn't interest my serious father, and I'm only a child. Later my mother puts the book so far back on the bookshelf that you can't see it when the glass door is closed. "A lovely reward for wearing out the steps every blessed Sunday," she says scornfully to my father. "And then he talks about scabs and being underpaid. Good Lord!" My father isn't allowed to have his happiness in peace, either.

12

TIME PASSED AND MY CHILDHOOD GREW THIN AND FLAT, paperlike. It was tired and theadbare, and in low moments it didn't look like it would last until I was grown up. Other people could see it too. Every time Aunt Agnete visited us, she said, "Goodness gracious, how you're growing!" "Yes," said my mother and looked at me pityingly, "if only she'd fill out a bit." She was right. I was as flat as a paper doll and clothes hung from my shoulders like from a hanger. My childhood was supposed to last until I was fourteen, but what was I going to do if it gave out beforehand? You never got answers to any of the important questions. Full of envy, I stared at Ruth's childhood, which was firm and smooth and without a single crack. It looked as if it would outlive her, so that someone else might inherit it and wear it out. Ruth herself wasn't aware of it. When the boys on the street yelled at me, "How's the weather up there, sister?" she sent a series of oaths and curses after them so that they ran off in terror. She knew I was vulnerable and shy and she always defended me. But Ruth wasn't enough for me anymore. Miss Møllerup wasn't either, because she had so many children to look after, and I was only one of them. I always dreamed of finding a person, just one, to whom I could show my poems and who would praise them. I had started thinking a lot about death, and I thought of it as a friend. I told myself that I wanted to die, and once when my mother went into town, I took our bread knife and sawed at my wrist, hoping to find the artery — all the while bawling at the thought of my despairing mother who would soon throw herself sobbing over my corpse. All that happened was that I got some cuts; I still have faint marks from them. My only consolation in this uncertain, trembling world was writing poetry like this:

> Once I was young and all aglow,
> full of laughter and fun.
> I was like a blushing rose.
> Now I am old and forgotten.

I was twelve years old then. Otherwise all of my poems were still "full of lies," as Edvin said. Most of them dealt with love, and if you were to believe them, I was living a wanton life filled with interesting conquests.

I was convinced that I would be sent to a reformatory if my parents ever saw a poem like this:

> It was joy I felt, my friend,
> when our lips met,
> knowing this was the moment
> we were born for — and yet . . .

> My vague young dream vanished.
> The door to life stands open.
> Life is beautiful, my friend, thanks,
> you christened me in passion.

I wrote love poems to the man in the moon, to Ruth, or to no one at all. I thought my poems covered the bare places in my childhood like the fine, new skin under a scab that hasn't yet fallen off completely. Would my adult form be shaped by my poems? I wondered. During that time I was almost always depressed. The wind in the street blew so cold through my tall, thin body that the world regarded with disapproving looks. In school I always sat and glared at the teachers, as I did at all grownups, finished people, and one day a substitute music teacher calmly came over to my seat, and said quietly but clearly, "I don't like your face." I went home and stared at it in the mirror over the dresser. It was pale, with round cheeks and frightened eyes. Across my top front teeth there were small dents in the enamel, which came from having had rickets as a child. I knew that from the school dentist, who said you got the disease from bad nutrition. I kept that to myself, of course, because it wasn't anything to talk about at home. When I couldn't explain my growing melancholy to myself, I thought that the worldwide depression had finally hit me. I also thought a lot about my early childhood, which would never return, and it seemed to me that everything was better then. In the evening, I sat up on the windowsill and wrote in my poetry album:

> Slender strings that break
> are ne'er tied together again,
> unless their tone does slake,
> unless a note does die then.

Then, unlike later on, there wasn't any Kai Friis Møller to whisper in my ear, "Watch out for inverted word order, Miss Ditlevsen, and for the word ne'er!" My literary models at that time were hymns, ballads, and the poets of the 90s.

One morning I woke up and felt really terrible. My throat hurt and I was freezing as I stepped out onto the floor. I asked my mother whether I could stay home from school, but she frowned and told me to spare her such nonsense.

She couldn't stand unexpected events or visits that weren't announced ahead of time. Burning with fever, I went to school and was sent home already during first period. By then my mother had collected herself and accepted that I was sick. I fell asleep as soon as I got into bed again and when I woke up, my mother was in the midst of a massive housecleaning of the whole apartment. She was hanging up clean curtains in the bedroom, and turned around when I called. "It's good you woke up," she said. "The doctor will be here in a little while; if only I get done." I was terribly afraid of the welfare doctor, and my mother was, too. When she had changed the bed linens and dug out my ears with a bobbypin, the doorbell rang and, flustered, she rushed out and opened the door. "Hello," she said respectfully, "I apologize for the inconvenience...." She didn't get any further before she was interrupted by his violent fit of coughing. Hacking and sputtering into his handkerchief, the doctor swept her aside with his cane. "Yes, yes," he bellowed when he caught his breath. "All those stairs — they'll be the death of me. And there's no room to breathe. It's no way to run a practice. I remember you well — you're the one with the teeth. But who in heaven's name is sick? Oh, it's your daughter — where the hell is she?" "In here." My mother led the way and the doctor pulled in his stomach with great difficulty as he went past the marriage bed over to me. "Well," he shouted and bent his face over me, "what's the matter with you? You're not playing hooky, are you?" He looked loathsome, and I pulled the comforter all the way up to my chin. He fixed his bulging black eyes on me and I felt like saying that even though we were poor, we were not in the least deaf. His hands were densely covered with hair and a thick black tuft stuck out of each ear. He roared for a spoon, and my mother just about fell over her own feet as she ran off to the kitchen to get one. He shone a little light down my throat and felt the sides of my neck and then said ominously, "Is there diphtheria in your school? Well? Any of your classmates?" I nodded. Then he grimaced as if he tasted something sour and shouted, "She's got diphtheria! She has to go to the hospital at once! God damn it!" My mother stared at me reproachfully, as if she'd never expected me to present a busy doctor with anything so impudent. The doctor grabbed his cane furiously and stomped into the living room to write up an admission form. I was horrified. The hospital! My poems! Where should I hide them now? Sleep overpowered me again, and when I woke up, my mother was sitting on the edge of the bed. She asked very gently if there was anything I wanted, and to please her, I asked for a piece of chocolate even though I knew that I couldn't swallow it. Thanks to Jytte, we always had chocolate in the house now. While we waited for the ambulance, I explained to her that I wanted to take my poetry album with me in case someone at the hospital would like to write in it. She had no objection. She sat next to me in the ambulance and stroked my forehead or my hands the whole time. I couldn't remember when she'd ever done that before, and it made me both embarrassed and glad. Whenever I walked down the street or stood in shops, I always looked with a mixture of joy and envy at mothers who held their small children in their arms or caressed them. Maybe my mother had done that once, but I couldn't remember it. At the hospital, I was put in a big ward where there were children of all ages. We all had diphtheria, and most of them were just as sick as I was. I put my poetry album in a drawer, and no one thought it strange that I had it there. Although I lay there for three months, I remember almost nothing about my stay. During visiting hours, my mother stood outside the window and shouted in to me. Shortly before I went home, she talked to the head doctor, who said that I was anemic and didn't weigh enough. Both things hurt my mother's feelings. During the first days after I came home, she made me rye porridge and other fattening foods, even though my father was unemployed again. During my long absence, Ruth had attached herself to the landlady's fat, white-haired Minna, who would soon be thirteen, and with whom she was now always hanging around the trash-can corner, even though she wasn't nearly old enough for that kind of promotion. I felt abandoned and alone. Only the night and the rain and my silent evening star — and my poetry album — gave me some slight comfort during that time. I wrote poetry exclusively like this:

> Wistful raven-black night,
> kindly you wrap me in darkness,
> so calm and mild, my soul you bless,
> making me drowsy and light.
>
> The rain quiet and fine
> drums so softly at the window.
> I lay my head on the pillow
> on the cool linen's incline.
>
> Quietly I sleep,
> blessed night, my best friend.
> Tomorrow I'll wake to life again
> my soul in sorrow deep.

One day my brother said to me that I should try to sell one of my poems to a magazine, but I didn't think anyone would pay money for them. I didn't really care, either, as long as someone would print them, but I would never come face to face with that "someone." Someday when I was grown up, my poems would of course be in a real book, but I didn't know how that would come about. My father probably knew, but he had said that a girl can't be a poet, so I wouldn't tell him anything about it. It was enough for me anyway to write the poems; there was no hurry to show them to a world that so far had only laughed and scorned them.

13

UNCLE PETER HAS KILLED GRANNY. AT LEAST THAT'S WHAT my parents and Aunt Rosalia say. He and Aunt Agnete picked her up on Christmas Eve and there was a violent snowstorm. All three of them waited at least fifteen minutes for the streetcar, and in spite of his fabulous wealth, it didn't occur to Uncle Peter to pay for a taxi home. By evening Granny had pneumonia, and they put her to bed on a sofa made up in the parlor, which of course is heated every Christmas, "But you know," says my mother, "how damp it is in a room that's only heated three days a year." There Granny lay all through the Christmas holidays and received visits from all of us, and she was completely convinced that she was going to die. The rest of us didn't believe it. She lay in a white, high-necked nightgown, and her slender hands that looked like my mother's constantly crept restlessly over the comforter, as if searching in vain for something very important. Now that she didn't have her glasses on, you saw that her nose was long and sharp, her eyes deep blue and very clear, and her sunken mouth had a stern, inflexible expression whenever she wasn't smiling. She talked nonstop about her funeral and the five hundred kroner that she lost when Landmands Bank scandalously folded. My mother and my aunts laughed heartily and said, "You'll have a fine funeral, Mama, when it comes time for that." I think I was the only one who took her seriously. She was seventy-six years old, after all, so it couldn't be much longer, I thought. We agreed on the hymns to be sung: "Churchbell, not for the big cities but for the little town were you cast," and "If you've put your hand to the Lord's plough, then don't look back." The latter was not, of course, a funeral hymn, but Granny and I were both so fond of it, and we sang it together so often whenever I visited her. On my part, there was also a little spite involved in the choice. My father hated that hymn more than any other because the line "If sobs strangle the voice, then think of the golden harvest" was proof, in his opinion, of the church's animosity toward the working class.

I wanted so much to write a hymn for Granny myself, but I couldn't. I'd tried so many times, but they always sounded like one of the old hymns, so sadly I had to give up. On the second day after Christmas, something terrible happened. The three sisters were sitting by Granny's bed and Uncle Peter was in the room, when suddenly the doorbell rang and one of my cousins opened the door to The Hollow Leg who, in an awful state, pushed his way in to the sickbed. Aunt Rosalia threw her hands over her face and burst into tears. The Hollow Leg swung at her and shouted that she damn well better come home now, or he'd break every bone in her body. Uncle Peter stepped forward and grabbed hold of the drunken man, and we children were shooed out of the room. There was a terrible uproar, women's screams, and, in the midst of it all, Granny's calm and authoritative voice, trying to appeal to any possible remaining decent side of his character. Then suddenly there was silence and we later learned that Uncle Peter had thrown him out bodily. He had never been allowed into their house before. It was the same thing at home on our street. Either the men drank — and most of them did — or else they harbored a violent hatred toward those who did. When Granny grew worse and the doctor said that she most likely wouldn't make it through the crisis, I wasn't allowed to visit her anymore. My mother was over there day and night, and came home with red eyes and discouraging news. When Granny died, I wasn't permitted to see her, either, but Edvin was. He said she looked just like when she was alive. But I did go to the funeral. I sat in Sundby Church next to my mother and Aunt Rosalia, and already during the sermon, I was gripped by an attack of hysterical laughter. It was so terrible that I held my handkerchief over my nose and mouth, hoping they would think I was crying like the others. Fortunately, tears ran down my cheeks too. I was horrified that I couldn't feel anything at her death. I had really loved Granny, and the hymns that we'd chosen together were sung. Why then couldn't I grieve? Long after the funeral, my comforter was replaced by Granny's — my mother's only inheritance. In the evening when I pulled it up over me, Granny's special smell of clean linen flooded over me, and then I cried for the first time and understood what had happened. Oh, Granny, you'll never hear me sing again. You'll never spread real butter on my bread again, and what you've forgotten to tell me about your life will now never be revealed. Every evening, for a long time, I cried myself to sleep, for the smell continued to cling to the comforter.

14

"God help you if you don't deliver that wringer in a hurry," says my mother, tossing the heavy machine over to me; I have to jump so it won't land on my toes. She's standing in the laundry room, bending over a steaming tub, and I know that she's half-insane on that one day of the month. But I'm in a terrible situation. She's given me ten øre to pay for renting the machine, and it costs fifteen øre an hour. It went up five øre last time, and then I had to promise to pay the remaining five øre next time. So they were supposed to get twenty øre today, and I had only ten. "Mother," I say timidly, "I can't help it if it's gone up." She raises her head and pushes the damp hair from her face. "Get going," she says threateningly, and I go out of the steaming room and up to the courtyard, where I look up at the gray sky, as if expecting help from it. It's late in the afternoon, and near the trash cans the usual gang is standing with their heads together. I wish I were one of them. I wish I were like Ruth, who is so little that she disappears in the middle of the crowd. "Hi, Tove," she yells happily, because she has no sense of having abandoned me. "Hi," I say and suddenly feel hope. I go over and signal Ruth to come over to me. Then I explain my errand to her and she says, "I'll go along — I'll get it delivered all right. Give me the ten øre — it's better than nothing." Everything is straightforward for Ruth, who never wonders at the grownups' behavior. I don't much, either, when it concerns my mother, whose unpredictable personality I've accepted. Over on Sundevedsgade,

I wait on the corner, ready to flee, while Ruth barges into the shop, throws the machine on the counter with the ten øre, and races over to me. We run all the way to Amerikavej and stand there, out of breath, laughing like in the old days when we'd pulled off something daring. "The bitch yelled after me," gasps Ruth. " 'It costs fifteen øre,' she shouted, but she couldn't get past the machine fast enough with that fat stomach. Oh God, that was fun." The clear tears leave streaks on the pretty little face, and I feel happy and grateful. As we go home, Ruth asks me why I don't want to join in at the trash-can corner. "They're such fun, the big girls," she says. "They have such a great time." If Ruth is old enough to be there, then I certainly am, too. When we reach the courtyard at home again, only Minna and Grete are in the trash-can corner. What Ruth sees in Minna, I don't know. Grete lives in the front building, and she's the daughter of a divorced mother who is a seamstress like my aunt. She's in the seventh grade, and I don't know her very well at all. She has on a knitted blouse that reveals two tiny little bulges in the front, what I'm so sadly lacking. When she laughs you can see that her mouth is crooked. It's almost dark in the corner, and it stinks terribly from the garbage cans. The two big girls are sitting on top of them, and Minna hospitably makes room for Ruth beside her. So I stand there, bolt upright like a milepost, and can't think of anything to say. This is a promotion that I've looked forward to for years, but now I don't know if there's much to it. "Gerda is going to have her baby soon," says Grete, banging her heels against the trash can. "It'll be retarded like Pretty Ludvig," says Minna hopefully. "That's what happens to children who are conceived during a drunken binge." "The hell it does," says Ruth. "Most of us would be retarded then." They always talk like that, and they have

73

something nasty and dirty to say about everyone. I wonder whether they talk about us the same way when my back is turned. Giggling, they talk about drinking and sex and secret, unmentionable liaisons. Grete and Minna won't keep their virginity more than an hour after they're confirmed, they say, and they'll be careful not to have kids before they turn eighteen. I've heard it all before from Ruth, and the conversation in the trash-can corner seems to me deadly dull and boring. It oppresses me and makes me long to be away from the courtyard and the street and the tall buildings. I don't know whether there are other streets, other court-yards, other buildings and people. As yet I've only been out to Vesterbrogade whenever I had to buy three pounds of ordinary potatoes at the grocer's, who always gave me a piece of candy, and who later turned out to be "The Drilling X." In the daytime, he quietly minded his little store, and at night he fooled the police by breaking into the city's post offices. It took years to catch him. I'm far away in my thoughts when Ruth suddenly says, "Tove has a boyfriend!" The two big girls crack up with laughter. "That's a damn lie," says Minna, "she's too holy for that!" "I'll be damned if it's a lie," maintains Ruth, giving me a big smile, completely without malice. "I know who it is, too. It's Curly Charles!" "Oh, ha ha!" They double over with laughter, and I laugh the loudest. I do it because Ruth just wanted to amuse us, but I don't think there's anything funny about it. Gerda goes across the courtyard, sway-backed and weighted down, and the laughter ceases. In her hand she has a net bag with beer bottles that clink against each other. Her short hair has gotten darker than before and she has brown spots on her face. I quickly wish that she'll have a beautiful little baby with a normal mind. A girl, I wish for her, with golden hair in a long thick braid down her back. Maybe Gerda was in love with Tin Snout, for no one can see into a woman's heart. Maybe she cries herself to sleep every night, no matter how much she sings and laughs during the day. Once she stood in the trash-can corner and shouted about what would happen when she turned fourteen. I don't want to follow tradition in that way. I don't want to do it before I meet a man that I love; but no man or boy has looked in my direction yet. I don't want to have a "stable skilled worker who comes right home with his weekly paycheck and doesn't drink." I'd rather be an old maid, which I guess my parents have also gradually resigned themselves to. My father is always talking about "a steady job with a pension" when I've finished school, but that seems to me just as horrible as the skilled worker. Whenever I think about the future, I run up against a wall everywhere, and that's why I want to prolong my childhood so badly. I can't see any way out of it, and when my mother calls me from up in the window, I leave the precious trash-can corner with relief and go upstairs. "Well," she says, very kindly, "did you get the wringer delivered?" "Yes," I say, and she smiles at me as if I've successfully completed a difficult task she had given me.

15

Miss Mathiassen has told me to ask at home for permission to go to high school, in spite of the fact that at the exams I couldn't say how long the Thirty Years' War lasted. I'll never learn to understand those kinds of jokes. Miss Mathiassen says I'm intelligent and ought to continue studying. That's what I'd like to do, too, but I know that we can't afford it. Without much hope, I ask my father anyway and he gets strangely agitated and talks contemptuously about bluestockings and female graduates who are both ugly and stuck-up. Once he was going to help me write a composition about Florence Nightingale, but all that he could say about her was that she had big feet and bad breath—so I consulted Miss Mollerup instead. Otherwise my father has written a lot of my papers and gotten good grades from Miss Mathiassen. It didn't misfire until he wrote an essay on America and ended it like this: "America has been called the land of freedom. Earlier it meant freedom to be yourself, to work, and to own land. Now it practically means freedom to starve to death if you don't have money to buy food." "What in the world," said my classroom teacher, "do you mean by that nonsense?" I couldn't explain it, and we only got a "B" for the effort. No, I can't continue my studies, and I can only remain a child for a short time yet. I have to finish school and be confirmed and get a job somewhere in a house where there's a lot to be done. The future is a monstrous, powerful colossus that will soon fall on me and crush me. My tattered childhood flaps around me, and no sooner

have I patched one hole than another breaks through somewhere else. It makes me vulnerable and irritable. I talk back
to my mother and she says, gloating, "All right, all right,
just wait until you get out among strangers. . . ." Their great
sorrow is Edvin, who I've gotten so close to since he clashed
with our parents. I don't have any deep or painful feelings
about him, so he can confide in me whatever he likes without fear. But my father has always believed that he would be
something great, because he had so many talents as a child.
He could sing and play guitar and he was always the prince
in the school play. All the girls in school and in the courtyard had a crush on him, and since we went to the same
school, the teachers always said to me with amazement,
"Are you the one who has such a smart, handsome brother?"
It pleased my father, too, that he was a member of DUI
and put body and soul into the party. My father always said
that he didn't respect government ministers who had never
had a shovel in their hands, so who knows what future he
once envisioned for Edvin? Now all of these dreams are
crushed. Edvin is just waiting for the golden day when he
becomes a journeyman and can bully the poor apprentices
himself. He's also waiting to turn eighteen, because then
he's going to move away from home and rent a room where
he can have his things in peace. He wants to live somewhere
where he can have girls visit him, because on that point my
mother is completely intransigent. In her eyes, all young
girls are enemy agents who are only out to get married and
be supported by a skilled worker, whose training his parents
have scrimped and saved to pay for. "And now when he's
going to be earning money," she says bitterly to my father,
"and could pay some of it back, he runs away from home, of
course. It's some girl who's put that into his head." She says
things like that when they've come to bed and think I'm

asleep. I understand Edvin completely because this isn't a home you can stay in, and when I turn eighteen, I'm going to move out, too. But I also understand that my father is disappointed. Recently, when he and Edvin were fighting, Edvin said that Stauning drank and had mistresses. My father turned bright red in the face with anger and gave him a terrible slap, so that he tumbled over on to the floor. I'd never seen my father hit Edvin before, and he's never hit me, either. One evening when my parents were lying in bed discussing the problem, my father said that they should give Edvin permission to invite his girlfriend home. "He doesn't have one — no one steady," said my mother curtly. "Yes he does," said my father, "otherwise he wouldn't be out every evening. You're chasing him away from home yourself this way." As always, when my father on a rare occasion insisted on something, my mother had to give in, and Edvin was asked to invite Solvejg to coffee the next evening. I know a lot about Solvejg, but I've never met her. I know that she and my brother love each other, and that they're going to get married when he becomes a journeyman. I also know that he visits her home and that her parents like him very much. He met her at a dance at Folkets Hus. She lives on Enghavevej and is seventeen just like him. Her father repairs bicycles and has a workshop on Vesterbrogade. She herself is a trained beautician and earns a lot of money.

The evening arrived and we all watched anxiously over my mother's movements. I helped her place our only white tablecloth on the table, and Edvin tried in vain to catch her eye in order to smile at her. He had on his confirmation suit that was too short at the wrists and ankles. My father had on his Sunday best and was sitting on the edge of the sofa, fumbling nervously with the knot in his tie, as if he himself were the guest. I got the platter with the cream puffs and

78

placed it in the middle of the tablecloth. Then the doorbell rang and my brother almost fell over his own feet as he ran out to open the door. Bright laughter sounded from out in the hallway, and my mother pressed her lips tightly together and grabbed her knitting, which she started working on furiously. "Hello," she said shortly and gave her hand to Solvejg without looking up. "Please sit down." She could just as well have said, "Go to hell," but it didn't look like Solvejg was aware of the tense atmosphere. She sat down, smiling, and I thought she was very pretty. Her blond hair was in a wreath on her head, she had pink cheeks with deep dimples, and her dark blue eyes had an expression like they were always laughing. She didn't notice how silent we were, but she talked in a cheerful and self-confident manner, as if she were used to giving orders. She talked about her work, about her parents, about Edvin, and about how happy she was to visit him at home. My mother looked more and more unyielding, and knitted as if she were doing piecework. Finally Solvejg noticed it after all, because she said, "It's really so strange! Since Edvin and I are going to get married, you'll be my mother-in-law, you know." She laughed heartily over this, but completely alone, and suddenly my mother burst into tears. It was excruciatingly embarrassing, and none of us knew what to do. She cried as she continued to knit, and there was nothing moving or touching about her tears. "Alfrida!" said my father admonishingly; he never called her by her first name. I desperately grabbed the coffee pot. "Won't you have another cup?" I asked Solvejg, and poured her a full cup without waiting for an answer. I thought that maybe she might think this was something quite normal for us. "Thank you," she said and smiled at me. For a minute everyone was silent. My brother looked down at the tablecloth with a dark expression. Solvejg made

79

much of putting cream and sugar in her coffee. Tears slid like rain out of my mother's fiercely downcast eyes, and suddenly Edvin pushed back his chair so it crashed against the buffet. "Come on, Solvejg," he said, "we're going. I knew she'd ruin everything. Stop blubbering, Mother. I'm going to marry Solvejg whether you like it or not. Goodbye." With Solvejg in hand, he rushed out to the hall without giving her time to say good-bye. The door banged hard after them. Only then did my mother take off her glasses and dry her eyes. "There, you see," she said reproachfully to my father, "what comes from his insisting on being an apprentice. That girl will never let go of such a goldmine!" Wearily he lay down on the sofa again and loosened his tie and opened the top button of his shirt. "That's not it," he said without anger, "but you're driving your children away like this."

Edvin never brought any girlfriend home again, and later when he got married, we first saw his wife after the wedding. It wasn't Solvejg.

16

My childhood's last spring is cold and windy. It tastes of dust and smells of painful departures and change. In school everyone is involved with preparations for exams and confirmation, but I see no meaning in any of it. You don't need a middle school diploma to clean house or wash dishes for strangers, and confirmation is the tombstone over a childhood that now seems to me bright, secure, and happy. Everything during this time makes a deep, indelible impression on me, and it's as if I'll remember even completely trivial remarks my whole life. When I'm out buying confirmation shoes with my mother, she says, as the sales-clerk listens, "Yes, these will be the last shoes we give you." It opens a terrifying perspective on the future and I don't know how I'll go about supporting myself. The shoes are brocade and cost nine kroner. They have high heels and, partly because I can't walk in them without spraining my ankles, and partly because — in my mother's opinion — I'll be as tall as a skyscraper when I wear them, my father chops off a piece of the heels with an axe. That makes the toes turn up, but after all, I'll only wear them on that one day, my mother consoles me. On his eighteenth birthday, Edvin moved to a room on Bagerstræde, and now I sleep on a bed made up on the sofa in the living room, which I perceive as still another unhappy sign that my childhood is over. Here I can't sit in the windowsill because it's full of geraniums, and there's only a view of the square with the green gypsy wagon and the gas pump with the big round lamp, which once

81

made me exclaim, "Mother, the moon has fallen down." I don't remember it myself, and in general the grownups have completely different memories about you than you yourself have. I've known that for a long time. Edvin's memories are different than mine, too, and whenever I ask him whether he can remember some event or other I thought we experienced together, he always says no. My brother and I are fond of each other, but we can't talk to each other very well. When I visit him at his room, his landlady opens the door. She has a black mustache and seems to suffer from the same suspicions as my mother. "His sister," she says, "that's a good one. I've never known a lodger who has so many sisters and cousins as he has." Things are not good with Edvin even though he now has a whole room to himself. He smokes cigarettes and drinks beer and often goes out to dances in the evening with a friend named Thorvald. They were apprentices together and want to have their own workshop someday. I've never met Thorvald, because neither of us can bring anyone home, no matter what sex they are. Edvin is unhappy because Solvejg has left him. One day she came up to his room where they could finally be alone together, and said that she didn't want to marry him after all. Edvin blames my mother, but I think Solvejg has found someone else. I've read somewhere, you see, that real love only grows greater with opposition, but I keep quiet about that because it's probably better for Edvin to believe that my mother has scared her away. His room is very small and the furniture looks like it's ready for the dump. I never stay very long at Edvin's because there are long pauses between our words, and he looks just as relieved when I leave as he looks happy when I arrive. I talk about little things from home. For example, I wear a pair of oiled leather boots that, as usual, I've inherited from him. My father varnished the soles of them so that they'll last longer and he also gave the toes a couple of swipes, so that they turned up and are completely black while the rest of the boots are brown. One day my mother threw some rags over to me, "Rub your boots with them and then throw them into the stove," she said. "My boots?" I asked happily, and she laughed long and hard at me. "No, you goof, the rags!" she said. Things like that make Edvin laugh too, and that's why I tell him about it now, when he's no longer part of our daily life. Nothing is like it was before. Only Istedgade is the same, and now I'm allowed to go there in the evening, too. I go there with Ruth and Minna, and Ruth doesn't seem to notice that there is something like hatred between Minna and me. Sometimes we go over to Saxogade to visit Olga, Minna's big sister who married a policeman and has it made. Olga minds the baby and I'm allowed to hold it in my arms. It feels unbelievably nice. Minna wants to marry a man in uniform too, "because they're so handsome," she says. Then they'll live near Hedebysgade, because that's what everyone does when they get married. Ruth nods approvingly and prepares herself for the same fate, which seems desirable to both of them. I smile in agreement as if I'm also looking forward to such a future, and as usual, I'm afraid of being found out. I feel like I'm a foreigner in this world and I can't talk to anyone about the overwhelming problems that fill me at the thought of the future.

Gerda has had a lovely little boy, and she strolls proudly up and down the street with him while her parents are at work. She's only seventeen, and you're first supposed to have children when you're eighteen. She's disliked because she won't admit by her attitude and bearing that things have gone awry for her and consequently politely accept the pity that the street offers her. Everyone is outraged that she refused to accept the basket full of baby clothes that Olga's mother had collected for her. There she goes, just like that, allowing her parents to support her beyond a reasonable age. "If only that were you," says my mother, "you'd have been kicked out long ago." Oh, how I'd like to hold my own little baby in my arms! I would support it and figure out everything some way or other. If only I'd gotten that far. At night when I'm in bed, I imagine meeting an attractive and friendly young man whom I ask with polite phrases to do me a great favor. I explain to him that I'd very much like to have a child and ask him to see that I get one. He agrees, and I clench my teeth and close my eyes and pretend that it's someone else this is happening to, someone who's of no concern to me. Afterwards, I don't want to ever see him again. But such a young man is not to be found in the courtyard or on our street, and I write a poem in my poetry album, which now lies in the bottom of the buffet drawer:

> A little butterfly flew
> high in the blue-tinged sky.
> All common sense, morality
> and duties did it defy.
>
> Drunk with the spring day's charm
> with trembling wings unfurled,
> it was borne by the sungold rays
> down to the beautiful world.
>
> And into a pale pink apple blossom
> which had just opened wide,
> flew the little butterfly
> and found a lovely bride.

And the apple blossom closed,
over was the wild flight.
Oh, thank you, little ones. You've taught me
how to love with delight.

17

MY GRANNY WAS HARDLY COLD IN HER GRAVE BEFORE MY father took us out of the state church. The expression was my mother's. Granny doesn't have a grave. Her ashes are in an urn at Bispebjerg Crematorium, and I feel nothing standing there looking at that stupid vase. But I go there often because my mother wants me to. She cries steadily every time we're there, and I have a guilty conscience when she says, "Why aren't you crying? You did at the funeral." Now that Edvin's gone, I'm always with my mother whenever I'm not in school or down on the street. I've also been to a dance at Folkets Hus with her, but it wasn't fun dancing with her because I'm a head taller than she is and I feel very big and clumsy compared to her. While she was dancing with a gentleman, a young man came and asked me to dance. That had never happened before, and I was about to say no, because I don't know any dance steps other than those my mother taught me at home in the living room when she was in one of her light-hearted moods. But the young man already had his arm around my waist and since he danced well, so did I. He was completely silent, and just to say something, I asked him what he did. "I'm in the courier corps," he said briefly. I thought it had something to do with "curing" and decided he was a doctor. That was certainly something different from a "stable skilled worker." Maybe he would dance with me the whole evening, and maybe he was already falling a little in love with me. My heart beat faster and I leaned against him just a little. "It's night, it's night, now the thieves are at work," he sang in my ear with the music. Suddenly it stopped and he set me next to my mother, bowed stiffly, and disappeared forever. "He was good-looking," said my mother. "If only he comes back." "He's a doctor," I bragged and told her that he was in the courier corps. "Oh, good God," laughed my mother, "that's just a messenger service!"

We're not members of the state church, and for that reason I'm going to have a civil confirmation. That separates me from all the girls in my class who go to a pastor, but it doesn't matter much since I've given up on being like them. They take turns visiting each other on Saturdays when Victor Cornelius plays for the radio's Saturday dances. Boys are invited then too and many of my classmates already have someone they're going steady with. We don't have a radio at home, and it's no fun anymore to put on the headphones and listen to the crackling of the crystal set my brother made at school. And even if we had a radio, my parents wouldn't have been inclined to give a Saturday dance in my honor. I'm taking exams now and I don't care whether I get good or bad grades. Maybe I'm disappointed after all that I can't go to high school. Only one of the girls in my class is allowed to. Her name is Inger Nørgård and she's just as tall and lanky as I am. She never does anything except study and gets A's in every subject. The others say that she'll be an old maid — that's why she's going to continue in school. I've never really talked to her, no more than with anyone else in school. I have to keep everything to myself, and sometimes I think I'm about to suffocate. I've stopped going around on Istedgade in the evening with Ruth and Minna because more and more their conversations consist of nothing but giggling references and coarse, obscene things that can't always be transformed into gentle, rhythmic lines in my increasingly sensitive soul. I only talk to my mother about very trivial things, about what we eat, or about the people who live downstairs. My father has grown very quiet since Edvin moved away, and for him I'm just someone who should "make a good start," with all the terrible events he imagines with that expression. One day when I'm visiting my brother, he says to my astonishment that his friend Thorvald would like to meet me. He's told Thorvald that I write poems, and he asks if Thorvald may read them. Horrified, I say no, but then my brother says that Thorvald knows an editor at *Social-Demokraten* who might possibly print my poems if they're good. He says this in between fits of coughing because he can't tolerate the cellulose lacquer he works with. Finally I give in and promise to come over with my poetry book the next evening, then Thorvald will look at my poems. Thorvald is also a journeyman painter, eighteen years old, and not engaged. The latter I verify since I've already started dreaming about him as the kind young man who, almost without a word, will understand everything.

With my poetry album in my school bag, I walk over to Bagerstræde the next evening. I look firmly at the people I meet because soon I'll be famous, and then they'll be proud that they met me on my way to the stars. I'm terribly afraid that Thorvald will laugh at my poetry as Edvin did long ago. I imagine that he looks like my brother, except he has a thin black mustache. When I enter Edvin's room, Thorvald is sitting on the bed next to my brother. He stands up and puts out his hand. He is little and solid. His hair is blond and coarse and his face is covered with pimples in all states of ripeness. He is visibly shy and the whole time he runs his hand through his hair so that it stands straight up in the air. I stare at him horrified because I think that I can't possibly show him my poems. "This is my sister," says Edvin completely superfluously. "She's damn pretty," says Thorvald, twisting his hair in his fingers. I think it's very kind of him to say that, and I smile at him as I sit down on the room's only chair. You shouldn't be swayed by people's appearance, I think, and maybe he really thinks I'm pretty. At any rate, he's the first person who's ever said that. I take the book out of my bag and hold it in my hands for a while. I'm so afraid that this influential person will think the poems are bad. I don't know whether they're any good at all. "Give it to him now," says my brother impatiently, and I hand it to him reluctantly. As he pages through it and reads with a serious, furrowed brow, I feel as if I'm in a completely different state of existence. I'm excited and moved and scared and it's as if the book is a trembling, living part of my self that can be destroyed with a single harsh or insulting word. Thorvald reads in silence and there's not a smile on his face. Finally he shuts the book, gives me an admiring look with his pale blue eyes and says emphatically, "They're damn good!" Thorvald's language reminds me of Ruth's. She can hardly form a sentence, either, without embellishing it with some seldom-varying swear word. But you shouldn't judge a person by that, and at the moment I think Thorvald looks both wise and handsome. "Do you really think so?" I ask happily. "God damn, yes," he avows. "You can easily sell them." His father is a printer, Edvin explains, and he knows all the editors. "Yes," says Thorvald with pride, "I'll take care of it, by God. Just let me take the book home and I'll show it to the old man." "No," I say quickly, and grab for the book. "I . . . I want to go there myself and show it to this editor. You just need to tell me where he lives." "That's swell," says Thorvald amenably. "I'll tell Edvin and then he can explain it to you." I pack the book away in my school bag again and am in a hurry to get home. I want to be alone to dream about my happiness. Now it doesn't matter about confirmation, it doesn't matter about growing up and going out among strangers, it doesn't matter about anything except the wonderful prospect of having just one poem printed in the newspaper.

Thorvald and Edvin keep their word, and a couple of days later I have a note in my hand on which it says: "Editor Brochmann, Sunday Magazine, *Social-Demokraten*, Nørre Farimagsgade 49, Tuesday, two o'clock." I put on my Sunday clothes, rub my mother's pink tissue paper across my cheeks, make her think that I'm going to take care of Olga's baby, and stroll out to Nørre Farimagsgade. I find the door in the big building with the editor's name on a sign and knock cautiously. "Come in," sounds from the other side. I step into an office where an old man with a white beard is sitting at a big, cluttered desk. "Sit down," he says very kindly and motions toward a chair. I sit down and am gripped by an intense shyness. "Well," he says, taking off his glasses, "what do you want?" Since I'm unable to utter a word, I can't think of what else to do except hand him the by now rather grubby little book. "What's this?" He leafs through it and reads a couple of the poems half-aloud. Then he looks at me over his glasses: "They're very sensual, aren't they?" he says, astonished. I turn bright red in the face and say quickly, "Not all of them." He reads on and then says: "No, but the sensual ones are the best, by God. How old are you?" "Fourteen," I say. "Hmm. . . ." Irresolutely he strokes his beard. "I only edit the children's page, you know, and we can't use these. Come back in a couple of years." He snaps shut my poor book and hands it to me, smiling. "Good-bye, my dear," he says. Somehow or other I edge myself out the door with all my crushed hopes. Slowly, numbed, I walk through the city's spring, the others' spring, the others' joyous transformation, the others' happiness. I'll never be famous, my poems are worthless. I'll marry a stable skilled worker who doesn't drink, or get a steady job with a pension. After that deadly disappointment, a long time passes before I write in my poetry album again. Even though no one else cares for my poems, I have to write them because it dulls the sorrow and longing in my heart.

18

DURING THE PREPARATIONS FOR MY CONFIRMATION, THE big question is whether The Hollow Leg will be invited. He has never visited us before, but now all of a sudden he's stopped drinking. He sits the whole day drinking just as many bottles of soda pop as he used to drink beers. My mother and father say it's a great joy for Aunt Rosalia. But she doesn't look happy, because the man is completely yellow in the face from a bad liver and apparently doesn't have long to live. The family thinks that's to her advantage, too. Now I'm allowed to visit them and it's no longer necessary to protect me from seeing and hearing anything that's not good for me. But Uncle Carl hasn't changed at all. He still mumbles gruffly and inarticulately down at the table about the rotten society and the incompetent government ministers. At intervals he issues short, telegraphic orders to Aunt Rosalia, who obeys his slightest gesture as she always has. The soda pop bottles are lined up in front of him and it's incomprehensible that any person is capable of consuming so much liquid. I wonder at my parents. When you go down into the basement for coal, you usually fall over some drunk who's sleeping it off wrapped up in the ruins of an overcoat, and on the street, drunken men are such an everyday sight that no one bothers to turn around to look at them. Almost every evening, a bunch of men stand in the doorway drinking beer and schnapps, and it's only the very young children who are afraid of them. But throughout our whole childhood, we weren't allowed to see Uncle Carl, even though it would have pleased Aunt Rosalia beyond words. After long discussions between my mother and father and between my mother and Aunt Agnete, it's decided that he will be invited to my confirmation. So the whole family will be there except for my four cousins, since there's just not room for them in the living room. My mother is in a good mood because of the big event, and she says I'm ungrateful and odd because I can't hide that I think all of the preparations have nothing to do with me.

The exams are over and we've had the graduation party at school. Everyone cheered now that they were leaving the "red prison," and I cheered loudest of all. It bothers me a lot that I don't seem to own any real feelings anymore, but always have to pretend that I do by copying other people's reactions. It's as if I'm only moved by things that come to me indirectly. I can cry when I see a picture in the newspaper of an unfortunate family that's been evicted, but when I see the same ordinary sight in reality, it doesn't touch me. I'm moved by poetry and lyrical prose, now as always — but the things that are described leave me completely cold. I don't think very much of reality. When I said good-bye to Miss Mathiassen, she asked me whether I'd found a position. I said yes, and chattered on with false cheerfulness about how I was going to home economics school in a year and until then I had an au pair job at a woman's home where I would take care of her child. All of the others were going to work in offices or stores and I was ashamed that I was only going to be a mother's helper. Miss Mathiassen looked at me searchingly with her wise, kind eyes. "Well, well," she sighed, "it's a shame though that you couldn't go to high school." As soon as my confirmation is over, I'm going to start my job. I went there with my mother to apply for it. The woman was divorced and treated us with cool condescension. She didn't look as if she would be interested in discovering I wrote poetry and just had to pass the time until I could go back to Editor Brochmann at *Social-Demokraten* in a couple of years. It wasn't very elegant in the apartment, either, even though there was of course a grand piano and carpets on the floor. She's at work during the day and in the meantime I'm supposed to clean, cook, and take care of the boy. I haven't done any of these things before, and I don't know how I'm going to be worth the twenty-five kroner I'm supposed to earn every month. Behind me is my childhood and school, and before me an unknown and dreaded life among strangers. I'm closed in and caught between these two poles, the way my feet are squeezed down into the long, pointed brocade shoes. I sit in the Odd Fellows Hall between my parents and listen to a speech about youth as the future all of Denmark is counting on, and about how we must never disappoint our parents who have done so much for us. All of the girls are sitting with a bouquet of carnations in their laps just like me, and they look as though they're just as bored. My father is tugging at his stiff collar and Edvin is suffering from fits of coughing. The doctor said he should change jobs, but that's impossible, of course, after he's been through four years of training to become a journeyman painter. My mother is wearing a new black silk dress with three cloth roses at the neck, and her newly permed hair frizzes around her head. She had to fight to have it done, partly because my father didn't think they could afford it, and partly because he thinks it's "new-fangled" and "loose." I liked her hair better when it was long and smooth. Now and then she puts her handkerchief up to her eyes, but I don't know whether she's really crying. I can't see any reason for it. I think about the fact that once the most important thing in the world was whether my mother liked me; but the child who yearned so deeply for that love and always had to search for any sign of it doesn't exist anymore. Now I think that my mother cares for me, but it doesn't make me happy.

We have pork roast and lemon mousse for dinner, and my mother, who gets angry and irritable at any domestic effort, doesn't relax until it's time for dessert. Uncle Carl is seated next to the stove and he sweats so much he has to constantly wipe his bald, round head with his handkerchief. At the other end of the table sits Uncle Peter, who is a carpenter and represents the cultured branch of the family along with Aunt Agnete, who sang in the church choir as a child. She has written a song for me because she has a "vein" that flows on all such occasions. It deals with various uninteresting events of my childhood and each verse ends like this: "God be with you on your way, fa-la-la, then luck and happiness will always follow you, fa-la-la." When we sing the refrain, Edvin looks at me with laughter in his eyes, and I hurriedly look at the song in order not to smile. Then Uncle Peter taps his glass and stands up. He's going to make a speech. It's like the one at the Odd Fellows Hall, and I only listen with half an ear. It's something about stepping into the adult ranks and being hard-working and clever like my parents. It's a little too long. Uncle Carl says, "Hear, hear!" every second, as if he'd been drinking wine, and Edvin coughs. My mother has shining eyes and I cringe with discomfort and boredom. When he's done and everyone has said "Hurrah," Aunt Rosalia says softly as she envelops me with her warm glance, "The adult ranks — Good Lord! She's neither fish nor fowl." I can feel my lips quiver and quickly look down at my plate. That's the most loving and maybe also the truest thing that is said at my confirmation. After dinner everyone can finally stretch their

95

legs, and they all seem to be in a better mood than when they arrived, maybe also because of the wine. They admire the little wristwatch that I got from my parents. I like it too, and think that it makes my thin wrist look a little more substantial. I got money from the others, more than fifty kroner, but it's to be put in the bank for my old age, so that doesn't excite me much.

After the guests have left and I've helped my mother clean up, we sit together at the table and talk for a while. Even though it's past midnight, I'm wide awake and very relieved that my party is over. "God, how he stuffed himself," says my mother, meaning Uncle Peter. "Did you see that?" "Yes," says my father indignantly, "and drank! When it's free he can really put it away." "And he pretended that Carl wasn't even there," continues my mother. "I felt bad for Rosalia." Suddenly she smiles at me and says, "Wasn't it a lovely day, Tove?" I think about how much trouble and expense this has cost them. "Oh yes," I lie, "it was a good confirmation." My mother nods in agreement and yawns. Then she's struck by an idea. "Ditlev," she says with a happy voice, "since Tove is going to be earning money now, can't we afford to buy a radio?" The blood rushes to my head with fright and rage. "You're not going to buy a radio with my money," I say hotly. "I have plenty of use for it myself." "I see," says my mother, cold as ice, getting up and stomping out the door, which she slams after her so that the plaster clatters down from the wall. My father looks at me, embarrassed. "Don't take it so literally," he explains. "We have a little in the bank — we can use that to buy a radio. You just have to pay for your room and board here at home." "Yes," I say, regretting my temper. Now my mother won't speak to me for days, I know. My father says good night kindly and goes into the bedroom, where I'll never again sit on the windowsill and dream about all the happiness that's only attainable by grown-up people.

I'm alone in my childhood's living room where my brother once sat and pounded nails into a board while my mother sang and my father read the forbidden book I haven't seen for years. It's all centuries ago and I think that I was very happy then, in spite of my painful feeling of childhood's endlessness. On the wall hangs the sailor's wife staring out to sea. Stauning's serious face looks down at me, and it's a long time since my God was created in his image. Although I'm going to be sleeping at home, I feel like I'm saying good-bye to the room tonight. I have no desire to go to bed, and I'm not sleepy, either. I'm seized by a vast sadness. I move the geraniums on the windowsill and look up at the sky where an infant star shines in the bottom of the new moon's cradle, which rocks gently and quietly between the shifting clouds. I repeat to myself some lines from Johannes V. Jensen's *Bræen*, which I've read so often that I know long passages by heart. "And now like the evening star, then like the morning star shines the little girl who was killed at her mother's breast; white and self-absorbed like a child's soul that wanders alone and plays so well by itself on endless roads." Tears run down my cheeks because the words always make me think of Ruth, whom I've lost for good. Ruth with the fine, heart-shaped mouth and the strong, clear eyes. My little lost friend with the sharp tongue and the loving heart. Our friendship is over just as my childhood is. Now the last remnants fall away from me like flakes of sun-scorched skin, and beneath looms an awkward, an impossible adult. I read in my poetry album while the night wanders past the window — and, unawares, my childhood falls silently to the bottom of my memory, that library of the soul from which I will draw knowledge and experience for the rest of my life.

97

YOUTH

I

I WAS AT MY FIRST JOB FOR ONLY ONE DAY. I LEFT HOME AT seven-thirty in order to be there in plenty of time, "because you should try especially hard in the beginning," said my mother, who had never made it past the beginning at the places where she'd worked in her youth. I was wearing the dress from the day after my confirmation that Aunt Rosalia had made. It was of light blue wool and there were little pleats in the front so that I didn't look quite as flat-chested as usual. I walked down Vesterbrogade in the thin, sharp sunshine, and I thought that everyone looked free and happy. When they'd passed the street door near Pile Allé, which would soon swallow me up, their step became as light as dancers', and happiness resided somewhere on the other side of Valby Bakke. The dark hallway smelled of fear, so I was afraid that Mrs. Olfertsen would notice it, as if I'd brought the smell with me. My body and my movements became stiff and awkward as I stood listening to her fluttering voice explaining many things and, in between the explanations, running on like an empty spool that babbled about nothing in an uninterrupted stream — about the weather, about the boy, about how tall I was for my age. She asked whether I had an apron with me, and I took my mother's out of the emptied school bag. There was a hole near the seam because there was something or other wrong with everything that my mother was responsible for, and I was touched by the sight of it. My mother was far away and I wouldn't see her for eight hours. I was among strangers —

I was someone whose physical strength they'd bought for a certain number of hours each day for a certain payment. They didn't care about the rest of me. When we went out to the kitchen, Toni, the little boy, came running up in his pajamas. "Good morning, Mummy," he said sweetly, leaning against his mother's legs and giving me a hostile look. The woman gently pulled herself free from him and said, "This is Tove, say hello to the nice lady." Reluctantly he put out his hand and when I took it, he said threateningly, "You have to do everything I say or else I'll shoot you." His mother laughed loudly and showed me a tray with cups and a teapot, and asked me to fix the tea and come into the living room with it. Then she took the boy by the hand and tripped into the living room on her high heels. I boiled the water and poured it into the pot, which had tea leaves in the bottom. I wasn't sure if that was correct because I'd never had or made tea before. I thought to myself that rich people drank tea and poor people drank coffee. I pushed the door handle down with my elbow and stepped into the room, where I stopped, horrified. Mrs. Olfertsen was sitting on Uncle William's lap, and on the floor Toni lay playing with a train. The woman jumped up and began pacing back and forth on the floor so that her wide sleeves kept cutting the sunshine up into little fiery flashes. "Be so good as to knock," she hissed, "before you come into a room here. I don't know what you're accustomed to, but that's what we do here, and you'd better get used to it. Go out again!" She pointed toward the door and, confused, I set the tray down and went out. For some reason or other it stung me that she addressed me formally, like a grownup. That had never happened to me before. When I reached the hallway, she yelled, "Now knock!" I did. "Come in!" I heard, and this time she and the silent Uncle William were each sitting on their own chair. I was bright red in the face from humiliation and I quickly decided that I couldn't stand any of them. That helped a little. When they had drunk the tea, they both went into the bedroom and got dressed. Then Uncle William left, after giving his hand to the mother and the boy. I was apparently not anyone you said good-bye to. The woman gave me a long typewritten list of what kind of work I should do at various times during the day. Then she disappeared into the bedroom again and returned with a hard, sharp expression on her face. I discovered that she was heavily made up and radiated an unnatural, lifeless freshness. I thought her prettier before. She knelt down and kissed the boy who was still playing, then stood up, nodded slightly toward me, and vanished. At once the child got up, grabbed hold of my dress, and stared up at me winsomely. "Toni wants anchovies," he said. Anchovies? I was dumbfounded and completely ignorant of children's eating habits. "You can't have that. Here it says . . ." I studied the schedule, "ten o'clock, rye porridge for Toni; eleven o'clock, soft-boiled egg and a vitamin pill; one o'clock. . . ." He didn't feel like listening to the rest. "Hanne always gave me anchovies," he said impatiently. "She ate everything else herself — you can too." Hanne was apparently my predecessor; and besides, I wasn't prepared to force a lot of things into a child who only wanted anchovies. "OK, OK," I said, in a better mood now that the adults had gone. "Where are the anchovies?" He crawled up onto a kitchen chair and took down a couple of cans, then he found a can opener in a drawer. "Open it," he said eagerly, handing it to me. I opened the can and put him up on the kitchen counter as he demanded. Then I let one anchovy after another disappear into his mouth, and when there weren't any more, he asked to go down to the courtyard to play. I helped him get dressed and sent him down the kitchen stairs. From the window I could keep an eye on him playing. Then I was supposed to clean house. One of the items said: "Carpet sweeper over the rugs." I took hold of the heavy monstrosity and navigated it onto the big red carpet in the living room. To try it out, I drove it over some threads which, however, did not disappear. Then I shook it a little and fiddled with the mechanism so that the lid opened and a whole pile of dirt fell out onto the carpet. I couldn't put it back together again; since I didn't know what to do with the dirt, I kicked it under the rug, which I stamped on a bit to even out the pile. During these exertions, it had gotten to be ten o'clock and I was hungry. I ate the first of Toni's meals and fortified myself with a couple of vitamins. Then came the next item: "Brush all of the furniture with water." I stared astonished at the note and then around at the furniture. It was strange, but that must be what was done here. I found a good stiff brush, poured cold water into a basin and again started in the living room. I scrubbed steadily and conscientiously until I'd done half of the grand piano. Then it dawned on me that something was terribly wrong. On the fine, shiny surface, the brush had left hundreds of thin scratches and I didn't know how I was going to remove them before the woman came home. Terror crept like cold snakes over my skin. I took the note and again read: "Brush *all* of the furniture with water." Whatever way I interpreted the order, it was clear enough and didn't exempt the grand piano. Was it possible that it wasn't a piece of furniture? It was one o'clock and the woman came home at five. I felt such a burning longing for my mother that I didn't think there was any time to waste. Quickly I took off my apron, called Toni from the window, explaining to him that we were going to look at toy stores. He came upstairs and got dressed and, with him in hand, I raced through Vesterbrogade so he could hardly keep up. "We're going home to my mother," I said, out of breath, "to have anchovies." My mother was very surprised to see me at that time of day, but when we came inside and I told her about the scratched grand piano, she burst out laughing. "Oh God," she gasped, "did you really brush the piano with water? Oh no, how could anybody be so dumb!" Suddenly she grew serious. "Look here," she said, "it's no use you going back there. We can certainly find you another job." I was grateful but not especially surprised. She was like that, and if it had been up to her, Edvin could have changed apprenticeships. "Yes," I said, "but what about Father?" "Oh," she said, "we'll just tell him the story about Uncle William — Father can't stand that kind of thing." A light-hearted mood possessed us both, like in the old days, and when Toni cried for anchovies, we took him with us down to Istedgade and bought two cans for him. A little before four o'clock, my mother and the boy went back to Mrs. Olfertsen's, where my mother got back the apron and the school bag. I never found out what was said about the damaged grand piano.

2

I'M WORKING IN A PENSION ON VESTERBROGADE NEAR Frihedsstøtten. It would be just as unthinkable for my mother to send me to another part of the city as to America. I start at eight o'clock every morning and work twelve hours in a sooty, greasy kitchen where there's never any peace or rest. When I get home in the evening, I'm much too tired to do anything except go to bed. "This time," says my father, "you have to stay at your job." My mother also thinks that it's good for me to be working, and besides, the trick with Uncle William can't be repeated. The only thing I think about is how I can get out of this dreary existence. I don't write poetry anymore since nothing in my daily life inspires me to do so. I don't go to the library either. I'm off every Wednesday afternoon after two o'clock, but then I go straight home to bed too. The pension is owned by Mrs. Petersen and Miss Petersen. They are mother and daughter, but I think they look like they're about the same age. Besides me there's a sixteen-year-old girl whose name is Yrsa. She's way above me, because when the boarders eat, she puts on a black dress, a white apron, and a white cap and bustles back and forth with the heavy platters. She's the serving girl and waits on the guests. In two years, the ladies promise me, I'll also be allowed to serve and get forty kroner a month like Yrsa. Now I get thirty. It's my job to see that there's always a fire in the stove, to clean the rooms of the three lodgers, the bathroom, and the kitchen. Even though I rush through everything, I'm always behind with it all.

Miss Petersen scolds, "Didn't your mother ever teach you to wring out a rag? Haven't you ever cleaned a bathroom before? Why are you making faces? For your sake I hope you never encounter anything more difficult than this!" Yrsa is little and thin, and she has a narrow, pale face with a snub nose. When the ladies take a nap before dinner, we drink a cup of coffee at the kitchen counter and she says, "If you didn't always have black fingernails, you'd be allowed to serve. That's what I heard Mrs. Petersen say." Or, "If you washed your hair once in a while, the guests would be allowed to see you, I'm sure of that." For Yrsa there's nothing in the world outside of the pension and no higher goal than to rush around the table at every mealtime. I don't reply to either her or the ladies' remarks, which come like pellets from a slingshot and never really hit the mark. While Yrsa and I do the dishes and the ladies cook in the big pots on the stove behind us, they talk about their illnesses that drive them from doctor to doctor, because they're not satisfied with any of them. They have gallstones, hardening of the arteries, high blood pressure, aches everywhere, mysterious internal pains, and gloomy warnings from their stomachs every time they've eaten. On Sundays they march past the Home for the Disabled on Grønningen in order to get into a better mood by looking at the invalids; and in general they put everything and everyone down with nasty pleasure. They have something in particular against the boarders and they know everything about their private lives, the intimate details of which they discuss while they dish out the food on to Yrsa's platters, complaining about how much those people can eat. Sometimes I think that their low, mean thoughts penetrate my skin so I can hardly breathe. But most of the time I find this life intolerably boring and recall with sorrow my variable and eventful childhood. In that narrow strip of the day when I'm awake enough to talk with my mother a little, I ask her about what's happening in the building and in the family and greedily devour every refreshing bit of news. Gerda is working at Carlsberg now, and her mother stays home to take care of the baby. Ruth has begun to go around with boys. "You could have expected that," says my mother. "You should never adopt other people's children." Edvin has lost his job and has started to come by the apartment again. "But you shouldn't feel bad about it," says my mother, "because now he doesn't cough so much." It still shakes me a little, because my father always said that skilled workers could never be unemployed. "My God," says my mother excitedly, "I almost forgot to tell you that Uncle Carl is in the hospital. He's terribly sick, and it's no wonder, considering how he's lived. Aunt Rosalia is over there every day, but it really will be best for her if he dies. And margarine has gone up two øre in Irma — isn't that steep?" "So it costs forty-nine øre," I say because I've always kept up on the prices, since I've either gone shopping with my mother or by myself. "If only Father can stay at the Ørsted Works," she says. "Now he's been there three months — even though it's no fun working at night." Her chattering voice spins softly around me in the growing darkness until I fall asleep with my arms on the table.

One evening I wake up as usual from this position at the sound of the clinking cups and the smell of coffee. As I sleepily raise my head, my eye is caught by a name in the newspaper: Editor Brochmann. I stare at it wide awake, and slowly I realize that it's an obituary. It hits me like the lash of a whip. It never occurred to me that he could die before the two years were up. I feel like he's deserted me and left me behind in the world without the slightest hope for the

108

future. My mother pours the coffee and puts the pot down over his name. "Drink now," she says and settles herself on the other side of the table. She says, "Pretty Ludvig has been put in an institution. His mother died, you know, and then they just came and took him away." "Yes," I say and again feel that we're infinitely far from each other. She says, "It'll be nice for you when you can get that bicycle. There's only two months left." "Yes," I say. I pay ten kroner a month at home, ten are put in the bank for my old age, and the remaining ten are my own. At the moment I couldn't care less about that bicycle — about anything. I drink my coffee and my mother says, "You're so quiet, there's nothing the matter, is there?" She says it sharply, because she only likes me if my soul is resting completely in hers and I don't keep any secret part of it to myself. "If you don't stop being so strange," she says, "you'll never get married." "I don't want to anyway," I say, even though I'm sitting there considering that desperate alternative. I think about my childhood ghost: the stable skilled worker. I don't have anything against a skilled worker; it's the word "stable" that blocks out all bright future dreams. It's as gray as a rainy sky when no bright ray of sun trickles through. My mother gets up. "Well," she says, "we've got to go to bed. We have to get up early, you know. Good night," she says from the door, looking suspicious and offended. When she's gone, I move the coffeepot and read the obituary again. There's a black cross over the name. I see his kind face before me and hear his voice, "Come back in a couple of years, my dear." My tears fall on the words and I think this is the hardest day of my life.

3

I SANK INTO A LONG-LASTING STUPOR THAT ROBBED ME OF all initiative. "You're going around asleep," said the ladies, whose reproaches made less of an impression on me than ever. I lost the desire to talk with my mother, and one evening when Edvin came with an invitation from Thorvald, I said no. I had no desire to go out dancing with that young man who had liked my poems. Maybe his father knew another editor who would also die before I was old enough to write real, grown-up poems. I'd gotten cold feet and didn't dare expose myself to any more disappointments. Summer had come. When I went home in the evening, the fresh breeze cooled my stove-flushed cheeks like a silk handkerchief, and young girls in light dresses walked hand in hand with their sweethearts. I felt very alone. Of the girls in the trash-can corner, Ruth was the only one I knew now, and she always yelled "Hi" to me when I went through the courtyard. I looked up at the front building's wall, flooded with life and memories, my childhood's wailing wall, behind which people ate and slept and argued and fought. Then I went up the stairs in my red dress with blue polka dots and puff sleeves — the only summer dress I had. Sometimes Jytte was sitting in the living room, smoking cigarettes, which she also offered to my mother. My mother smoked awkwardly and ineptly and always got smoke in her eyes. Now Jytte was working in a tobacco factory. My father said that she stole the cigarettes, but my mother didn't care. She always had to have a girlfriend who was much younger than her, because she was so youthful. But there were gray streaks in her black hair and she had put on weight around her hips. That's why she often went to the steambaths at the public bathhouse on Lyrskovgade, and when she came home, she gleefully told us about how terribly fat all the other women were.

One evening the pension's kitchen doorbell rang, and when I opened the door, Ruth was standing outside. "Hi," she said, smiling, "are you going home now? There's something I want to tell you." "Yes," I said, "just wait outside." I poured out the last of the dishwater, took off my apron, and slipped out to her, as if she were a secret contact that no one must discover. What did she want with me? It was a long time since anyone had wanted me for anything. She had on a white muslin dress with a wide, black patent leather belt around her waist and short sleeves. She was wearing lipstick and her eyebrows were plucked like my mother's. Even though she was still slightly built, she seemed to me very grown-up in appearance. We didn't speak until we reached the street, but then Ruth began to chatter on as if there'd never been any question of a separation between us. She told me that Minna had finished school and now had a live-in job in Østerbro. "In Østerbro?" I repeated, dumbfounded. "Yes," said Ruth, "but she's always had a screw loose." It didn't fill me with the joy you would have expected. I just thought that Ruth never missed anyone. She had written Minna off with a shrug of her shoulder, just as she presumably had written me off a year ago. There was no room for deep or lasting feelings in her heart. When we reached Sundevedsgade, where I usually turned off, we stopped. "But you know," said Ruth, "you haven't even heard what I wanted to tell you." Reluctantly I continued on with her, because now my mother would have

111

to wait for me in vain, and if too much time passed, she'd go over to the pension and ask for me. Then when she found out that I'd left, she would be sure that some accident had occurred. But Ruth radiated faintly some of the old magic and power to get me to do things that I never would think of myself. Ruth said that she had a sweetheart, a boy sixteen years old, whose name was Ejvind and who lived on Amerikavej. He was an apprentice mechanic and someday they would get married. He had taken her virginity, and it was "damned great." And then she'd gotten to know a very rich man who was an antiquarian bookseller and lived on Gammel Kongevej. It was him that she wanted me to visit with her. She had visited him alone but he'd tried to seduce her, and that, she said, she wouldn't do to Ejvind. The rich man was named Mr. Krogh, and his best friend was Holger Bjerre, whom he was going to persuade to make Ruth a chorus girl. "You too," she said, "he's promised me." "Me?" A gleam of hope streaks through my soul. A chorus girl is on stage dancing every evening, and in the daytime she can do whatever she wants. I know, of course, that they'd never permit it at home, but the world is never totally real when I'm with Ruth. "And you know what," she says eagerly, "he's very old and he's sick, too. When I was over there, I thought he was going to die of a heart attack, he coughed and puffed and gasped so much. He lives all alone and if we're really nice to him, maybe he'll will us everything he owns, and then Ejvind can get his own workshop." She looks up at me delightedly, with her clear, strong eyes, and the crazy plan puts me in a good mood. I know very well what it is Ruth wants of me, and I say, "I won't do it, but I'd like to meet him." Ruth laughs and holds her hand in front of her mouth while wiping her nose with her thumb at the same time. She says that he looks horrid, but I should think about the money and our future as chorus girls. Mr. Krogh lives on the top floor of a building that doesn't at all look like it houses millionaires. When we've rung the bell, we hear a violent coughing on the other side of the door. "There, you can hear he's not long for this world, by God," whispers Ruth. After a lengthy rattling with security chains and keys, the door is opened a crack and Mr. Krogh's face appears. He looks at us suspiciously for a moment, then he loosens the chain and lets us come in. "Oh," I exclaim, "what a lot of books!" The living room is practically wallpapered with books and large paintings like I've otherwise only seen in museums. Mr. Krogh doesn't say anything until we sit down. He looks at me intently and asks kindly, "Do you like books?" "Yes," I say and look at him more closely. He's not as old as Ruth said, but not young either. He's completely bald and has plump, red cheeks, as if he were out in the fresh air a lot. His eyes are brown and a little melancholy like my father's. I like him very much and sense that he likes me too. He makes coffee for us and Ruth asks whether he has spoken to Holger Bjerre. "No . . . I'm afraid he's on vacation right now." When he looks at Ruth, his glance slides searchingly up and down her body, but luckily he doesn't seem to be interested in mine. He offers us cakes and talks about the fine weather and about the city's young ·girls who spring up from the cobblestones like flowers. "It is," he says, "a refreshing sight." Ruth is bored and kicks my legs under the table. I say, "Do you think I could be a chorus girl too, Mr. Krogh?" "You!" he says astonished. "No, you're not suited for that at all." "Yes, she is," protests Ruth, "if she gets a permanent and make-up and things like that. She's pretty without clothes on." I blush and for the first time in my life I feel irritated with Ruth. Mr. Krogh looks from her to me and says, "How in the world did you two ever find each other?" I ask if I can take a look at his books, and when he hears that I prefer reading poems, he shows me where they are. I take out a volume at random and open it. Delighted and happy, I read:

> — the pitchers are filled with wine,
> the twilight-veiled earth.

Baudelaire: *Les fleurs du mal* I read on the title page, and I go over to Mr. Krogh and ask him how it's pronounced. He tells me and says that I can borrow the book if I promise to return it. I promise and sit down again at the table. Only now do I notice that Mr. Krogh is in his dressing gown. He has a coughing fit again, during which he turns bright red in the face and, wheezing for air, he asks Ruth to thump him on the back. While she does this, she laughs soundlessly at me, but I don't laugh back. Between Mr. Krogh and me there's a silent understanding that I don't remember having experienced with anyone else before. I wish fiercely that he were my father or my uncle. Ruth notices this and frowns, annoyed. "I have to go home," she says sulkily, "I'm going to meet Ejvind." When we're about to leave, Mr. Krogh tries to kiss Ruth but she turns her sweet face away, and I feel sorry for him. I wouldn't have anything against kissing him, but he just gives me his hand and says, "You can borrow all the books from me that you like, just as long as I get them back. I'm always home this time of the evening." When I get home, my mother is sitting at the table with a swollen face and red eyes. She asks me where in heaven's name I've been and where I got that book from. I say that I've been over at Edvin's and that his cough really has gotten better. The book I borrowed from one of the lodgers.

114

When I get into bed, the thought strikes me with terror that Mr. Krogh could die like my editor. I desire with all my heart to make contact with a world that seems to consist entirely of sick old men who might keel over at any moment, before I myself have grown old enough to be taken seriously.

4

UNCLE CARL IS DEAD. "HE DIED QUIETLY IN HIS SLEEP," says Aunt Rosalia, and he died with his hand in hers. She is sitting on the edge of a chair, with her hat on and her sewing over her arm like always, even though she doesn't have anything to go home to now. Her eyes are completely swollen from crying and my mother can't really find any way to comfort her. My mother has always thought it would be best for Aunt Rosalia if Uncle Carl died, but it doesn't look like Aunt Rosalia thinks so. At the funeral we're all present, including Uncle Peter and Aunt Agnete, who didn't want to have anything to do with Uncle Carl when he was alive. My three cousins are there too. They're little and fat and pasty-white in the face, and my mother says gloatingly that they'll never get married, and so what do their parents have to be so stuck-up about? She and my father have always put down Aunt Agnete and Uncle Peter, and yet they still play cards with them a couple of times a week. It irritates me when I get home from work, because then I can't go to bed until they've left. While the minister preaches over Uncle Carl, I don't laugh like at my Granny's funeral, but I think about the fact that no one except Aunt Rosalia has known him or knew what he was really like. First he was a hussar, then he was a blacksmith, then he drank beer, and finally soda pop. That's all that the rest of us know. We have coffee in a restaurant near the cemetery, and there's an oppressive mood because Aunt Rosalia refuses to be cheered up by anything whatsoever. Her tears fall into her coffee cup and she has to keep lifting the black veil of her funeral hat to dry them away. "He was handsome as a young man," she says to my mother, "wasn't he, Alfrida?" "Yes, he was," says my mother. "He was handsome then." Then Aunt Rosalia says, "I know that none of you liked him because he drank. He suffered a great deal because of that. His own family didn't like him either." It's embarrassing, and no one answers, because she's right, of course. "Well," says Edvin, getting up, "I have to go now. I have to meet a friend." After he's gone, I look around at my family, at these faces that have surrounded me my whole childhood, and I find them tired and aged, as if the years that I've used to grow up in have exhausted them completely. Even my cousins, who are not much older than me, look worn out and used up. My father is very quiet and serious, as always when he's wearing his Sunday suit. It's as if it's lined with dark and depressing thoughts that he puts on along with the suit. He's talking with Uncle Peter in a low voice, mumbling. Even at the funeral they discuss politics, but they don't get excited about it like they usually do. My father is still working at the H. C. Ørsted Works, and my mother has finally gotten the radio that she wanted me to pay for. She has it on all day long and only turns it off when there's someone in the living room she wants to talk to. When my father's home, he's always lying on the sofa, sleeping. Then when my mother turns off the radio, he wakes up with a start and says, "It's damn near impossible to sleep with that God-awful noise." We think that's really funny. But I'm not really involved with all that goes on at home anymore — not like before. I'm really only alive when I'm at Mr. Krogh's. I visit him as often as I dare, without provoking my mother. I say that I'm visiting Yrsa, but my mother can't understand why we're suddenly friends, since I've always said that I didn't like her. I borrow books from Mr. Krogh and return them again after I've read them. He always greets me in his silk dressing gown, with red slippers on his feet; he pours us coffee from a silver coffeepot. If he doesn't have any pastry, he gives me fifty øre to go down and buy some. We drink coffee at a low table with an etched brass surface. Mr. Krogh has long, white hands that always tremble slightly, and he has a low, pleasant voice that I love to listen to. He does most of the talking when I'm there, because he doesn't like me to show my curiosity. One evening when I asked him why he wasn't married, he said, "You're not supposed to know everything about a person — remember that. Then it stops being exciting." I don't know, either, whether Ruth still comes there, whether she's going to be a chorus girl, or whether Mr. Krogh even knows Holger Bjerre at all. Ruth doesn't think so. Whenever I meet her in the courtyard or on the street, she says, "That Krogh is full of lies, and he's a dirty old man. Hasn't he made a pass at you yet?" "No," I say and think she's talking about someone completely different than the Mr. Krogh I know. "Well, I don't dare go there alone," she says. Another day she says that he's stingy since he never gives me any presents. "Why should he?" I ask. She gives me a look bursting with impatience. "Because," she says, "he's old and you're young. He's completely crazy about young girls, and he has to pay for that — what else?" One evening when Mr. Krogh has lit the candles in a tall silver candleholder that's standing on the table between us, I gather my courage and say, "Mr. Krogh, when I was little, I wrote poems." He smiles. "Yes," he says, "and you want to show them to me?" I blush because he's guessed what I want from him, and I ask him how he knows. "Oh," he says, "either that or something else. People always want something from each other, and I've known all along that you wanted to use me for something." When I make a protesting gesture, he says, "There's nothing wrong with that — it's completely natural. I want something from you, too." "What?" I ask. "Nothing in particular," he says, taking his long thin pipe out of his mouth. "I just collect eccentrics — people who are different, special cases. I'd like to see your poems. Thump me on the back." The last comes out in gasps, and he gets quite blue in the face. He coughs at each thump I give him and he doubles up so that his arms hang down to the floor. I wonder what kind of illness he suffers from. I don't dare ask whether it's fatal, but already the next evening I rush up to him with my poetry album, half-convinced that he's no longer among the living. But he is, and as soon as we're sitting at the coffee table, I hand him the book, very afraid of disappointing him, accustomed as he is to reading the greatest poetry. He puts his pipe down and pages through the book, while I tensely watch his face. "Yes," he says, nodding, "children's poems!" He reads aloud:

> Sleeping girl, I'll sing a hymn for you.
> No sight has ever brought me joy so true
> as you lying motionless and sweet,
> smiling in your dreams, the white sheet
> barely covering your young breast,
> oh, how that sight to me was blest,
> but you were unaware.

There are four or five verses, and he mumbles them all to himself. Then he looks at me kindly and gravely and says, "That's interesting. Who were you thinking of when you wrote that poem?" "No one," I say, "well, yes, maybe Ruth." He laughs heartily. "Life is funny," he says then.

"You realize it first when you're about to lose it." "But Mr. Krogh," I say terrified, "you're not that old — not any older than my father." "Oh no," he says, "but even so, I've lived a long time." He shuts the book and puts it on the table. "These poems," he says, "can't be used for anything, but it looks like you're going to be a poet someday." A wave of happiness floods through me at these words. I tell him about Editor Brochmann, who said that I should come back in a couple of years, and he says that he knew him well. He also says that someday when I write something good, something that other people will take pleasure in reading, I should show it to him and then he'll see that it's published. The candles flicker in the holder and the dark evening sky is full of stars. I'm so terribly fond of Mr. Krogh, but I don't dare tell him so. We're silent for a long time. From the bookshelves there issues a pleasant smell of leather, paper, and dust, and Mr. Krogh looks at me with a sorrowful glance, as if what he wants to tell me will never be said, exactly like my father has always looked at me. Then he gets up. "Well," he says, "you'd better go. I have some work to do before I go to bed." Out in the hallway he puts his hand under my chin and says, "Will you give an old man a kiss on the cheek?" I kiss him carefully, as if my kiss could bring about his feared death. It's a soft, old man's cheek that reminds me of my Granny's.

5

HITLER HAS COME TO POWER IN GERMANY. MY FATHER says that it's the reactionaries who've won and that the Germans don't deserve any better since they voted for him themselves. Mr. Krogh calls it a catastrophe for the whole world and is gloomy and depressed as if from some personal sorrow. The ladies at the pension cheer and say that if Stauning were like Hitler, we wouldn't have unemployment, but he's weak and corrupt and drunken and everything he does in the government is wrong. They listen to the news on the radio instead of taking a nap before dinner, and they come back with shining eyes and say that the Reichstag fire was set by the Communists and now it will certainly be proved at the trial. My father and Mr. Krogh say that the Nazis started it themselves, and if I have any opinion at all, it's to agree with them. But most of all, I'm terrified — as if the swells from the great ocean of the world could capsize my fragile little ship at any moment. I don't like reading the newspapers anymore, but I can't avoid them entirely. My father shows me Anton Hansen's dark, satirical drawings in *Social-Demokraten,* and they increase my fear. There is an old Jew with a large sign on his back, surrounded by laughing SS-men. On the sign it says: "Ich bin Jude, aber ich will mich nicht über die Nazis beschweren." * I have to tell my father what it means. Mr. Krogh subscribes to *Politiken.* He shows me a drawing of Van der Lubbe and the caption

---

* "I am a Jew, but I don't want to complain about the Nazis."—Trans.

121

underneath:

> Tell us what you know
> about Torgler and the fire.
>
> —
>
> You know, we want to know, damn it.
> Say that Dimitroff
> and Popoff were waiting by the stairs,
> then you'll save your neck.

"Oh yes," he says, "now the German intelligentsia is in for
it." I ask him what "German intelligentsia" means and he
explains it to me. Among other things, it means the artists.
A poet is an artist, and Mr. Krogh has said that I'll be a poet
someday. The ladies read *Berlingske Tidende,* and there,
they say, the truth is written about Hitler, who may save all
of Europe and create a kind of paradise for us all. More than
ever I want to get away from the pension's close, filthy
kitchen and the people I'm with there every day. My father
is always sleeping when I come home and a couple of hours
later he leaves for work. One evening when he wakes up, I
ask him whether I can look for another job. I say that I hate
washing dishes and cleaning and doing any kind of domestic
work at all. I would rather work in an office and learn to
type. "Not yet," he says, "first you have to learn to take
care of a house properly and cook for your husband when he
comes home from work." "She'll learn that soon enough,"
my mother comes to my aid, "when she has use for it one
day." She also says, "You talk like she's going to get married tomorrow. She's only just turned fifteen." My father
presses his lips together and frowns. "Is it you or me who
decides?" he says. Then my mother keeps quiet, but she's
insulted too, and the atmosphere in the living room is tense.

When my father has left, she puts down her knitting and smiles. "We'll pretend," she says, "that one of the lodgers has made a pass at you. Then you can look for another job." "OK," I say relieved, astonished that I never thought of that before. A couple of days later, my father is sitting on the sofa when I come home. "Well," he says, "Mother told me what happened. Now you've reached the age when you need to watch out for yourself. You're not to go back there. Mother can go and pick up your paycheck, and then you'll have to start looking for another job." Then I stay home for a while. We buy *Berlingske Tidende* and I send in replies for many office jobs but get no response. I also go around Vesterbro and apply for those jobs where you're supposed to appear in person. I talk to fine gentlemen in big, light offices and they all ask me what my father does. When I tell them, they figure that I'll have to live on my salary and it's never intended for that. But finally I succeed in getting a job where the director just asks me whether I'm a member of the union. When he hears that I'm not, he hires me immediately for forty kroner a month. It's in a nursing supply company on Valdemarsgade and I'm to be stock clerk. "Scab company," says my father when he hears the part about the union, but he gives in anyway, because even for a girl it's not easy to find a job.

While all of this was going on, I didn't have a chance to visit Mr. Krogh. He had never asked me where I lived and was not inquisitive in general, just as he didn't like others to be, either. One evening I go out to see him again. It's winter and I have on Edvin's made-over coat, which is more warm than beautiful. I'm looking forward to seeing my friend again and to telling him about my new job, which for now I'm happy with. I cut through the usual passageway from Vesterbrogade, and when I reach Gammel Kongevej, I stop as if paralyzed, completely uncomprehending. The yellow building isn't there anymore. Where it had stood, there is just a space with rubble, plaster, and rusty, twisted water pipes. I go over and brace my hand against the low remains of a wall, because I don't think my legs will support me any longer. People go past me with closed faces, wrapped up in their own evening errands. I feel like grabbing one of them by the arm and saying, "There was a building here yesterday — can you tell me where it is? Where is Mr. Krogh?" He must be living somewhere else now, of course, but how do you find someone who has disappeared? I don't understand how he could do this to me. But maybe he knew so many young girls and I was just one of them. He'd said that he collected eccentrics, but maybe I wasn't eccentric enough. As I walk slowly home, still half-numbed by this misfortune, I think that this wouldn't have happened if I'd written good poems. I don't think it would have happened, either, if he'd desired my body, as he obviously desired Ruth's, but no one has yet shown any interest whatsoever in me in that way; my father's warning is completely unnecessary. At home on my street, Ruth is standing with her apprentice mechanic in front of the stairwell to the front building. I stop and button my coat at the neck because the wind is icy cold, which I first notice now. "Mr. Krogh's house is torn down," I say. "Do you know where he's living?" "Nope," she says over the young man's shoulder, "and I don't give a damn, either." They disappear into each other's embrace again and I walk past, across the courtyard. As I go up the stairs to the back building, I'm gripped by the fear that I'll never get away from this place where I was born. Suddenly I can't stand it and find every memory of it dark and sad. As long as I live here I'm condemned to loneliness and anonymity. The world doesn't count me as anything and every time I get hold of a corner of it, it slips out of my hands again. People die and houses are torn down over them. The world is constantly changing — it's only my childhood's world that endures. Up in the living room it looks like it has always looked. My father is sleeping and my mother is sitting at the table knitting. Her gray hair is gone because, in the greatest secrecy, she has it dyed — wherever she gets the money from for that. . . . Once in a while my father says, "It's strange that your hair is still black. Mine is completely gray now." He's naive and believes everything we say, because he himself never lies. "Where have you been?" asks my mother, looking at me suspiciously. "At Yrsa's," I say, not caring whether she believes me. She says, "It's cold in here; put some more coals in the stove." Then she puts the water on for coffee and I decide that, like Edvin, I'm going to move out when I'm eighteen. I won't be allowed to until then. When I live somewhere else — away from Vesterbro — it'll be easier for me to make contact with people like Mr. Krogh. While we're drinking coffee, I glance through the newspaper a bit. It says that Van der Lubbe has been executed and that Dimitroff made a complete fool of Göring at the trial. I turn to the obituaries, but don't find Mr. Krogh's name among the dead. It strikes me that it was as if he lost interest in me when Hitler came to power; again my little ship trembles with a vague fear of being tipped over.

6

I HAVE TO BE AT WORK AT SEVEN O'CLOCK IN THE MORNING and, with Mr. Jensen, I clean the rooms and put them in order before the office personnel and the director arrive. Mr. Jensen is sixteen years old, tall and thin and silly. He blows up condoms and lets them fly around over my head while I'm washing the floor, and he tries to kiss me so that, laughing, I have to defend myself with the rag in one hand. He's just a boy, and I'm not offended by his coarseness. In the director's office, he sits in the chair with his feet up on the desk and a cigarette between his lips. "Don't I look like him?" he asks, twisting his long bangs around his fingers. He says that I'm prudish because I'm a virgin and because I won't kiss him. "If you were in love with me," I say, "then I would." He insists that he is, but I don't believe him. One morning when I'm in the process of washing the floor in the director's office, the director suddenly comes through the door and, as I feverishly gather up the scrub brushes and bucket, he takes hold of me from behind and grabs my breasts with both hands. He does it rather like the way my mother touches the meat at the butcher's, and I turn red with shame and outrage and slip past him with the bucket and scrub brushes without saying a word. I tell Mr. Jensen about it and he says I should have slapped his fingers because he always goes to bed with the female employees, and I shouldn't put up with that. He's married and has lots of children because he's a Catholic. But afterwards I don't feel very bad about it. He is the first man who has shown interest in my body, and I've gotten it into my head that without that, I will never get ahead in the world. When the two office secretaries and the stock room supervisor arrive, the orders have to be taken care of. It's my job to pack the goods at the long counter in the stock room. Thermometers, absorbent cotton, vaginal syringes, hot-water bottles, condoms, trusses. Mr. Jensen has carefully explained what everything is used for, and sex seems to me extremely complicated and not very appealing. One thing is for before and one thing is for afterwards; during Mr. Jensen's explanations, which certainly don't present it very simply, I feel quite inadequate. The stock room supervisor is named Mr. Ottosen, and the pretty secretaries are openly in love with him. When they stand at the counter with their papers, explaining something to him, he slips his arm around their waists, and they lean toward him, starry-eyed. Two pretty, chic young girls with tiny curls all over their heads, high heels, and wide patent leather belts around their waists. Someday when I work in an office, I want to try to look just like them. I'll try to pay attention to what dresses I wear and how my hair looks. But I put off these exertions because they bore me. I'm wearing a brown smock that the company issued me. When I'm looking for a job, I rub my cheeks with my mother's tissue paper, and that's all I've ever done for my appearance. My hair is long, blond and straight, and I wash it with brown soap whenever I think it needs it. Mr. Krogh said that I had beautiful hair, but maybe he couldn't find anything else to praise me for. In any case, I very often stand next to Mr. Ottosen, and I've also tried leaning ever so slightly against him, but he never puts his arm around my waist or seems to notice my weak overture at all. I think about that a lot and reach the conclusion that most women exert an irresistible attraction over men — but I don't. It's both sad and strange, but it does protect me from having children too soon, like most of the girls on my street. One day Mr. Jensen asks me if I'd like to go to the movies in the evening. I say yes, because ever since I was a child I've wanted to be allowed to see a movie. My parents wouldn't let me. For once I tell the truth at home, and my mother looks very excited. She wants to know everything about Mr. Jensen, and in her mind she has me married to him at once. But I don't know what his father does or what plans he himself has for the future, so I can't satisfy her curiosity. My father is very happy that he's a member of Danish Socialist Youth (DSU) which, to his regret, Edvin won't join. "Without a doubt," he says, twisting the ends of his mustache, "a very sensible young man." So for the first time I'm sitting in a movie house next to a very scrubbed Mr. Jensen, who is wearing his confirmation suit that ends just short of his not completely clean wrist. We've hung our coats over the backs of the seats. First there's someone who plays the piano. Then the lights go out and flashing commercials flicker across the screen. When they're over and the lights go on again, I'm about to get up because I think that's all there is, but Mr. Jensen pulls me down in the seat again. "It's just starting now," he says patiently. The film is called *The Cabin Boy,* and the boy is the handsome and touching Jackie Coogan. I'm completely enchanted and forget where I am and who I'm with. I cry as if I were being beaten and mechanically accept the handkerchief Mr. Jensen puts into my hand. When he puts his hand on my knee, I push it away as if it were a dead object. With the captain, the cabin boy goes down with the ship, sacrificing his life for a beautiful, violently sobbing woman and her little girl. I bawl loudly and can't stop when the lights go on. "Shh . . . ," says Mr. Jensen embarrassed, taking me by the

128

arm as we go out. "Why aren't you crying?" I ask. "Don't you think it was sad?" "Yes, I do," says Mr. Jensen, "but to come right out and cry at the movies!" We walk down Søndre Boulevard and Mr. Jensen laces his fingers through mine. I give him a sidelong glance and discover that he has long eyelashes. Maybe he really is in love with me. The snow creaks under our feet and the sky is bright with stars. His arm shakes a little, but that could be from the cold. Home in the dark doorway, he embraces me and kisses me. I don't resist, but it doesn't make me feel anything. His lips are cold and hard as leather. "Why don't we use our first names?" he asks in a hoarse voice. "OK," I say, "what's your name?" His name is Erling, and we agree to still use our last names at work.

Whenever there's nothing to do in the stock room in the afternoon, I'm sent up to the attic to put lead boxes in order in long rows. I like the work because I'm all alone in the dark and dusty room. I lie on the floor and place the boxes in even rows according to what it says on them: zinc salve, lanolin. I sink into a sweet melancholy and rhythmic waves of words stream through me again. I write them down on brown wrapping paper and conclude sorrowfully that the poems are still not good enough. "Children's poems," said Mr. Krogh. He also said, "In order to write a good poem, you have to have experienced an awful lot." I think that I have, but maybe I'll experience even more. But one day I write something that is different from anything I've written before, only I don't know what the difference is. I write the following:

> There burns a candle in the night,
> it burns for me alone,
> and if I blow at it,

it flames up,
and flames for me alone.
But if you breathe softly
and if you breathe quietly,
the candle is suddenly more than bright
and burns deep in my own breast,
for you alone.

I think it's a real poem, and the pain at Mr. Krogh's disappearance springs up again, because I want so much to show it to him. I want so much to tell him that now I understand what he meant. But for me he's just as dead as the old editor, and I can't find any new wedge into the world that is moved by poems and, I hope, by people who write them. "You were gone a long time," says Erling when I come downstairs. He acts the whole time as if we are going steady. He's standing there packing a douche bag (it's used afterwards, he has explained to me), and says, as he bends the red tubes under the monstrosity, "Why don't we sleep together at a hotel on Saturday? I've saved up for it." "No," I say, because if I can write real poems now, it doesn't matter that I'm a virgin. On the contrary, I may have use for it when I meet the right man. "God Almighty," says Erling irritated, "are you saving it for the coroner?" "Yes," I say, laughing so I can hardly stop. I don't really know myself what virginity and poems have to do with each other, so how could I explain the strange connection to Erling?

7

Every Saturday evening, Erling and I go to the movies. He waits for me, leaning against the wall of the front building, his hands buried in the pockets of his father's coat, which he inherited just like I've inherited my brother's. If I keep him waiting too long, he chews on matches and twists his hair in his fingers. As we go out through the doorway, my mother opens the window and yells, "Good-bye, Tove." That means she approves of the relationship, and Erling takes it to mean that too. He asks me whether he's going to meet my parents soon. "No," I say, "not yet." My mother asks whether Erling has a clubfoot or a harelip, since they aren't allowed to meet him. I don't want to visit Erling's parents, either, because then they'll think that we're engaged. It would be both easier and more fun for me if I had a girlfriend, but I don't anymore; so Erling is better than nothing. I like him a lot because he's also a little strange, and he's like me in many ways. His father is a laborer and often unemployed. He has a grownup sister who is married. He himself wants to be a schoolteacher, but he can't get into the teacher's college until he's eighteen. He's saving money for it. He says that it's outrageous that they use unorganized labor in the company, but if he joins the union, he'll be thrown out. He earns twentyfive kroner a week. I pay for myself when we go to the movies, both because he can't really afford to pay for the two of us, and because 1 think it makes me more independent. All of these evenings proceed in the same way. When the movie is over, he walks me home, and inside the dark doorway, he embraces and kisses me. I observe him with a certain cold curiosity, wanting to see how excited I can make him. If I were in love with him, I would be passionate too, but I'm not, and he knows it. At a certain moment I loosen his cold hands from around my neck and say, "No, don't do that." "Oh yes," he whispers breathlessly, "it doesn't hurt at all." "No," I say, "but I don't want to." I feel sorry for him and kiss his leathery lips before I go. He asks me when I will want to, and just for something to say, I promise to do it when I turn eighteen, because that's still such a terribly long way off. I also feel a little sorry for myself because his embraces don't make the slightest chord in me sing. I wonder whether I'm abnormal in that way too. "Damned great," Ruth had said, and she was only thirteen. All of the girls in the trash-can corner said the same thing, but maybe they were lying. Maybe it was just something that they said. "When do we get to meet your sweetheart?" says my mother upstairs in the living room. "When I met your father, I invited him home right away." She also says that he's obviously only out after one thing, and if I let him have his way, he won't want anything more to do with me. "And you can't come back here with a kid," she says. One evening I say that she wasn't nearly so eager for Edvin to bring his girlfriend home, and she says sharply that it's totally different with a boy. There's no rush, and a man can always get married, but a girl has to be supported and she always has to think of that. My father says that she should stop pestering me. He says that it's smart of Erling to want to be a schoolteacher because they make good money and are never unemployed. "White-collar workers," says my brother, who fortunately has found work again, "and they're the worst kind." My brother is annoyed that I've got a boyfriend because he's always teased me that I'd never get married. He is listening to the news on the radio about Crown Prince Frederik's wedding, which greatly interests my mother. "Turn off all that royalty junk," says my father from deep in the sofa. "Now we have one more mouth to feed, that's all." At work, the office secretaries are completely ecstatic over the enchanting Crown Princess Ingrid. They take up one of their usual collections and trip through the stock room with a long list on which they write down what everyone donates for a bouquet for the royal house. I've given a krone, and a few days ago I gave a krone for the director's daughter's confirmation. He has so many children that there are constantly collections for their christenings or birthdays. "Before you know it," says Erling, "your whole salary is used up for that nonsense." Erling is a Social Democrat like my father and my brother, and he dreams of a revolution that will lift the masses. I like to hear him develop this plan, because it would further my own personal interests if the poor came to power. Erling wants to change the social democracy and make it more red. "Actually," he says, "I'm a syndicalist." I don't ask him what that is because then I'll get a long, incomprehensible speech about politics. Once he takes me along to a meeting at Blågårds Plads, but things get violent and the police take out their nightsticks and break up the brawling factions. "Down with the cops," yells Erling, who is in his DSU uniform, and immediately he gets a bop on the head that makes him give out a howl. Terrified, I grab him by the arm, and hand in hand we run down the street that echoes with the fleeing steps of the crowd. That's not for me and I never do it again. At work, besides us, there are two laborers and a driver. We all eat lunch together in a little room behind the stock room. It's not heated and that too, says Erling, is outrageous. As a rule, we all sit with our coats on. We sit on upside-down beer crates, and I get along well with this little group of people. I'm not shy with them — not even when they ask me, for example, if I really know what a truss or a vaginal syringe is used for. But I tell them that they should join the union, and one day when I'm in a light-hearted mood, I climb up on one of the beer crates and imitate Stauning when he speaks: "Comrades!" I stroke my invisible beard and drop my voice to a low pitch, and my audience is very appreciative. They laugh and clap, and then I forget all about it. A little later, Mr. Ottosen comes in and says that the director wants to speak to me. I haven't been alone with him since that day he grabbed my breasts, and I'm afraid that he wants something like that from me. "Sit down," he says curtly, pointing to a chair. I sit down on the very edge and, to my horror, I see that his face is dark with anger. "We can't use you here," he says hotly. "I won't have Bolsheviks in my company." "No," I say, not knowing what Bolsheviks are. He pounds the desk, so I jump. Then he gets up and comes over to my chair and sticks his red face right down into mine. I turn my head away a little because he has bad breath. "You've urged my people to join the union," he yells, "but do you have any idea what would happen then?" "No," I whisper, even though I really do know. "They'd be fired," he roars and again pounds his hand on the desk, "just like I'm firing you now — without a reference! You can pick up your check at the front office." He straightens up and goes back to his place. I feel like I ought to burst into tears, but instead I'm filled with a dark joy that I can't define. This man regards me as dangerous, as significant in an area I know nothing about. "There's nothing to laugh about," he yells, so I must have been sitting there smiling. "Get out!" He points to the door and

I hurry to get out. "I never want to see you again," he screams after me and slams the door. Over in the stock room Mr. Ottosen and Erling are standing looking astonished. They ask me what in the world is the matter and I tell them proudly. Mr. Ottosen shrugs his shoulders. "You're young," he says, "and badly paid, so you can easily find some other work to do. And you just have yourself, of course. I have a wife and four children, so I'll keep my mouth shut." Erling says that I should have kept my opinions to myself, and I get furious with him. "There'll never be a revolution here in Denmark," I say hotly, "as long as there are people like you that won't risk their own neck." Then, indignantly, I go in to the secretaries and ask for my check, which is already waiting for me. The snow is piled high in the streets as I go home and an ice-cold wind whistles right through my coat. I've suffered for what I believe in, and I'm eager to tell my father about it. I feel like a Joan of Arc, a Charlotte Corday, a young woman who will inscribe her name in the history of the world. The poetry writing is going too slowly anyway. With straight back and head held high, I go up the stairs, and full of wounded dignity I step into the living room, where my father lies sleeping with his backside to the world. My mother asks me why I'm home already and when I tell her, she says that I shouldn't get involved in things that don't concern me. She says furiously that it was a good position and that no man will marry a girl who is constantly changing jobs. This time she doesn't back me up, and I clear my throat loudly and make a bit of racket at the table so my father will wake up. And he does. When he sits up, rubbing his eyes, my mother says, "Tove was thrown out. It's because of all your blabber about unions that she's gotten into her head." When my father hears the details, his face takes on a furious expression. "Who the hell do you think you are," he yells, pounding his fist on the table so that the light fixture dances on its hooks. "Here you've finally gotten a decent job and then you're thrown out for such foolishness. You don't know anything about politics. These are bad times and there are so many scabs that you could feed the pigs with them. But the next job you get you'll have to keep or else you'll be just like your mother." They glare angrily at each other like they always do when there's trouble with Edvin or me. I keep quiet and really don't know what I had expected. But in the space of a few minutes, I've lost my suddenly awakened interest in politics, in red banners and revolutions. Erling and I go to the movies a few more Saturdays — then he stops leaning against the wall waiting for me. I miss him a little, because he made me less lonely, and I especially miss the attic with the lead boxes, where I wrote my first real poem. "What's become of your young man?" asks my mother, who had dreamed of being mother-in-law to a schoolteacher. "He found someone else," I say. My mother has to have very concrete reasons for everything. She says, "You should take more trouble with your appearance. You should buy a spring suit instead of that bicycle. When you're not naturally pretty," she says, "you have to help things out a bit." My mother doesn't say such things to hurt me; she's just completely ignorant of what goes on inside other people.

8

"CAN YOU TELL WHO I LOOK LIKE?" MISS LØNGREN IS
staring at me with her bulging eyes, and I really can't see
who she resembles. She smiles, raising and lowering her
eyebrows. Maybe she looks a little like Chaplin, but I don't
dare say that, since she's easily insulted. Now she's already
frowning impatiently. "Don't you ever go to the movies,
young lady?" she says. "Yes, I do," I say miserably and
wrack my brain in vain. "In profile, then," she says, turning her head. "Now you can see it. Everyone says so." Her
profile doesn't tell me anything either other than that she
has a crooked nose and a weak chin. In the middle of my
ordeal, the phone rings. She takes it and says, "I. P.
Jensen." She always says it in a high, threatening tone, so I
don't understand how the person on the other end dares
state their business. It's an order, and she writes it down,
holding the receiver at her right ear with her left hand. After
she has hung up, she says, "Greta Garbo—now you can
see, can't you?" "Oh yes," I say, wishing I had someone to
laugh with. But I don't. In a strange way, I'm all alone here.
I'm employed in the office of a lithographer's shop. In the
innermost room resides the owner, who is called Master.
Whenever he's in, his door is always closed. In the front
office there are two desks. Carl Jensen, one of the sons, sits
at one of them with his back to Miss Løngren's chair. She
sits across from me by the telephone and the switchboard,
and at the end of our desk there's a little table with a typewriter, which I'm supposed to learn to use. But all day long

I have practically nothing to do, and no one seems to know why I was hired. There is an apartment upstairs above the offices, and this is where the other son, Sven Åge, lives. He is a lithographer and works across the courtyard in the print shop. Carl Jensen is thin and quick in his movements like a squirrel. He has brown, close-set eyes that are slightly crossed, which gives him a shifty appearance. He never speaks to me, and when he and Miss Løngren are both there, they act as if I were invisible. They flirt a lot with each other, and sometimes Carl Jensen turns in his chair, which can spin all the way around, and tries to kiss Miss Løngren. She swats at him and laughs loudly, flattered; I think it looks ridiculous because they're so old. Whenever Master goes through the office, they bend low over their work, and I quickly write down some figures or words that I afterwards slowly and carefully erase. Carl Jensen is not there very often, and I feel Miss Løngren's peering and attentive glance constantly resting on me. She comments on every move I make. "Why are you always looking at the clock?" she says. "It won't make the time go any faster." She says, "Don't you have a handkerchief? That sniffing is getting on my nerves." Or, "Why is it always me who has to get up to close the door? You're young, too." The word "too" astonishes me. One day she asks me how old I think she is. "Forty," I say cautiously, because I'm certain that she's at least fifty. "I'm thirty-five," she says, insulted, "and people even say that I look younger than that." Whenever I make an effort to be completely still and rest my gaze on a neutral spot, she says, "Are you falling asleep? You've got to do *some* work for those fifty kroner that you get a month." I happen to yawn, and she asks me with her manly voice whether I ever sleep at night. All day long I have to listen to these remarks and when I get home in the evening, I'm just as tired as when I was working at the pension. But I was the one who wanted to work in an office and I have to stay until I'm eighteen, even though it's a shocking thought. I enter the work orders in a book and I'm finished with that in an hour. Miss Løngren doesn't like me to practice on the typewriter because it makes such a racket. One day Master asks her timidly whether I could take care of the switchboard, and she says angrily that she doesn't want to sit with her back to the customers. Behind me there's a counter where the walk-in business takes place. Master seems to be just as afraid of her as I am. He's a heavy little man with a blue, spongy nose, which Miss Løngren says he didn't get for nothing. Whenever she has to find him, she always calls Grøften restaurant in Tivoli, which seems to be his permanent abode when he's not in his office. Once in a while he calls me in and gives me some slips of paper that I have to type up for him. They're letters and they all start with "Dear brother" and are signed "With fraternal greetings." Sometimes they're about a brother who's passed away, and as I write about all of his magnificent qualities, especially in relation to the brothers, I can be quite moved, and I think there's a rare and beautiful closeness in that family. But one day when I venture to ask Miss Løngren how many brothers Master has, she breaks into loud laughter and says, "They're his lodge brothers, all of them. He's a member of the Order of Saint George." Afterwards, she tells the son about it and he turns his chair all the way around to see what such an idiot looks like. Every Friday evening I go around the print shop and hand out the pay envelopes. It's something of an ordeal because the workers make witty or fresh remarks to me, and I can't find a response right off the top of my head. I'm not one of them like in the nursing supply company. This job, my father says, is the best one I've had and I have

139

no excuse for not staying there. Everyone is in the union — I am too. Master pays the dues, and I'm supposed to go to shorthand class, which Master will pay for too. I don't know why I'm supposed to learn shorthand since I'm only allowed to write to the brothers. Miss Løngren writes the invoices and the business letters. I get the impression that she was against hiring me and now is keeping me from learning anything at all. I sit and stare at her from eight in the morning until five in the evening, and it's hard and exhausting work. I've never met such a person before. Sometimes she's friendly and asks me, for example, whether I'd like an apple. She gives it to me, but when I crunch it in my mouth, she wrinkles her brow and says, "Can't you even eat an apple without making a racket?" And if I visit the bathroom too often, she asks me whether I have indigestion. One day she says that her niece is going to be confirmed and she asks me whether I know anyone who could write a confirmation song. Just to surprise her, I say that I can, and she looks at me doubtfully. "It has to be good," she says, "like the ones you read in the kiosk display windows." I promise that it'll be good, and reluctantly she lets me try. I write the song to the required tune, "The Happy Coppersmith," and Miss Løngren is impressed. "It really is," she says, "just as good as the ones you pay money for." She shows it to the son and he says to her, "Well, I'll be damned," and "you wouldn't have thought that of Miss Ditlevsen." He turns his chair around and stares curiously at me with his shifty eyes. To me he doesn't say anything, as usual. "Yes," says Miss Løngren, "something like that is a gift." I find them both very stupid. Miss Løngren can't even speak correct Danish. For example, she says "anyways" and she says it often. Whenever she wants to give her words emphasis, she says, "I say, and I'll keep on saying, that... ," etc. But naturally she

140

doesn't keep on saying it. I have to spend two more years in this pointless way, and I find the thought almost unbearable. When I get home in the evening, Jytte is almost always there, and it wears me out listening to her and my mother talking. Jytte is big and blond and pretty, and she herself says that she'll never get married because she so quickly tires of men. She's had a long series of lovers and is always entertaining my mother with stories about the latest one. They laugh a lot about it, and here too I feel myself left out. My father snores loudly and I can't go to bed until he leaves for work and Jytte has gone over to her own apartment. But I can't understand why I can barely tolerate people or how they ought to talk so that I'll listen willingly. They should talk the way Mr. Krogh talked; when I'm walking in the street I always think that it's him turning the corner or cutting across the street. I run to catch up, but it's never him. They're in the process of putting up a new building where his once stood, and I never look in that direction when I go through the passage on my way home. I know that I could look him up in the telephone book, but my pride stops me. I didn't mean anything to him. I just amused him for a moment — then he shrugged his shoulders and turned his back. But I'm withering in this existence, and I've got to figure out something. I remember a column in the *Politiken* classified section headed "Help Wanted: Theater and Music." That would be something to do in the evening, and now I'm allowed to stay out until ten o'clock. Music is a closed realm for me, but I'd like to be an actress. In great secrecy I send in a reply to an ad looking for actors for an amateur theater. I get a letter from "Succès Theater Company," which meets in a café on Amager, where I'm told to appear on a certain evening. I dress in my brown suit which, at my mother's insistence, I bought

141

instead of the bicycle, and take the streetcar out to the restaurant. There I say hello to three serious young men and a young girl, who, like me, is there for the first time. We sit at a table and the leader says that he is thinking of putting on an amateur comedy called *Aunt Agnes*. He has the scripts with him, and after a short, appraising look, he decides that I'm to play Aunt Agnes. It is, he explains, a comic role that I'm wonderfully suited for. The woman is about seventy years old, but that can easily be taken care of with a little make-up. In the play, there's a young couple —the man will be played by himself and the girl by Miss Karstensen. I look over at the young girl and find her very beautiful. Her hair is platinum blond, her eyes deep blue, and her teeth white and perfect. I can easily see that I couldn't play her part. Still, I hadn't imagined my debut as a comic woman of seventy. When the roles are handed out and we've been ordered to meet again after we've learned them, we drink a cup of coffee and part. Miss Karstensen and I walk together to the streetcar. She asks if she may call me by my first name. Her name is Nina and she lives in Nørrebro. I ask her why she answered the ad. "Because I was dying of boredom," she says. She sways her hips a little as she walks, and I already feel happy in her company. Nina is eighteen and I'm sure that we're going to be friends.

9

THE LEADER OF OUR THEATER COMPANY IS CALLED GAM-meltorv. He is twenty-two and has a wife and child. We rehearse at his house, and his wife is mad because the noise wakes up the baby. "She doesn't have any feeling for art," says Gammeltorv apologetically. But *he* does. When he directs us, he uses his head and arms and legs like famous conductors. He rages and yells at us and begs us, practically in tears, to put more soul into the lines and to throw ourselves totally into the roles. Aunt Agnes is a very silly and gullible person, constantly being made a fool of by the young couple; that's the comic part of the play, because the lines themselves are not funny. They are few and brief. The climax occurs when the woman comes into the living room with a tea tray in her hands. When she sees that the couple is sitting in a tight embrace on a love seat, she drops the tray, claps her hands, and says, "God save us all!" When she says that, the hall is supposed to roar with laughter, says Gammeltorv, and I'm saying the words as if I were reading them out of a book! "Over again!" he roars, "over again!" At last I succeed in putting enough astonishment into the lines, and he says that it will work when there are real cups on the tray. These his wife refuses to supply for me. At home in our living room, I act out Aunt Agnes for my mother, who is very enthusiastic. "Maybe," she says, "you'll be a real actress. It's a shame that you can't sing." Nina can — she has to trill a love-song duet with Gammel-torv, and in my opinion she does it very beautifully. The

143

play is going to be performed in Stjernekroen on Amager, and Gammeltorv thinks there will be a full house because there's a dance afterwards. Nina and I are really looking forward to it. Nina is from Korsør, and her fiancé, who is a forester, lives there. He's coming to the opening. Nina works at Berlingske Tidende in the classified ad department, and she lives in a rented room in Nørrebro. It's a depressing and unheated room, where we sit on the edge of the bed with our coats on and confide our future plans to each other while we can hear the fire roaring in the family's stove on the other side of the thin wall. Some day Nina will marry her forester, because she wants to live her life in the country, but until that time she wants to have fun and enjoy her youth in Copenhagen. She says that when we're not so busy with the play anymore, we'll go to taverns and find someone to dance with. A girl can't sit in a pub alone, but when there are two, it's OK. I remember Mr. Krogh's remark that people always want to use each other for something, and I'm glad that Nina has some use for me. Since I've met her, I don't think about Ruth as often. For that matter, she and her parents have moved away, so I never see her anymore when I come home in the evening. Nina grew up with her grandmother, who owns a hotel in Korsør. Her mother lives in Copenhagen with a man she's not married to. She is poor and cleans house for people; Nina says that some evening I should come home with her to meet her. My mother has no desire to meet Nina. "Why does she live in Copenhagen," she says, "when her fiancé is in Korsør? Your girlfriends are always a bad influence." At the office, Miss Løngren says sternly, "You've been looking so happy lately. Has something nice happened at home?" I deny it, terrified, and try to look less glad. I'm taking a course in shorthand on Vester Voldgade, and it's lots of fun. Sometimes I think exclusively in shorthand symbols. One evening when I leave the office for home, Edvin is standing outside, looking very happy. As we walk home together, he tells me that soon he's going to marry a young girl whose name is Grete and who is from Vordingborg. They're going to be married in secret, and they've already found an apartment in Sydhavnen. I'm filled with a dark jealousy and have trouble sharing his enthusiasm. My mother and father are not to know until the wedding is over. "They'll be furious," I say, and feel a little sorry for them. "You know Mother," he just says, "she freezes my girls out." I tell him that on that point I'll have it easier, because my mother was delighted with Erling, even though she never got to meet him. He says that's the way it is most places, and there's nothing very strange about it. He asks how it's going with my poems and whether I will try another editor. "They can't all die, you know." I say that I've gradually begun to write better poems, but until I can do it well enough, I don't want to try again. But Edvin thinks that the children's poems are just as good as the ones you read in schoolbooks and newspapers, and I can't explain the indefinable difference between a good and a bad poem, because I've just recently found out myself. We stand there talking in front of the doorway at home for a little while as we stamp our feet to keep warm. Edvin doesn't want to come up with me because then my mother will suspect that we walked home together and she doesn't like us to have anything together that she's not part of. He hasn't gotten over his old grudge against my father for the four hard apprentice years, either. "He's the one I can thank for my cough," he says bitterly and a little unjustly. Edvin is twenty years old now, and around his jaw the skin is dark after shaving. His black curls fall over his forehead, and his brown eyes resemble my father's and Mr. Krogh's.

Some day I'll marry a man with brown eyes. Then maybe my children will have them too; I think I'll have the first one when I'm eighteen. Nina is completely horrified that I still have my virginity, and she thinks it's a defect that should be remedied as soon as possible. She says she was afraid too, because you hear so many things, but in reality it was wonderful. Nina has bought a long, slinky silk dress for the dance at Stjernekroen. It's cut low in the back, and she bought it on credit. It cost two hundred kroner, and I can't understand how she's ever going to pay for it. She laughs and says that of course she wasn't crazy enough to give her real name. I'm impressed — as always when someone dares to do something I don't. Over at Stjernekroen we're busy getting dressed and putting on make-up. I'm wearing Gammeltorv's grandmother's black dress. It reaches to the floor and underneath I have a pillow bound around my stomach. On my head I have a wig made of gray yarn, and Gammeltorv has drawn black lines on my face. They're supposed to be wrinkles. I have to walk bent over like a jackknife because I'm plagued by rheumatism in various places. We peek out through a hole in the curtain. We look down at our families and count to see if they're all there yet. They fill only the first three or four rows, and the rest of the hall is almost empty except for a few young people who are sitting, yawning, totally uninterested because they've only come for the sake of the dance. Nina shows me her forester, who is sitting right behind Aunt Rosalia. He looks like he's aloof from it all, but then Nina has told me that he's very much against her living in Copenhagen. "What's he mad about?" asks Gammeltorv, who's looking with us. Then the band strikes up and the curtain lifts. My heart pounds violently from excitement, and I'm not sure that my Aunt Agnes will make anyone laugh. But it's an unusually receptive audience. They clap and enjoy themselves, and after every act Gammeltorv says that it can't help but be a success; have we seen that man writing on a notepad? That's a reporter from *Amagerbladet* and he's obviously been sent over because it's a big event. Finally the moment comes when, with the tray in my hands, I surprise the young folks on the love seat. I drop the tray, clap my hands, and cry out, "God save us all!" At the same moment, a door is opened behind the stage entrance and the wig blows off my head. Horrified, I want to pick it up, but Gammeltorv shakes his head from the sofa because a hearty laughter swells up toward me from the hall. Laughter and clapping and stamping on the floor. Only Nina sends me an offended look because isn't *she* the star? When the curtain falls, Gammeltorv takes both my hands. "You've saved the whole show," he says, "you'll have the leading role in the next play." My family praises me too, and Edvin says that I have talent. He thinks he does too, but he's never had a chance. He dances with me a lot, and I'm grateful to him for that. He dances well, and Nina gives him a sidelong glance as she dances past with her forester. He's shorter than her and in general doesn't look like much. Edvin also dances with my mother and with both aunts, and at twelve o'clock my mother says that we have to go home, so I have to leave my friends. The next time we meet at the café on Strandlodsvej, Gammeltorv shows me a clipping from *Amagerbladet*, where, among other things, it says, "A quite young girl, Tove Ditlefsen, was a great success as Aunt Agnes." Even though my name is misspelled, it's a strange feeling to see it in print for the first time. "And here," says the enterprising Gammeltorv, "are the scripts for the new play, *Trilby*. Trilby is a poor little girl who's in a magician's power. He forces her to sing and she sings beautifully." "And who," says Nina coolly, "is going to

147

play Trilby?" "Tove is," he says, "and since she can't sing, she just has to open and close her mouth. Then you stand in the wings and sing." Nina gets red in the face with anger. She takes her purse and gets up. "I won't have any part of it," she says. "You can sing yourself while she opens and shuts her mouth. I've had enough." I stare at her, horror-stricken. "I don't want any part of it, either," I say. "Nina is prettier than I am. So why should I play Trilby?" Suddenly we're all standing up. Gammeltorv pounds the table. "Is it your theater company or mine?" he yells. "Ha," snorts Nina, "Succès Theater Company! Any idiot can put an ad in a newspaper and pretend that he's somebody. I'm leaving!" "Me too," I yell, and rush out on her heels. I have to run to catch up with her. Suddenly we stand still, as if by mutual agreement. We're standing between two lampposts and the road is completely empty of people. There's a touch of spring in the air. Nina's narrow face wreathed with the fine halo of hair is still dark with anger, but suddenly she breaks into laughter and I do the same. "So you were supposed to be the star," she laughs. "Oh, how funny." We imagine how I was supposed to stand, opening and shutting my mouth without a sound coming over my lips while Nina sang with full voice, hidden from the audience. We laugh so we can hardly stop, and we agree that neither of us has talent for the theater. We'll have fun ourselves instead of entertaining others. We'll cut loose in the big, exciting city and find some young men we can fall in love with. Some young men who are nice to look at and who have money in their pockets. Now that we're not going to spend any more evenings with the idiotic rehearsals for *Aunt Agnes*, we have lots of time. The only tiresome thing about it is that I have to be home at ten o'clock, but for the time being there's nothing to be done about that.

10

Aunt Rosalia is in the hospital. One day when my mother went out to visit her, Aunt Rosalia said, laughing, "I'm young again, Alfrida." My mother said that she should go to the doctor, but my aunt wouldn't. Like my mother, she only goes to the doctor under dire circumstances. My mother told me about it in the evening when I came home from the office. I didn't understand what the mysterious remark meant, but my mother explained that my aunt had started to bleed after it had stopped many years ago. Although my mother has never informed me about anything regarding those matters, she always assumes that I know all about it. But there were obviously gaps in the trash-can corner's sex education. It took my mother a long time to persuade my aunt to go to a doctor, and when she finally did, he put her in the hospital at once. Now she's going to have an operation, and she talks about it as if it were a picnic. "It's cancer," says my mother gloomily. "First her husband — now her. And just when she was going to have some good years, now that she's gotten rid of that beast." My mother is sincerely worried and unhappy about it, because she's much more fond of Aunt Rosalia than of Aunt Agnete. I visit her with my mother the day before the operation. She's lying there eating oranges and talking cheerfully with the other patients in the ward. I can't believe that my mother is right, because she doesn't look sick and she's not in pain. But when we've said good-bye and come out into the hallway, a nurse comes over and asks my mother who

149

my aunt's nearest relatives are. When she hears that we are, she asks my mother to come in and talk to the doctor. In the meantime, I wait outside on a bench. My mother comes back with red eyes. She blows her nose loudly and leans on my arm as we leave. "I thought so," she sniffs. "I was right. They don't know whether she'll survive the operation." On the way to the office, I call Nina and say that I can't come over to her house that evening. I don't feel that I can leave my mother, and Jytte is no help when you're feeling bad about something. At the office, Miss Løngren says suspiciously, "Well, so how was your aunt?" "She has cancer," I say solemnly, "and she might die." "Well, well," says Miss Løngren callously, "we're all going to die, you know. Get to work now. Here are some letters." I type letters to the brothers, and I've taken them in shorthand myself from Master's dictation. Carl Jensen comes in from the print shop and sits down in his revolving chair. He's wearing a gray smock and has a yellow pencil behind his ear. As far as I can see, he never does any work, but with Miss Løngren he doesn't have to pretend to do any, either. I can see that there's something he wants to say to her and that my presence is embarrassing him, but I calmly keep tapping at the typewriter, and I'm beginning to get faster at it. "Løngren," he says, leaning back so his face is close to hers, "Sven Åge has his silver wedding anniversary in two weeks. Do you think it'd be possible to get someone to write a song for him?" His shifty eyes pass over me for a moment, but I don't look up. "Oh God, yes," says Miss Løngren, "Miss Ditlevsen could, couldn't you?" The last words come loudly and shrilly and I don't dare pretend that I didn't hear them. "Yes," I say, addressing myself to Miss Løngren, "sure I can." "Sure she can," she says to Carl Jensen. "She just needs some information, you know. What's happened through the years, things like that." "She'll have it," says Carl Jensen, relieved. "I'll bring it tomorrow." I look at him sideways and suddenly I realize that it's a strange form of shyness that makes him unable to speak to me directly. That makes it less uncomfortable and puts the problem on his shoulders. The next day, I write the song while people walk past outside in the sunshine — independent people who can move about freely in the world between nine and five and who all have some personal goal that they've determined themselves. I write the ridiculous song while my aunt is being operated on and no one knows whether she'll survive. The telephone rings and Miss Løngren hands the receiver to me looking as if it's burning her fingers. "It's for you," she says sternly. "It's a young woman." Bright red in the face, I go around the desk and take the telephone as I stand close to Carl Jensen and Miss Løngren, who are completely silent. It's Nina, and I've forbidden her to call me. "Hi," she says. "Just listen — I met a really sweet guy yesterday in the Heidelberg. He has a friend who's cute too. Tall, dark, and everything. You'll like him. I promised that we'd be there tonight. Then they'll both be there." "No," I say in a low voice, "I can't tonight. I have to be home." "Why?" she asks and, embarrassed, I whisper that I'll tell her some other time. I'm busy now. Nina is insulted and says that I'm strange. When she's finally found a young man for me, and I don't want to meet him. "I've got to go," I say. "I'm busy. Good-bye." Fumbling, I put down the receiver. "Thank you," I mumble, and go back to my place. "Was that your girlfriend?" asks Miss Løngren after a long and oppressive silence. When I answer affirmatively, she says, "She sounded rather frivolous. At your age, you have to be careful about the kind of girlfriends you have." "That's true," says Carl Jensen, adding philosophically, "In some ways, it's better to have a boyfriend — at least you know what's going on." I keep working on the song, annoyed that there's nothing that rhymes with Sven Åge. Boa, Noah, protozoa, Balboa. Sven Åge is just as silent as his brother is talkative. He's fat like his father and his head is always tilted slightly, as if one neck muscle were too short. It gives him an endearing look. The brothers practically don't talk to each other at all because Sven Åge lives upstairs free of charge while Carl Jensen has to pay rent himself somewhere else. Furthermore, Sven Åge, as the oldest, is going to take over the press when Master dies. "Sad," says Miss Løngren sentimentally, "that blood ties aren't stronger." When I'm through with the song, I type it up on the typewriter, and when Master suddenly appears, I tear it out and stuff it away in the drawer because I'm not getting paid to write poetry for special occasions. When the product is done, I give it to Miss Løngren, and she's almost more enthusiastic than the time before. She stares at me as if I were a new Shakespeare and says, "It's amazing — look here, Carl Jensen." He takes the song and reads through it and agrees with her and stares at me for a long time without saying a word. Then he says to Miss Løngren, "I wonder where she gets it from?" "It's a gift," determines Miss Løngren, "a gift you're born with. I had an uncle who could do it, too. But it wore him out. It was as if all strength left him when he was done with a song. It's the same with mediums — they're completely exhausted by it, too. Aren't you tired, Miss Ditlevsen?" No, I'm not tired and my strength hasn't left me. But I want so badly to have a place where I can practice writing real poems. I'd like to have a room with four walls and a closed door. A room with a bed, a table and a chair, with a typewriter, or a pad of paper and a pencil, nothing more. Well, yes — a door I could lock. All

152

of this I can't have until I'm eighteen and can move away from home. The attic with the lead boxes was the last place where I had peace. That and my childhood windowsill. I walk home, caressed by the soft May air. Now it stays light for a long time in the evening and I'm not cold in my brown suit. The jacket just reaches my waist and the skirt is pleated. I have a pleasant feeling of being well dressed when I wear it. Nina says I should have a bigger wardrobe, but I don't have any money. I pay twenty kroner a month at home now that I get all my meals there; ten kroner goes in the bank; and then there's twenty kroner left, a little less when medical insurance is paid for. Most of it I use for candy, because it's an inner battle to pass unscathed by a chocolate store. I also need money for the soda pop that I drink when I go to dance halls with Nina. The young men who might pay for it unfortunately don't show up until ten o'clock, when I have to say good-bye to the joys of nightlife. I think a little bit about what kind of young man Nina had chosen for me, and regret that I didn't get to meet him. But if my aunt is dead, I can't let my mother be alone. I always peek into baby buggies when I walk home, because I love to look at the little children who are lying asleep with up-stretched hands on a ruffled pillowcase. I also like to look at people who in one way or another give expression to their feelings. I like to look at mothers caressing their children, and I willingly go a little out of my way in order to follow a young couple who are walking hand in hand and are openly in love. It gives me a wistful feeling of happiness and an indefinable hope for the future. Up in the living room my mother is sitting waiting for me. She's very pale and she has recently been crying. I'm fond of my mother, too, whenever she's prey to a simple and sincere emotion. "She didn't die," she says solemnly, "but the doctor said that it's only a

153

reprieve. The important thing now is that she doesn't find out what's wrong with her. Don't ever tell her." "I won't," I say. My mother goes out to make coffee, and I look at my sleeping father's back. Suddenly I see that he is aged and tired. There's nothing definite to point to, it's just an impression that I get. My father is fifty-five years old, and I've never known him as young. My mother was first young, and then youthful, and she's still standing at that shaky stage. She lies without compunction that she's a couple of years younger, even to us, who know very well how old she is. She still gets her hair dyed and goes to the steambath once a week; these exertions fill me with a kind of compassion because they're an expression of a fear in her that I don't understand. I just observe it. When she puts the cups on the table, my father wakes up, rubs his eyes, and sits up. "Have you told her?" he says grimly. "No," says my mother calmly, "you can do it." "We've gotten a new apartment," he says bitterly, "over on Westend. It costs sixty kroner a month and I don't know where the money's going to come from when I'm unemployed again." "Nonsense," says my mother harshly. "Tove pays twenty, you know." I'm horrified, because they shouldn't plan their future around my contribution. They shouldn't count on me in any way when they make plans behind my back. I ask them why they haven't told me before, and my mother says that they wanted to surprise me. There are three rooms and I'm to have one of them. And it looks out on the street so you can see what's going on. I feel a little happy after all, because I've always dreamed of having my own room. "What the hell," snaps my father, "is she going to do in that room? Sit and bite her fingernails or pick her nose? Huh?" I get mad because he doesn't know anything about his own children. And whenever I get mad I always say something that I

154

regret. "I want to read," I say, "and write." He asks what in hell I want to write. "Poems," I yell. "I've written lots of poems and once there was an editor who said they were excellent." "There, you see," says my father, rubbing his face with his big hand, "she's crazy, too. Did you know that she was fooling around with things like that?" "No," says my mother curtly, "but that's her own business. If she wants to write, it's clear that she has to have her own room." In offended silence, my father takes his lunchbox and puts on his jacket to go to work. When he puts on his cap, he stands there a little, looking uncomfortable. "Tove," he says with a tender voice, "can I see your... uh... poems sometime? I know something about that kind of thing." My anger disappears completely. "Yes, you can," I say and he nods at me awkwardly before he leaves. My father can regret and repent — an ability that my mother doesn't possess. When he's left, she tells me about the new apartment that we're going to move into on the first. "Three enormous rooms," she says, "that are almost like ballrooms. It'll be nice to get away from this proletarian neighborhood." When she's gone into the bedroom, I look around at our little living room. I look at the old dusty puppet theater that we were once so happy with when my father made it. It will probably not survive a move. I look at the wallpaper that bears various spots, many of whose origins I remember. I look at the sailor's wife on the wall, at the brass coffee service on the buffet, at the door handle that broke one time when my mother slammed the door after her and that has never been repaired. I look out the window over at the courtyard with the gas pump and the gypsy wagon. I look at all this, which has remained unchanged, and I realize that I detest changes. It's difficult to keep a grasp on yourself when things around you change.

155

II

Summer is over and fall has come. The wildly colored leaves blow through the streets, and it's cold for me to go out in the brown suit. Since Edvin's made-over coat doesn't fit me anymore, I buy a coat on credit. It's totally against my father's advice. He says that you should pay everyone their due and make sure that you don't owe anyone anything, because otherwise you'll end up in Sundholm. We live on Westend now, on the ground floor, in number 32. My room is called the parlor whenever I don't take outright possession of it, and it's only separated from the dining room by a flowered cotton curtain. There's a table with crooked legs, two leather armchairs, and a leather sofa — all bought used and quite worn. I sleep on the sofa at night and its curved back makes it impossible for me to stretch out completely. "Then maybe you won't grow much more," says my mother hopefully. I myself often wonder how tall a person can continue to grow, but with me it doesn't seem to have any end. I'll soon be seventeen and I'm earning sixty kroner a month. My salary is according to union scale. I don't get much pleasure from my room because if I go in there in the evening, my mother yells through the curtain, "What are you doing now? It's so quiet." Usually I'm not doing anything other than reading my father's books, which I've already read. "You can read just as well in here," yells my mother in a voice as if heavy steel doors separated us. When she's in a good mood, she sticks her head in around the curtain and says, "Are you writing poetry, Tove?" But usually I'm not home in the evening anymore. I go to the Lodberg or the Olympia or the Heidelberg with Nina, and we sit with our soda pop and watch the dancing couples in the middle of the floor — as if we haven't come there to dance ourselves. As a rule it's Nina who is chosen first. I smile at the young man who wants to dance with her, as if I were her mother, certain that now she's in good hands. I continue to smile approvingly as they dance past me, and I also look at other people in the room with interest. I imagine that people will think I'm studying my surroundings with the intention of writing a book about them sometime. For my sake, people can think what they like, just not that I'm an overlooked girl who's only out to get engaged. Once when I get up to dance with a young man who has taken pity on me, a man at the neighboring table mumbles, "Even an ugly duckling can find a mate." It ruins the whole evening for me. Nina says that it first gets to be fun after ten, and can't I get permission to stay out until twelve? But my mother won't hear of it. Nina also wants to fix me up a bit. Together we go out and buy a bra with cotton padding and a black and red cossack dress on credit. I don't dare tell them that at home, so I say I got it from Nina. These items help a good deal, to my astonishment, since I'm still the same person, whether I have cotton padding or not. "The world wants to be fooled," says Nina, satisfied, because she really wants me to be just as big a success as she is. One evening a handsome and serious young man asks me to dance. He's badly dressed, and while we dance, he tells me that the next day he's leaving for Spain to take part in the civil war. He lays his cheek against mine as we dance and even though it scratches a little, I like his caress. I lean a little closer to him and I can feel the warmth of his hand on the skin on my back. I get a little weak in the knees and feel something that

157

I've never felt before at anyone's touch. Maybe he feels the same, because he stays standing with his arm around my waist until the music starts again. His name is Kurt and he asks if he can walk me home. "You'll be the last girl I'm with before I leave," he says. Kurt has been unemployed for three years and he would rather sacrifice his life for a great cause than rot in Denmark. He lives on welfare. When he was working, he was a driver for a taxicab owner, and he's never learned anything other than how to drive a car. He sits down at our table, and Nina smiles happily because I've finally found a young man I may be able to hold on to. We've agreed to keep away from unemployed young men, but it's hard to find one who's not. At ten o'clock, Kurt walks me home. It's clear moonlight and my heart is rather moved. I'm walking through the streets with a man who soon will suffer a hero's death. That makes him different in my eyes than all the others. His eyes are dark blue and almond-shaped, his hair black, and his mouth red like a small child's. At home in the entryway, he takes my head in his hands and kisses me very tenderly. He asks me if I live alone and I say no. He himself lives in a room with a vile landlady who doesn't let him have girls visiting. While we're standing embracing each other, my mother opens the window and yells, "Tove, get up here now!" We jump apart terrified, and Kurt says, "Was that your mother?" I can't deny it, and now we have to part. And Kurt has to go down by Trommesalen in order to get food from a sandwich store where it's handed out at midnight, but you have to get in line a couple of hours ahead of time. I stand watching him as he walks down the almost empty street. He's not wearing an overcoat and he has stuck both hands in the pockets of his jacket. He's going to die soon, and I'll never see him again. When I get upstairs, I make a scene over my mother's inter-

158

ference, but she says that I can just invite the young men up so she can see that there's nothing unsavory about them. She doesn't want me to go around with people who can't bear the light of day. And for that matter, she has other things to think about, because soon Aunt Rosalia is coming home from the hospital, where she's now been several times. She's coming home to us to die. That's what the doctors have told my mother. There's nothing more they can do, and there's no room in the hospital for people that the doctors can't do anything else for. Aunt Rosalia will lie in my father's side of the bed next to my mother. So my father will sleep on the sofa in the dining room. "All of this," says my mother, "wouldn't have been possible in the old apartment," so it was as if an inner voice spoke to her when she begged my father to move.

One evening when I come home without a cavalier, I meet my father in the entryway. He's on his way out, as I'm going in. He looks enraged and bitter. "Edvin's sitting up there," he says. "He's gotten married without saying a word to any of us. He's got a wife and apartment, and there's probably a kid on the way, too. Ha! — and him we've sacrificed so much for. Good-bye." Before I let myself in (for now I have a key), I put on an astonished expression. "Oh," I say, "are you here?" They're sitting in my room because Edvin is a guest now, and that's what you use a parlor for. My mother is bawling and Edvin looks very ill at ease. Maybe he regrets his pig-headedness, which also seems to me a little extreme. "It was to surprise you," he says meekly, "and so you wouldn't have the expense of the wedding." That only makes matters worse. My mother asks, offended, whether he thinks they couldn't afford a little wedding present, "but I suppose we're just not fine enough." Then Edvin shows us a picture of his wife. Her

159

name is Grete and she has a round face with dimples. My mother studies it with a frown. "Can she cook?" she asks and stops crying. Edvin has no idea. "She doesn't look like she can," says my mother. My mother herself is no great shakes in the kitchen, and everything edible that she makes has a cementlike consistency because she digs too deeply into the flour bag. While we drink coffee and eat pastry, she asks how much Edvin's rent is and whether his wife is going to work as long as there aren't any children. She's not, and my mother wonders how she'll manage to pass the time. It's very clear that she's already formed an unfavorable opinion of Grete that won't change for the better through personal acquaintance. The clock strikes eleven in the dining room and Edvin gets up to go. "We'll come on Sunday, then," he says dejectedly. When he's left, my mother wants to talk, and I want to be alone. I want to be alone to think about Kurt, and I want to write down some lines that came to me as I watched him go down the street without once turning around. At the corner of Westend and Matthæusgade there's a tavern where a band by the name of "Bing and Bang" blares until two in the morning. Because of that, we practically have to shout at each other; it was far quieter in the old apartment. My mother asks me what kind of a young man I was standing there kissing. "One I danced with," I say. "Other than that I don't know." She says that I should always make a date before the young men leave. She suffers from a nagging fear that I'll never get engaged, and is prepared to receive any young man royally if he's just the least bit interested in me. "You're too critical," she says point-blank. "You can't afford to be that way." Finally she leaves and I sit down at the table with the crooked legs and take out paper and pencil. I think about the handsome young man who's going to die in Spain and then I write a poem that is good. It's called "To My Dead Child" and has no obvious connection with Kurt. Still, I wouldn't have written it if I hadn't met him. When it's done, I'm no longer sorry that I'll never see him again. I'm happy and relieved and yet melancholy. It's so sad that I can't show the poem to a living soul and that everything still has to wait until I meet a person like Mr. Krogh. I've shown Nina my poems and she thinks they're all good. I've shown my father the poem I wrote in the attic with the lead boxes, and he said that it was an amateur poem and that things like that were a good hobby for me—like when he did crossword puzzles. "You train your brain with things like that," he said. I can't explain to myself, either, why I want so badly to have my poems published, so other people who have a feeling for poetry can enjoy them. But that's what I want. That's what I, by dark and twisting roads, am working toward. That's what gives me the strength to get up every day, to go to the printing office and sit across from Miss Løngren's Argus-eyes for eight hours. That's why I want to move away from home the same day I turn eighteen. Bing and Bang roars through the night; drunk people are thrown out into our courtyard from the café's back door. There they yell, swear, and fight, and not until morning is there silence in the courtyard and on our street.

12

Rumors of my poetic abilities have reached the print shop, and now orders come in every day. Carl Jensen receives them and brings them to Miss Løngren, who is still the only one I stand in direct contact with. I write songs for all kinds of occasions and when I go over to hand out the pay envelopes, the workers thank me, embarrassed, and just as embarrassed, I say that there's nothing to thank me for. I write songs and in shorthand I take important messages to the brothers or obituaries of dead brothers. They're printed in the Order of Saint George newsletter. All of this doesn't have much to do with office work, but Miss Løngren won't train me; when she was on vacation, everything was on the verge of collapse because I didn't know the first thing about anything. When I turn eighteen, I'll apply for a real office job and no longer work as a trainee. Then I can get a much higher salary. When I turn eighteen the world will be different in every way, and Nina and I will have the whole night at our disposal. Then I'll also have to see about getting rid of my virtue — Nina is very set on that. She herself was only fifteen when the forester took hers. Whenever we go out in the evening, she takes off her engagement ring. She only goes to bed with those young men who are not unemployed, and I haven't told her about Kurt. That's an experience I want to keep for myself. If I had lived in a room, I would have taken him in. But I don't know whether I would have taken in other young men who have walked me home and kissed me in the entryway. One day when

Nina is pressuring me again because of my scandalous virginity, I tell her that I want to be engaged first. That's not something that I've thought about before, but the decision relieves me. In reality there has only been one real prospective buyer for my virtue, and it's a little embarrassing, because Nina talks as if everyone is out after it. Now that Aunt Rosalia is lying at home sick, my mother is a lot less concerned with what I'm doing. All day she sits in there by my aunt's bed, talking and laughing, and in the evening she goes to bed early and lies there, talking on until one of them falls asleep. My father has become totally superfluous in her world, and I think she would be completely happy if my aunt wasn't going to die. My aunt is yellow in the face and her skin is so stretched over her bones that you're continually reminded of her skull's existence. Her skin is so tight that she can't even close her mouth all the way anymore. If she's awake in the evening when I come home, she calls me in and I sit down by her bed for a while. I try to hold my breath the whole time because there's a terrible smell around the bed, and I hope that my aunt doesn't notice it herself. When she's in pain, my mother phones from the café on the corner for a nurse, who comes and gives her an injection of morphine. It makes her hazy, and she often mistakes my mother and me for each other. "I'm going to die, Alfrida," she says to me one evening. "I know it. You don't have to hide it from me." "No," I say unhappily, "you're just sick. The doctor says you'll be well soon." "It was the same with Carl," she says. "The doctor said that I shouldn't tell him." I don't answer, just put her emaciated hands underneath the comforter, turn off the light, and go into my own room where I can hear my father's snoring through the cotton curtain. I would have liked to speak honestly with my aunt because I'm sure that it would have made her happy, but I don't dare because of my mother, who acts out her sad comedy while my aunt pretends that she doesn't know anything. I think that I would want to know the truth when I'm going to die someday. I also think that if I meet a young man I like, I can't invite him up, as my mother always requests, because the smell from my aunt fills the whole apartment. We've all been out to Sydhavnen to visit my brother and his wife. They have a two-room apartment with a few pieces of furniture that were bought on credit, which made my father put on a foreboding expression. Grete is tiny and plump and smiling, and she sat on Edvin's lap the whole time, while my mother looked at her as if she were a vampire who would suck all strength out of him before long. She hardly spoke to her, and conversation was difficult, too, since my mother carefully avoided addressing her directly. I'm so tired of my family because it's as if I run up against them every time I want to move freely. Maybe I can't be free of them until I get married myself and start my own family. One evening when we're sitting in Lodberg over our soda pop, a young man asks Nina to dance and steps onto the dance floor with her, and I sit as usual with my maternal smile, watching youth amuse itself. Then a young man bows before me and we step out onto the crowded dance floor. He hums in my ear to the music, "The young man from Rome, don't count him out." "That's Mussolini," I say. I happen to know that because my brother was outraged by the song that Liva Weel often sings. "Who's that?" asks the young man, and I say that I don't know. I only know that it's a man in Italy who's just like Hitler, and that you shouldn't write Danish songs that praise him. "Your girlfriend is dancing with my friend," he says. "His name is Egon. And I'm Aksel. What's your name?" "Tove," I say. Aksel dances well and he's in no way

fresh during the dance like most of them. "You dance well,"
he says, "better than most of the girls." I tell him that I've
never learned to dance and he says that it doesn't matter. I
have rhythm in my body. It's very rare that any of the
young men say anything while you dance with them, and I
like Aksel. We dance past Nina and Egon; I smile at Nina,
and Egon and Aksel say hi to each other. When the music
stops, Aksel asks if they can sit at our table and I say yes.
Nina's beautiful eyes shine with happiness when we reach
our table. She asks, "Don't you think Egon is handsome?"
and I say, "Yes, I do." "He's a carpenter," she says, "and
he lives in a house on Amager with his parents, and Aksel
lives across the street with his parents. In a house too."
Then they come over and sit down and I look closer at
Aksel. He has a round, friendly face and everything about
him reminds you that he was once a child. The light curly
hair is a little damp on his forehead, the blue eyes have a
trusting expression, and he has a deep cleft in his chin,
which is only erased when he laughs. There's a faint scent
of milk about him. Egon is shorter than he is, dark, and
apparently somewhat older. Nina asks him how many rooms
there are in his house, and I can see that she's far away in a
dream about two rich men's sons who will lift up two poor
girls into their carefree world. Maybe she's even considering
giving the forester the sack. I have the impression that he's
heavy and serious, and that Nina has a much too romantic
picture of the future he'll provide for her in the country.
When she's being very silly she calls him The Shrub, but no
one else is allowed to. She's with him every weekend and
I'm not permitted to meet him. He's not allowed to meet
me, either, because she thinks that he'll think I'm a bad
influence, like my mother thinks Nina is a bad influence on
me. "And what do you do?" Nina asks Aksel as we drink

165

the beers we ordered. "I'm a collection agent," he says, smiling charmingly at her. I don't know what that is, but Nina looks disappointed. "Oh," she says, "you go around with bills and things like that?" "Drive," he corrects her with a certain conceitedness. "I drive a van." Her face brightens a little and suddenly she suggests that we all celebrate our meeting. We drink to that, and I would much rather have had a soda pop. I don't like beer. Since it's past ten, I admit dispiritedly that I'll have to leave. Aksel jumps up gallantly and buttons his jacket, which is very broad across the shoulders. He's tall and extraordinarily knock-kneed. He takes me easily by the arm as we walk across the room together, and out in the cloakroom he helps me with my coat. As we walk through the cool streets, where the city's lights outshine the stars, he tells me that he's an adopted child and that his parents are quite old, but very nice. And to my astonishment, he asks me whether I feel like coming over to meet them someday. "Sure," I say. "I want so much to have a steady girlfriend," he says childishly and forthrightly. "And the old folks want me so badly to get engaged." At home in the entryway he kisses me according to program, but I can tell that he doesn't feel anything special by it, not even when I press myself lovingly against him. He says, "The four of us can have fun together." "Yes," I say, and promise to come out to visit him next Sunday. He asks curiously if I'm a virgin and I admit that I am. He grabs my hand and shakes it heartily. "I respect that," he says warmly. Disappointed and confused, I go to bed. I think about whether you can get engaged to a collection agent. I have a suspicion that it's just a nicer expression for bicycle messenger, except that he drives a van.

13

Aksel and I are formally engaged after knowing each other for two weeks, and treating each other as chastely as if we were brother and sister. Nina told Egon that I wouldn't go to bed with Aksel until we were engaged, and Egon told Aksel, who suggested the engagement as his own spontaneous idea. Now I'm an engaged girl, and my mother is thrilled. She thinks Aksel looks stable; just as she could tell that Edvin's wife couldn't cook, she can tell that Aksel doesn't drink. He behaves very gallantly toward my mother. "Anyone can see," she says to my father, who doesn't contradict her, "that he's an educated person." After spending several evenings with him, my father says, "You know, he's never learned anything except how to drive a car." "Well," says my mother offended, "isn't that good enough? Maybe you know how to drive a car?" Aksel has promised to take my mother out driving someday; I don't give it much thought, however. But one day, while I'm innocently sitting in the office, there is a loud honking outside and Miss Løngren stares out the window. "Who on earth is that?" she says astonished. "They're waving over here. Is it someone you know?" I deny it, blushing, because Aksel and my mother are waving like mad and leaning out the window while Aksel honks the horn, long and rhythmically. "It must be for the people upstairs," I say miserably. "What nerve," says Miss Løngren, drawing the curtains tighter together. When I get home, I say furiously that I don't want any part of that stupid waving, and my mother says that she

167

and Aksel had so much fun all day. They went to a pastry shop and Aksel treated her. Her eyes shine, as if she were the one who was engaged to him. Aksel's parents are both tiny and old and tremendously nice. They live in a bungalow in Kastrup. The father is a foreman in a factory and there's an air of affluence over the house. Aksel has his room down in the basement. He has a radio and a phonograph and over three hundred records, arranged on tall shelves like books. The room next door is a billiard room where all four of us play billiards when Nina and Egon are there. Aksel's parents call him Assemand and treat him as if he were a little boy. He's very loving toward them just as he is toward me. He has a warmth in his being that makes you feel secure and comfortable. One day Nina says that we're going to have a little party out at Aksel's. We're going to drink his father's homemade wine and we've gotten permission for this from Aksel's parents. We're also going to dance and play billiards and afterwards I must give Aksel the great pleasure of going to bed with him. "When you've been drinking," says Nina encouragingly, "it doesn't hurt a bit." Egon also thinks it's about time, Nina tells me, and it's really as if Aksel and I aren't even consulted. We don't talk about it at all and he still respects me to a fault. Nina and I go out there together and Aksel is a conscientious host. He opens the bottles and puts on records and we all get giddy from the wine, which doesn't taste nearly as terrible as beer. Egon sits and kisses Nina in between dances. She laughs and says if only The Shrub could see this, because she's told her secret to Egon, who makes fun of The Shrub, whom he imagines sitting on the doorstep, tamping his evening pipe as he watches the sunset. We all laugh loudly at this stereotype. "Nina comes out," elaborates Egon, encouraged by his success, "with three sniveling kids hanging onto her

168

dress, dries her hands on her apron and says, 'Papa, it's time for evening coffee.' " Aksel doesn't kiss me at all and as time goes on, he grows more and more serious. I almost feel sorry for him because in so many ways he seems like a child. I myself have gotten very animated from the wine and I'm really set on going through with it now. It surely won't be any worse for me than for so many others. Sometime after midnight, Nina and Egon sneak into the billiard room and close the door behind them. "What are you doing in there?" Aksel yells unnecessarily. Then he looks at me, uncertain and afraid. "Well," he says, "I'd better make the bed." He does this with slow, careful movements. "Take off your clothes," he says miserably, "at least some of them." It's like being at the doctor's. "Why don't we talk a little first?" I ask. "Sure," he says and we sit down in separate chairs. He fills our glasses to the top and we empty them greedily. "You should see about getting your front teeth filled," he says gently. "Yes," I say astonished. Unlike the other procedure, though, it costs money to go the dentist. "I can't afford it," I add. Then he offers to pay for it and since I don't feel that I can accept, he says that he's going to support me someday anyway. So I thank him and agree to let him pay for the fillings. "It's a shame," he explains, "because otherwise you're so pretty." Suddenly there's a strange howl from the billiard room, and both of us gasp. "It's Egon," explains Aksel. "He's so passionate." "Are you too?" I ask cautiously, because I'd like to be prepared for it if he's actually going to roar. "No," he says honestly, "I'm not very passionate." "I don't think I am either," I admit. A glimmer of hope appears in his eyes. "We could," he says optimistically, "wait until another time?" "Then they'll think we're crazy," I say, nodding toward the billiard room. "No. Well, we could turn out the light." Aksel turns out the light. I clench my teeth and lie listening to his warm, kind, reassuring words. The whole thing isn't so bad, and he doesn't utter any animal-like sounds. Afterwards he turns on the light again, and we both laugh with great relief that it's over and that it wasn't anything special. "I want to tell you," he confesses, "I've never been to bed with a virgin before." Nina and Egon appear in the door with flushed cheeks and shining eyes. They look from the bed to us and then at each other, as if it were all their doing, but nothing is said about it. We continue dancing, because when I'm with Aksel, I'm allowed to come home late. With him I can do anything, so this wouldn't upset my mother, either, if she found out. Later Nina asks me if it wasn't wonderful, and of course I say yes. She says that it gets better and better each time. I hadn't considered that the procedure would be repeated. In reality I think that it was a completely insignificant event in my life — not nearly as important as my brief meeting with Kurt and what that meeting could have developed into. But still, I write in my diary that I've kept since I got my own room, "As Nina gave herself to Egon with all of her warm, passionate body in the billiard room, I answered Aksel's question about whether I was innocent with a pure and chaste 'yes,' etc." In my diary everything is sheer romanticism. I store it in the top dresser drawer in the bedroom at home. I've had an extra key made for it. In the drawer are also my two "real" poems, three thermometers, and five or six condoms. The latter items I stole from the nursing supply company because at one time I thought of opening a nursing supply store. But I was thrown out before my stock was large enough. To my great relief, Aksel continues to treat me exactly as before, and he never refers to the embarrassing interlude. I think that he does everything that Egon tells him to do, just as I tend to do whatever Nina wants me to. When I'm alone with Nina, I pretend that Aksel and I are frequently together and maybe he does the same when he's with Egon. During the day Aksel drives around with my mother, who sits in the delivery van and waits while he's with customers. He works for a furniture company, and he tells me that there are many whores among the customers. My suspicious mother has discovered that he stays an especially long time with them, but he just says that it's difficult to get the money from them. My mother says that I shouldn't trust him, but actually I couldn't care less whether he goes to bed with the whores. I don't think it's any concern of mine or my mother's. It's worse that I sense a certain coolness from his parents whenever I'm visiting. I can't figure out how I've offended them. Once in a while I catch his mother staring at me sharply when she doesn't think I'll notice. She's very tiny and always dressed in black like my grandmother. She has wise brown eyes and completely white hair. I've never seen her without an apron. "Has Aksel promised to pay your dentist bill?" she says one evening. "Yes," I say, feeling uncomfortable. "He doesn't make very much," says his mother. "I'm afraid that you may have to pay it yourself." There's something that I don't understand at all. One evening when I'm invited to dinner, I get there a little before Aksel. His parents look very serious. His mother says that Aksel isn't the man for me. He'll never be able to support a wife, and I'm too good for him. "Let me," says his father, waving at her with his hand. "The thing is," he says, "many times we've paid the company back when there've been funds missing. I mean, when Aksel has taken money that isn't his. When it comes to money, he's a child. We thought it would help when he got engaged to a nice girl, but it hasn't helped. He's our only

171

son and our greatest sorrow. He's run away from eleven apprenticeships, and the only things he thinks about are cars and records." He's a good boy," his mother defends him, wiping her eyes, "but reckless and irresponsible." "I like him a lot," I say. "And I don't need to be supported. I can make a living writing poetry." The latter slips out of me involuntarily and I look at Aksel's parents, horrified. They don't look very surprised. "I knew you weren't an ordinary young girl. You can see that," says his mother. Then Aksel drives up and stops out in the gravel with screeching brakes. He often drives home in the company van. As he rings the bell, his mother says, "Now you can't say that you weren't warned." I think it over for a few days and am very glad that people can see I'm not ordinary. It wasn't so many years ago that I was unhappy about that. I think a lot about my fiancé and I reach the conclusion that he's not suited to be a lifelong mate to a girl who wants to break into high society someday. But I can't get myself to break the engagement. I feel sorry for Aksel, who is still gallant and kind and respects me. But my mother also starts to wonder why Aksel always has money in his pocket and why he stays so long with the whores. She stops accompanying him in his van and she advises me to see about finding someone else, someone like Erling who wanted to be a schoolteacher, whom I spurned as if there were a whole line of young men waiting at my door. Nina is in the midst of a serious crisis, because she's considering breaking off with The Shrub and marrying Egon. When I tell her what I know about Aksel, she advises me to end things with him as soon as my dental work is done. The fillings are almost invisible, and when they're finished, Nina thinks that I can get whoever I want. She says that I've finally gotten some "class," and that's what men notice. But I'm so happy when

I'm with Aksel because I'm really fond of him. I'm happy and secure in his company. I stop visiting his parents, and he stops visiting mine. My mother treats him coldly now and my father asks him questions that only serve to show his ignorance. "What do you think about the Olympics? Huh? Isn't it scandalous?" my father says to him. He means the Olympics in Berlin where our girl swimmers are, but Aksel knows nothing about any Olympics. He only knows a little about Hitler and the world situation, and he hasn't read *The Last Civilian* by Ernst Glaeser. I have, and so I know a lot about the persecution of the Jews and the concentration camps, and all of it fills me with fear. It's so pleasant with Aksel because he knows nothing about all the things that could terrify a person these days. That doesn't mean that he's an idiot, but my father's interrogation is only aimed at showing that he is. He senses that and stops visiting. So we're homeless when we're together and only have the taverns and the streets. One day he picks me up outside the office and, silently, we walk down H. C. Ørstedsvej. It's clear that there's something he wants to tell me. Finally it comes. "I've been thinking," he says, "that we ought to take off our rings. I've never really been in love with you." "And I haven't been in love with you, either," I say. "No," he says, "I know that." He takes great strides, out of sheer embarrassment, and I have to jog to keep up with him. "And I'll be eighteen soon," I say, not knowing what that has to do with anything. "Yes," he says, "then you won't be a minor anymore." We walk for a while without saying anything. "And my mother says you're too good for me," he explains. "You should marry someone who has a lot of money and reads books and things like that." "Yes," I say, "I think so too." At home in the entryway, he kisses me tenderly as always and then twists the ring off his finger. He

173

puts it in his pocket and mine goes there too. "Maybe," he says, "we'll see each other again." His short, stiff eyelashes scratch my cheek for the last time. Then he walks down Westend with his scissors-shaped legs and his supple boy's back. He turns around and waves at me. "Bye," he yells. "Bye," I yell back, waving. Then I go up, taking a deep breath before I put the key in the door, because the smell is getting worse and worse. I go in to my mother and Aunt Rosalia. "Now I'm not engaged anymore," I say. "That's fine," says my mother. "He wasn't much good." "Yes, he was," I say and then keep quiet. I can't explain to my mother what was good about Aksel. "There's something good about everyone, Alfrida," says my aunt gently from her bed. And we both know she's thinking about Uncle Carl.

14

ONE MORNING WHEN I TURN THE CORNER ONTO THE ROAD in Frederiksberg where the printer's is located, I see that the flag is at half-mast in the little front yard of the office building. My first thought is that perhaps it's Miss Løngren who is dead, which fills me with perverse glee. Then I'll be allowed to mind the switchboard and talk on the telephone. And I can call Nina as often as I like. In a rather good mood, I go up the stairs, but when I step in the door, Miss Løngren is sitting at her usual place and blowing her nose with a great blast. It's all red, as if she's been sitting in the hot sun. "Master is dead," she says with a breaking voice, "quite suddenly. He was with the brothers at the lodge. In the middle of a speech he fell over the table. A heart attack — there was nothing to be done." I sit down at my place and say nothing. Master was a very taciturn man that everyone was afraid of, even his sons. He had difficulty expressing himself in writing, and I always embellished the language in the letters to the brothers and in the obituaries, because he couldn't remember what he had dictated. Aside from dictating letters, he'd never spoken to me. Miss Løngren stares at me reproachfully while I enter the work lists. "You could at least offer your condolences," she says. "What's that?" I ask. She doesn't condescend to give an explanation, but continues her reading of the newspapers. "Did you hear King Edward's abdication speech?" she asks. "It was gripping. To give up a throne for the sake of a woman! And he's so handsome. Princess Ingrid didn't get her hands on him after all." "He looks like Leslie Howard," I venture to say, and now it's her turn to ask who's that. She shows me a picture of Mrs. Simpson and says, "It's just so strange that he would fall in love with such a middle-aged woman. I could understand it better if it had been a young girl." She runs her fingers through her old maid hairdo, as if the thought crosses her mind that the world would have better understood it if it had been for her sake. "He was handsome when he was young," she says dreamily, meaning suddenly Master. "Carl Jensen looks like him, don't you think? I'll buy a black suit for the funeral — I owe him that. What are you going to wear? Well, you can wear your suit, since it's spring." The death and the abdication have made her talkative. She says that there will certainly be big changes now, and these changes will probably mean that I'll be let go. It was completely Master's idea that I was hired at all. These bright prospects fill me with joy and comfort. There's only half a year until I turn eighteen and it's about time that I move out. In every way the air is too thick to breathe.

Aunt Rosalia doesn't have long to live, and the light-hearted conversations with my mother have stopped completely. My aunt is unable to eat and she is in a lot of pain. My father tiptoes around like a criminal because my mother snaps at him as soon as she sets eyes on him. Edvin and Grete still haven't been to visit us because my mother doesn't have the energy for housekeeping chores in her sorrow-laden condition. She sleeps very little at night, so I've gotten myself an alarm clock and make coffee myself in the morning. Every evening I'm with Nina, who — after an inner battle — has broken off the relationship with Egon because she'd rather live in the country with The Shrub. And almost every night, when the taverns have closed, I stand downstairs in the entryway kissing some young man who's usually unemployed and who I never see again. After a while I can't tell one young man from the next. But I've begun to long for the intimate closeness with another human being that is called love. I long for love without knowing what it is. I think that I'll find it when I no longer live at home. And the man I love will be different from anyone else. When I think about Mr. Krogh, I don't even think that he needs to be young. He doesn't have to be particularly handsome, either. But he has to like poems and he has to be able to advise me as to what I should do with mine. When I've said good-bye to the night's young man, I write love poems in my diary, which has taken the place of my childhood poetry album. Some of them are good and some of them are not so good. I've learned to tell the difference. But I don't read many poems anymore, because then I easily end up writing something that resembles them. Master's funeral is a terrible trial for me. Carl Jensen gives a speech out in the cemetery for both the workers and the family. The wind carries the words in the other direction and I don't hear any of them. I stand behind the youngest and most insignificant of the personnel, and next to me is a delicatessen worker who is very pregnant. It starts raining and I'm freezing in my suit. Suddenly the thought strikes me that I could be pregnant, and it's odd that I haven't thought of that before. Aksel apparently didn't think of it either. How do you know if you're pregnant? Suddenly I think that there are all kinds of signs that I am, and if it's true, I don't know what I'm going to do. Nina has confided to me that she can't have children; otherwise she would have gotten pregnant long ago. She says that the young men never use anything; they couldn't care less. I think about my mother, who always says that I can't come home with a kid, but I especially think about how it will hinder me in

177

my vague wandering toward an equally vague goal. I would like very much to have a baby, but not yet. Things must come in the proper order. When the speech is over and everyone is going over to drink coffee or beer, I tell Miss Løngren that I have to go home because my aunt is about to die. She looks like she doesn't believe me, but I don't care. I rush home and look at myself in the mirror in the hallway. I think I look bad. I feel my breasts and imagine they're tender. I think about cream puffs and imagine I feel nauseous. I smooth my hand over my flat stomach and imagine it's gotten bigger. At five o'clock I'm standing in Pilestræde, outside Berlingske Tidende, waiting for Nina. I confide my fear to her and she says that I should go to the doctor. The next day I stay home from work and go up to old, mean Dr. Bonnesen; with difficulty I manage to blurt out my errand. "You knew very well what could happen," he snaps in a harassed tone, "before you started these highjinks." He gives me a urine bottle and the next morning I deliver it full. The next few days Miss Løngren asks me where my thoughts are, since I'm not listening to what is said to me. Her own thoughts are still jumping from Master to the Duke of Windsor and back again. I feel her searching glance on me like a physical pain and fervently hope for the promised layoff. Several days later I finally find out that I'm not pregnant, and I'm filled with enormous relief. "I'm very romantic," confesses Miss Løngren as she pages through a magazine full of pictures of the world's most celebrated couple. "That's why I can cry over something like this. Can't you? Aren't you at all romantic?" Such questions always contain a lurking reproach, and I hurry to assure her that I'm very romantic. The word makes me think of dark Bedouins with scimitars, of moonlit nights by the river, of dark blue, star-filled nights. I think of loneliness and the

178

complete lack of family or relatives, of a garret room with a candlestick and a pen scratching across the paper, and of a man whose face and name are hidden from me for the time being. "Yes," says Miss Løngren thoughtfully, "I think you are, too. Otherwise you wouldn't be able to write such beautiful songs." She also says, "Why don't you set yourself up as a freelance poet? You could earn a lot of money at it." I think for a moment that I could have a sign in the window at home: "Songs composed for all occasions." And then my name underneath. But my mother probably wouldn't want a sign like that in the window.

One night shortly after Master's funeral, my mother wakes me up. "Come," she says, "I think it's about to happen." Her face is totally unrecognizable from crying. My aunt has tensed her body into an arc and cast her head back so the hard sinews of her neck look like thick ropes under the yellow skin. Her throat rattles eerily and my mother whispers that she's unconscious. But her eyes are open and roll around in their sockets as if they want to get out of them. My mother says that I should go and call the doctor. I dress quickly and borrow the telephone in the café on the corner where Bing and Bang play noisily in the background. The doctor is a kind man who stands for a long time, looking sadly at my aunt. "Should she be given the last one?" he says as if to himself as he draws the syringe. "Yes," pleads my mother, "it's terrible to see her suffer like this." "All right." He injects her in her bony leg and a little later all of her muscles relax. Her eyes close and she lies back and starts to snore. "Thank you," says my mother to the doctor, following him out without thinking about her wrinkled nightgown. Then we sit together by the deathbed and neither one of us thinks of waking my father. Aunt Rosalia is ours and only a minor character in his life. Late into the night, my aunt stops snoring and my mother puts her ear to her mouth to see if she's breathing. "It's over," she says. "Thank God she found peace." She sits back on the chair again and gives me a helpless look. I feel very sorry for her and I feel that I ought to caress her or kiss her — something completely impossible. I can't even cry when she's looking at me, although I know that someday she'll say that I didn't even cry when my aunt died. She'll mention it as a sign of my heartlessness and maybe it will happen when I move away from home soon. I've never told her that I'm going to. We sit close to each other but there are miles between our hands. "And now," says my mother, "just when she was going to enjoy life." "Yes," I say, "but she's not suffering anymore." In spite of the late hour, my mother makes coffee and we sit in my room drinking it. "Tomorrow," says my mother, "I'll have to go over to tell Aunt Agnete. She's only visited her three times in all the time she's been lying here." When my mother begins to be outraged at other people's behavior, she's temporarily saved from the deepest despair. She talks about how Aunt Agnete has never come through when it mattered — even when they were children. Then she always told on the other two and she always had to be a little better than them. I let my mother talk and don't need to say very much myself. I'm sorry that Aunt Rosalia is dead, but not as much as I would have been as a child. That night I sleep with an open window in spite of the ruckus from Bing and Bang, and I look forward to having the rotten, suffocating stench seep out of the apartment. Death is not a gentle falling asleep as I once believed. It's brutal, hideous, and foul smelling. I wrap my arms around myself and rejoice in my youth and my health. Otherwise my youth is nothing more than a deficiency and a hindrance that I can't get rid of fast enough.

15

"IT WAS ALL FOR YOUR SAKE THAT WE MOVED," SAYS MY mother bitterly. "So that you could have a room to write in. But you don't care. And now your father's unemployed again. We can't do without what you pay at home." My father sits up and rubs his eyes. "Yes," he says fiercely, "yes we can. Things are pretty bad if you can't get by without your children. You sacrifice everything for them and just when you're going to have a little pleasure from them, they disappear. It was the same with Edvin." "It was a different matter with Edvin," says my mother. "He's a boy." She says it out of sheer contrariness, and I breathe a little easier, because now it's become a fight between the two of them. We're sitting in the dining room eating dinner. It's become a habit that, because of my father's varying work schedule, we eat a hot meal at noon, even though it doesn't make any difference now. Because I'm unemployed too. I was laid off from the office two weeks before my birthday. But I've found a new job that I'm to start the day after tomorrow, and I've also found a room. I'm moving there tomorrow, and I've told my parents. While I carry the plates out, they argue about it. "She's heartless," says my mother crying, "like my father. The night Rosalia died, she sat stiff as a board without shedding a single tear. It was really spooky, Ditlev." "No," snaps my father, "she's good enough at heart. You've just brought these children up all wrong." "And you," yells my mother, "haven't you brought them up? To be socialists and dry their snot in Stauning's beard.

No, since Rosalia died, and now that Tove is moving out, I have nothing more to live for. You're always lying around snoring, whether you've got work or not. It's deadly boring to look at." "And you," says my father furiously, "you have nothing but your family and royalty in your head. As long as you can run off to the beauty salon every other minute, you don't care whether your husband is starving." Now, fortunately, my mother is sobbing with rage and not with sorrow over my moving. "Husband," she howls, "it's a hell of a husband I have. You don't even want to touch me anymore, but I'm not a hundred years old, and there are other men in the world!" Bang! She slams the door to the bedroom and throws herself onto the bed, continuing to sob so that you can probably hear it all over the building. I take the tablecloth off the table and fold it. Since we've moved to a better neighborhood, we don't use *Social-Demokraten* as a tablecloth anymore, and I don't have to look at Anton Hansen's gloomy drawings from Nazi Germany. My father rubs his hand hard over his face, as if he wants to move all of his features around, and says tiredly, "Mother's in a difficult age. Her nerves aren't good. You ought to consider that." "Yes," I say uncomfortably, "but I want to live my own life, Father. I just want to be myself." "That's what you have your own room for, you know," he says. "There you can be yourself and write all the poems you want." I despise it when they mention my poems — I don't know why. "It's not just that," I say on my way behind the curtain. "I want to have a place where I can invite my friends." "Well, yes," he says, rubbing his face again, "and Mother won't allow that. But at any rate, you take good care of yourself." "Yes," I promise, slipping at last into my own room. There I pack up my few possessions, but I have to wait to empty the dresser drawer in the bedroom until my mother has gone into the dining room again. I've rented a room in Østerbro because I don't think moving would be complete if I stayed in Vesterbro. I don't like my landlady, but I took the room anyway because it cost only forty kroner a month. I'm paying off my winter coat and my dentist bill, but I'll have enough money to get by, because at the Currency Exchange I'll get a hundred kroner a month. My landlady is big and heavy. She has wild, bleached hair and a dramatic demeanor, as if something catastrophic were about to happen any minute. In the living room there hangs a big picture of Hitler. "Look," she said when I rented the room, "isn't he handsome? Someday he'll rule the whole world." She's a member of the Danish Nazi Party and asked me whether I wanted to be a member too, because they wanted to include the Danish youth. I said no, I didn't have any sense for politics. And it's none of my business what she's like. The main thing is that the room is cheap. I move out there the next day. I ride over in the streetcar with my suitcase and my alarm clock, which won't fit into the suitcase. It starts to ring between two stops and I smile foolishly as I turn it off. It's a very temperamental alarm clock that only I can operate. It's crabby and asthmatic like an old man, and when it gets too sluggish and creaky, I throw it onto the floor. Then it starts ticking, all gentle and friendly again. The landlady greets me in the same loose-fitting kimono that I saw her in the first time, and she looks just as dramatic too. "You're not engaged, are you?" she asks, pressing her hand to her heart. "No," I say. "Thank God," she lets out her breath, relieved, as if she's avoided a dangerous situation. "Men! I was married once, dear. He beat me black and blue whenever he'd been drinking, and I had to support him too. Things like that aren't allowed in Germany. Hitler won't stand for it. If people won't work, they get put in concentration camps. Does that alarm clock ring very loudly? I have such trouble sleeping and you can hear every sound in this house." It rings so a whole county can hear it, but I swear that it's as good as soundless. At last she leaves me and I can calmly look over my new home. The room is quite small. There's a sofa with a flowered covering, an armchair in the same style, a table, and an old dresser with crooked, dangling handles on the drawers. There's a key in one of them, so I can really have something all to myself. In one corner there's a curtain with a rod behind it. It's supposed to serve as a wardrobe. There's also a chipped wash basin and pitcher. Furthermore, it's ice-cold here, like in Nina's room, and there's no stove. When I've put my clothes behind the curtain, I go out and buy a hundred sheets of typing paper. Then, with my last ten-kroner note, I rent a typewriter, which I place on the rickety table when I get back. I pull the armchair over to it, but when I sit down in it, the seat falls apart. All that I wanted for my forty kroner was a table and chair, but maybe you have to go up to a higher price category to get that. I go out and knock on the door to the living room where the landlady is sitting listening to the radio. "Mrs. Suhr," I say, "the chair broke. Could I borrow an ordinary chair?" She stares at me as if the news were a real misfortune. "Broke?" she says. "That was a perfectly good chair. It dates all the way back to my wedding." She rushes in to inspect the damage. "You'll have to give me five kroner for damages," she says then, putting out her hand. I say that I don't have money until the first. Then she'll add it onto the rent, she says angrily. I follow her when she goes out again, begging her for an ordinary chair. "It's highway robbery," she huffs, massaging her heart again. "It doesn't pay at all to rent out rooms. You'll probably wind up dragging men into my home, too."

She sends Hitler an imploring glance, as if he personally could throw out any men who might appear. Then she goes into the other room where there is a row of stiff, upright chairs along one wall. "Here," she says crossly, as she selects the most worn of them, "take this one, then." I thank her politely and carry it into my room. It's a good height for the table. Then I begin to type up my poems, and it's as if it makes them better. I'm filled with calm during this work, and the dream that this will someday be a book develops with stronger and clearer colors than before. Suddenly my landlady is standing in the doorway. "That thing," she says, pointing to the typewriter, "makes a horrible racket. It sounds like machine guns." "I'm almost done," I say. "Otherwise I only type in the evening." "Well, all right." She shakes her yellow-haired head. "But not after eleven. You can hear every sound here. Say, wouldn't you like to hear Hitler's speech tonight? I listen to all of his speeches — they're wonderful. Manly, firm, resonant!" She gestures enthusiastically with her arm so you see her voluminous bosom. "No," I say alarmed, "I . . . don't think I'll be home tonight." But I *am* home because Nina has a visit from her forester, so I don't have anywhere to go. I sit and freeze even though I have my coat on, and I can't concentrate on writing because Hitler's speech roars through the wall as if he were standing right next to me. It's threatening and bellowing and it makes me very afraid. He's talking about Austria, and I button my coat at the neck and curl up my toes in my shoes. Rhythmic shouts of "Heil" constantly interrupt him, and there's nowhere in the room I can hide. When the speech is over, Mrs. Suhr comes into my room with shining eyes and feverishly flushed cheeks. "Did you hear him?" she shouts enraptured. "Did you understand what he said? You don't need to understand it at all. It goes

185

right through your skin like a steambath. I *drank* every word. Do you want a cup of coffee?" I say no thanks, although I haven't had a thing to eat or drink all day. I say no because I don't want to sit under Hitler's picture. It seems to me that then he'll notice me and find a means of crushing me. What I do is "entartet Kunst," * and I remember what Mr. Krogh said about the German intelligentsia. The next day I start my job at the Currency Exchange typing pool and Hitler invades Austria.

---

* "Decadent art"—exhibit of "Decadent Art" in Munich, 1937— products of "cultural Bolshevism." — Trans.

16

"CAN YOU DANCE THE CARIOCA?" I LOOK UP FROM MY shorthand and say no. I look at the secretary who I'm taking shorthand for; he's really handsome, but he doesn't take his work seriously. He sits lazily leaning back in the chair, now and then taking a gulp of the beer at his side. He yawns noisily without holding his hand in front of his mouth. "Well," he says tiredly, "where were we?" We're sitting in a large room on the top floor. Here there are lots of desks with many secretaries. Whenever they need a typist, they phone down to our office and the supervisor sends one of us up. I like this work, but the secretaries bring me to despair. They would rather talk, and in the meantime the case lies in a blue folder on which it says *"urgent!"* in red letters. There are applications for all kinds of things, and with each application there's a compelling letter implying that refusal of the enclosed will lead to suicide. Every single applicant writes about pressing, strictly personal reasons why *he* should be allowed to import his goods. I can dance the carioca just fine, but this is company time and I'm getting a high salary now, more than I've ever gotten before. "Stop frowning," says the secretary smiling, "the wrinkles will end up being permanent." I run down all the stairs and into the office to type up the letter. It's a rejection, and I try to make the tone of the letter kinder and less businesslike, just like I changed the letters to the brothers, but it isn't allowed here. I have to type it all over again and am requested to hold myself to the shorthand. There are about twenty of us

187

young girls in the office, which looks like a schoolroom. There's a girl at every desk, and the desks are in three long rows. Farthest forward sits the supervisor, facing us like a teacher, and when the noise gets too intense, she hushes us sternly. All the other girls are very chic, with tight dresses, high heels, and a lot of make-up on their faces. One day one of them decides to make up my lips, my cheeks, and my eyes, and they all think I look much better that way. They say that I should use it every day, and I start to borrow Nina's cosmetics when we go out in the evening. After I've typed up all of my poems, I can't stand sitting in my room with my teeth chattering from the cold. So I continue my nightlife with Nina, and even though it's rather monotonous, the days and nights fly by during this time, like a drumroll just before something's about to happen on stage. The terrible years at I. P. Jensen have passed; I'm eighteen; I've broken away from my family. One evening in the Heidelberg, I dance with a tall, blond young man who isn't like any of the usual young men and doesn't talk like them, either. He asks if he can treat me to a sandwich. I say that I'm with my girlfriend. He says that doesn't matter — then all three of us can have a sandwich. Nina looks at him approvingly and a little astonished when he introduces himself. His name is Albert and he's better dressed than the others. Maybe he's even a university student. We have sandwiches and beer, and I fumble with my knife and fork and watch to see how the others use the utensils. At home we cut up the food with the knife and then eat it with the fork. Albert asks me where I live and what I do. He asks me how much I earn and whether I can live on that. It's nothing special, but the other young men have never talked about anything but themselves. I have a tremendous desire to tell Albert everything about myself and my life. "Maybe," I say, "I'll soon be able to earn more. I write poems, you see." I don't like to say it, and especially not here, where there's so much noise, laughter, and music. But I don't feel that I can wait any longer and I don't know whether I'll ever see Albert again. "Oh," he says surprised, "I didn't expect that. Are they good?" He smiles at me from the side, as if he's privately amused at me. That annoys me and I can feel that I'm blushing. "Yes," I say, "some of them are." "Can't you remember one of them by heart?" he says, munching. "Yes, I can," I say, "but I don't want to say it here." "Then write it down," he says calmly, pushing a napkin over to me. He takes a pencil out of his pocket and hands it to me. Which verse should I write? Which is the best of all? I feel that it's enormously important what I write, and after chewing on the pencil for a while, I write:

> I never heard your little voice.
> Your pale lips never smiled at me.
> And the kick of your tiny feet
> is something I will never see.

He looks thoughtfully at the verse for a long time and asks me what the poem is about. "A child," I say, "stillborn." He asks whether I've ever had a stillborn child, and I say no. "I'll be damned," he says then, regarding me with great curiosity. Nina is dancing with a young man and she winks at me encouragingly as they dance past the table. She thinks that I should make something of the situation, and I will too, in my own way. Albert follows my glance. "Your girl-friend," he says, "is very pretty." "Yes," I say, thinking that he wished it were her he had chosen and not me. But I don't care about that side of the matter now. "Do you know," I say stubbornly, "where you can send a poem like

189

this to be published?" "Oh, sure," he says, as if I'd asked about something perfectly ordinary. "Do you know a journal called *Vild Hvede?*★ I don't, and he tells me that it's where young, unknown people can get their poems and drawings published. It's edited by a man named Viggo F. Møller, and he writes the name and address down on another napkin. "I was out to see him recently," he says so casually that it's clear that he's proud of it. "He's very nice and he has a great understanding of young art." I ask cautiously if he writes himself, and he says just as casually that in his spare time he has committed some verses to paper and a number of them have already been published in *Vild Hvede.* The news makes me totally speechless. I'm sitting next to a poet. It was more than I've ever dreamed of. I'm still silent when Nina returns. She lifts her fine eyebrows and thinks that Albert and I haven't gotten any further. "In Heidelberg I lost my heart to the magic of a pair of eyes. . . ." Everyone stands up and sings, as they swing the full beer steins back and forth. Albert has stood up too, and all of a sudden his posture expresses a certain impatience. I follow the direction of his glance and see, on the other side of the dance floor, a slight young girl, who's sitting alone and is very serious. When the music starts, Albert pays the bill, bows a little awkwardly to both of us, and asks the serious girl to dance. "It was your own fault," says Nina annoyed. "He was really cute." But actually I don't care. I've gotten hold of a corner of the world that I long for and I don't intend to let that corner go. I put the napkin in my purse and smile mysteriously at my girlfriend. "I'm going home to type," I say. "If only the witch doesn't wake up." "You've gone from the frying pan into the fire," Nina says.

★ *Wild Wheat* — Trans.

190

"She's not a bit better than your mother." I work my way to the cloakroom and get hold of my coat. I walk the whole way home even though it's bitter frost, and I feel very happy. A name and an address — how many years it can take to get that far. And maybe that's not even enough. Maybe this man won't want my poems. Maybe he'll die before they reach him. Maybe he's already dead. I should have asked Albert how old Viggo F. Møller is. I turn the name over and over and wonder what the "F" stands for. Frants? Frederik? Finn? What if my letter never arrives because the postal service loses it? What if Albert has given me a totally wrong name and was putting one over on me? Some people think that kind of thing is so funny. Yet — deep inside I believe that this will work out. It's two in the morning when I tiptoe into my room. I fold the sofa blanket over several times and put it under the typewriter to dull the sound of it, and then I choose three poems that I send with a short, formal letter, so that the man won't think it's very important to me. "Editor Viggo F. Møller," I write, "I am enclosing three poems in the hope that you will publish them in your journal, *Vild Hvede*. Respectfully and sincerely yours, T. D." I run out to the nearest mailbox with the letter and look to see when it will be picked up. I want to figure out when the editor will get it and when he'll be able to answer it. Then I go home to bed, after first setting the alarm clock. I put all of my clothes on top of the comforter, but I still lie shaking from the cold for a long time before I fall asleep.

17

EVERY EVENING I RUSH HOME FROM THE OFFICE AND ASK
Mrs. Suhr if there's a letter for me. There isn't, and Mrs.
Suhr is very curious. She asks if someone in my family is
sick. She asks if I'm waiting for money in the mail, and
reminds me of the five kroner that I owe her for the ruined
chair. Once in a while she also asks me if I'm hungry, but I
never am, even though I seldom eat dinner. Sometimes I eat
at Berlingske Tidende's canteen with Nina. It's cheap, but
it's only for employees. My landlady also says that I'm getting thinner and thinner and if I were her daughter she'd
fatten me up all right. When I notice the smell from the
dinner that she's cooking, I get hungry after all, but then, of
course, it's too late. Usually I drink a cup of coffee at Øster-
port station before going home, and I eat a piece of pastry
with it. But that's a luxury that I really can't afford because
I'm on a very strict budget. So are all of the girls in the
office, even though most of them live at home. Toward the
end of the month, they all borrow from each other, and
they'd borrow from me too if I had anything to lend them.
They're not hurt if you refuse. Their poverty isn't oppressive or sad because they all have something to look forward
to; they all dream of a better life. I do too. Poverty is temporary and bearable. It's not any real problem. Nina has her
mother to borrow from and she has The Shrub. Nina's
mother is a fat and friendly woman who doesn't take anything too much to heart. She makes a living cleaning for
people and she lives with a man who is the father of Nina's

twelve- or thirteen-year-old half brother. You can tell immediately that Nina didn't grow up in that home but is only visiting. She's also only visiting in Copenhagen, and it's incomprehensible to me that she really wants to live in the country. While I'm waiting for the letter, I don't go out in the evening, but sit freezing in my room, listening for sounds from the hallway. I know that express letters can be delivered outside of the normal delivery times. There's no reason whatsoever why I should receive an express letter, but I listen for the doorbell just the same. One evening there's a political meeting at Mrs. Suhr's, and a bunch of boot-clad men swarm into the living room where there is soon a terrible uproar. In the living room they click their heels together and shout "Heil!" at the picture of Hitler. There are also a number of women present. Their voices are shrill like Mrs. Suhr's, and as usual I hope that none of them will catch sight of me. They sing the Horst Wessel song and stamp on the floor so that the wall shakes from it. Mrs. Suhr comes into my room, her cheeks red and her hair sticking out in all directions. She's still wearing her kimono and looks as if she's come running out of a burning house. "Oh," she gasps, "won't you drink a toast to the Führer with us? Come in and say hello to all of these splendid fellows. Join us in fighting for our great cause." "No," I say terrified, "I have something I have to finish. Overtime work from the office." I set myself to tapping at the typewriter so that they'll think I'm working, while I think with sorrow and uneasiness about the darkness that is about to descend over the whole world. But I don't forget to keep an ear tuned toward the hallway. Express letter, telegram — you never know. . . . Several days later Mrs. Suhr is standing in the hallway with a letter in her hand when I let myself in. "Well," she says with sensation-hungry eyes, "here's that letter you've been waiting for." I grab it out of her hand and want to go into my room but she blocks the way. "Open it now," she says breathlessly, "I'm just as excited as you are." "No," I say with a pounding heart, "it's strictly private, confidential. It's a secret message, I must tell you." "Oh God!" she puts her hand to her heart and whispers, "Something political?" "Yes," I say desperately, "something political. Let me get by." She looks at me as if I were a modern-day Mata Hari and finally backs away, deeply impressed. At last I'm alone with my letter. It's much too thick, and I grow weak in the knees with fear that the editor is sending it all back. I sit down by the window and look down at the little courtyard. The dusk wraps itself around the trash cans and the lights are being turned on in the building opposite. I open the envelope with an effort, take the letter out, and read, "Dear Tove Ditlevsen: Two of your poems are, to put it mildly, not good, but the third, 'To My Dead Child,' I can use. Sincerely, Viggo F. Møller." I immediately tear up the two poems that, to put it mildly, are not good, and then read the letter once again. He wants to publish my poem in his journal. He is the person that I've waited for all my life. I have a copy of *Vild Hvede* that I bought with money I borrowed from Nina. In it there's a poem by a woman — Hulda Lütken — and I've read it many times because I can't forget that my father once said that a girl can't be a poet. Even though I didn't believe him, his words made a deep impression on me. I have to share my joy with someone. I don't feel like talking about it at home, and Nina wouldn't understand what it means to me. The only one who might is Edvin. He was the first to say that my poems were good, after he made fun of them. But that doesn't matter; we were only children then. I take the streetcar out to Sydhavnen. Grete opens the door and smiles, surprised at seeing me. "Come in," she says hospitably, and then runs in and sits down on Edvin's lap, which apparently is her main occupation as a newlywed. I think he looks completely defenseless in the deep armchair. "Hi," he says happily, "how are you?" He has to move Grete's head in order to look at me. "How are Mummy and Daddy?" asks Grete between two kisses. My mother can't stand this affectionate form of address, but Grete is completely insensitive to the coldness my mother exudes. I don't care much for Grete either, because I had always imagined that Edvin would have a beautiful, proud, and intelligent wife and not a little, smiling housewife of the Rubenesque type. But that doesn't really matter because my feelings aren't nearly as strong or as passionate as my mother's. I tell Edvin what has happened and show him the letter. He asks Grete to make coffee while he reads it. "Wow," he says impressed, "you should get paid for this. He doesn't write a damn word about that. Be careful he doesn't cheat you." I haven't thought about that at all, not for a moment. "He earns money selling the journal, you know," explains Edvin, "so he shouldn't have unpaid contributors." "No," I say. Not even Edvin understands what a miracle has occurred — no one understands it. "Now listen here," he says. "You call him up and ask him what you're going to get for it." "Yes," I say because I would like to call him up. I would like to hear his voice, and this is an excellent excuse. Grete sets the table and chatters on about nothing, and Edvin tells her about the letter. "Oh," she says happily, "then I'm related to a poet. I'll write that to my parents. Would you like a couple of slices of bread?" "Yes, thank you," I say and ask how Edvin's cough is. The doctor said that he'll cough as long as he is spraying cellulose lacquer. He'll cough until he finds some other occupation. The doctor also says that it sounds worse than it is. He won't die from it, not even get really sick. His lungs are just black and irritated. While we drink coffee, I look at my brother. He doesn't seem happy, and maybe marriage isn't what he had expected. Maybe he had imagined a wife that he could talk to about something other than love and the evening meal. Maybe he had imagined that they could do something else in the evening other than sit on each other's lap and declare how much they love each other. I think, at any rate, that it must be just terribly boring. "Don't you need a new dress soon?" says Grete. "I've never seen you in anything except that cossack dress. You should get a permanent," she says, "like mine." Grete's hair sits on top of her head in lots of little curls, and in her ears she has two large rings that clink when she shakes her head. "Isn't it strange to have such a handsome brother?" she says. "I think it must be very strange for you." Edvin gets tired of her conversation and quickly sits down in the armchair again. After the cups are carried out, Grete settles herself on his lap once more and twists his black curls in her fingers. I think my brother has married her in order to escape sitting in his rented room with the stern landlady, because what other way out did he have? I don't intend to live at Mrs. Suhr's for the rest of my life either. Being young is itself temporary, fragile, and ephemeral. You have to get through it — it has no other meaning. Edvin asks me whether I've told them the news at home, and I say that I want to wait until the poem appears in the journal. Then I'll show it to them, not before. Edvin reads the poem and is deeply impressed. "But you're still full of lies," he says with wonder in his voice. "You've never had any dead child." He says that Thorvald has gotten engaged to a very ugly girl, and it annoys me a little. I could have had him but I didn't want him. Still, I

liked it that he wasn't attached to anyone else. Before I
leave, I borrow ten øre from my brother to make a call.
I have to let myself out because Grete is in the middle of a
long whispering in Edvin's ear. In the telephone booth on
Enghavevej, I look up Viggo F. Møller's number and ask
for it with my heart in my throat from excitement. "Hello,"
I say, "you are speaking with Tove Ditlevsen." He repeats
my name inquiringly and then he remembers it. "Your poem
will come out in a month," he says. "It's excellent." "Will I
get any money for it?" I ask, very embarrassed. But he
doesn't get angry. He just explains to me that no one gets an
honorarium because the journal runs on a deficit, which he
pays for out of his own pocket. I hurry to assure him that it
doesn't matter, it was just something my brother said. Then
he asks me how old I am. "Eighteen," I say. "Good God —
not more?" he says with a little laugh. Then he asks me
whether I would like to meet him and I say that I would.
He'll meet me the day after tomorrow, six o'clock, in the
Glyptotek café, so we can eat dinner together. I thank him,
overwhelmed, and then he says good-bye. I'm going to meet
him. I'm going to talk to him. He undoubtedly wants to do
something for me. Mr. Krogh said that people always
wanted to use each other for something, and that there was
nothing wrong with that. It's quite clear what I want to use
the editor for, but what does he want to use me for? Next
evening I go home anyway and tell everything. My mother
is home alone. She's very happy to see me, and I have a
guilty conscience because I come over so seldom. My
mother has grown very lonely since Aunt Rosalia's death.
The building is just "fine" enough that you don't simply go
running over to visit other people, and my mother doesn't
have a single girlfriend she can talk to and laugh with. She
only has us, and we deserted her as soon as she and the law

would permit it. We drink coffee together and I can see that her imagination is hard at work. "You know what," she says, "that editor — he probably wants to marry you." I laugh and say that she never thinks of anything except getting me married. I laugh, but when I get home and into bed, I think about whether he's married or not. If he's single, I have nothing against marrying him. Entirely sight unseen.

18

He has on a green suit and green tie. He has thick, curly gray hair and a gray mustache, the ends of which he often twists between his fingers. He has an old-fashioned wing collar, and his double chin hangs over it a bit. His eyes are bright blue like little babies' eyes, and his complexion is pink and white and transparent like a child's. He has round, wide-sweeping arm movements and small, fine hands with dimples at the knuckles. He is warm and friendly, and I quickly forget my shyness in his company. He doesn't resemble Mr. Krogh in appearance and yet he reminds me of him a little. He studies the menu for a long time before he chooses a course and, without knowing what it is, I ask for the same. He says that he's very fond of food, and that you can probably tell by looking at him. I say politely no. I admit that I never notice what I'm eating and he says, laughingly, that you can certainly tell by looking at me. I'm much too thin, he says. We drink red wine with our meal and I make a face because it's sour. He says that's because I'm so young. When I get older, I'll learn to appreciate good wine. He asks me to tell him a little about myself, about how I found my way to him. I'm nervous and light-hearted and want to tell everything at once. I also mention Albert, and he shrugs his shoulders as if he's no one in particular. "You never can tell with young people," he says, twisting his mustache. "You believe in some of them, and then they don't amount to anything. Others you don't believe in, and it turns out that they're good after all." I ask him whether he thinks I'm any good, and he says that you can't tell. He says that those who don't amount to much are those young men who come with a poem and say, "I wrote this in ten minutes." If they say that, he knows that they're not any good. "And what then?" I ask. "Then I advise them to be streetcar conductors or something else sensible," he says, wiping his mouth with his napkin. I'm glad that I didn't write anything about how many minutes it took me to write "To My Dead Child." I don't even know myself. I think the editor is a magnificent man and I think he's handsome. Maybe others don't think he's handsome, and Nina would think that he's too old and fat, but I don't care. He gives me the menu so that I can order dessert, and I ask for ice cream because everything else looks much too complicated. The editor wants fruit with whipped cream. "I have a sweet tooth," he says, "because I don't smoke." The waiter treats him very respectfully and calls him "the Editor" the whole time. He calls me "the young lady." "May I pour for the young lady?" I bravely drink the sour wine and grow warm and relaxed from it. It's getting to be dusk outside and the wind is blowing softly in the trees on the boulevard. They're already in blossom, and soon Tivoli will open. Viggo F. Møller says that he loves spring and summer in the city. The trees and the flowers bloom, and the young girls blossom too, like beautiful flowers out of the cobblestones. Mr. Krogh said something similar, and he wasn't married. That's probably something that married men have no sense for at all. Finally I have the courage to ask him if he's married, and he says no with a little laugh. "No one," he says gesturing with his hand apologetically, "has ever wanted to have me." "I was formally engaged once," I say, "but then he broke it off." "And now?" he asks. "Aren't you engaged now?" "No," I say, "I'm waiting for the right one to come along." I try to look him deep in the eyes, but he doesn't see the meaning behind it. It's just that I've gotten used to the fact that everything is urgent, and I almost expect that he'll propose to me right then and there. You never know where a person will be tomorrow. He could get a letter from another young girl who writes poems — Hulda Lütken, for example — invite her out, and forget me completely. He must be the kind of man who can have whomever he chooses. With growing jealousy I ask how Hulda Lütken is, and he laughs loudly at the thought of her. "She wouldn't like you," he says. "She's insanely jealous of other women poets, especially if they're younger than her. She's temperamental enough for ten. Once in a while she calls me and says, 'Møller, am I a genius?' 'Yes, yes,' I say, 'yes, you are, Hulda.' Then she's satisfied for a while." Then he asks me if I'd like to come to a *Vild Hvede* party next month. It's a party where the "Top Wheat" and the "Top Rusk" are chosen. Those are the poet and the illustrator who, during the year, have had the most contributions in the journal. I ask what I should wear, and he says a long dress. When he hears that I don't have one, he says that I can borrow one from a girlfriend. That makes me think of Nina, who got herself a long, backless dress for the dance at Stjernekroen. I say that I would love to go to that party. We have coffee in very thin cups and the editor looks at his watch, as if it's time to go. I would have liked to sit there for a lot longer. Outside, my daily life is waiting for me with its urgent matters at the office, the evenings at the taverns, the young men who accompany me home, and my cold room with the Nazi landlady. My only consolation in this existence is a handful of poems, of which there are still not enough for a collection. And I don't know, either, how to go about publishing a poetry collection. When the bill is paid, Mr. Møller suddenly places his hand over mine on the colorful tablecloth. "You have beautiful hands," he says, "long and slender." He pats my hand a couple of times, as if he knows very well that I'm sorry to leave and wants to assure me that he won't disappear from my life right away. I notice that I'm about to cry, and don't know why. I feel like putting my arms around his neck, as if I'm very tired after a long, long trip and now have finally found home. It's a crazy feeling and I blink my eyes a little to hide that they've grown moist. Outside we stand together for a while and look at the traffic. He's shorter than me, and that surprises me because you couldn't tell when he was sitting down. "Well," he says, "I guess we're going different ways. Stop by some day. You know the address." He swings his green, wide-brimmed hat in an elegant arc, puts it on his head, and walks quickly down the boulevard. I stand looking after him as long as my eyes can follow him. I think that I'm always having to say good-bye to men — standing and staring at their backs and hearing their steps disappear in the darkness. And they seldom turn around to wave at me.

19

I'VE BEEN MOVED OVER TO THE STATE GRAIN OFFICE ON THE other side of the street, and I like it much better. There are just the two of us women in the office. I take care of the switchboard and I write letters for the office manager, Mr. Hjelm. He's a tall, gaunt man with a long, grim face that is never softened by anything resembling a smile. Whenever there's a pause in the dictation, he stares at me as if he suspects that I have something other than grain in my head. The other girl is named Kate. She's quick to laugh and childish and we have a lot of fun together when we're alone. I'm waiting for my poem to be published in the journal, because then I'll visit Viggo F. Møller — not before. I'm going to have summer vacation soon, and that's always been a problem for me. Nina wants us to join the Danish Youth Hostel group and go hiking in the country and stay at youth hostels. But I don't like people in groups and I'm not interested in it. But if my poem comes out soon, maybe I can stay with the editor during my vacation. While I wait, I still look at the little children and the lovers who are driven out of the buildings by the heat. I look at the dogs too, the dogs and their masters. Some of the dogs have a short leash that's jerked impatiently every time they stop. Others have a long leash and their masters wait patiently whenever an exciting smell detains the dog. That's the kind of master I want. That's the kind of life I could thrive in. There are also the masterless dogs that run around confused between people's legs, apparently without enjoying their freedom. I'm like that kind of masterless dog — scruffy, confused, and alone. I go out in the evening less often than before, and Nina says I'm getting to be downright boring. I stay in my room now that the cold doesn't chase me out anymore. I read my poems over and over again, and sometimes I write a new one. The two that were, to put it mildly, not good, I've long ago removed from my collection. I think they were hideous, but if the editor had written that they were good, I would have believed that. Sometimes I go home for a visit. My father is unemployed again and there's a cool atmosphere between him and my mother. Usually he's lying on my sofa, sleeping or dozing, and my mother sits knitting with a dis-approving look on her face. She thinks it's about time I visit the editor because she's more and more convinced that he wants to marry me. "Fat people," she says, "are happy and good-natured. It's the lean ones that are grumpy." She asks how old he is, and I say that he's about fifty. That too she thinks is fine because then he's sown his wild oats and will make a faithful husband. She says that soon I can probably quit my job and be provided for. I say nothing because all of this has to wait. "We'll hold the wedding," says my mother, and I think about what my editor will say about his mother-in-law. He's older than she is, I'm pretty sure; but that doesn't bother my mother. I always leave soon because now my mother is demanding something of me. My father says that there's no rush and that it's up to me whom I want to marry. "You've never cared much about it," says my mother, "but now you can see what's happened to Edvin. That's what you get for your indifference." Then the battle has turned away from me and I have no qualms about leav-ing them. One day when I come home from my parents', I find a written eviction notice from Mrs. Suhr. "Since it has become known to me," she writes, to my astonishment,

204

"that you have participated in conspiratorial activities, I no longer wish to live under the same roof with you." I remember the political letter that I received and my unwillingness to take part in her Nazi meetings. Then I find another room on Amager, not far from the editor's residence, and ride out there with my suitcase and my alarm clock in my hand. It's with a family that has grown children. A daughter has gotten married and it's her room that I move into. It's nicer and bigger than the other one and only ten kroner more. And on top of that, there's a stove. I immediately call Viggo F. Møller to tell him my new address, and he says it's good that I called because the journal has come out and he was just about to send it to me. He says it as if it were quite an everyday thing, as if I'd had dozens of poems published and this was just one of them. He says it in a friendly, ordinary tone, as if journals and books with my works were flooding the world so that it didn't matter so much whether such a trivial thing as a single poem got lost. But he is, of course, used to being around people like Hulda Lütken, people he's on a first-name basis with. Every time I think of her, I feel a stab of jealousy in my heart. I wonder whether Viggo F. Møller will ever tell peculiar things about me to other people? Will he say, "Tove called recently, by the way, and said such and such. Ha, ha." And twist his mustache and smile. The next day two copies of *Vild Hvede* arrive in the mail and my poem is in both of them. I read it many times and get an apprehensive feeling in my stomach. It looks completely different in print than typewritten or in longhand. I can't correct it anymore and it's no longer mine alone. It's in many hundreds or thousands of copies of the journal, and strange people will read it and may think that it's good. It's spread out over the whole country, and people I meet on the street may have read it. They may be walking with a copy of the journal in their inside pocket or purse. If I ride in the streetcar, there may be a man sitting across from me reading it. It's completely overwhelming and there's not a person I can share this wonderful experience with. I rush home to show it to my father and mother. "I think it's good," says my mother, "but you should have a pen name. The one you have isn't good. You should take my maiden name. Tove Mundus — that sounds much better." "Her name is good enough," says my father, "but the poem is much too modern. It doesn't rhyme in the right way. You could learn a lot from Johannes Jørgensen." I'm not offended by my father's criticism because he has always wanted to protect us from disappointments. According to his experience, you should never expect anything from life, then you'll avoid disappointments. Still, he asks to be allowed to keep the journal, and he holds it in the same careful way as he does his books. On the way home, I go into a bookstore and ask for the latest edition of *Vild Hvede*. They don't have it but they can order one. "We don't sell any of them as single copies," the man explains to me, "it's mostly by subscription." "That's too bad," I say, "you see, I've heard there's an excellent poem in it." He takes down my name so I can get it in a couple of days. "It's a very little journal, you know," he explains talkatively. "I think there are only five hundred copies printed. Strange that it can make a go of it." Insulted, I go out of the store again. But I'm not the same as before. My name is in print. I'm not anonymous any longer. And soon I'll visit my editor, even though he didn't repeat his invitation on the phone. He has, of course, many other things to occupy him besides talking to young poets. A week after the journal came out, I'm called into Mr. Hjelm's office. His long face is, if possible, even crabbier than usual and on the desk in front of him is

Vild Hvede open to the page where my poem is. The thought flashes through my mind that he's going to praise me for it. "I bought this journal," he says, "because I thought that it had something to do with grain. And then I see" — he strikes my poem with a ruler — "that you apparently have other interests than the State Grain Office. I'm sorry, but unfortunately we can't use you here any longer." He looks at me with his fish eyes and I don't know what to say. I feel bad because I was happy here, but there's also something comical about it that will make Kate and Nina laugh when I tell them. "Yes," I say, "there's nothing to be done about it." I edge my way out of the office and go in and tell Kate about being fired. She laughs that Mr. Hjelm thought *Vild Hvede* was an agricultural journal, and I laugh too, but I'm still a girl who has lost her job and will now have the trouble of finding a new one. Kate says that I should report to the union and have them find a new position for me, and I think that's a good idea. The same evening I call Viggo F. Møller and he says that he would be happy to see me the following evening. Then it doesn't matter so much that I've been thrown out of the grain office. Maybe the editor can find a solution that is better than Kate's. I have so many expenses now that I can't allow myself to be unemployed.

20

"WOULDN'T YOU LIKE," SAYS VIGGO F. MØLLER, "TO have a collection of poems published?" He says this as if it were nothing special. He says this as if it were quite common for me to publish poetry collections; as if it weren't what I've wished for, most fervently of all, for as long as I can remember. And I say with a thin, ordinary voice that yes, I would rather like that. I've just never thought of it before. But now that he mentions it, it would be great fun. I hope he can't tell how joyfully and excitedly my heart is pounding. It's pounding as if I were in love, and I look closely at this man who has caused such joy in my soul. He's sitting on the other side of the table, which is covered with a bottle-green tablecloth. We're drinking tea from green cups. The curtains are green, the vases and the pots are green, and the editor is wearing a green suit like before. The bookshelves reach almost up to the ceiling and the wall is completely hidden by paintings and drawings. It all reminds me of Mr. Krogh's living room, but Viggo F. Møller doesn't remind me much of Mr. Krogh. He's much less secretive and I'm welcome to ask him about anything I want to know. The sun is about to go down and there's a soft twilight in the living room that sets an intimate mood. I help my new friend carry the cups out to the kitchen and he asks me if I'd like a glass of wine. I say yes, thank you, and he pours wine into green glasses, lifts his and says, "Skål." Then I ask him how you go about getting a poetry collection published, and he says that you send it to a publisher. Then they take care of the rest, if they accept the poems. It's very simple. I'm to show him all of the poems that I have so he can see if there are enough and if they're good enough. I don't care for the wine, but I like the effect. I'm very taken with the editor's soft, round arm movements, with his silver-gray hair and his voice, which wraps itself soothingly and refreshingly around my soul. I'm already fond of him, but I don't know what his feelings are for me. He doesn't touch me and doesn't try to kiss me. Maybe he thinks that I'm too young for him. I ask him why he's not married and he says gravely that no one wanted him. It's sad, he says, but now he figures that it's too late. He has a smile in his eyes when he says this, and I frown because he doesn't take me seriously. I tell him about my life, about my parents, about Edvin, and about how I've just lost my job because of the poem in *Vild Hvede*. The latter amuses him greatly and he says that it will amuse his friends too, when he tells them about it. His friends are celebrities, and some of them have asked him who the poor young girl is who wrote so beautifully about her dead child. So it's not just my family who thinks everything you write is true. "Oh," he says, slapping his forehead, "I almost forgot. Did you see Valdemar Koppel's review of the journal in *Politiken* recently? He writes very positively about your poem." He takes out the clipping and shows it to me. It says: "A single poem, 'To My Dead Child,' by Tove Ditlevsen is justification enough for the little journal's existence." "Oh," I say overwhelmed, "how happy that makes me. May I keep it?" He gives it to me and he pours more wine into the green glasses. Then he says, "It makes a strong impression on a young person to see their name in print for the first time." "I'm so glad that I met you," I say. "It's as if nothing bad can happen when I'm with you. When I'm here, I don't believe there'll be a world war." Viggo F. Møller grows suddenly serious. "It looks very bleak otherwise," he says. "I can probably do something or other for you, my dear, but I can't prevent the world war." It's the wine that makes me say such things. All the grownups withdraw from me whenever they start thinking about the world situation. In comparison, my poems and I are just specks of dust that the smallest puff of wind can blow away. "No," I say, "but you're not going to suddenly die and this house isn't going to be torn down." I tell him about Editor Brochmann and Mr. Krogh. The former he knew, but not the latter. "No," he says seriously, "in that sense you can rely on me. Why don't we use our first names?" We toast our friendship and he turns on the lights in the green-shaded lamps. "Call me Viggo F.," he says then. "Everyone calls me Viggo F. or Møller — no one calls me Viggo except my family." His parents, he says, are dead, but he has a brother and a sister whom he rarely sees. "Families," he says, "never understand artists. Artists only have each other to rely on." He asks me if I'd like to sit next to him on the sofa, and I sit down by him. I sit close to him so that our legs are touching each other, but it apparently doesn't make any impression on him. Maybe I'm not pretty enough; maybe I'm not old enough. He tells me that he's fifty-three years old, and I say politely that he doesn't look it. He doesn't either, aside from the fact that he's fat. His skin is pink and white and totally free of wrinkles. I think my father looks much older. But for that matter I don't care a bit about how old people are. Viggo F.'s father was a bank director and his brother is, too. He himself works for a fire insurance company, which he doesn't care for, but you've got to earn a living somehow. He has also written books, and I'm embarrassed that I haven't read them. I haven't even run across his name in the library. My ignorance irritates me and I tell my friend that I was supposed to go to high school but I wasn't allowed to. We couldn't afford it. Gently he puts his arm around my waist and a hot stream races through me. Is this love? I'm so tired of my long search for this person that I feel like crying with relief, now that I've reached my goal. I'm so tired that I can't return his tender, cautious caresses, but just sit passively and let him stroke my hair and pat my cheeks. "You're like a child," he says kindly, "a child who can't really manage the adult world." "I once knew someone," I say, "who said that all people want to use each other for something. I want to use you to get my poems published." "Yes," he says, continuing to caress me, "but I don't have as much influence as you think. If the publishers don't want your poems, I can't do anything. But we'll take a look at them. I can advise you and support you, at any rate." When I go out to the bathroom, I see that Viggo F. has a shower, and it overwhelms me. I ask him if I can take a shower, and he says yes, laughing. Otherwise I go once in a while to the public baths on Lyrskovsgade, but it costs money, of course, so it's never been very often. Now I stand delighted under the shower, twisting and turning, and thinking that if we really get married, I'll take a shower every single day. When I come out of the bathroom, Viggo F. says, "You have nice legs. Lift up your dress so I can see them properly." "No," I say, blushing, because I have a run in one stocking. "No, they're only nice from the knees down." It's gotten to be twelve o'clock and I have to go home to my wretched room. Viggo F. offers to pay for a cab home, but I say that I can certainly walk the short distance. And I add, "I can't figure out what I'm supposed to give the cabbie as a tip, anyway." "Remember to call him 'driver,' not 'cabbie.' That sounds too colloquial." The remark hurts me and I get furious at my whole upbringing, at my ignorance, my language, my complete lack of sophistication and culture, words I hardly understand. He kisses me on the mouth when he says goodbye, and I walk through the mild summer night and recall all of his words and movements. I am not alone anymore.

21

I'VE BEEN WITH MANY CELEBRITIES. I'VE SEEN THEM, I'VE
talked to them, I've sat next to them, I've danced with
them. As soon as I stepped in the door, I was moving on a
completely different plane than usual. I walked in a glaring
light and cast the rays of the celebrities back like a mirror.
I reflected their images, and they liked what they saw. Flattered, they smiled and gave me many compliments. They
even praised my dress, although it is Nina's and it's too big
for me. But it hid my shoes, which are old and worn and
need to be replaced. The celebrities constantly gathered in
clusters around Viggo F.'s green shape, which appeared and
disappeared like duckweed on a windy pond. It swelled
back and forth before my eyes, and I repeatedly sought it
out because it was my protection and my security among all
the celebrities. Viggo F. introduced me to them with pride,
as if he had invented me. "My youngest contributor," he
said to the press photographers, smilingly twisting his mustache. I was photographed with him and some of the celebrities, and the picture was in *Aftenbladet* the next day. It
wasn't very good, but Viggo F. said that it was important to
be friendly toward the press. And I was friendly. I smiled
the whole evening to all of the celebrities who wanted to
meet me, and in the end my cheeks hurt from it. My feet
also hurt from dancing, and when I finally left, the whole
thing was as unreal as a dream. I couldn't remember who
had become the "Top Wheat" and the "Top Rusk." But a
young man I danced with said that everyone was chosen

eventually. I, too, would someday be the "Top Wheat," it was just a matter of writing a lot for the journal, regardless of whether it was good. The young man also asked me if I wanted to go to the movies some evening, but I turned him down coldly. I had quite different plans for my future. I've gotten a job as a temporary through the union and now I'm earning ten kroner a day. I've never had so much money in my hands before. I've paid the dentist bill and I've bought a light gray suit with a long jacket because the brown one had gone out of style. I don't spend much time with Nina anymore, because now I'm totally uninterested in meeting a young man who might want to marry me. After Viggo F. looked at my poems and selected some of them, I sent them to Gyldendal Publishing Company and now I'm going around waiting for an answer. "If they don't want them," says Viggo F., "you just send them to another one. There are plenty of publishers." But I'm certain that they'll want them, since Viggo F. says they're good. He knows the director, who is a woman. Her name is Ingeborg Andersen and she dresses like a man. "But she's not the one who will decide," says Viggo F., "it's the consultants." They are Paul la Cour and Aase Hansen, and I don't know either of them. I don't know any of the celebrities because I almost never read newspapers and have only read authors long since dead. I've never realized before that I was so dumb and ignorant. Viggo F. says that he'll take care of getting me a little education, and he lends me *The French Revolution* by Carlyle. I find it very exciting, but I would rather start with the present day. One evening when I'm visiting Viggo F., the doorbell rings and I hear a low female voice out in the hallway. Viggo F. comes in with a sparkling, plump, dark little woman who shakes my hand as if she means to tear it off, and says, "Hulda Lütken. Huh... so that's what you look like. You're becoming so celebrated it's almost unbearable." Then she sits down and speaks the whole time to Viggo F., who finally asks me to leave, because there's something he wants to talk to Hulda about. Later he explains to me — what he has already hinted at — that Hulda Lütken can't stand other female poets. While I'm waiting to hear from Gyldendal, I sometimes go home to visit my parents. My father says that of course it would be fun if I had a poetry collection published, but that you can't make a living as a poet. "She won't have to, either," says my mother, eager to fight. "That Viggo F. Møller — he can support her." I tell them about the shower and in her thoughts, my mother also stands under Viggo F.'s shower. I tell them about the wine in the green glasses and in her thoughts, my mother drinks from them too. They have cut out the picture from *Aftenbladet* and put it in the frame of the sailor's wife. "It's good," says my mother. "You can really see that you've had your teeth fixed." She says with pride, "The doctor says that I have high blood pressure. I also have hardening of the arteries and a bad liver." She's gotten a new doctor because the old one was no good. Whatever you said was wrong with you, he said that he suffered from the same thing. The new doctor agrees with all of my mother's suspicions and she is devoted to him. Since Aunt Rosalia died and both Edvin and I have moved out, she's very absorbed with her health, even though she never gave it a thought before. She's going through the change of life, the doctor said, and the people around her must be considerate of her. That's what she told my father, who never dares lie down on the sofa anymore, which she always has nagged him about. He sits up and reads and sometimes he falls asleep with the book in his hand. I never stay home for very long because I get tired of listening to my mother's alarming symptoms from her inner organs. But I feel sorry for her because she never had very much in this world, and the little she had, she lost. One day when I come home from work, there is a big, yellow envelope lying on the table in my room. My knees grow weak with disappointment because I know what it contains. Then I open it. They have sent my book back with a few apologetic sentences, to the effect that they only publish five poetry collections a year, and they've already chosen them. I take the letter and go over to Viggo F. with it. "Oh well," he says, "it was to be expected. We'll try Reitzel's Publishing Company. Don't let yourself be beaten by something like this. Trust in yourself, otherwise you'll never get anyone else to." We send the poems to Reitzel's and a month later they're sent back. I think it's starting to get interesting because I know that the poems are good. Viggo F. says that almost every famous writer has been through the mill — yes, there's almost something wrong if it goes too smoothly. Finally the poems have almost made the entire rounds, and it's hard to keep up my courage. Then Viggo F. says that it's a question of money. The publishers make almost nothing on poems; that's why they're reluctant to publish them. But *Vild Hvede* has a fund of five hundred kroner meant for cases like mine. He'll give the money to a publisher to publish the poems. He'll talk to his friend, Rasmus Naver, about the matter. Mr. Naver agrees to publish the poems at his company, and I am happy. He comes over to Viggo F.'s to talk to him about it. He's a kind, gray-haired gentleman with a Fyn accent, and I smile at him sweetly the whole time so that nothing about me will make him give up the idea. He says that Arne Ungermann would probably draw the cover without a fee, and he likes the title: *Pigesind*. Finally it's worked out and I don't know how to show Viggo F. my gratitude. I kiss him and ruffle his curly hair, but he is so absent-minded lately. It's as if he does want to do something for me, but he has something more important on his mind at the moment. One evening he tells me about the concentration camps in Germany and says that all of Europe will soon be one concentration camp. He also shows me a journal in which he has written an article against Nazism and he says that it will be dangerous for him if the Germans ever come to Denmark. I think about my poetry collection that will come out in October and have a strange feeling that it will never appear if the world war breaks out. "If they go into Poland," says Viggo F., "the English won't stand for it." I say that they have put up with so much. I tell him about my time at Mrs. Suhr's. I tell him that every time I heard Hitler speaking through the wall on Saturday, he invaded some innocent country on Sunday. Viggo F. says that he can't understand why I didn't move out before, and I think that he doesn't know what it is to be poor. But I don't say anything. Arne Ungermann comes over one evening and shows me the cover drawing. It depicts a naked young girl with bowed head, and it's very beautiful. The figure is chaste and devoid of all sensuality. He and Viggo F. talk about the world situation and are very serious. Now I'm almost always at Viggo F. Møller's, and my mother thinks that I might just as well move in with him. "When," she says impatiently, "do you intend to marry him?"

22

EDVIN HAS LEFT HIS WIFE. NOW HE'S LIVING AT HOME IN MY old room behind the cotton curtain, and my mother is happy, even though he's going to move as soon as he can find a room. My mother says that she can understand why he left Grete, because she only had clothes and nonsense in her head and no man can put up with that. But my brother won't allow anyone to put Grete down. He says that the mistake was his. He didn't love her, and that wasn't her fault. That's also why he has let her keep the apartment. She gets to keep the furniture too, and Edvin will continue to make the payments. I like coming home now that my brother is there. We talk about my poetry collection, and Edvin can't understand why you don't get paid for something like that. "It's a piece of work," he says, "and it's despicable that it's not paid for." We also talk about Edvin's cough and about all of my mother's new illnesses. We talk about my work at a lawyer's office in Shellhuset, where I get to observe many disagreements between people. And we talk a lot about Viggo F. Møller and the world that he has opened for me. I have to tell my family everything about his apartment — how the furniture is arranged, how many rooms there are, and what books are on the bookshelves. I tell my father that Viggo F. writes books himself, and he says that he thinks he's read one of them once, but that it was nothing special. My father also says, "Isn't he too old for you?" My mother protests and says it's not age that matters, and it never has bothered her that my father is ten years older than she is. She says the most important thing is that he can support me, so I can quit working. They all talk as if he has already proposed to me, and when I say that I don't know if he will have me, they brush the question aside as a minor detail. "Of course he will have you," says my mother. "Why else would he do so much for you?" I think about that and come to the same conclusion. The different thing about me is that I write poetry, but at the same time there's a lot that is ordinary about me. Like all other young girls, I want to get married and have children and a home of my own. There's something painful and fragile about being a young girl who makes her own living. You can't see any light ahead on that road. And I want so badly to own my own time instead of always having to sell it. My mother asks me what Viggo F. makes at the fire insurance company, and she thinks it's strange that I have no idea. "He's just a white-collar worker," says my father, full of contrariness, invoking an indignant stream of words from both my mother and Edvin. "If I were a white-collar worker," says Edvin angrily, "I would never have gotten this damned cough." "At any rate there's no risk," my mother seconds him, "of him being unemployed at any minute and loafing around with a book while decent people go to work. Feel my neck," she says to me suddenly. "It's as if there's a knot right here. I'll have to show it to the doctor. We'll hire a cook for the wedding — he's of course used to the best. Soup, roast, and dessert — I remember well how it was at the places where I worked. Couldn't you invite him home some day?" I don't know why I don't do that. My family is mine. I know them and am used to them. I don't like having them displayed to someone from a higher social class. Viggo F. has even asked me if he could meet my parents. He says he would like to meet the people who have produced such

219

an odd creature as me. But I think that can wait until we get married. My father and Edvin also talk about the imminent world war. Then my mother gets bored and I lose my good humor. Suddenly it's a fact. England has declared war on Germany, and I stand with thousands of other silent people and follow the neon headlines on Politiken's building. I stand next to my brother and my father and I don't know where Viggo F. is at this fateful hour. When we go home, I have a painful, sinking feeling in my stomach, as if I were very hungry. Will my poetry collection come out now? Will daily life continue at all? Will Viggo F. marry me when the whole world is burning? Will Hitler's evil shadow fall over Denmark? I don't go home with them but take a streetcar out to my friend's. There are a lot of celebrities at his house, and he doesn't seem to notice me. They're drinking wine from the green glasses and talking very seriously about the situation. Ungermann asks me what I think of his drawing, and I thank him for it. So the book will probably come out after all. I go home without really having talked to Viggo F., and at night I dream uneasily about the world war and *Pigesind*, as if there really were a fateful connection between them. But already the next day it's clear that daily life will go on as if nothing had happened. At the office the divorce cases, property line disputes, and other heated disagreements between people pile up. Excited people stand at the counter asking for the attorney, who is seldom there, and I have to listen to them present their special, terribly important case, and no one seems to remember that a world war broke out yesterday. My landlady tells me that pork has gone up fifty øre per kilo, and Nina comes over to confide in me that she's met a wonderful young man, and she's thinking of dropping The Shrub again. Nothing at all has changed, and when I go over to Viggo F.'s, he is again in a good mood, radiating calm and coziness in great, warm waves. "In three weeks," he says, "your book will come out. Soon you'll have to read the proofs, but you shouldn't let it get you down. Reading the proofs, you never think it's good enough. It's like that for everyone." Viggo F. isn't the least bit interested in ordinary people. He only likes artists and only spends time with artists. Everything about me that is quite ordinary, I try to hide from him. I hide from him that I like the new dress that I've bought. I hide the fact that I use lipstick and rouge and that I like to look at myself in the mirror and turn my neck around almost out of joint in order to see what I look like in profile. I hide everything that could make him have misgivings about marrying me. He's right about the proofs. When they arrive, I don't care for my poems at all anymore, and I find many words and expressions that could be better. But I don't correct very much because Viggo F. says that then the printing will be too expensive. In the days before the book comes out, I stay home in my room all the time that I'm not in the office. I want to be there when my book is delivered. One evening when I come home, there's a big package lying on my table, and I tear it open with shaking hands. My book! I take it in my hands and feel a solemn happiness, that isn't like anything I've ever felt before. Tove Ditlevsen. *Pigesind*. It can't be taken back anymore. It is irretrievable. The book will always exist, regardless of how my fate takes shape. I open one of the books and read some lines. They are strangely distant and foreign, now that I see them in print. I open another book because I can't really believe that it says the same thing in all of them. But it does. Maybe my book will be in the libraries. Maybe a child, who in all secrecy is fond of poetry, will someday find it there, read the poems, and feel something from them, something that the people around her don't understand. And that odd child doesn't know me at all. She won't think that I'm a living young girl who works, eats, and sleeps like other people. Because I myself never thought about that when I read books as a child. I seldom remembered the names of those who wrote them. My book will be in the libraries and maybe it will be in the windows of bookstores. Five hundred copies of it have been printed, and I've been given ten. Four hundred and ninety people will buy it and read it. Maybe their families will read it too, and maybe they'll lend it out like Mr. Krogh lent out his books. I will wait to show the book to Viggo F. until tomorrow. Tonight I want to be alone with it, because there's no one who really understands what a miracle it is for me.

Translator's Notes

Childhood

Page

12 Zacharias Nielsen (1844–1922).
Author of many novels and short story collections depicting Danish country life and centering on the conflict between traditional religious values and the new ideas of the 1870s and 80s.

15 *Ditte menneskebarn.*
Novel by the Danish author Martin Andersen Nexø (1869–1954). Translated into English and published in three volumes: *Ditte: Girl Alive!* (1920), *Ditte: Daughter of Man* (1921), and *Ditte: Towards the Stars* (1922).

Thorvald Stauning (1873–1942).
Leader of the Social Democratic Party and Prime Minister of Denmark 1924–1926, 1929–1942. He grew up in a working class neighborhood of Copenhagen. From 1891 until 1893 he worked in a cigar factory in Fredericia. He became involved in union organizing and the labor movement, and in 1906 he was elected to the Folketing (Parliament). His politics were clearly influenced by his concern for the well-being of the poor and his desire to improve their lot.

23 Jylland dialect.
Jylland, commonly called Jutland in English, is the western Danish peninsula which borders Germany.

50 Vilhelm Bergsøe (1835–1911).
Author and zoologist whose short stories and novels have a significant place in Danish post-Romanticism.

224

Page

56   Johannes V. Jensen (1873–1950).
One of Denmark's most important authors, and recipient of
the Nobel Prize in 1944.

57   Herman Bang (1857–1912).
Author of short stories and novels which played an important role in the development of Danish realism and natural-
ism. Noted for his eccentric appearance and undisguised
homosexuality. His first novel, *Haabløse Slægter* (*Hopeless
Generations*) was declared "immoral" by court ruling.

Agnes Henningsen (1868–1962).
Novelist whose works all deal with women's role in society
and the sexual double standard. In 1918 the conservative
press succeeded in starting a campaign against her novels
Den elskede Eva (*The Beloved Eva*) and *Den store Kærlighed*
(*True Love*).

59   Folkets Hus.
Literally, "the people's house." Meeting places for workers
established by the unions in the 1930s.

64   Kai Friis Møller (1888–1960).
Author, journalist, literary critic, and translator. From 1913
to 1918 and again from 1925 to 1931, he was literary critic
for the Danish newspaper *Politiken,* and much respected by
his contemporaries.

97   *Bræen.*
Published in 1908, the first in a series entitled *Den lange
Rejse* (*The Long Journey*), which depicts Jensen's vision of
the development of human history, through myth, from the
ice age to Christopher Columbus' voyage of discovery.

Youth

Page

121 Reichstag fire.
The destruction of the Reichstag building in Berlin by arson on February 27, 1933. Hitler accused the Communists of setting the fire. The incident was used as an excuse for declaring a state of emergency and revoking constitutional rights for "protection against Communist violence." In the Reichstag trial before the high court September 21–December 23, 1933, the Dutch Communist Marinus van der Lubbe was sentenced to death. The other defendants (E. Torgler, G. Dimitrov, and others) were acquitted. From the beginning, there were indications that the Reichstag fire had been set by a terrorist group of the Nazi party. However, the circumstances surrounding the fire have never been fully disclosed.

Anton Hansen (1891–1960).
Illustrator who grew up in Vesterbro and experienced poverty and deprivation, which greatly influenced his art. Called a "proletarian artist," he was known for his satirical cartoons and drawings depicting scenes of war and social injustice.

133 Blågårds Plads.
Common gathering place for rallies and demonstrations by workers. Located in Nørrebro, a working class neighborhood.

173 *The Last Civilian.*
A book by Ernst Glaeser, originally published in Zürich under the title *Der letzte Zivilist* in 1935. Translated into more than twenty languages.

193   Horst Wessel (1907–1930).
Student, Nazi Storm Trooper, killed by Communists in
Berlin in 1930. The song he wrote was elevated to a national
anthem alongside "Deutschland über alles" by the Nazi
party.

194   Hulda Lütken (1896–1946).
Poet who debuted in 1927 with the poetry collection *Lys og
Skygge* (*Light and Shadow*). From the mid-30s she wrote
poetry in free verse.

206   Johannes Jørgensen (1866–1956).
Poet and editor of the literary journal *Taarnet*, which
appeared in 1893.

216   Rasmus Naver (1894–1976).
Publisher who specialized in art books.

Fyn accent.
Fyn, often called Funen in English, is the central Danish
island situated between Sjælland (the island on which
Copenhagen is located) and the peninsula of Jylland. The
Fyn accent is said to be somewhat more melodic than the
Copenhagen accent.

Arne Ungermann (1902–1981).
Well-known Danish illustrator who designed almost all of
the covers for Tove Ditlevsen's books.

Pigesind.
Tove Ditlevsen's first published book. The title is difficult
to translate as it is an invented word, combining the word
for girl and the word meaning psyche/soul/mind. Despite
highly favorable reviews, only about a hundred copies of the
original edition of five hundred were sold.

Ibsens' Play's
    The Wild Duck –
    Enemy of the People –

Call Lois & Cathy

Love Medicine — aug. 3 [?]
Louise Erdrich   maybe

Beet Queen — Sept.
Louise Erdick —